HAVING FUN WITH
ALIEN
TECHNOLOGY

HAVING FUN WITH
ALIEN
TECHNOLOGY

A.C. WELLS

TATE PUBLISHING
AND ENTERPRISES, LLC

Published by Tate Publishing & Enterprises, LLC
127 E. Trade Center Terrace | Mustang, Oklahoma 73064 USA
1.888.361.9473 | www.tatepublishing.com

Tate Publishing is committed to excellence in the publishing industry. The company reflects the philosophy established by the founders, based on Psalm 68:11,
"The Lord gave the word and great was the company of those who published it."

Book design copyright © 2014 by Tate Publishing, LLC. All rights reserved.
Cover design by Lisa Lebrun
Interior design by Mary Jean Archival

Published in the United States of America

ISBN: 978-1-63122-637-3
1. Fiction / Science Fiction / Action & Adventure
2. Fiction / Science Fiction / Alien Contact
14.05.21

CONTENTS

EUROPEAN INTERVENTION

R ex did not like this dream. He was now strapped to the card table in the dark room of the torture facility. Hernandez, Lena, and Strudenhamme were there. Vance watched the proceedings over an altered Combine monitor. And the doctors were cutting him open, watching his innards squirm while he screamed and moved atop the table, restraints bolting him into place, smiles growing on each face at his horrible screams. A streamer of blood jutted from one vein, and Lena laughed nastily, features turning into the white-suited Overwatch with their evil red lenses glaring down at him impassively, laughs morphing into amused chuckles, someone starting up a power saw while another stuck needles full of evil red fluid into his arteries.

Rex awoke with an inhuman roar completely shocked that he was still alive, dully noting that a portion of the wiring for the headgear was still in the port. His eyes were giving him the odd black-white scale for background, and layered color heat registry for living things, allowing him to distinctly pick out the ten or so Judicators inside of the steel crate with him. The Restrictor prods holding him down were nothing to Rex now, the implant's noises so silent in his mind that the world seemed to have upped his hearing dramatically somehow. Ripping free from his restraints,

Rex grabbed one of the knives on the torso sheaths, and began using it to kill the first Judicator to his immediate right before any of the others knew what was happening. His surroundings were suddenly a crimson blur of guts flying, blood spurting, bones cracking, armor plate buckling under his left fist like it was a panel of packing material, someone's head torn free from torso in a flash, and a Judicator pleading for his life as a booted foot crushed skull easily.

Rex almost slid in the gray matter on the floor as he raged amongst the close quarters, a pulse rifle landing in his right hand almost as if it was meant to be as a traitor screamed all the way to the deck, one foot-long blade jutting from his chest. Rex began wheeling around to empty the weapon at the furthest of the Judicators now, one still alive next to the wreckage of torn restraints and ruined metal dying with fifteen energy rounds, until the weapon was again knocked from his hands. Rex turned to the offender with hate boiling up over the levies, the last of the Judicators yelling out with a staccato burst of pain as Rex drove his pointed fingers into the traitor's throat, his left hand forming a knife that cut through everything, thanks to the brute force driving behind it.

Pulling his left hand free from the bloody cavity in the traitor's throat, Rex reached up with his right hand and pulled the portion of headgear, still jammed into the port, loose. Sighing heavily as his vision returned to normal, he began looking around for his knives, while thanking the bladesman for the pitch-black sheaths that the Combine did not remove from his torso. Shifting things around on the bloody deck, Rex cursed as he noted his right arm was indeed altering in color, the veins appearing to be heavy black shadows under graying, rhino-like skin. Peeling off the armor vest, he confirmed the fact that it was affecting his entire body, and suddenly he felt ashamed.

Was he even human anymore? What had done this to him all of this time away from the Combine scientists? And as he stumbled across the question in his mind, Rex knew what the cause was: The implant that had been jammed into his chest was changing him, a gift that was slowly becoming a curse. Strapping the knives on under the armor vest, this time to keep them fully concealed, Rex stooped to grab one of the alien rifles and felt the deck shift under him. Planting his feet firmly, Rex felt his guts quiver at the feeling of a slight drop, and instantly he knew he was airborne. For how long—he had no idea, but Rex was not planning on showing up to where they wanted to take him so easily. Approaching the far end of the crate and using bodies as a way to easily keep standing upright on the now-pitching deck, Rex stopped at the segmented wall and began to bash it open manically.

As he began to see daylight through the cracks of the segmented doors, something above him whined loudly, and suddenly he was in freefall, guts, blood, and various other innards rising up from the deck to float around in the air. Passing up a kidney, liver, and length of coiled intestine as he too floated around, Rex knew instinctively that this was not going to end well. As he predicted, the fall, that took forever to complete itself, ended as the dipping back end of the huge container slammed down into a building or something just as well-built. Rex bounced around numbly in the interior until his consciousness ended with one of the segmented doors falling inward, smashing him up against the ruined restraining wall.

—◦◦◦—

This dream was much more like it. He was sitting on a folding chair, sipping at a fancy alcoholic drink, while he watched the sunset from a beach, water lapping at the shore softly, Molly off to one side building a sand castle, Maurine next to him in a skimpy bathing suit.

The dream was quickly ruined as a headcrab burst through the sandcastle Molly was making, Maurine saw Rex's skin mutate entirely akin to his arm and screamed, and a huge Combine dropship fell from the sky. A Dragon hovered over the Whale as it lowered the transport crate, blue flashes of energy dicing Molly and the headcrab to cutlets and Overwatch firing at Maurine as she ran away, bolting across the beach and dying with pulse bolts to the back.

They were overwhelming him before he knew what to do...

—⟨∾∾∾⟩—

Waking up with a groan, he pushed upwards on the length of blue metal pinning him down, and snarled as it refused to budge momentarily, shoving it aside and standing amongst the carnage, knee-deep in corpses. Adding to his anger was the fact that all of the weapons inside of the container were now junked, and smashed to pieces during the fall. As he tried to stand on the tilted portion of the container that was now the floor, something under him groaned, and the entire side of the container broke free, Rex cursing as he fell amongst the corpses yet again to land heavily on a concrete floor. The segmented door section missed him by a few feet, but still inspired him to get his ass up and move quickly, looking around the area cautiously.

Drawing one of the three blades, Rex advanced out of the room he was in, apparently a storage area on the top of some type of an apartment complex he guessed, emerging into a stairwell leading downwards. A metal grating or fencing wrapped around the sides to either prevent people from falling over the side of the stairs, or more than likely, cages for an elevator shaft. Continuing down to the next floor, he entered the first door as it opened for him, and began navigating the darkened rooms. Rex found plenty of evidence that it was some type of manager's suite, and that it was large enough to take up the entire floor. And as he arrived at a pair of glass-lined double doors, he heard the distinct noises of CPs breathing through their masks, speaking to one another.

"What was that?"

"Not sure. Shook the whole building, I think. Knocked Unit 55 out cold. Appears to have struck a table while falling over."

"Not good. We need to find out what happened. Then report. Go down to the 3rd floor and see if the others are intact, and get them up here. I'm going to scout out the area."

"Roger."

A cocking of a weapon followed the last of the dialogue, and Rex retreated into the shadows, waiting in the darkness as the glass-lined doors opened up and one of the white-masked abusers walked by, oblivious to his presence. Creeping up slowly behind the CP, he used the knife to hack at the neck and throat of the CP with several blows, almost decapitating the CP in the process, and preventing it from reporting any activity effectively, destroying the throat mic that was part of the headgear easily.

Sheathing the blade, he grabbed the small weapon from the dead CP, and in the darkness, he examined it carefully; a smaller version of the H&K MP7, using smaller magazines that fit into the rear pistol grip of the weapon, and a different fold-down forward grip. Checking the chamber, he found it loaded with specialized 4.3mm ammunition, and the top rail was absent of any sights. It was completely unlike the previous MP7s he'd used, with their stranger forward-loading magazine receiver, 9mm chambers, barrels, and the standard issue laser peep sight.

Interestingly enough, he found another of the H&K USPs on the corpse, but only a single spare magazine of .45cal for the pistol and no extra ammunition. Leaving the corpse behind, Rex advanced into the lit area beyond the glass-lined double doors, and gasped as he found a man strapped into a barber's chair, converted to use for the Combine, the purpose clear enough.

The man in the chair was wearing odd brown-and-tan mottled fatigues, and had clearly been tortured using riot prods and beatings, as well as a strange heat device that left the skin mottled and cooked. Taking the pair of dog tags from the necklace of the soldier, Rex found the patch for a foreign fighting force, sewn into the right shoulder, but it was in Cyrillic or something and he couldn't read it. There was also a small bag of colors similar to the fatigues sitting on one desk, and as he opened it up, Rex found it full of random papers in the same language, as well as half-dozen fold-out maps.

Zipping the bag shut and hanging it across his chest, Rex quickly pocketed the dog tags and took up the small weapon into a two-handed grip, shifting the USP around in the belt of his pants, and wishing the Combine hadn't taken all of his tactical gear. Rex cursed under his breath as it became the least of his worries, the sounds of feet on the wooden floors advancing to the room he was in, taking precedence over his preferences for carrying things. Smashing the lightbulb with his left hand and crouching in the dark, Rex listened as the movements suddenly slowed down and became more cautious as they grew closer.

"That light isn't supposed to be out. I can't contact Unit 78 over the radio, and it sounds like his gear has been destroyed. Watch for hostiles."

As the CP finished speaking, Rex advanced out to the entry hall leading to the room, and opened fire on the first CP that was in his line of fire, the traitor leading five others. It took nearly ten rounds from the machine pistol to drop the CP, and as he fired into the next in line, the weapon suddenly emptied, his target falling backwards to avoid the bullets, now cutting up one wall. Retreating with the weapon still in his grasp, Rex began to run through the darkened rooms once again, arriving at the staircase and beginning to make his way downwards as fast as possible. Noting that the door to the room on the second floor was half-caved inwards, Rex continued down to ground level easily, reaching for the doorknob of the entry and laughing as he found it open as well.

Stepping out into an odd courtyard in the middle of a small city was a nice change of pace, especially now that Rex could see it was late day, and the sunset didn't look as horrible as it did in other areas he'd been to, so he was mildly elated. All of those thoughts disappeared as someone from across the courtyard spotted him, and suddenly he had nearly half a dozen CPs turning to look at him, emerging from the building. Rex swore aloud this time as he slammed the door shut, bullets racing by mere inches from him, then riddling the door with holes as he moved back and away, dropping the empty MP7 and pulling up the USP in a panic.

A grenade thrown from the exterior destroyed the door and sprayed the area with wood shards, the doorknob making ringing sounds as it bounced from the walls. The first enemy to enter the ruined doorway was a CP with a USP of his own, and Rex shot the Combine twice in the head from his vantage point. Approaching the body quickly, he took the second USP and the single grenade on the corpse, before bolting back up the stairwell. Rex stopped at the second floor, however, as he heard the sounds of more CPs advancing on his position from above, and instead of continuing onward, he moved to the half-collapsed doorway, crawling over the pile of concrete and wood blocking it.

Grabbing a hunk of concrete, Rex stacked it over the grenade, jamming the explosive at the bottom of the pile. He used the hunk of poured material to pin the tang down and prevent it from popping off easily as he yanked the pin, bolting away from his little booby trap and running through the rooms to check the windows for fire escapes or quick evac routes. Livid cursing emanated from his lips as he found them all barred and locked shut. Looping around to a position in the kitchen area, Rex found a small hole in the floor, and began ripping the wood slats apart, to make the passage big enough for him to slip through.

Stopping at the last second, he turned the gas valves on the nearby stove all the way up, smiling as the still-intact lines began to flood the room, and dropping through the hole in the floor easily. Moving through the pitch-black rooms as easily as possible, Rex found the exit door, noted it was braced shut with a chair, and removed the obstacle, testing the knob and finding it unlocked. Peering out, Rex found no one on the first floor or ground level; all the noises were coming from above, indicating that the CPs were crawling into the room he'd trapped, following his path.

Emerging onto the first floor, Rex began to run downstairs with the pair of USPs at the ready in his akimbo grip, until a Combine from the next floor up shouted in surprise, spotting him. As Rex opened fire on the CP that saw him with both of the pistols simultaneously, another enemy inside the room above stumbled across the grenade trap and cursed aloud over the radio band. Combine soldiers began yelling in shock, and the CP remaining on the outside of the doorway fell back away from the elevator gating to the pile of stone outside the second floor entry, avoiding Rex's gunfire as best as possible.

"Get rid of it! Toss it in the next room if you have to!"

Rex could barely hear the words as they were shouted, but he knew what was coming next, and as he tucked one USP away in favor of grabbing the dropped MP7, he began running for the doorway. Rex was still unable to clear the room as the explosion of the grenade hit the natural gas, creating a massive fireball, the sounds of an elephant herd stomping through the area combined with a shockwave that was enough to fling him out into the courtyard. The CP in the staircase behind him was still screaming as superheated pressures tore him apart. Landing roughly in the middle of a battered street, Rex picked himself up from the cracked and pitted pavement.

Looking around, he found the street to the north blocked off by a large blue energy field, the intersection to the southwest barred by a massive blue-steel gate with energy barriers beyond, and only the avenue to the east unblocked. Gathering himself together, still slightly stunned from the detonation with the implant playing physical prose in his ears, Rex stood up and glanced back at the smoking remains of the building. He marveled at the fact that he couldn't go five minutes in an area without blowing something up, and as he put the second USP away, Rex began to examine the area for more CPs.

Without warning, an APC roared down a side street from the north, and just as it reached the barrier, a rocket trailing behind it struck the rear half and flung it through the barrier. The vehicle crashed heavily in the center of the street, exploding in a flaming mess of debris and popping ammunition stores. A wheel rolled away from the barred street, ensuring that even Rex wouldn't be able to approach through the sparking, fiery mess, and effectively cutting off the route, despite his ability to ruin force fields.

Heading across the courtyard in an easterly direction, Rex easily thumbed the empty magazine loose from the weapon in his hands, and began to examine the MP7 closer, when another of the buildings caught his attention. This time, it was one to the north, and it appeared to be the only other six-story-or-higher building surrounding the courtyard, turning itself into a hive of CPs, pouring from the dual doorways on ground level. And at least seven or more of the traitors were accompanied by a handful of the electric blue-eyed half-breeds, all heavily armed, and no doubt bloodthirsty after the deaths of their fellow fighters were reported via radio.

Rex began to run away now as fast as he could manage, the blast of an energy round searing by his right side and the sounds of a bolt-action, being worked at echoing along as he moved. He barely cleared the corner of the courtyard around one building's edge before hearing it peppered with gunfire, inspiring him to double his pace. Running straight up the long street in front of him, he slid to a halt as he found a massive crater running through the middle of it, the edges and bottom still glowing cherry-red from one hell of an explosion. With no way to run across the wall of heat, around the crater's edge or the ability to walk across molten rock, Rex made a split-second decision. Turning to the shattered-out window frame of a candy store on his right, he ran inside just as another of the sniper's rounds ricocheted off of an exposed steel support beam.

Locating the emergency fire exit easily, Rex shoved it open and swore vapidly as the age-old fire alarm actually began to function, slamming the door shut once again behind him and using the empty MP7 as a doorstopper. Metal and plastic complained loudly as he lodged the empty machine pistol under the door, wedging it in between the steel-core safety door and the concrete stoop. With a show of force, he bent the rear half down with his left hand and jammed the stock into the pavement to make it more effective. Looking around, Rex found himself in an alleyway, just on the other side of the candy store, and as he ran back out to the side of the street, he found the crater behind him and no longer impeding his path, allowing him to bolt ahead to the next intersection.

One of the half-breeds might've spotted Rex as he hit the next intersection, but realizing their own path was blocked, he could hear them now attempting to batter the barred door down by force. Taking a second to map out his path, Rex noted that there was a massive, dried-up water fountain here in the center of the large intersection, and that the lane ahead was again blocked off by another massive blue metal barrier. He chose to take the way open to the right, moving in what he guessed was a southerly direction, pausing at one darkened doorway. Rex was breathing heavier than he could recall ever before, and it took major effort to slow it down, so he could remain quiet, grabbing two of the three hunting blades this time, their custom handles giving him a perfect grip.

Soon enough, he could hear what he was really waiting for, the CPs and the half-breeds coming around the corner of the intersection—like a bull in the china cabinet—loud, angry, and shooting at bodies lying in the street. Rex finally noticed the corpses, and just how decayed they were, signaling that he'd really pissed off the Combine if they were now angrily shooting off rounds at the dead. The bodies were no doubt left behind by the very same group that was trailing him, and the fact that the soldiers were still firing at them signaled that the Combine were possibly expecting a ploy like a body standing up to shoot back at them.

Tucking that little nugget of information away for later, Rex paused his breathing entirely, felt the implant begin to actually rumble in his body at the prospect of more bloodshed coming up, and waited until the last Combine half-breed passed his position before moving out silently. The large blade in his left hand jammed through the rear of the skull to emerge through the faceplate, Rex catching the corpse silently, and taking the last of the three blades from the torso sheaths in his left hand again. Rex crept up to the two blue-eyed monsters that were next in the group. Using both blades at the same time in a forward stabbing motion, the knives cut through the alien armor and padding easily, reaching the innards beyond. The blades reached their hearts easily, and again he caught the bodies as they fell. But the Combine on his left gurgled, and Rex was forced to scramble to pick up both of the alien pulse rifles from the bodies.

With one rifle in each hand, and crouching to brace himself for the recoil, Rex waited for the last pair of the half-breeds to turn around and face him before squeezing both triggers. He didn't bother snarling as the weapons shredded through the members of the so-called *Transgenic Forces* and caught the entire group of CPs by surprise. The weapons emptied as the last of the Civil Patrol fell back, wounded but still ready to fight.

Dropping the rifles, Rex advanced without a weapon at the ready, his left hand begging for something to do, and the traitor providing a nice opportunity. Smacking away the USP effortlessly as the CP tried to raise it, Rex used the same hand to strike the wounded patrolman in the gut as hard as possible, organic material deep inside the body shuddering from the impact, and the traitor screaming through the mask.

Using his right hand to pin the man down, Rex slowly began to peel the mask from the face, and found what appeared to be an albino human staring back at him, tubes running through the back of the head and in through the front right nostril as well. Rex tore the mask off completely, and the traitor began to scream louder, writhing under him. Apparently the bastard was coming along the way to becoming a full-fledged half-breed quite nicely, but Rex ended that by pounding the traitor's face with his left hand several times, caving the features inwards. The only thing that stopped Rex was the realization that he was pounding brain and bone into the pavement, the mask cackling in its strange radio tones as someone else spoke through a vocoder or throat mic.

"Unit 566, come in. Unit 566, report. Unit 566, your heart monitor is not in place. What is happening?"

Smiling grimly to himself, Rex began to grasp the fact that the mask and wiring, perhaps even the tube up the nose, were all monitoring systems. Pull the systems free, and there was nothing the headgear could do to report—it was neither receiving information, nor transmitting it. Perhaps the wetware the Combine enjoyed employing relied more on the brain and the synapses of the nerves than most people knew. But on the other hand, their more-advanced equipment no doubt *replaced* portions of the human mind to make them more alien in thought patterns and the like.

Dismissing the thoughts running through his battered head for later, Rex understood he could easily make that kind of experiment now, with the bodies all around him. But sooner or later, the Combine soldiers were going to send additional troops here, simply because one couldn't report back and the others were dead. Hurrying to retrieve the blades and the rifles, he again began cutting up pieces of the alien padding and armor, using them to fashion together a decent tactical belt and sling assembly. Locating more of the small ammo pods for the rifles and a few spare magazines for the USPs, Rex also found a large alien sniper rifle from the first Combine he'd killed. Leaving behind the smaller MP7 models some of the CPs once carried, Rex decided they weren't worth the plastic they were made of. He kept moving down the street to the next intersection, hearing the mask finally beep loudly as it reported a missing unit, rather than a dead one.

Curiously, Rex realized there was none of the female voices droning here to coordinate enemy soldiers, so he guessed that perhaps this wasn't too much of a high-priority area. But as he spotted the next intersection, buildings collapsed across the southerly route and the southeastern path, Rex estimated that, more than likely, the area had simply been bombed into submission by particle and HE weapons, any of the citizens or civilians here simply target practice. It would certainly fit with the state of things, Rex gathered, but the presence of the soldier strapped into the chair had Rex confused—was Maurine wrong? Did the Seven-Hour War *not* finish off the troops here? Or were these simply a new kind of resistance, in uniform, and more militarized?

Rex wished he knew exactly where he was, and that history class wasn't so lacking of real details in his youth. Taking the street that was unblocked to the north, with one of the pulse rifles in his arms, he froze as he reached the main street here. Hunkering down and spying the building across the way, Rex could see that it was massive and ornate, amazingly enough still in one piece, a park on its left side stretching north as far as he could see, and a large lot to the south. A parking area with a sandbag and concrete bunker in the center of it, a pair of massive twin 20mm or larger AA guns pointing straight up, as well as a duo of smaller antipersonnel mounts, each with *Twin 50's*, scanning the area.

The lettering on the building was shot to Swiss cheese however, but from what he could piece together, it looked like a national opera house of some kind, and he wondered curiously who really occupied it now. Rex was about to turn around and see if he could get a better vantage point elsewhere, until the cocking of a large weapon and a bore being pressed to the back of his head forced him to stop. Slowly, he let the alien rifle droop, set it down carefully, and began to raise his hands while standing, but someone pushed him back down, and he landed on his knees roughly.

"That won't be necessary, you Combine piece-of- crap. Prepare to meet your masters."

Rex didn't have time to complete a sentence before the next attack came. "Wait, I'm not—"

Someone struck him from behind hard, directly on his right kidney, and he realized he'd just been shot. The body armor deflected the round, but Rex reflexively winced at the bruise that was going to develop later, the implant already inducing him into a numbing buzz. Some of his nerves began to go just short of twitching as his entire body begged him to release his terrible rage and power against the offender. His mind was still human enough however to hold him back, preparing to spring into motion, every muscle tensed. Voices continued speaking behind him, and it took a very large amount of effort to grit his teeth, restraining himself from growling out his own response.

"Why didn't he go down when I shot him?"

"Beats me. Combine armor is worthless. Check him to see what it is."

"Fine."

Someone moved closer to Rex, and a weapon was being gestured at his face as the man circled around to look at him. The stranger was wearing the same fatigues as the tortured soldier Rex found earlier, but had a different patch on his arm, the older one apparently torn off and replaced. Rex could clearly see the pistol he was being threatened with now, one his father commonly spoke about, and showed him in older gun magazines from before the storms:

It was an AutoMag IV, a beautifully constructed seven-round weapon, this one the standard .357, .44, or perhaps the ultra-rare .50cal version. All of it was polished gunmetal gray and in great condition, other than what appeared to be a small patch of rust just below the cartridge ejection slot on the slide. The man gasped as he spotted Rex's face and the armor, and immediately he knew something was wrong, or right, either of which he couldn't exactly tell; the man looked both surprised and somewhat sick at the same time, and almost appeared to…salute. What the hell?

"Who is it, Mott?"

"I-I-I think he might be an American soldier. A Warrant Officer."

What? What the hell was this bullroar? And where did it come from? What was causing this man to assume he was a *soldier*? A berserker, yes, perhaps even a revolutionary on some sort a level, but all too much of a monster to be human, he knew, and definitely not worth of having the title or distinction of being a soldier, not after what he'd watched Cap go through.

"Mott, you have got to be kidding me. All of the Americans around here are dead, mate."

"I'm not going tits-up over this for no reason, look at this, man!"

A second male in the same fatigues came into view, except this one had longer hair at shoulder level, odd in comparison to his partner, who had it close-cropped, military style. And the weapon the other man carried was also interesting, appearing to be a British-made L85; except at a second glance, it was clearly the better SA80 carbine version. Another rare weapon, this one kept ornately clean, and handled quite well by the scruffy-haired, would-be sniper. Of course, this man gasped at Rex as well, except there wasn't too much shock in his tones.

"Wow! Is that an MCV!?"

The man walked closer, helped Rex to his feet, and smiled as he spotted the rank tabs that Rex himself clearly had ignored, or simply didn't understand, the sniper looking fondly at the armor vest. "It is, Mott! It's a damned mobile combat vest! I thought those things were impossible to get your hands on, even in the military. And a chief warrant officer, eh? Wouldn't one of those be quite a bit older than this guy?"

The sniper noticed the graying skin with the black veins raised close to the surface of the flesh, and finally looked a slight horrified at the sight. Rex grimaced while shaking his head, damning Strudenhamme with his thoughts. For a second, he wondered what Combine underling would find the shriveled heart of the dead doctor in the pocket of his tactical gear, before turning his attention back to the present.

The man named *Mott* grabbed his pulse rifle from the ground and handed it over sheepishly, apologizing profusely. "Sorry, mate, I—"

Rex cut him off in mid-sentence, trying not to sound angry as he spoke, thinking of the enemy close on his tail. "We don't have time for this. There are bound to be more Combine following me, they should be here soon."

Neither of the two men appeared to be very concerned at his words, and Rex swore under his breath. Was it going to be another exercise in explaining things? Perhaps another go-around with people he was trying to ally with, attempting to kill or abandon him? "Look, relax, man. We control the area around here at the opera house. Don't worry. The Combine generally tend not to pursue anyone for very long here, and frankly there aren't many readily available reinforcements. Besides, Me, n' Nate here, we're not the only two standing watch at this point. We've got a few other nests active in the area. No worries."

A hip radio on Nate's gear belt sprang to life, and suddenly the tone changed. The sniper grabbed the radio off his belt as it squawked, preparing to respond.

"Outer Defense to Nest 5. We've got two inbound APCs, perhaps on a run-through course. Rocket Defense 3 is taking them on, but there's also Combine radio chatter about another of the Behemoths dropping off reinforcements in the courtyard. Something really bad happened there, and Nest 2 wasn't active at the time. They saw nothing."

"Roger, Dodger. Keep up the pressure, and we'll keep the area clear."

Mott turned to Rex now, somewhat more serious as he spoke, "Look, I'd better get you into the station before those APCs arrive. If they report anyone on the ground as open targets around here, they'll just bomb the area later, so I'm guessing the commander wants our quad mounts to take them out, rather than leaving people out here to get shot at. Casualties we don't need, but if someone destroys a mounted launcher, we can always repair it again." Just as Mott was about to lead the way, he pointed to Nate. "You got this area, pal. Don't let it fall, got me?"

"I hear ya, man."

Mott continued across the street casually, and Rex took the time to check his equipment, feeling slightly disappointed. Not only was he down to scavenging again, but he'd lost his store of ammo, weapons. Not to mention the pride in being heavily over-armed, forced down to stealth-killing and missing out on the savage butchery he could be reveling in. Turning his focus on the man leading the way, Rex found it surprising that the man was armed with only the heavy handgun. But as he spotted a bandoleer covered in camo paint, Rex noted that the man had more than enough ammunition for the pistol, with little or no body armor, making him a somewhat effective scout or spotter he supposed. Finally as they reached the parking lot and began to move to the rear of the building, the scout began to talk casually.

"So, uh, sorry about shooting you, Chief, but wha—"

"Look, I'm not a chief warrant officer. This armor was my father's. I guess he didn't tell me a few things. And about shooting me, I'm surprised you aimed for anywhere other than my head."

"Yeah. Well, if you're not a CWO, what are you?"

"Name's T-Rex. Was a Revolutionary at one point. Guess I'm something…else now. But I'm not fond of talking about my past."

"I hear you, mate. No one here is eager to relive what pasts they have, especially with anyone else. By the way, boy-o, I saw what you did to the Combine on that street, but I wasn't sure what you really were. I've never seen anything like that before."

Rex considered it for a moment before speaking again. "Yeah, well neither have I. Guess I'm just lucky."

Something deep inside Rex was laughing at the thought of that concept. If he had any luck, it went from bad, to worse, to miserably disappointing, and beyond even that. No, the only thing he had that was keeping him alive was his need for survival, and the need to kill every Combine he saw, if he had the chance. Something he felt would serve only to undermine any alliance he made with anyone else right now, so Rex decided not to speak of it.

"Changing the subject, that's a nice AutoMag you have there."

"Thanks. Found it in an old Russian lockup we've been pillaging for almost a year now."

A year? Time was passing too quickly. Far too quickly. Perhaps time shifted when he was in Kiev, or before that. Rex had no idea. Perhaps there were only minutes and seconds between certain hops. Maybe the man in the blue suit cared nothing for the pitiful contrivances of time and space altogether and simply bent them to suit his purpose. If so, Rex still had a chance, however slight, that he would simply reappear from where he started all of this madness, standing in the teleportation chambers, Molly sound asleep next to Maurine, the cot ready and waiting for the rest he desperately needed. That too was also very unlikely for it to actually happen for him.

"Here we go," Mott spoke as they reached the side doors, leading into the backstage area of the opera house, and immediately the scout began to jog by the well-armed sentries with Rex following closely. Rex received odd stares from a few of the guards, but quickly discerned that the bulk of the people simply ignored him and went about their business. Some were repairing radios, others cleaning weapons and loading magazines, while still more attended to the wounded along one rear wall. Mott led the way past two more sentries into another area completely converted into a well-made kitchen area. None of it matched the rest of the opera house's ornamentation, but however industrial it was, it ran like a well-oiled machine and smelled great.

They moved all the way to the back, Mott opening a pair of double doors that were original fixtures, and smiling as it led into a massive dining area. It was full of people eating at a long table that once only saw use for conferences. The two of them walked through another pair of double doors to the right this time, and they were suddenly descending a set of stairs that led down for quite a ways. At the bottom of the stairs, they began through another area that looked like living spaces for those that used to tend to the giant opera house, and their path finally dead-ended at a closet of the last room. Three knocks and it slid aside to reveal a square-shaped, hand-dug room of earth, another heavily armed and armored sentry here waving them down another set of stairs, these carved out of the bedrock and shaped by human hands.

Finally as they reached the bottom, they arrived at a door that appeared to be made of old wooden wine casks. And as it creaked open, Rex realized it was a good ten or so inches thick, layered wood and metal forming quite a sturdy, if makeshift, vault-like door, sealing the room effectively. The area here was damp and warm, with the electric lighting strips buzzing loudly from the low ceiling. Moving along, Mott guided Rex through another man-dug tunnel with cylindrical definition, and Rex whistled as the tunnel ended at what appeared to be an old concrete bunker deep under the opera house.

The door was marked with Russian lettering and rusted heavily, but clearly operable, even if it apparently dated back to the Russo-Japanese War. The huge steel door opened to the sight of thick concrete bunker walls heading in a straight path, and Rex could see now that the tunnels looked quite utilitarian in nature, with exposed duct and conduit running along the ceiling. It was so long of a tunnel in fact, that Rex could tell they used small transports down here, Mott climbing into one that looked like a repaired golf cart. Rex hopped in alongside as the man motioned for him to do so, and Mott started them off quickly.

It took nearly fifteen minutes for the ride to complete, and Rex was wholly surprised to see a modern-day piece of artwork hanging on the wall to his left at the arrival station. It was a painting of a woman constructed of greened copper, holding three stars above her head like she was celebrating a triumph over something. Down at the bottom, was a small plaque that read "The Statue of Liberty," but clearly this was not the Lady Liberty that his father liked to reference, recalling the picture of the once-great statue before it was torn in half by a massive portal storm. Rex also remembered the story his father hated to repeat, but he could not resist hearing, about the day the storm happened, about the arc of energy that buzzed through the conductive statue like AC current.

The arc superheated it at an odd diagonal, the metal slagging and tearing while it glowed white hot for a brief second. The ocean began boiling as the upper half toppled in head first, steam rising as it cooled the molten copper. Shaking the thoughts clear from his mind, he turned back to Mott, and found the man waiting at a second steel door with a puzzled look on his face, but Rex ignored the glance and continued on through. One step forward and he found himself in a tight, metal-lined loading bay, a large object in the center covered over with a giant patchwork tarp, Mott gesturing forward and into the room beyond.

As the door closed behind him, Rex realized Mott wasn't coming with him, and as he glared into the dark room, he found it was a firebombed office space. It had been recently restored and decorated with makeshift furniture, including what was probably the only intact mahogany desk in the world. There was a small doorway to another room, this one lined with gun cages and lockers, but Rex didn't bother going in just yet, clearing his throat and hearing a surprised grunt from behind the desk.

The patched leather chair rotated around, and a hand flicked on a small lamp, the bare bulb harsh, but a source of light nonetheless. The man in the chair was an aging black fellow, at least fifty or greater in age, wearing the same camo fatigues and newer patch, as well as a tan beret with two stars on it. For a second, neither one of them spoke, both of them sizing each other up, until the commander spotted the small cloth bag Rex took from the tortured soldier.

"It's alright, Tanya, he's clear."

A door Rex couldn't see in the dark slid to the side, letting in another pillar of light from the ceiling fixture inside, a woman and two men standing inside heavily armed, and apparently just waiting for Rex to make a mistake so they could shoot him down where he stood. As they came into the main room, however, they all seemed to relax a hair, the woman crossing the room and opening yet another door leading to a small antechamber, opening a second door ahead of her as the first closed behind. Rex's attention was suddenly drawn to the sight of the commander behind the desk thumbing free a rather sizable revolver and setting it on the desk, chewing on the stub of a cigarillo.

"Awright, look here, outsider. We already know there's only one real reason you're here, what with the Combine killing anyone in sight, and frankly you're going to need to prove why we should recruit you. Even if you are an American and a solder, you'll have to prove yourself if you expect—"

Rex cut him off before the older gentleman could continue. "Look, *commander*, I'm not here to join up. I'm here supposedly because you may need help. I guess. Otherwise I don't think the man in the blue suit would have stuck me here." Rex added the last casually, guessing that they wouldn't know the man that was controlling his teleportation locations. However he was surprised as he received steady, recognizing nods rather than nonplussed features at the reference, and Rex gathered that perhaps things were so lax here for a reason.

Pulling the camo bag from over his shoulder, Rex tossed it down onto the desk surface and continued. "Now get this straight, I'm not here for good, so you'd better make use of me while you can. And just so you know, I got that gear bag from one of your men." Grabbing the set of dog tags, Rex tossed them over as well, and stiffened as the two men to either side of the commander leveled their weapons at him. One was a battered FAMAS with broken stock and the other a pistol-grip Beretta pump-action shotgun moving in unison. "Before you get all trigger happy, you should know that I found those on the body of a man that had been severely tortured. I managed to recover the bag before the CPs that did it to him. They look like they might come in handy."

The soldiers slowly lowered their weapons again, and the commander began thumbing through the pages contained within. "Very well. I must study some of these, and I shall return. You can sleep here for now, unless you wish to make the trip back to the opera house?"

"No. This will be fine. I only ask that you leave me a copy of a few maps, so that I may orient myself."

"I...will leave one or two. Although I recommend you get some sleep. You look like you've been through hell."

With that said, the commander grabbed up his revolver, locked a few items into a desk drawer, and left only one map behind before exiting through the antechamber with the two others following him. Rex guessed he could probably make it through any locking assembly or rudimentary security system these people had to get into the same room where the commander was now. But he wasn't about to risk it, knowing that the Commander already had two twitchy gunmen with him, not to mention who else was in there. Instead Rex decided to take advantage of what was present in the room, using his left hand to easily pull the desk drawer open.

It came apart regardless of the simple lock, and he located a second map to use with the first, an inventory of the gun cages, and a keyset for both the lockers and the cages. Going over the first map carefully, Rex found himself staring at a big section of Latvia, with sections outside of Riga circled. The second map was actually an overlay of the first, this one including markings where Combine soldiers had set up camp, barriers, nests, bunkers, and other larger buildings. Rex noted one demolished section of town marked with a large *secured* stamp, around something referenced as the *Cool Stepal*.

Taking in the shorthand descriptions of a section just beyond the secured area, Rex used it in conjunction with the inventory to guess the best way to drop the structures scouted out. It included a tower or outlook post, a pair of massive metal walls separated by a space in between them, a building marked as a weapons factory just beyond that. And even further from the previous areas sat a massive drawing of a circular structure, taking up impossibly enormous amounts of space if he accurately translated the distance on the map's key.

Once Rex had a decent list of items prepared, he used the keys to unlock the cages and lockers, smiling as he found himself able to upgrade what he was carrying. Dropping both of the pulse rifles and the USPs, Rex decided to keep the strange sniper rifle, stripping off the makeshift sling and belt assembly he'd made from the Combine armor and padding. Rex found a decent set of old MP gear to replace it with, including a holster and set of pistol mag pouches. Locating a nice .45 Long Slide and a set of magazines for the weapon, he sighed as he loaded the .45cal piece, recognizing that it was nothing compared to his beloved 10mm Delta Elite. But it was a genuine Colt by God, and it would do well enough, with a decent double-stack capacity rare for this type of pistol.

Storing the rest of the twelve-round mags into the proper pouches, Rex holstered the gray metal pistol into the MP rig, the duo fitting together like they were meant to be. A second pair of larger tactical pouches on an old leather belt were quickly added to his new MP gear, and Rex thanked the stars as only one of them were enough to relieve his overloaded pockets of the large cases of pulse-rifle pods. Continuing on his spree, Rex picked up a small Type 79 submachine gun, the weapon reminding him of the PLA soldiers and he eagerly added it to his arsenal. Collecting three mags of the 7.62mm ammunition, Rex attached the weapon to the gear belt using a lanyard ring. Turning his attention back to the sling assemblies he'd left behind, Rex used his skill at making makeshift items to turn it into another of the carryalls he'd rigged together before, strapping it to his back and using the inventory to find what he needed next.

Running over the plans he'd made deciphering the maps, Rex decided first that he needed a decent grenade launcher, or at least a few hand grenades would substitute nicely. Fortunately for Rex, the forces here had an entire cage full of the newer Russian GM-94 launchers, smiling as he pulled one of the four that was there free, the only with a folding stock. Removing four of the 43mm cartridges from the ammo tins, Rex loaded the pump-action launcher and hung it on the makeshift tac gear, feeling like he was almost ready for anything. Only four shots loaded into the launcher at the same time, but it would have to suffice.

Next was the problem with dealing with the dual walls between him and what he guessed was the objectives beyond, and that was readily solvable by discovering the locker holding some of the much older gear. It included a small cache of arms donated to the Russian stockpile during or after WW1, the contents consisting of a few boxes of obsolete ammo for a .30–06 Springfield that was marked off of the inventory as in use, along with a few other weapons. It also had what Rex was looking for, a boxed set of old plastic explosives that looked to be dated right after WW2 started, four sealed canisters of the material still waiting to be used, and he hoped they still worked after all this time.

The locker included a detonator for the charges, but unfortunately the device needed to be powered by feeds to a battery, and as he thought about it, Rex recalled that there was a garage here at this facility, and he'd find some of what he required there. Turning back to the inventory, he found it also included a pair of what was marked as 180mm shells, but Rex knew that couldn't be right, and located where the two were stored, in a massive crate along one wall. Opening it up, he found two of the biggest tank shells he'd ever laid eyes upon, marked with Combine signatures.

But at a certain point, he could see a human mind had influence in the shaping of this weapon, almost as if the invaders were taking the best ideas from the very peoples they conquered, absorbing it into their fold. Immediately, Rex began a careful inspection of the crates, and found that he could easily disassemble each of them, and did so cautiously. In the end, Rex could only manage to take one of the two warheads at first, but as he reread the list, he found a suitable solution in a small bag that would hang at the small of his waist for now, so that he could carry them, but only so far.

With his search and raid of the room complete, Rex had to decide whether or not he was going to stick around long enough for the commander to okay his plan, or come up with a new one. And after only a moment, Rex chose to side with his instinct to get things over with, hustling over to the garage area. As he arrived, Rex found three others inside, two men armed and a third that appeared to be an engineer, pulling the tarp down over the large object in the bay as they chatted.

The man holding a Steyr AUG was the first to notice Rex, and a single nod from the soldier to his friends was enough to quiet the conversation and turn their attention over to Rex. He wasn't about to let stage fright hold him back, however, so Rex eagerly began speaking.

"Ah, an engineer, just the man I needed to see. And a pair of fine solders. You'd do well on a quest to kick some Combine ass."

Everyone perked up and walked over cautiously, Rex pulling free the largest map in his possession, the paper still marked where he'd copied the overlay.

"As you can see, the Combine have this oversized structure here…" Pointing out the massive object above the smaller one, noting that the small writing on the overlay indicated the project wasn't completed, Rex stabbed it with his index finger. "…and I intend to see that it does not get completed, permanently."

Instantly, Rex had three volunteers on his hands, the man with the AUG conducting introductions. "I'm Devarov, this guy is Estes, and the man with the toolset here is Dmitri."

Estes took one hand off of his PPS-43 to wave at him, and that was about all of an introduction that was required, Dmitri not saying a word, merely looking a bit tired.

"Well, I have a plan to take all of these structures off of the grid, for good, and really we just need a way to get there, a little luck, and some backup in case things go awry. You two would be the backup, incidentally. Dmitri, I need a spool of cable compatible with a detonator like this one, and a car battery, or something similar, if you have it. And all that's left is a way there."

A smile spread across Dmitri's features. "We have that, too."

"Good. By the way, my name is Rex. Let's do some damage."

Dmitri had him a car battery and the wiring before Rex could comment further, and after disappearing for a moment, the other two soldiers reappeared. They were fully loaded with weapons and stores of ammo, both checking each other's thin Kevlar body armor before arriving back at the draped object. Dmitri waited to unveil whatever it was until the soldiers got close enough, doing so now with a flourish, the patchwork cover kicking up dust, but it was nothing that couldn't be ignored in favor of the object before him.

Long ago in another life, it was either a work truck or a rich man's toy, a 4X4 raised up on massive independent hydraulics systems, bearing giant turf-biting tires. It had a bare-frame look, covered only by long gleaming panels of reinforced and armored solar arrays, a large *Dominator* grill mounted on the front taken from a police cruiser somewhere. It also had the beautiful sight of a modified Russian DTM light machine gun mounted solidly atop the cab, a belt of rounds snaking out of the weapon and down to a large set of crates bolted to the frame of the bed.

Estes hopped up into the driver's seat and Devarov took shotgun, while Dmitri began to tinker with a few portions of the vehicle to ensure they were ready for use. Taking his time, Rex hauled everything up to the bed, thankful that someone had at least left the liner intact. Rex set the heavy battery down next to the large charges, as well as the small canisters of plastic explosives. Manning the DTM, Rex continued preparing by checking the 200-round box of ammunition, and while he noticed that while the belts could not be linked together, the modified receiver was easier to load and unload.

Dmitri soon nodded his affirm, and Estes started the bad boy up, the sound of a large V8 engine roaring and producing a smile on everyone's face. The engineer thumbed a button and the vehicle raised up, the ceiling parting and allowing Rex to see the signs of obviously newer construction. And Rex bet that the forces here weren't wasting time the Combine gave them, every second allowing them to grow stronger here. Hope was not as lost as it seemed.

Soon a second pair of doors opened above them, leveling out with the ground, and as the vehicle reached the surface, Rex could recognize they were rising up in the middle of a section of a park. The copper lady statue stood right behind them, still intact and no doubt a sign of human resistance. The vehicle roared down into the park at high speed before slowing and dipping down into what appeared to be a ruined canal. The water level was low and filthy, evaporated completely most areas. And a quick check of the map confirmed Rex's suspicions: The walls the Combine had constructed blocked the paths off, and would not allow them where they needed to go, but as soon as the problem presented itself, he had a solution. Leaning down to the cab, Rex leaned in, pointed on the map as he held it in front of Devarov, and shouted over the roar of the wind and the engine. "Pull up into the forward half of this ruined area here"—Indicating a section of buildings just beyond the *Cool Stepal* area on the map, he motioned inwards and to a halt.—"and hold position! I'll close the distance to the tower and the walls! Do you have anything that could be used as signals?"

Devarov paused, reached into the section in between the seats where a large bucket holding a dozen different items sat, and pulled up a handful of smoke and light flares. Grabbing two light flares and the smoke signal device, Rex continued shouting.

"I'm going to use the flares as distractions if I need any! When you see the smoke, and believe me, you will, ride up fast and hard! I'll leave some gear aboard, and collect it when you meet me at the device! After that, we'll play it by ear!"

A steady nod was all he needed in response, and Rex gave the map to Devarov to explain the plan to Estes, focusing his attention on manning the gun and collecting his thoughts. Should he have waited for the commander? Probably not. Time was of the essence, and Rex had been seriously derailed from whatever objective he was assigned to accomplish here. There was no telling what the effect of these events had on where he was supposed to be arriving next. No doubt the man in the blue suit wouldn't care too much, merely send him on another goddamned task—but Rex had to admit, he was starting to feel useful.

On the other hand, Rex was feeling terrible about Maurine and Molly. All he wanted to do was get back to them. But he estimated that wasn't going to happen for a long time, so Rex stuck his head back where it belonged, in killing Combine, destroying their goddamned Pillars of Dominance and Structures of Supremacy before their metaphorical fingers of alien and human half-breed flesh could wrap ever tighter about Terra. Soon enough the vehicle he was fond of thinking of as *homicidally vehicular* roared up the side of the dried out ravine and up onto a solid surface.

Rex looked at all of the buildings here, recognizing that most of them were decimated to spidery structures barely a story in height. Spotting a prime section of undamaged roofing over a ground-level entry in the largest of the buildings, Rex waved them over to it. They pulled up inside of what was once a reception area or showcase of a dealership, the shadows effectively hiding them. Devarov was immediately out of the truck and moving, however, grabbing a large device from the side of the vehicle, where a gas tank once might have sat, and pulled it out to the fading daylight, unfolding a solar collector and unraveling a cable to the truck, which was now shut off.

Rex knew they were trying to gather all the energy they possibly could, and with a quick gaze, he ensured they had a clear view of the area Rex was about to assault.

"See you soon."

Grabbing his first set of gear, having earlier divided it into thirds, Rex ran down the section of paved area to the grassy, overgrown hills. It was an easy approach from this side and allowed Rex to move as quietly as possible, closing the distance between him and the tower rapidly. He paused only once long enough to grab the sniper rifle from his back and look down the odd scope, noting that it allowed him to zoom in extremely close. Instantly, he could see two blue suits patrolling the tower, just outside of the wall, the wall with a small station at midpoint but no windows.

Checking the rifle again, Rex found it to be almost a part-for-part rip-off of the Arctic Warfare Magnum rifle, with a side-loading mechanism for the Combine pods and a bolt-action that looked more like it was merely used to limit the firing rate to one shot at a time. It mattered little to him however, slinging the weapon and growing closer in the darkness. Stopping at a massive boulder in the clearing near the tower, Rex spotted a strange trench that had been dug up to the tower's base from his position, guessing that the channel was originally defended before shortages in manpower.

As he peeked out to his right on the side of the boulder to get a better look at the trench, Rex was suddenly pinned by a beam of light and the sounds of gunfire striking the rock. The Type 79 was the first weapon in his hands as he landed backwards behind cover, opening fire on the tower above and smiling at how effective the small weapon was. He easily took out the spotlight in only a few shots, but was still unable to hit either of the half-breeds on the tower, as they hid behind metal panels and stanchions. Hanging the weapon back on the lanyard ring, Rex focused on a plan, decided distraction was the best option, and grabbed the flares from his pocket.

Bright red and originally designed for roadside use, they would do fine here and now, amongst the cool wet grasses and the night air that was slightly chilly as the sun continued its fall. Rex thumbed off the caps one-handed and dragged them across the surface of the boulder dramatically. He waited a half-second for them to flare-up and set alight before tossing them to his left, watching them land on the turf a few feet away, the source of light instantly taking fire. Selecting the GM-94 launcher from his pack, Rex leaned out to the right of the rock, took aim, adjusted for distance, and let fly at the tower.

He had to resist the urge to laugh before it could grow, as the 43mm cartridge struck tried and true, exploding loudly and ripping one blue suit apart, sending the other enemy falling to the turf some twenty feet below. Pumping the weapon to reload it, Rex hung it on his side and scrambled out from cover over to the trench, running up its length as Combine soldiers began to emerge from the small structure atop the Outer Wall. Rex selected the Type 79 again and opened fire upon the unsuspecting-yet-rapidly-reacting Combine, hitting one with a glancing blow and reloading as the weapon emptied of rounds. Rex took down a second soldier for good, the half-breed toppling from the wall as the rounds struck his legs. As Rex arrived at the triple supports of the tower near the wall, his vantage point was cut off, the Combine firing late in response to his persistent shooting and missing him by a wide margin.

Opening one canister of the plastic charges, Rex smeared it along one of the legs of the tower, stuck in a pair of contacts connected to the det cord, and ran along the side of the wall to his left. Rex got as far as he could get in a short time, turned back, and pulled the car battery free from the carryall, setting it down on the muddy ground. Looping the feeds on the other end of the spool through the detonator before snapping them onto the contacts of the battery, Rex slung it back into the carryall and gripped the detonator with both hands.

Holding his breath, Rex pulled up, twisted, and closed the connection on the plunger device, smiling as the charge did as it was meant to do and cut the leg of the tower effectively. The still-flaming mess toppled over to land in the trench leading back to the boulder, vibrating the turf and echoing loudly off of the Outer Wall. Rex was already moving as the tower finished its fall, pulling free a second case of the plastic charges, tearing the coating free in motion. As he got close, Rex smeared it onto the face of the Wall next to him, and connected the new feeds after snipping off the old pair first.

Uncoiling the cord behind him as he ran back to the footpad of the tower, Rex sat where it once did and again pulled up the plunger, gave it a twist, and closed the connection. This detonation was much louder than the first, the explosives each apparently in a different state of potency, and he only hoped what he had would suffice. Pulling the single smoke signal from his bag as he ran forward, Rex felt relief wash over him as he spotted the now-gaping maw in the Outer Wall, and pulled the tab free on the device, tossing it into the center of the clearing.

The red flares were enough to illuminate the smoke, thanks in large part to their proximity, and soon the truck was roaring up into the clearing. Devarov was standing on the bed of the truck with his AUG up at his shoulder, picking off Combine as they scrambled across the hole in the wall.

Rex bolted over to the modified vehicle, grabbed another canister of the charges, and spoke to the others as he switched his load of gear. "I'm breeching the second wall. As soon as I come back out through that first hole, wait for me to hop in, and then we can charge right through to the factory, or whatever it is." Rex paused to ensure everything was intact on his person, nodded to Devarov and Estes sharply, and charged back up to the wall. The Type 79 was a light weight in his grasp, taking his mind off of the hunger in his belly, the implant roaring in his chest, or the madness he felt as Rex realized his body was changing all too quickly, and not helping him hold onto what remainder of human was left in him. The space in between the walls was devoid of grass, all of the dirt kicking up thick clouds of dust as he moved, no similar structure on the Inner Wall to provide with him some sense of security in the fact that he could potentially pull this off.

However, it was too late to second-guess his plans, already tearing the charge out of the next canister as he arrived at the wall, mashing it onto the navy-blue metal surface. Sticking in another set of feeds and dashing away again, Rex began moving across the face of the wall and sliding along the dirt as he halted, grabbing the detonator in one hand. Another sequence of up, twist, and down was followed by one more blast of similar proportions to the last, and as the smoke cleared Rex ran back to the Outer Wall. There he found the truck already there and waiting at the first ragged hole, Estes and Devarov smiling from inside the cab. Leaping up onto the bed of the vehicle, Rex picked up the last charge of explosives, slipped it into one pocket, and gripped the handles of the light machine gun again, pounding on the metal flooring with one foot as he yelled. "Let's rock and roll!"

The truck growled loudly at once, and then roared into motion through the hole in the Outer Wall, quickly closing the distance to the Inner Wall. Rex spotted a trio of the Combine half-breeds examining the second opening, slapping the hood of the cab with an open palm, and yelling to Estes. "Run 'em down!"

One enemy stood his ground and tried to open fire, but it was far too late for any of the blue-eyed soldiers to escape, the Dominator grill tearing into the blue suit standing at the center. The monster tires ground the other two into the turf below, Rex opening fire with the mounted DTM steadily as he identified a group of half-breeds guarding the entrance to an old human building rebuilt to Combine standards. The truck swerved to the right and Rex tracked his fire as the Combine broke their lines and ran for cover, rather than attempting to overwhelm the vehicle with numbers. Their actions were odd in comparison to how they normally operated in combat against humans.

Finally the truck jerked back to the left to halt facing the structure, and Rex generously applied the ammunition from the Russian-made weapon to the opening. The pounding of the mounted machine gun was slow and steady, yet effective nonetheless. Neither overheating nor underperforming due to age, the modified DTM was truly a marvel of weapon crafting. As the 200-round box ran dry, Rex realized that Estes was ready and waiting to load and man the weapon next, allowing him to gather the next charge from the bed and leap out of the truck. Devarov had already taken a position underneath the vehicle and was providing cover with his deadly aim, covering Estes until the LMG was ready again, Estes opening fire on the structure.

No more Combine dared to pour out of the building now, and Rex came to the conclusion that he was going to be very busy soon, the Type 79 in his hands again like a reliable old friend. Waving off Estes from firing, Rex charged in through the bullet-ridden doorway, one Combine in his path falling to punctuating bursts from the small submachine gun. Another enemy died as he forcefully opened the doors, leading deeper inside, Rex shooting the half-breed while the bastard lay prone on the floor.

Quickly reloading with the last spare magazine for the Chinese weapon, Rex stepped into the interior of a massive automated weaponsmith shop. And as he cleared the structure for signs or presence of the blue-suited bastards, Rex found that they had to have been reassigned, even the light security detail here now obliterated. Pausing as he moved along the tables, he spotted an old blueprint-styled schematic set on one screen of a smithing bench, cursing. Rex could easily tell from the design of the alien weapon that it was not something any human had faced so far— the weapon was long and compact simultaneously.

A compensator was set to be mounted on the main barrel, and a second barrel protruded under the first—this one clearly marked with energy emitters and projection chambers. The weapon had two magazines, one bullpup styled and long, similar to a banana shape and the forward magazine, which appeared to be modeled after the M14 BAR or the standard Galil AR.

A quick check confirmed that none of the weapons were here anymore but no doubt Rex would be seeing them soon, and he only hoped they wouldn't be used against him as effectively as they were designed. After one quick run-through, Rex selected a few prime boxes of Combine pulse-rifles, one of the newer sniper rifles, another of navy-blue metal auto shotguns designed by the aliens, and a few stores of ammo, gathering them at a point by the doorway and moving out to the truck.

"Devarov! Get in here and haul this stuff to the truck for me!"

The soldier quickly ran up and followed Rex inside of the structure, laughing as he spotted the pile of weaponry. Devarov began to haul what he could, and paused as he spotted more within the building. "What about the rest?"

"I need it to help level this place."

"Gotcha. Moving out."

Rex began gathering the rest of the arms to a pile at the dead center of the main floor, loaded weapons, ammo tins, crates of grenades, and everything he could manage to find stacked together. Discovering a choice stash of newer, Combine-modified HK MP7s in the process, he examined these with larger 7.62mm rifle barrels extended to carbine length, larger forward receivers in between the two grips to accommodate the bigger round, and folding stocks rather than the smaller, and somewhat useless, collapsible stock. The upper rail was also equipped with a Combat Weapon Sight far better than a simple laser dot peep sight, and much more desirable for medium-to-long distances.

Dropping the nearly spent Type 79 in favor of one of the MP7M weapons, Rex collected as much ammo as he could carry, and shifted the crate outside to Devarov's waiting hands before reentering the building for the last time. Tossing the last canister of the old plastic explosive onto the pile, Rex stepped out slowly, ensured he had a clear shot, and pulled up the GH-94 launcher, yelling at the soldiers to move the truck. "Move that thing back! Better yet, get to the other side of the Inner Wall! I have no idea if this will work or how big the blast will be!"

Pausing long enough to allow the vehicle to get beyond the hole in the massive Combine barrier, Rex then focused his attention on the building ahead of him, adjusted for distance, and fired off the second cartridge in the weapon, taking cover by hitting the ground. The grenade began a chain of explosive reactions inside of the factory, and soon enough, what had to be a box of grenades touched off the plastic charge. The final detonation did not throw large hunks of the building outward dramatically, but rather crippled it from the interior fatally, the structure collapsing in on itself, even as the last of the rounds continued to pop off unabated.

Moving back to the Inner Wall's breech, Rex located the duo waiting in the cab of the truck silently for him, either in shock or awe, and as Rex hopped into the bed of the vehicle, he prepared the warheads, and waved the driver in through the maw again. Pointing them to a spot where there once sat an intersection for streets long ago, it was now the only clearing at the edge of a massive length of crushed and firebombed buildings. As soon as they were in position, Rex leaned in to the rear cab window and spoke to them softly,

"You'll have a prime view of what I'm going to do to that tower from here. As soon as it falls, wait ten minutes, and meet me back at the Inner Wall."

Effortlessly, Rex lifted the warheads into his bag and began to move at a swift jog over to the giant structure, finally giving it a place in his line of thoughts. It was enormous in size even though it was only three rings stacked upon one another, with some 2,000 or more feet of distance between each of them. It was taller than any building remaining in the area, and at almost 10,000 square meters in circumference, it was monstrous to say the least. Rex had no idea what it could have been used for once completed, but he wasn't about to find out, double-timing his motions with the MP7M in his hands, looking for any Combine activity and failing to find it.

Finally, he arrived at a section of the structure that was close to the dried-up canal, and as Rex scouted the area, he closed in on the Y-shaped support that was nearest him. Closing the distance, he noted that the ground here had been razed horridly, leaving only loose, shifting dirt and soil with no roots to stabilize it, and as he neared the support itself, he realized that the section under his left foot wasn't solid. Slowly sidestepping off of the spot, Rex cleared it away gently, pulling up on one of the timbers he found underneath with his left arm, and it snapped in half from weight of the soil on it and rotting age. Removing the shattered remains of wood exposed a deep dark shaft straight down into the crust, perhaps a mineshaft or emergency escape shelter for hundreds of people, now covered up and no longer operable.

Stepping back, Rex measured the distance from the foot of the support to the shaft, coming up with a total of mere inches. Looking upwards as he reformulated his plans, Rex found the support was actually one whole spire of steel jutting straight upwards, no doubt awaiting a second piece of similar proportions to be stacked up atop of it. Continuing with his previous plan, only slightly altered, Rex chose a point halfway up the support as a perfect spot for the oversized Combine warheads, stripping off some of his gear and climbing up the side of the support steadily.

Rex realized it was getting closer to dawn as he moved into position, wiring up the warheads and bracing them into exposures on the supports, using some spare det cord to tie them down effectively, before looping free some of the cable. As he began climbing down, Rex let the cord unravel from the spool as he moved, reaching the ground again. He was sweating like a pig, his right hand aching from gripping onto the metal support like a vice, but glad the job was almost complete. Bolting from his handiwork after recovering his gear, Rex froze as he heard the echoes of buzzing machinations, and turned to the sound of a dozen of the little flying razorblades coming down to investigate the area. They were being followed by, what appeared to be, a floating bipedal robot or other Combine-styled creation, perhaps an engineering machine of sorts, as well as a pair of the orange-eyed floaters, with their flash weapon and kamikaze bombing tendencies.

Knowing he couldn't allow the flying razors to clip his lines to the warheads, Rex grabbed the first thing he could reach. The GH-94 launcher was probably not the best weapon for the job, but he needed to take out a whole lot of enemies at once, and it would have to do, if only he could use it properly. Pumping the action, Rex took aim, and after firing the third cartridge, he laughed as it detonated right in the center of the mecha-razorblades, taking out all of them in one fell swoop. Pumping the slide again, he fired at the engineering bot and almost panicked as the cartridge missed the bot, or it evaded the well-aimed shot. The cartridge itself bounced from an upper portion of the support, beginning to fall to the bottom, where he'd placed his charges.

Thankfully, his luck quotient leapt up the scale, the orange-eyed blinder on the right of the engineering bot swooping in underneath the falling grenade cartridge. The explosion destroyed one blinder, stunned the second into a kamikaze fall to the loose soil, and damaged the engineering bot so severely that it began retreating, clearly not up to the task all by its lonesome. Slinging the empty launcher, Rex turned his attention back to the task at hand, and completed his run to the dried-out canal, unspooling the last of the det cord behind him. Sliding down the side of the canal, he stopped ankle-deep in a small puddle surrounded by garbage, grabbed the detonator, and prepared it for its last use by his hands.

Dramatically, Rex paused once more for his own pleasure, pulled up on the plunger, twisted it, and let the connection close again.

This time, the detonation was a storm of noise, a cacophony that went on for a good ten minutes, Rex pinned to the side of the canal as the ground vibrated and shook ferociously. Hunks of rock and metal bounced over the edge, and at one point, a large mass mashed into the center of the canal, several feet to his left. As the chaos halted, Rex dared to crawl back up the side and witness the destruction he'd wrought with the warheads and the simple, perhaps rushed, plan.

The support had clipped free of itself from the portion dug into the soil, and it had fallen straight into the exposed cavity in the crust, the stub at the bottom speared up into the first ring as it reached ground level. The impalement prevented it from drifting very far, but the reverse happened for the upper two levels—as soon as the structure fell, the top two rings smashed down onto the first, destroying it completely. But as the support pulled free, falling deeply into the shaft, the upper two rings were freed from the sound engineering and pulled hard on the other supports, yanking several down and tearing loose from the rest, landing in a diagonal heap on the ground.

Cheering a war cry from his vantage point, Rex felt relieved at the sight before him, but even as this burden lifted from him, another was still squarely in place. He had to get back to Molly and Maurine—by any means necessary. Gathering himself, he began to jog along the side of the canal, bypassing the remains of the factory and arriving at the Inner Wall with a sigh, noting that he'd arrived just before the others, their vehicle pulling up now.

Dmitri yelled out to him as Rex ambled over, "Hop in!"

Both of the revolutionaries wore large grins, and Rex couldn't help but smile as well, hopping into the truck. He unstrapped the GH-94, leaving the empty launcher on the bed of the truck, sitting up against one of the wheel wells tiredly, speaking to them with a weary tone. "Let's get outta here." Estes and Devarov clearly agreed, and as the drive back began, Rex began to wonder what would be next on his agenda. Turning and speaking to the others through the empty rear window frame, Rex absentmindedly picked at the mud dotting his clothing. "So what did you think of those fireworks?" Pulling the heavy battery from the carryall, Rex chuckled at their simultaneous response.

"Outstanding."

"I agree."

Grabbing loose the spool of det cord, he tossed it next to the battery and the spent launcher, continuing his end of the conversation. "So what are you going to tell your boss about this, then?"

Picking free the detonator, Rex set it down with the rest of the gear, feeling his implant wind down slowly, listening to them speak.

"Only that we blew up and killed every Combine in sight!"

"Yeah, wait'll Mott gets a load of this. He prolly wanted to be in on this raid, too."

"Hah! Like he deserved the chance! That bastard always gets the prime assignments. And here we were stuck to guard duty in the goddamned garage again."

"Well, it sure as hell turned out a lot differently this time, thanks to you."

As Devarov questioned the lack of response, he turned and found the American named *T-Rex* no longer sitting in the truck bed. They backed up, looked for him until dawn, but still they found no sign of him. Disappointed that the stranger was gone so quickly, and with plenty of explaining to do to the commander, they climbed back into the vehicle and drove off towards their base.

———❦———

Rex felt the shift slowly, and suddenly it was on him, the vehicle speeding off, and as he turned to see what was happening, the world flashed, and he was stuck in the blackness. Again. Damnit, he wanted to go home. Enough of this. He needed to see Molly again.

"Where the hell are you?!"

All this time in passing and still he didn't know the name of this new, finely dressed tormentor.

"Come out here!"

No reaction. Nothing. Was this how it he would end up? In the blackness, screaming at nothing, with no way home?

"Why so angry, Rex?" Rex spun about to see the man in the blue suit standing right behind him, with a creepy smile on his face. "Ah, I see the changes are starting to affect you. Then I suggest you complete your next task before you're no longer human enough to ever see Molly again."

Rex wanted to leap at the man in the suit, to tear his throat free from the body, but he knew he had no chance of doing it. The man in the blue suit would simply leave him here, in his eternal nothingness, and so resignedly, he shook his head and responded gently. "Yes. I should. What's next?"

The man in the blue suit smiled, no doubt already knowing what Rex was thinking as he spoke. "Well, you see the…tardiness of your arrival in certain areas, and the surprising presence of a group of now-rogue Combine recruits in action, I've been forced to change plans. I never expected the Combine to actually capture you and take

*you so far off course. It almost looked like they were attempting to...
re-recruit you, if my estimates are no doubt correct."*

*Rex saw the smile on the man's lips, knew he lied about not knowing
Rex would be nabbed, but the latter parts, perhaps they were the truth.
He guessed that if the man had gone this far to lie about his knowledge
of Rex's kidnapping, then perhaps he guessed it would happen after
Rex had the time to accomplish something in Kiev, perhaps something
involved with the crew of Combine recruits he'd rescued.*

"And? Does this mean what I think it does?"

*"Perhaps, Mr. Rex. Perhaps. But even I do not know just how
far away you are towards your...own goal, having witnessed the
incredible...efficiency you dispatch your foes with. So perhaps there is
hope after all, yes?"*

*Rex froze at the quotations of his own thoughts, and realized he
was in deeper than he truly ever had known, especially when it came
to the abilities of the blue-suited gentleman, especially those he didn't
know about yet.*

"Perhaps."

*"Good to hear, Mr. Rex. In any case, I need you to...assist a few
others I wish to keep...intact, so be cautious in this quest, Mr. Rex,
they are all required beyond your...scope of understanding. And do not
fail me, Mr. Rex, or those thoughts of yours will come to life."*

*Another rapid flashing of background, and he faded into the blurred
world of a field of grasses, a tree a few feet to the left, a massive island
beyond in the distance.*

*"And, Mr. Rex, I promise, if you do your task well, you will know
more than you do now, I am...certain of that fact."*

*Flash. Blinding, and overwhelming. Ringing in his ears.
Sensations similar to those of the transporter Lena had run him
through. Instantly he had thoughts and dreams of being home, oh so
soon, far later than he hoped, but sooner than he expected. As things
resolved, he realized he knew this area, but it wasn't home, was it?*

—⌇∽⌇—

BLACK MESA EAST

Rex appeared in some kind of cage-bound system totally thrashed to hell, and as he felt the floor materialize under his feet, he kicked at the tilted cages barring him in. As they fell forward, he stepped off of the device, which now began to spark and destruct further. Things were living nightmares here for scientists, everything destroyed by hand he could tell, and there were several splashes of red blood on the walls, crimson pools on the floor, now coated with burnt ashes of papers and fragments of circuit boards and metal. Everything that was once was now destroyed, but Rex knew this area vaguely.

This was the last place he'd seen Dr. Vance, when they tried to bring him over, before everything went askew. Something was seriously wrong if one of the most well-stocked and supposedly most intelligent groups of humans were suddenly decimated. Rex slid on the remains of something once alive, ignored it, and noted the elevator was gone, perhaps fallen to the bottom floor or stuck at the top. Doorways leading straight ahead from the ruined device collapsed downwards, forming a wall of concrete he could most likely move, but not without considerable effort.

Turning his attention to the only pair of doors not blocked to the north of the room, Rex walked through them and emerged into an access area, containing a ladder that reached all the way up to the surface, as well as a staircase. Rex cursed as he heard sounds, not only from up above him and down below in the staircase, but also behind him, at the pair of double doors he'd ignored situated at the southern section of the room.

A group of spindly, almost-human creatures emerged into the same room he was in, screeching and walking forward slowly. And as one halted, preparing to do something Rex wasn't about to witness, he pulled up the MP7M, and cut the group of five screeching parodies of human life down with a single magazine of the blessed 7.62mm ammo. Reloading with one of the four forty-five-round mags he had left, Rex focused his attention on the noises below him first, rushing down to the next floor of thrashed equipment, spotting a squad of blue-suited half-breeds.

Crouching from his vantage point in the corridor, Rex realized this had been little more than a storeroom, and began wondering why the Combine was here. Using the gleam of a shorted-out elevator through cage doors on his left side, as a decent source of illumination, Rex easily cut his enemies down with the newer MP7, thanking the Combine for creating it and leaving it in his loving hands. With the half-empty weapon at the ready, Rex crept inwards, found a loaded pulse rifle, and jammed it into the carryall, never knowing when he'd blow through all of his ammo next, and concentrating on listening to the sounds of enemy troops moving about on the floor above him.

Tactically reloading while he had the chance, Rex crept up the staircase now, the floor above the labs empty of everything, except for more destroyed equipment. Rex began to get the general idea behind some of the destruction. The last few people to pass through here were on a scorched earth policy, burning everything they could and perhaps taking measures to sow the ground with salt so that it would never bear any fruit again, preventing the Combine from gaining more than what they had now. But as he moved up to the next floor, Rex cursed under his breath, finding more Combine just standing at the entry to a room that had been seriously blocked off. The four of them were chatting as if the sounds of gunfire were nothing to be wary about, most likely guessing that their own friends below met some humans, and had vaporized them.

"So you think there are more survivors behind here?"

"Yeah. Not positive, but we found this area marked as a medical wing, so I'm guessing some were here when we first struck. Unit 668 is upstairs scrambling another transport with a demo crew. Evidently someone forgot to send one of those groups out here with us, no doubt a tac leader is going to hear an earful for making such a stupid decision."

"What about the humans that escaped?"

"Not sure. Command reports that they killed most of the advance scouts before we got here, and they're guessing the humans were responsible for destroying all of the equipment. Word is that Breen has Vance, and is going to torture the answers out of him, slowly."

"Nice. Guess these human scum are about to learn the lesson of not siding with our Benefactors."

Rex had heard enough, and as he advanced a little closer out of the staircase, he took careful aim at the first Combine in his line of fire, the bastard thumbing a section of the collapsed stone wall free to look at it. The soldier died as he laughed, the first shot ripping through the temple, thanks largely in part to the CWS, Rex using only headshots to kill the others looking around wildly for the source of the incoming fire.

Immediately Rex moved to the collapsed entry, and found it in the same condition as the ingress downstairs in the lab, one massive slab of set concrete tilted down covering the doorway. Rex hung the MP7M on its small sling and began to grab at the concrete sections, lifting it back and up with inhuman strength.

Just as it cleared the floor, a hand with a USP gripped within leaned out around the corner, a voice screaming. "Die you Combine bastards!"

Almost falling back with the slab in his arms, Rex finally hocked it to his left side casually while regaining his balance. A snarl formed across his face as he responded, pushing the firearm aside, and the bullets missing him by a wide margin. "Goddamnit, stop firing! I'm…human!"

"Really?! Hell, we thought no one was left to help us!"

"Well, stand back and don't shoot, for Christ's sakes! There might be more Combine already on the way!"

"Fine, fine, get to work! We want the hell out of here!"

It took only a minute to deconstruct the rest of the fallen debris enough for the group to crawl out of the single entrance room. The bunch of survivors consisted of a man with one hand; an older, huskier male; a blond woman in a scientist's smock; and another woman, this one with reddish hair cropped short. The redhead wore garments that reminded him a lot of the scavenged clothing Maurine wore when he first saw her, including an armband with the Lambda symbol encased in a circle spray-painted orange. The similarities shocked him, but not as much as the last survivor to crawl from the opening, another of the brown-skinned aliens with the red eye, whom seemed to recognize him right away, yet said nothing to the others.

"Alright, everyone grab the weapons from the Combine bodies here, and if you can, strip off the torso armor."

The last request was taken with an odd look, but Rex had no time to explain to their already-strained responses, noting that his odd skin tone and mottled arm was not drawing the best of their attentions, dully realizing that this discoloration was more than likely affecting his face as well. He needed a mirror, but with no time to give to such vanities, Rex began to hustle the small group, noting that the man with one hand was struggling and helped his efforts, getting the armor free from the four Combine bodies. Rex also became aware of the fact that while the alien needed neither armor nor a weapon and made outfitting the group one measure easier, he was still uncomfortable around the creature. He tried not to let it mask the fact that the situation was going swimmingly so far as a rescue, but also not able to accept it wholly on the other hand.

Focusing on getting the new recruits armed was simple, the scientist, revolutionary, and heavyset man getting pulse rifles, but the one-handed man somehow ending up with a pump-action shotgun. Turning to him again, Rex traded him the shotgun for the sniper's rifle, which could be loaded with the firing hand, hoping that the bandages around the stub of what was left on his left hand wasn't paining him too much. It was also handy that the entire group of dead Combine wore more of the USPs as backup weapons, allowing the one-handed man with two handguns and the others all a single backup piece, with a spare mag of .45cal each to go around to the survivors.

"Alright. Let's hustle. Down to the bottom floor, the lab, I think. We're not sticking around for anymore Combine to show up and shoot at us." Quickly Rex led the group back down to the lab and stopped them at the collapsed doorway, turning to his new recruits and realizing he needed their names in order to get things going cohesively.

"What're you're names?"

The one-handed man spoke first, "Oz."

The lady scientist was next, voice wavering, "Alexia."

The female revolutionary took her turn. "Rinzinka."

The husky man was next, sweating still from the run. "Harry."

Rex turned to the alien, and tried to hold back the old feelings of revulsion still brewing within. "And you?"

"I have taken the name Diazepam."

"Good for you. Hopefully, you'll do well without a weapon. Your brothers on Xen did."

"We know this, and more, T-Rex."

Smiling hollowly, he turned to the rest. "Now we're introduced. If you didn't hear the brownskin, I'm T-Rex. Let's get the hell out of this place. Oz, I need you to cover the stairwell. Rinzinka, go with him. Alexia, Harry, in the storage area downstairs is a group of dead Combine. Collect their ammo, and get back up here to divvy it out, pronto. Diazepam, you're with me." As everyone began to move, Rex explained to the alien what he intended. "We clear this pile, and I'll lift this massive hunk here. You get everyone on the other side, and I'll follow, with you doing your best to keep it up in case I lose it."

"A wise plan, odd one."

Harry and Alexia were already finished with their task even before Rex and Diazepam had cleared the rubble, but just as Rex began to heft the center hunk of collapsed concrete, Oz yelled out, letting his sniper rifle speak for him after his one word warning. "Combine!"

"Fine! Fine! Get in here and get under this damned breech!" Rex roared as he lifted up the massive hunk of material, immediately feeling his muscles complain, knowing he'd overworked himself so far, pushed himself to the limits, and felt his body only increase in resolve each time. Now Rex didn't know if he could manage it. All of the survivors scrambled under the slab as he lifted it, and just as he leaned in where they stood, preparing to release it, a Combine half-breed ran into him from behind at full tilt. The blue-eyed prick was visibly surprised as he managed to knock Rex backwards, falling down into the group as the massive section of concrete mashed the enemy trooper. Breathing a sigh of relief, Rex helped himself up as well as the others that had caught him, thanking them with a slight nod before focusing ahead on the thick door to blackness up to their right, or the bent door straight onwards.

"Alright, I'm now officially out of ideas. Where do we go to next?"

Rex was breathing hard now, as well as everyone else, but it was the female Revolutionary that spoke first, her voice solid and ready for everything.

"I suggest you lift that door there, and we get through Ravenholm. There's greater chance going through zombieland rather than waiting for the Combine to cut us down in the junkyards' main grounds."

The female scientist immediately disagreed, a quick verbal rebuttal that was short and to the point. "No. There's a way to get out through the main yard, and we should try that. Ravenholm is off-limits for a reason."

Rex considered it as the two women began to lambaste each other. Before it could get any further along, Rex spoke up. "Main yard it is. I'm not particularly fond of going through anywhere named *Ravenholm* that has the word *zombieland* attached to it as one of its primary descriptors. Let's go."

Moving up to the bent pair of double doors, Rex cursed as he found the interior door inoperable, and smashed his fist into the control panel in response, shattering the monitor and making Alexia shriek. Ignoring the reaction to his brutal move, Rex laughed to himself as the doors finally squealed and opened up. The group moved in through the outer yard quickly, and as they passed up a strange fenced-in barrier, they arrived to the well-lit inner yard, surprised to find a few Combine bodies alongside a number of human corpses. There was a minimal amount of ammo to be scavenged, and as Rex did so, the two women began arguing again.

Alexia was yelling so loudly that it reverberated down the concrete and metal around him and made his ears ring, his teeth clenching tightly. "Well, this is genius! You say the exit tube is up there, but how the hell are we supposed to get to it?!"

And Rinzinka was not letting up, firing back a salvo of her own in return. "You won't even let me finish!"

"Enough!" Rex commanded attention as he spoke now, and realized he was much different than the scared little child that started off on this trek. He was jabbing the finger on his right hand as he roared at them both.

"You. Finish your task and get us up there. Rinzinka. You'll shut your mouth around her. If you need someone to get into a pissing contest with, it'll be me! Not a goddamned civvy! You got that?!"

Angry, but submissive, nods followed.

"Now stop arguing! We have to work as a group to get outta here and to safety, and there's no telling when the Combine *demo team* will get here, and accomplish that little feat! Move!"

Alexia had Harry help her with opening a massive shipping crate at the far end of the yard, moving in herself and driving out with a large stepladder truck. It was apparently a cherry picker or engineering lift in a previous life, now modified with a large ladder along its length, taken from what looked to be an old firefighter's ladder unit, the lifter arm and bucket replaced with the stepladder unit bolted to its side. Harry, once an operator of heavy equipment, knew easily just how to modify the position and movement of the ladder, creating a great path up.

As Rex stood at the bottom of the ladder unit, covering the group while they moved to the top, he turned at just the right moment and noticed they were all waiting for him, Oz covering for him with the rifle as he ascended the ladder. Arriving into the tunnel, Rex realized the entry was very deceptive, a smaller tube used to mask the larger passageway of pipe beyond, obviously a hidden setup for escape, and one he was glad they'd chosen. But before they moved on, there was something he needed to do.

"Wait. Oz, over here with that rifle."

Oz humped over awkwardly in the dark tunnel, carrying the bolt-action Combine weapon cautiously, having already modified the bandage that was holding his left arm to his chest by wrapping part of it about the rifle to keep the weapon steady in his grasp. "One second."

Rex leaned out to the entry tube, and grabbed the top of the outer rim to give him some leverage, planting feet firmly on the top step of the ladder on the truck. Bracing himself between the pipe entry and the ladder threshold, Rex began shoving outward with both feet on the top step, a deep throaty growl growing from within as he pushed. Rex finally roared aloud as he moved the truck down at the bottom visibly, tilting it up onto two wheels, and finally pushing it over on its side. The vehicle continued to fall as the off-balanced ladder weighed it down even more, the entire device on the truck snapping free as the vehicle rolled over onto its top.

Laughing at his show of exertion so far, Rex wondered just how long he could keep this up, sweat pouring down his back in rivulets, making the now-ratty shirt he had on underneath a poor barrier between his back and the heavy armor vest. Pulling himself back inside the pipe slowly, Rex could hear a distant thump of what could have been an explosion, most likely the Combine demolition crew trying to get past the heavy stone obstacle in the lab.

"Oz, you're up. Blow that vehicle to hell. Make sure the Combine can't use it."

"Right."

"The rest of you, get moving. Diazepam, you're in charge until we catch up."

"As you say, odd one."

Oz turned around at the last of the statement. "We?"

"What, you thought I was going to leave you here all by your lonesome? No, my orders are to protect all of you. Even a one-handed sniper."

Rex smiled and prodded Oz into motion.

"Now blow that thing to kingdom come so we can get the hell out of here."

Oz nodded imperceptibly, already taking aim through the fancy Combine scope with nearly unlimited zooming capacity, taking his time and ensuring his first shot was the only one required, the small duty truck going up in a fancy ball of flames. Rex bet that it was probably one of the only gas-fueled vehicles still functioning nowadays in this area, but he realized there was no choice other than to destroy it. The Combine were hot on their tails, so anything that served to keep the offenders as far back as possible only satiated him further.

"Alright, you lead the way. The scope is NV capable, I think, so you'll have an easier time of it."

Oz was already moving again, reloading the weapon and practicing his bolt-action motions, responding dryly. "What, now you're gonna use the one-armed sniper as a body shield?"

Rex smiled. "Anything that keeps me from being in between those two women and their arguing is acceptable."

Oz laughed aloud, obviously recalling something from inside the Medlab, where the group had been trapped, most likely for quite some time before Rex arrived.

"Let me guess, you've seen them do worse, right?"

Oz nodded his head but didn't speak about it. "Believe me, you don't wanna know."

The two of them kept up a steady pace well behind the rest for some time, until Diazepam's voice came into Rex's thoughts, disturbing him thoroughly.

"Problems here, odd one."

Immediately Rex moved Oz faster down the tunnel, and as they both arrived, Rex was glad to see most of the problem was over, a group of headcrabs now dead and Alexia providing some basic first aid to a nasty wound on one of Harry's thighs. But alas, the worst wasn't over, Alexia and Rinzinka starting up on each other for the third time.

"Damnit! Can't you open your freaking mouth when you see a group of headcrabs coming for us, rather than just shooting at them?!"

"I was a little busy, if you couldn't tell! You've got a gun and a pair of eyes too! Why don't you use them?!"

Rex moved ahead of Oz, knowing he had to get this under control now. "Stop it! Both of you!"

Both of them turned to face Rex, and for a split second, he thought they'd turn on him.

"Alexia! Don't start with her! Shut up and heal Harry! We need you to keep everyone in tip-top shape! Not complain why you have a sudden task!"

"Yeah, and—"

Rex grabbed Rinzinka by the arm, flung her around hard. "Stop. It." Staring right into her face, Rex tried it again. "What the hell did I tell you?! We work as a group now, and even if that scientist windbag brings something up with you, you bring it to me! It's clear I can't trust either of you to act somewhat reasonable around each other, but by God, Allah, and whoever else is keeping us alive, you *will* get along while I'm here! No exceptions!"

"Who the hell do you think you are?!"

Rex smiled as Rinzinka said it, almost exactly as Maurine did so long ago. Holding the scary grin in place, he used the same tactic as before.

"I'm the prick that's killed more Combine with my bare hands than I care to count, brought down two of the biggest alien structures I've ever seen before, wiped out nearly three square miles of Combine aircraft factories, toppled a Combine train from its tracks, slaughtered zombie hordes, traitorous masses, and mechanical creations alike, and, oh yeah, saved your sorry ass from a Combine Death Squad not more than fifteen minutes ago!"

Rinzinka recoiled at the response, clearly fearful of what Rex might do to her but not raising her weapon.

"And now I've been given the task of keeping you and *everyone* else in this group *alive* and in *one piece*. I can't have you screwing around, especially since you're one of the only combat-experienced people I have right now! Get your head into the damn job, and *scout!*"

As Rex pointed the way forward down the tube, Rinzinka followed it dutifully now, clearly not interested in testing his resolve anytime soon. Rex sighed as he took on gazes from the rest of the group for a moment, but the others followed the scout, leaving him behind for Tail-End Charlie. Picking through the best of the headcrab remains, Rex grabbed the biggest, fattest, and pretty much nastiest one he could find, treading softly behind the group. Unfortunately, they'd all been through quite a lot, exhaustion showing through slow movements and raised tempers, and it wasn't long before they'd halted in the tunnel.

Diazepam began explaining the situation to Rex as he approached. "They're all quite tired, odd one, and seek rest."

"Very well. Do you think you can make this…thing edible?"

Rex passed over the headcrab slowly, and Diazepam seemed to smile, as far as Rex could make out, that is.

"Yes. It will be palatable and somewhat nutritious, but a little…bitter."

Rex nodded his affirm. "Go ahead. We'll need sustenance, and there isn't much around here."

"As you desire, odd one."

As the group slept, Rex waited farther down in the tunnel, counting the minutes as they passed by, mostly to keep time, but also to help him derail his thoughts, force his concentration on what was coming in the tunnel, and avoid his own approaching exhaustion. After about four hours, he stood up tiredly, and made his way back to the group, Diazepam stopping him to present him with the cooked and trimmed headcrab.

"Here you are, odd one. A request of a question, if I may do so?"

"Go ahead."

"Long you have been from home, we see. Why?"

Rex paused. Didn't the creature know already? The alien had been roaming through his thoughts as easily as Rex might have thumbed the pages of a book.

"The man in the blue suit. He…uses me as a weapon, I think. And I only have one choice: Obey, or never see Home again."

"Thank you, odd one."

Rex knelt at Oz's shoulder and shook the man awake, using the cleanest of his three knives to cut the headcrab into pieces, taking the smallest portion and handing the rest over to the startled fighter.

"Wake the others up and give them some. Divvy it up evenly between them, and when they're done, join me up ahead in the tunnel—it's time to move on."

Navigating the tunnel became easier as it widened in dimensions, curving several times, and convincing Rex that whoever had designed this as an escape route clearly had not finished his job. The lack of transportation was a true pain in the ass, and the discovery of headcrabs every once in a while was not exactly comforting. To Rex, it all meant that either the course was never finished because of the presence of the creatures, or the escape transport was already used to get to the other end. If the latter was true, there was no doubt the person attempting to escape found that it was now invaded with the creepy-crawlies, most likely something to do with the other end being discovered by the Combine or more unsavory beings.

But all of this was speculation in Rex's mind, and as the hours passed drearily, conversation never picked up between the group members, most of it only a basis for argument, and that, Rex had decided, he would have none of. After what felt like they'd spent about eighteen hours walking silently through the empty tunnel, Rex decided they needed a real break, especially if more of this tiring travel was what they could expect to encounter later on. Stopping the group, Rex turned to them. "Alright. We need a real stop for rest. Diazepam, I know you don't sleep, so I'm going to ask you to cover the route behind us, alright? Expect eight to ten hours at most."

"At once, odd one."

As Diazepam shuffled off down the tunnel, Rex continued speaking. "Okay. I'll take last two hours or so to sleep, so the rest of you, go ahead."

As they began to lie down, Rex moved forward in the tunnel and halted again a few feet from the group, wondering just how the hell he was supposed to keep them all alive, and what he'd done in a past life to deserve babysitting the two women like this. It was so much to think upon that before he knew it, two hours had passed, and one of the others approached him from behind. Turning slowly, he found it was Oz, the man smiling visibly as he took a seat. "Not sleeping?"

"Oh, I will, I just wanted to thank you."

"For what?"

"Heh, getting my ass out of that room back in BME."

Rex was puzzled, and questioned the abbreviation. "BME?"

"Yeah, Black Mesa East. Or at least it *was* BME before the Combine showed up."

"Why is it called BME?"

"For a couple of reasons. One is that Doc Vance and all the others that lived and worked there, including his daughter, strangely enough, were all survivors from the Black Mesa Incident in New Mexico."

Rex found himself roaring back at the discovery. "You mean they're all part of the reason of the portal storms occurring?!"

Oz looked a little taken aback. "What crate have you been locked up in, man? All this is common knowledge."

Rex pushed it aside. "Look, never mind. Let's just say I was never very well-informed. Now what's the other reason?"

"Alright, man. The second reason is theoretically that they were not only working on the same technology as in Black Mesa, but supposedly they had some kind of link to Black Mesa itself, or at least one of the old labs, for a while."

"For a while?"

"Yeah, apparently one of the satellites they were using to bounce signals to each other was discovered by the Combine and zapped down. Doc Vance was trying to bounce a signal using the Xen relay coordinates to reach them, but it wasn't working. All of that was happening just before the Combine came in. I'm not sure because I was in the lab getting this taken care of, but Rinzinka had been patrolling through there looking for Alyx, and when she came back up, she told me some of what was going on, but not all. Some guy named *Freeman* was down there with Alyx, in the junkyard, and Rinzinka didn't get to talk to her about it."

"Alyx?"

"Oh yeah, Vance's daughter."

"And what happened to your hand?"

Oz looked upset. "I'd rather not talk about it."

Rex looked at his skin, and the mutated left arm. "I know what you mean."

"Look, I'd better get back and sleep some more. Still a little tired."

Rex nodded in the darkness. "Go ahead, I gotcha covered."

TUNNEL RUNNING

H is thoughts were still roiling over themselves rapidly for another two hours or so, when he was approached again, this time by Rinzinka. As she sat down, she didn't look happy.

"I know who you really are."

Rex smiled. "Oh really? Enlighten me, sister."

"Don't call me that, scum. You're the one Vance talked about. The one that wore Combine headgear and had the messed-up arm. You're *nothing* to me."

"Hah. I'm enough for you to try and confront. Strange enough to form a target you can't resist hating, strong enough for you to attempt to overcome to prove to yourself you're stronger, smart enough to acknowledge your weaknesses, bold enough to reveal them to you, and still I persist, an obstacle to which you compare yourself and demand you overcome. I'm more than just one that wears the Combine gear, I'm one that kills them while I do it, reminding them, body by body, blood for blood, of what they did to me and the ninety others that died to make me what I am. And if I'm nothing to you, then you have no clue what I bring: The Death of any Combine near me. And as any Revolutionary, you should know better than to shun those that bear such hearty gifts, even for the likes of you."

"Likes of me? You're one to talk!"

"Yes I am! I'm the one that sees the hate in your eyes at the very mention of my semblance in your thoughts! I have not done *anything* to you to deserve such things, and yet you bear the brunt of that disgust for which you hold only to the damned Combine on me, even though I am *nothing* like them!"

"Nothing like them?! The entire reason Vance wanted to bring you over so desperately is because he thought you *were* Combine, that somehow you held the weakness for them all in your blood, and he wanted you only to dissect you! I helped guard the labs, and I know what happened, I heard him talk to Meredith and the others about you! He said he couldn't believe that they were down to cooperating with a bloodthirsty Combine *traitor* just to keep humanity alive!"

Rex snarled low and deep. "If you think I've *ever* fought alongside the Combine that tortured me, that did this to me, you're dead wrong. I've seen the faces of real traitors: Strudenhamme as I took his heart and spread him around, Griswold after another human gutted him behind me, even the face of the first Judicator after I broke him, and a Civil Patrolman as I ripped the mask from his still-screaming features. And Breen is on that list, and as I kill him, I will enjoy it just as much."

Rinzinka went pale as a ghost now, obviously rejudging her take on Rex as a traitor, and fled slowly from his presence, perhaps to think upon such things as she slept. He decided now would be the optimal time to take his two, and as he lay down far from the group, he realized his dreams might haunt him, but he ultimately had no other choice.

—⟨∿∿⟩—

Rex was walking along a war-torn beach now, and as he looked to his left, he found the sea, long, deep, intimidatingly cold, and perhaps infested with things that were not of earthen origin, a large island to his right. Advancing up out of the water, Rex realized that his feet were bare here, his pants torn and ragged, the armor vest stained with blood, but otherwise intact. The shirt he once wore was now simply tatters about his neck and shoulders, and as he advanced up the sandy soil, something large and nasty began to approach the shore, and he realized he bore no weapons to kill the massive thing with.

Dully Rex realized he was being watched, the man in the blue suit sitting on a distant hill, observing what was happening.

As the beast advanced, a trio of smaller sand-burrowing creatures came up through the soil much closer, Rex deciding the sand insects needed to be taught a lesson, even if he had to do it with his bare hands. He killed the first as it came at him with his left hand, tearing the angular head from the body and laughing as the corpse fell still. Rex threw the head at a second incoming insect and watched the chitinous material crunch together brutally, caving in both the insectile skulls, disembodied and intact alike. The last of the three died as Rex grabbed a bunch of legs in his right hand, the head in the left, and tore it apart like cheap rope in a one-man tug of war game.

The bigger beast however was upon him quickly, and as it struck him in the chest with its forehead, Rex was flung back several feet to land on the ground, the implant suddenly like a blazing fire, the liquid heat pouring through his veins. As Rex stood up now he realized he was much bigger, the height of the beast attacking him. Rex's right arm looked like something out of a steroid-pumping weightlifter magazine before the storms, and his left now indescribably nightmarish, the blackened limb muscular and scaled with thickened armor, fingers long and sharp, animalistic.

And the sudden rage of red that curtained over his vision, it was like madness multiplied, forming a fury beyond comparison, the need for bathing in the blood of his enemies, and divining their flesh almost immeasurable. Charging ahead, Rex used the left arm to cut deeply into the head of the beast, and it dropped in a single swipe of deadly claws. His steel-like fingers worked like daggers, tearing out massive valleys of sand creature flesh. However, his thirst stood unsatiated, and Rex began to move ahead with great velocity, right for the man in the blue suit.

Things suddenly flashed and Rex was almost normal again, standing on the hill next to the man in the blue suit, the man holding a knowing glance. All around him, the wind roared, and Rex could see now the island was essentially bare along the surface, hilly, unfarmed, and simplistic, except for the massive tower dominating the center. It was another damned Combine spire, rising up into the sky and touching the stars, strange vibrations through the ground telling him that deep below odd machinations were occurring.

"What is this place?"

"The End, Mr. Rex. The End."

———◦⦾◦———

Rex woke up gasping. What the hell was that all about? Looking around, he still wore his boots, armor, the shirt, weapons, and he relaxed as reality sunk in. It was just another bedamned nightmare, but somehow Rex let the tower on the island embed itself into his thoughts. As Rex finally sat up, he realized the female doctor was sitting over him, and he almost recoiled backwards instinctively from her proximity.

Reflexes had him ignoring her warm smile and soft hands in order to focus on where he was in the tunnel, ensuring the world hadn't taken another 180-degree shift on him, like it had before so long ago now…Turning his attention back to the doctor, he watched as she continued taking notes and examining his arms with a small device. Rex pulled himself together mentally, putting any slight complaints to the back of his mind, and removing his hands from under the scanner in order to search his person.

"What the hell are you doing?"

Hanging the MP7M on its sling, Rex pulled the pump-action shotgun free from the carryall, and found it to be quite strange. Trying to ignore the unsettling feeling of the doctor there near him, Rex focused studying it in order to identify how it functioned or perhaps where it came from, until the doc interrupted his reverie. "Excuse me, Mr. Rex."

Looking up slowly, he wondered what she wanted this time. "What is it? Why aren't you sleeping?"

Alexia looked a bit nervous but spoke up anyway, "Was what Rinzinka said correct? Are you the one from the Black Mesa labs?"

Rex smiled, recalling Maurine and Molly's features. Soon he knew he would forget what they looked like, smelled like, their names, the sounds of their voices and laughter. Shaking his head, Rex turned back to the present. "Yeah, I am. I only wished Doc Hernandez told me that their teleporter wasn't functioning 100 percent properly before they sent me through it a second time."

The doc stuck out her hand. "Doctor Alexia Robbins. I was the psych that was supposed to evaluate you when you arrived. Goodness, wasn't that a long time back? Before Freeman arrived at least."

Rex shook her hand resolutely, not wanting to be overtly rude. "T-Rex. And yeah, it was a lot longer ago than I tend to realize, or want to, in any case." He received an odd look in response to the statement, but nodded for her to continue onwards anyway as he spoke again. "Whatever. What is it you wanted to say about me, Doc?" Rex didn't like this, talking to a shrink, but perhaps he was just messed up psychologically enough to get away with chatting amicably with her and not receive any kind of diagnosis.

"Well, I don't have Charlie with me; that poor bastard. Anyway, he was a biology expert, and he was also supposed to converse with you, get a look at your genetics, other things. So it makes what I have to say pretty one-sided. To me it looks as if whatever the Combine has done to you, it's altered your physiology in ways that your mind cannot adapt to. I have no clue what you must be going through, but in my professional opinion, you need at least a few months away from combat, a gene therapist, and at least five or six psychiatrists to diagnose the mental problems you must be going through. Gene scans and repetitive heart rate monitoring indicates your body is *definitely* not the same as the person Hernandez scanned and sent the vital readings for over, and that previous scan was off the charts in human advancement. Now however, all the readings I'm getting are way too…alien or something. My entire suite of gear might've helped me, but that's back in BME; not even this med unit"—Alexia pointed out the complex machinery and pouches of supplies on the fancy belt she was wearing, obviously something for the doctor to help operate on patients with expedited efficiency, also allowing her to perform her duties without the need of a nurse or staff. Now that Rex considered it, he was glad she was in the group; if anyone was injured, she could patch them up on the go, making survivability a more likely scenario.—"can tell me everything I need to know or see in order to properly diagnose just what happened to you."

Rex snorted derisively. "Look, Doc, I don't need a goddamned shrink now, especially when I can't afford to lock myself up for months on end—humanity is in danger, and I need to be here to fight the bastards that threaten it. And I can *tell* you what happened to me. I was freaking *there*. Ninety other people died around me while the Combine tortured me, experimented upon me, cut me open, and shoved something inside. Do you want to know what *real* guilt is? I have ninety other souls I carry around with me because I was the only one to survive. I was the one those traitorous bastards chose to work on, and they killed the others in order to learn more about keeping their precious experiment alive.

"As for me still being human? Hah. As long as I know which side I'm fighting for, whom I'm fighting for, I'll always have my shred of humanity, the only part I ever needed. If the Combine's downfall meant that I would have to stay this way forever, then so be it."

The doctor did not look surprised by his state of being or the response he used, obviously having heard similar words before from comparable head cases. "And what if the Combine is driven from our world? What then?"

Rex considered it for a moment, hands running gracefully along the upper section of the shotgun, now able to identify it as a South African-made unit commonly named after the company that produced it, the *Neostead*. Opening the dual-tube magazine breeches atop the weapon, Rex found both of them fully loaded, and wondered how the hell a Combine trooper had gotten his hands on one of these. His only guess was that a half-breed took it off the corpse of a Revolutionary just recently ventilated somewhere. With the weapon loaded to the brim with twelve shots of 12ga. buckshot shells, Rex closed the dual magazine breeches, and pumped the weapon forward back in its odd reversal of the atypical shotgun loading mechanism.

"Well, then I'll be the only monster on this world, won't I? And perhaps I'll go elsewhere, or maybe I'll just end it all like that fool Hemingway did, with a 12ga. shell to the face. It's not very likely, but possibly I'll get the chance to follow the bastards back to their own home world, and blow it up right under their noses, damning their supposed interstellar empire right in their own backyard. There certainly won't be any place in this world for me when all of my enemies are gone, but I guess I'll find out eventually."

Standing up, Rex took charge again, felt his body react like a wild, berserker killing machine, and knew he was back up to snuff; whether or not it was temporary, he had no clue.

"Get back to the group, Doc. We're moving out now."

Alexia looked like she had something more to say, but only bore a piteous look on her features as she walked back to the others. She gathered up her energy rifle and obeyed the orders as he gave them, feeling like he'd just changed again somehow, but Rex couldn't quite put his finger on it.

EXPECTED EMERGENCE

Several hours of walking later, the group began to see a light at the end of the tunnel, and as Rex paused, he waited for the group to catch up, halting them as well.

"Oz, tell me what you see up there."

The one-handed sniper moved into position next to Rex, acting as a spotter as best he could, and waiting to hear what Oz would say. The man responded softly, "I've got two CPs in range. They're just standing there, guarding the tunnel maybe? I doubt they know exactly where it leads."

Rex waved him back to the rest of the group and began to consider the situation. "No, they don't know where it goes, but there's no doubt that they are guarding the entry here, as well as any other entries or exits along the area. They most likely blanketed the area with troops in order to cut off anyone escaping from BME."

Rinzinka cleared her throat, and Rex looked back, noting she had something to say.

"Go ahead."

"When Freeman came in through BME, we were getting reports all over about the Combine coming down hard on local outposts. These are more than likely just reinforcements for those soldiers and CPs, meant to cut off and kill groups leaving not only BME, but all of the outposts that lead back up to it. That means Route Kanal is compromised."

The group seemed to be lost in thought for a moment, the doctor speaking up tenderly. "This exit isn't part of Route Kanal. It leads across the tops of the ridgeline near it, I think, an old pipeline for water or fuel. We should come up in the old industrial area near Kleiner's Labs. There's a good chance he still has Outpost Alpha in contact; maybe we can hook up with them, get supplies, and start up work there."

Rex paused again before he spoke, considering his tone before actually talking, "How did that info get sent to BME, Alexia?"

The doc froze as Rex turned to her, icy stare boring into her gaze. "Landline. It's near this tunnel, and runs to his labs. I knew it would mean a direct route, especially since this was excavated long before the Combine arrived.

"And along with that data Hernandez sent, what else was in it?"

The doctor looked almost as if she didn't want to respond. "Coordinates for the transporter here at BME, one for a Xen relay, another for a third structure in Russia somewhere, near the Urals I think."

Rex considered the information for a moment, and wondered if that meant he could get back home somehow, with those coordinates in his possession. He guessed that the man in the blue suit would do something to try and stop him, but it was worth the effort in his mind to get back to Molly.

"Alright. Oz, cover me from here. Diazepam, you keep the group quiet and settled 'till I return. I'll be back soon."

Grabbing up one of the three hunting knives in his right hand, Rex slowly began to approach the end of the tunnel, and just as he was a few feet away from the guards, he froze, observing the area, listening for a chance to gather info, biding his time for the perfect moment to strike. The tunnel wasn't really supposed to end here that he could tell, collapsed inwards after being struck by bombardment no doubt, half-covered in dirt, but the exit was wide and clear, if a bit jagged on the edges. To no surprise, the CPs began talking to one another, giving away position and leaning against the entry lazily.

"What the hell are we standing here for? I want to go beat some civvies or shoot something."

"We were ordered here for a reason, now quiet down."

A slight pause followed, and curiosity won out.

"But why did we get orders to stand all the way out here? There's obviously no one coming. All of the rebels in this area were put down when Delta-3-29 swept through here looking for Freeman."

"Not all of them, damnit. We've even had reports of some kind of sniper topside south of here, so watch your side."

Another pause broke through, this one slightly longer before the talking continued.

"But that bastard was south of here, like you said, and he was reported when Freeman had already come through. Delta-3-29 had to have taken care of it."

"Really? Then why hasn't Delta-3-29 reported back in yet, eh? Maybe because they were killed off to the last man when Freeman hit the canals! Damn, don't you even listen to those reports?"

"Then Gamma-77 should have been called down here instead of us or Delta-3-29."

"Why the hell would they pull one of the biggest squads of Transgenic Overwatch from around the Citadel to come down here, when it's obvious that Freeman is headed in the other direction?"

"Because Charlie-33 and Whiskey-92 could have taken care of Citadel and the routes there; don't they already have Nova under control?"

"Hold on. I'm getting another report."

It was hard to decipher at such range, but Rex caught the gist of it as it came through, but only in bursts.

"Unit 366 down, shore—ine route comp—mised, pos—sighting of Free—Fox-86 encou—resis—force sma—outer perim—breach, Nova Pros—aler—all force—Unit 309 not res—scram—additional force—bound you—"

As it continued to broadcast, Rex realized his time was now, and he stood up while creeping forward a few steps, throwing the knife at the CP on his right, the soldier still eagerly awaiting a sit rep from his squad as it landed. Rex rushed forward at the CP on his left as the knife struck the first with the butt of the grip in the temple, knocking the traitor down efficiently. The position allowed Rex to rip the facemask off of the guard under him with his left hand, crumpling the unit in his blackened palm as the traitor screamed like the previous one had. He was still reveling in the sounds of music as he spun and crushed the larynx of the bastard behind him with another swift strike. His right hand formed a five-fingered blade and caught the second CP perfectly as the soldier tried to stand, still dazed. Rex snarled as the traitor went down again gasping, the throat mic crushed from the blow.

Picking up the fallen knife from the floor of the tunnel, Rex slammed it home into the torso of the CP on his left side to stop the bastard from screaming any longer, turning back to the lone-surviving CP. Rex began laughing as he watched the prick try to breathe through a crushed windpipe, watching him die slowly before retrieving the blade. Gathering the weapons together that the CPs had, Rex shifted the bodies farther into the darkness, and advanced slowly out of the tunnel.

The Neostead 12ga. shotgun was in his hands as Rex scouted out the area, finding it to be a small valley on one side of a hill, Rex crawling up to the outer edge and peering down. The hill was one on the edge of the small industrial area ahead as the doctor had suggested, but Rex also noticed it bordered on a much larger just beyond that, and as he spotted the tower here, Rex paused again, reminded of the other's he had dropped.

But this one was bigger somehow, already opened and ready to spew units out into the world, apparently at yellow alert or DEFCON 3, but Rex knew this wasn't his target. The man in the blue suit gave him people to babysit rather than the tower, the spawning vats of the Combine, and he could only wonder why. Perhaps it had something to do with this *Freeman* person he kept hearing about. And instinctively Rex wanted to know more about this strange man. But that would all have to wait for later, and as he turned back to the tunnel, Rex found the group already following him, words flooding his thoughts as he spotted Diazepam.

"We knew, odd one, we knew."

Slowly they spread out along the ridge of the hill, and Rex slowly realized they'd turned to him for direction. Perhaps leading a group wasn't so bad, Rex considered.

"Alright, we head down into the area, slowly and surely. If you see a Combine or CP, fall back and tell me. We don't need to let them know we're here just yet. Follow me, soldiers."

Leading the way and feeling like John Wayne in his prime, Rex began the slow descent along the rest of the uncovered piping, using it as cover just in case anyone looked up expecting to see them, waving his group into the shadows and continuing to move. It took quite a while to reach the fence around the outer edges of the industrial area, and as the squad of makeshift troopers crouched in the darkness behind him, Rex moved ahead, grabbed a fistful of the gate where it met the ground, and peeled it upwards easily, forming a large entry into the grounds.

Moving just inside the fence with the Neostead shotgun in his hands, Rex covered the group cautiously as everyone followed suit, motioning towards the nearest building, and listening for the sounds of enemy movements. As Oz arrived at the building with the rest of the group, he signaled to Rex that it was all clear. Rex easily trod over to them, kneeling at the corner of two buildings where they lead deeper into the area. But first, he wanted some standing orders.

"No firing. If you see a CP or Combine, only shoot if you're going to die otherwise. Don't let them see you or hear you as best as you can possibly manage. We're going to need to get closer to this lab that belongs to your friend, Kleiner, before we can make a break for it, and the closer we are before they discover us, the better. If they happen to spot us as we're making entry; however, that will be the worst possible moment, so we may end up causing a distraction once we get far enough inside the zone. Keep down, stay in the shadows."

Rex began by leading through example, hugging the wall in the shadows and peering cautiously around each corner, noting that there weren't too many soldiers patrolling this area. Most of the CPs and half-breeds were inside the structures manning stations, or at least that's what it sounded like as they passed several up, listening intently for anyone trying to exit the buildings, before leaving them behind cautiously. Rex hated letting Combine or CPs live when they were in his range of contact, but he had no other choices. He had zero desire to get into a full-fledged firefight while a bunch of people were with him, people he needed to keep alive, not spend their resources fruitlessly in the middle of a big showdown with the half-breeds and traitors.

It took them several hours to navigate the industrial area without getting spotted, and just as they were about to leave the area, Rex had them all halting behind a dumpster of a meat-packing facility turned into God-knew-what now, pushing them down and sticking the shotgun into his carryall. Just up ahead, voices could be heard as two blue-eyed freaks in their suits of armored padding emerged through a side door, and Rex moved ahead while signaling the group to stay behind. As he closed the distance, Rex pulled two of the blades free, held them in a downward-angled grip, and halted, tensing his legs like springs being coiled for launch.

Rex dully realized they were chatting with each other as he launched himself up into the air, barely making out identical voices over throat mics as he landed hard right behind them, the blades slamming down into each upper back simultaneously, all the way to the hilts. One tried to spin about to return fire, and Rex finished him off with a nasty strike to the face. His blackened fist shattered headgear and broke bones in the altered facial features of the half-breed to his right, the Combine on the left slumping down to the ground, already dead.

Removing his blades again with a quick jerk on each, Rex returned each of the bloodstained knives to their matching sheathes, kicked the bodies over to retrieve sparse amounts of ammo, and waved his group forward. It was easy to realize that once they crossed the battered street into the more residential-industrial mixed portions ahead, they were leaving behind a score of enemies to their rear. And they were now wandering into more territory even heavier occupied, scores of troops no doubt searching for signs of revolutionaries.

"Alright. When we get into the center of the area, scout out a good building; we'll rest until nightfall, and theoretically it should be easier going on the final approach to Kleiner's lab. Stay sharp, people."

Now with the Neostead at the ready once again, Rex took point for a while, identifying a few structures. But he quickly dismissed them as unusable due to being already occupied or battered beyond any condition of being defensible. Rex finally let Oz take over as he realized the one-handed sniper had the best view using the infrared scope. Returning to the rear line, Rex waited until Diazepam was walking alongside him and continued to keep his eyes open. The group stopped when Oz motioned to do so, pointing to a large redbrick building on the edge of a train yard and moving over.

Everyone followed suit, entering through a fire exit that had already been pried open a long time ago, Oz waiting until last to enter, and Rex bracing the door shut with a hunk of cinder block just inside, like it was meant exactly for that purpose. Rex began to make a sweep of the building as the rest of the people gathered together on the main floor, picking a spot in the center, back-to-back, everyone covering everyone. As Rex arrived on the top floor, he recognized the tower off in the distance as he looked off to the horizon, wondering how long it would take the sun to fall.

FINAL THRUST

After a decent break, the sun finally set, and Rex returned to the bottom floor to see the group talking peacefully amongst themselves. He couldn't help himself from smiling at the progress they were making, readying his own mind for what would come next. "Alright, settle down." Everyone turned to face Rex as he sat just a bit away from them. "I've been scouting the area from the windows up on the third floor. It looks like I've been able to spot where you need to go through, but it'll be tough. About four buildings over on this side of the street, there's a large white building with windows that we can use to get down to street level if we need to, but a few buildings beyond that is another redbrick building that's got a gaping hole in the side of the roof, and there's at least a dozen Combine guarding it.

"Even worse is the fact that street level is heavily dominated by CPs, at least one armored personnel carrier, and this giant nasty thing with three long legs, at least twenty feet tall or more. Thankfully, the giant thing and the APC aren't patrolling now, but there is still a big load of CPs patrolling down there, with a bunch of floating cameras or whatever the goddamned things are filling in the gaps. The way I see it is I'm the distraction, and you're the prize. The goal is to get you all into that white building, and get below ground level. Alexia, I think you can take navigating the areas from there on in. Do you have a paintstick on that thing?" Rex pointed at her med unit in reference to the age-old marking system used by most armed forces, but Rinzinka surprised him by coming up with one of her own.

"Good. Mark off the areas you clear and make a path to the lab with Kleiner. Something tells me it is close, especially with the heavy presence. Now I'll go up to the third level first. When I get to the building at the far end occupied by the Combine, I need you all to go out through the same windows here while I'm centering their attention on me, and you all get to the white building, get through those windows. Then haul ass to the lab by any means necessary. Once I'm done here, I'll catch up."

Everyone paused as the commands sunk in, the group realizing this might've been the last time they ever saw Rex alive. He stopped at Rinzinka's side and motioned towards her armband. "You think I could have that? I'm not quite as easily…recognized as a Revolutionary where I go."

She pulled the armband off and handed it over, with a handshake following. As he pulled the armband up over the graying skin on his right bicep, Rex responded kindly, "You and Oz keep everyone alive. Alexia, get them to the labs, in one piece. Harry, don't know much about you, but keep on fighting the good fight. And Diazepam. Keep things cool, if you can. Good working with y'all. I might see you again, if I'm lucky. Now get moving. I got Combine to kill, and you'd better be ready to hustle when the time comes."

Rex stood and jammed the shotgun back into the carryall, selecting the MP7M instead with steady hands as he moved back up the staircase. A snarl began growing on his features, excitement and anticipation feeding his engine, revving himself up as he reached the third floor. Rex readied the micro assault carbine in his arms, and kicked the entire metal frame of the heavy, leaded windows in front of him, roaring like King Kong as the frame filled with glass panels fell three stories to smash onto a five-man group of CPs gathered around a console below.

A spotlight struck him from ground level, and Rex immediately blew it out by peppering the source of light with rounds, killing three more CPs and a half-breed blue suit, before someone finally managed to react to the first spot going out. A second cone of light cast him in white illumination, rounds screaming off of the walls and window frame around him, something heavy bouncing off of the armor vest. Rex began moving along the ledge outside of the building as fast as possible, following the curve of the building and leaping across to the next ledge.

The spotlight was unable to catch up in time as Rex stopped, fired on more CPs, avoided sloppily aimed rounds spitting in his direction, and skittered across a broken portion on the ledge, finding the time to halt, before reaching the next ledge. Rex quickly killed the second source of light pinning him to the side of the building, leaving only a few scattered fires amongst rubble as illumination, casting shadows and glowing eerily, the flashes of weapons being fired at where he once stood strobing manically.

As Rex leapt across to the third building, he emptied the magazine in the weapon into a CP scanning the darkness fruitlessly and found himself suddenly attracting all the attention in the world. Slapping the last fully loaded magazine into the weapon with a grin, Rex laid into a pair of half-breeds taking cover at the end of the street behind him. Their sloppy and wide-spaced fire was ineffective in comparison to the accuracy he could achieve with the mounted CWS, picking them off easily with headshots. A group of CPs in newer riot gear came through one of the blue-metal barriers blocking off another street as it opened up, massive hydraulics moving the slabs of navy-blue steel silently and effortlessly. The repetitive sounds of 9mm MP7 variants echoed loudly as they snapped off rounds in his direction a slight more accurately in steadied bursts, forcing Rex to continue onto the ledge of the fourth building.

Rex could hear the bricks chewed to dust by bullets behind him as he ran, diving onto the fifth building's ledge and almost falling off, noticing this was the route in and down he's seen earlier, spying a staircase through the window, but hauling ass onwards anyway. Another leap to the sixth building had given him the range advantage over the smaller 9mm rounds, and immediately Rex noticed the drop in incoming fire, spinning about and tapping out single shots. Rex snarled as the riot gear provided the CPs with enough protection to die only after he'd shot them three or four times each, his anger adding inaccuracy. But as he calmed himself, Rex cleared out the nest they'd formed behind one waist high barrier of liquid glass, or whatever the hell their impregnable shielding consisted of.

Turning his attention to the next row of ledges, Rex bolted ahead in the sparse light, darkness shadowing his movements, and giving him the slight advantage as he spotted the trio of blue suits emerging through the gaping hole in the roof of the building, two in front of him and one floor up. But the ledges here were wider, providing him with the ability to crouch behind the side of the roof on his end, using it as cover, and firing as accurately as possible at the trio. The first enemy dropped with the single shot Rex started the fight off with, the second taking one to the temple and another to the jugular before falling, the third turning and running through the gaping hole.

Rex was able only to hit the bastard once in the back before the soldier moved around the chimney stack and out of sight. Checking the weapon in his hands and finding seventeen rounds left with another eighteen in the other magazine on his hip, Rex hung the weapon on its sling. He planned on consolidating the rounds into a single magazine later and grabbed the fully loaded Neostead pump-action from the carryall. Rex could feel the wind shift slightly, becoming colder now than it was a moment before. Running ahead in the dark, he spotted the wide gap, leapt, and barely made it without sliding over the edge, running up the diagonal face of the roof, and thanking his father for the boots with their excellent treads.

Rex emerged at the top of the roof unscathed and prepared for almost anything as he passed the chimney, his vision adjusting to the blackness on the interior of the hole in the roof. It didn't last long as a half-breed spun around the edge of the hole in the roof, opening fire with a pulse rifle and lighting up the dark, barely missing Rex as he responded in kind with the shotgun. Two shells later, the Combine was dead, and Rex added the energy weapon to his arsenal, jamming it into the carryall. Numbly, he realized that he was going to end up dropping the shotgun next, with no readily available source of ammunition. But as he considered it, Rex decided he'd hold onto the weapons long enough to drop them into human hands, letting them get stuck with finding replacement ammo. He had neither the time nor the means for such a search.

The entire area under the roofing here was empty of a few shattered wooden crates and a pile of paint cans, so Rex immediately turned to the staircase, bolted down, and found the door here had been removed by force. The rotting corpse of a civilian sat in one corner of the room he'd entered, and he tore his vision away as he moved through the next empty doorway to the sight of a woman tied down to a radiator. She'd died long ago, a small television set at her feet droning onwards with Breen on the screen, but Rex had no time to pay attention to the speech or pause and respect the dead.

Stepping over the woman's corpse, Rex spotted another Revolutionary tied down to a bedstand leaning against the far wall, with a clear view of the woman on the radiator. No doubt, the poor bastard and the woman knew each other, and one had been forced to watch as the other was tortured. Who had stormed through here inspiring such atrocities to be committed upon these people? The only name that surfaced was Freeman. He was the only one that could have set the Combine's blood to boil; the only other person was himself, Rex guessed, and as far as his blurred memory could piece it together, he'd never been in this area before. Although he had to admit, it was getting rather hard to tell just where he'd been, and more importantly, where he was going.

But as Rex moved out into the hall past a pair of glass doors that had been permanently opened, he simply marked it down as where he needed to go, get a job done, and get back to Molly after he was finished. And part of him wanted to know just how much more crap he had to go through to get home, but in kicking aside an empty filing cabinet blocking the hall and emerging into a long winding staircase, he disturbed a group of CPs a few floors below, and the train of thought was put on hold.

Rex switched to the pulse rifle from the carryall and continued navigating his way around the stairs, firing through the elevator safety cages as the trio came into view. They had come charging up the stairs with stun sticks and MP7s, most likely just 9mm variants he guessed at this range. Rex emptied thirty rounds in a blur and cycled in the next ammo pod, stuffing the pulse weapon into the carryall and taking up the shotgun once again.

The bottom floor had been previously cleared, but as Rex stuck his head through the next doorway leading out to the street, a pair of blue-eyed Combine to the north of his position took advantage of their surprise attack to launch one of the energy grenades at him. And as Rex dove to the ground outside, rolling to avoid the ball of white-hot energy trying to consume him, he realized the second Combine bastard had thumbed a second grenade free, lobbing the damned thing a foot away and forcing him to get up and scramble for time. Rex was barely able to fall over the wreck of an old civilian car in time to avoid the energy grenade as it struck the conventional HE device, sound, energy, force, and fire combining in order to form a more deadly and shocking explosion, sending Rex to the ground.

The ringing in his ears now was actually the implant on full alert, but Rex couldn't really tell the difference between the two.

With distance too long for the Neostead to be effective, Rex had the MP7M in his hands in no time at all, aiming through the combat weapon sight carefully and using the last seventeen rounds in the magazine to effectively shred the half-breeds' headgear as they popped up out of cover to fire. Unconsciously Rex was laughing raucously at the death he was dishing out, reloading with the last eighteen rounds of 7.62mm and standing from cover. Sounds of booted feet on pavement had him spinning around to face another group of the CPs in heavier riot gear. As he sprayed ammunition at them, two dropped, while the other three dully realized this was no mere riot, attempting to fall back behind the closing barricades.

One died slowly as Rex charged forward, shoving the last CP in between the massive blue metal panels, the traitor screaming as he was crushed in betwixt the huge slabs of alien metal. A sudden silence fell on the area and as Rex pulled back away from the large barrier of navy-blued steel, he let the MP7M hang by its tiny strap, grabbed the Neostead from the carryall, and began to make his way back to the ground-level entry. As he approached the bottom floor of the large white building, its seamless surface interrupted, a thick steel door painted white to blend in with the wall squealing loudly as a human stuck his face out into the open.

Rex froze as he realized the man was also wearing the bodysuit of the atypical Civil Patrolman, and carrying one of the alien energy rifles. And as he raised the shotgun for his first response, the human held hands up, palms out, and yelped. "Whoa! Hold on there! I'm a friendly."

Rex allowed himself to relax a hair and the muzzle of the shotgun lowered ever so slightly, the man with black hair and a few days stubble smiling at the sight of the armband. "Who the hell are you, and what are you doing wearing *that*?"

The man seemed somewhat sheepish to explain himself, but the sight was quickly replaced with another of the harsh droning sounds echoing above them, the man taking a tactical crouch and waving over Rex hastily.

"Come on! We'll have time for introductions later!" Rex hustled over and found the man was equally prepared for the run that followed, moving through the main level of the building. Rex dully awakened to the fact that they were heading through maintenance halls, rather than through the main section of the floor, and as they stopped at a set of stairs, the man grinned.

"Down we go."

The flight of stairs took a while to descend, and soon they'd arrived in a basement of sorts, with an elevator right across from the exit of the staircase, the man in the CP uniform guiding him along a paved floor and warehouse architecture. They finally stopped at a canned water machine, a gaping hole in the wall to his left and a shaft leading straight down a few floors. A coin click, a couple of button presses, a slap on the machine, and the front of it opened up like he was back in some weird-ass science fiction movie made in the sixties. The strange man stepped through the entry and led Rex into another large room, the group of survivors there talking with each other, and another man in a scientist's smock petting…a *docile* headcrab. The sight brought back instant recollection, and as he looked at the creature, it seemed to focus on him as well, a name he'd heard in his dreams escaping his lips.

"Lamar?"

Everyone ceased what they were doing to look at him, even the man in the CP uniform. The scientist cleared his throat and set the headcrab down, the four-legged creature ambling off to the side, into a pet carrier.

"Excuse me, have we met?"

Rex decided he wasn't about to go explaining his odd dreams to strangers. "No. And we're not really meeting now. I'm dropping these survivors off, and you're going to help me get the hell out of here."

The man in the CP suit turned to face him head-on. "Now just wait a minute here…"

Rex saw the man's hands move to the pulse-rifle, and Rex classified him as a threat immediately. Hauling the man up into the air with the blackened fist, Rex plucked the rifle from his hands and tossed it down loudly at his booted feet. But before it could escalate further, the scientist halted them with a loud, nasal yell.

"Enough, you two! Barney, you need to get out there and regroup the people in the streets. Alyx and Freeman are in Nova right now, and they'll need a clear path to leave with."

As Rex and the man named *Barney* separated, the man in the CP suit did not looked pleased, but grabbed his rifle from the floor and left anyway.

"And as for you, all. When Barney returns we'll prepare a group to head out from here. We're going to need all the help we can get."

Rex felt like he was being ignored. "Whoa, hold on a second. I'm not here to help you anymore. My task was to get these people here and get the hell back home. Word is you and your teleporter have the coordinates I need to get home, and you're gonna help me, damnit."

"We need that ready to receive Alyx and Gordon should they require it. Doctor Robbins, just who is this man?"

The female scientist appeared that she didn't like being asked that question, but obviously had no choice but to respond. "This is the subject, the one Doctor Vance spoke of. He did send you the data, didn't he?"

The scientist looked shocked. "My God. This is the 91st subject?"

"Yes, Doctor Kleiner. He's arrived about a month or two late, but this is him."

The old, balding scientist adjusted his glasses, reached for a small notepad, and seemed quite excited. "Then this is wonderful! Another to fight for the cause, and what the recruit!"

Rex was starting to get angry. "Damnit, listen to me. I'm not here to assist in any way further than what I've done already!

Freeman is here for that tower, and I'm done. Now I know you have those damned coordinates, so send me back!"

The entire group looked somewhat crestfallen, even the older scientist. It was almost like a visual guilt trip, and Rex was not about to fall for it.

"Let's go! I don't have all goddamn day!"

The older male led the way to the far wall, did something to a picture, looked into a crevice stuffed with machinery, and suddenly the far wall slid open to the right, Rex advancing inside as the elder scientist followed. Another of the cage-bound devices were here, and Rex instantly recognized it, recalling trying to materialize into one so long ago. And more recently, actually managing to arrive in BME far too late, appearing in the center of the shattered remnants once identifiable as a transporter. The doctor took a small lift up to a set of controls for the teleporter, and as he worked at the device, a small yellow length of paper streamed out from a bulk printer, the man gesturing to it.

"Tear that off and take it with you. You'll need it for the sequence ahead."

Rex grabbed the small sheet, tore it free, and goggled at the numbers, almost incomprehensible to him, and felt puzzled. "What do you mean, sequence ahead?"

A strange look came to Doctor Kleiner's features, and he tried to explain it as simply as possible. "To put it bluntly, I don't know where these coordinates lead to. But they need to be done in sequence to arrive at Black Mesa. It's a security precaution to prevent unwanted arrivals, but unfortunately it was never utilized properly, and now after so long, I'm not even sure the relay sites are functioning."

Rex began to consider the situation, remembering his discussion with Robbins, and piecing together what little he knew. "Well look. One is definitely Black Mesa. The next has to be the relay site on Xen. I was there, helped clear the area, saw that it was restored. I'm assuming that I was supposed to go there from Black Mesa, then to the next relay site, and finally here, in order to arrive, so it has to work like that in reverse."

"But what about the last site? We have no clue where it is or if it's functioning."

Rex thoughtfully softened his tone as he spoke now, realizing he was just putting everyone on edge by being so tense. "I discussed it with Doc Robbins back there. The last relay is in Russia, the Urals, she guessed. Do you remember any sites there?"

Kleiner seemed to be lost deeply in thought over the matter for several seconds, and Rex almost thought he'd fallen asleep standing up, when the scientist spun back to face him with a look of recognition sparkling in his eyes, a smile warming the somewhat chilly room. "Yes! We had a minor experiment running there with an agreement the US once had with Russia…long ago, but hopefully the facility is still working. We mothballed it months before the…portal storms started happening, so everything should still be there, intact and stored away for later use."

Rex smiled at the sound of good news, stepping into the transporter as the cages lifted up, and closed down behind him. Turning in the device, he jammed the piece of paper into the old gear belt, tossed the shotgun over the top of the cage, and felt the device lift him up. Stripping off the MP7M, he tossed it down with the shotgun, and checked the pulse rifle in the carryall, noting that it had sixty rounds in it, and stood waiting as machinery hummed. "Thanks, Doc. Sorry I pressured you, but hopefully you guys can deal with things here without me. Say 'hi' to Freeman for me if you think about it."

The doctor smiled widely, pushed a button, and waved as he spoke. "Good luck out there, whoever you are."

Things were slower and louder here, and not one word beyond what was already said passed between the two of them as the machine finally kicked in, a feeling of energy around him pulling inside to a core, his sight inverting, and a flash…

FALSE PRETENSES

There was no time for him to be caught in the blackness this time, and as Rex materialized, he realized he was ankle-deep in snow. It was damned cold here, snowing, wind blowing, and his awareness came to full scope, taking in the large flat space he was standing on. He easily spotted a pair of long-dead markers and guessed this was once a landing pad of sorts, now long unused and covered in six inches of powder. A sudden gust of wind had him stumbling to the right, and as Rex slid in snow, his head turned to face the sight of one of the Dragons rising up on his left. A mounted spotlight pinned him to the white surface, forcing him to raise his hands, shielding his eyes from the glare and identifying the swiveling ball turret next to the affixed light.

The long, nasty weapon barrel that jutted out from the turret spun to focus on Rex as he stood there resolutely, the pulse-rifle in his arms and a smirk on his features. As the living ship opened fire upon him, Rex abandoned his steady stance in favor of a sprint across the surface, halting at the far end, grabbing the edge of the concrete platform with his blackened fist as energy lined a path behind him. He barely escaped the flow of accelerated particles, but lost his grip on the rifle as the heavy rounds struck it instead, sending it twirling down into the emptiness below. Snarling as he waited for the ship to come around over the top, Rex planned out his moves to attempt avoiding it again, possibly seeking shelter in a cavern, if there was one. Instead, the Dragon swept around low and was under him now, the turret pointing up, ready to fire.

Changing tactics, Rex pulled his legs up and braced his feet against the side of the poured concrete platform, waiting a half-second to gather energy for what was coming next. As soon as he felt it was the best timing, Rex shoved off hard against the side of the mountain. He propelled himself up and away from the platform, his arc defined shortly thereafter by the trails of energy the Dragon was attempting to track him with. The beast was suddenly far too close for his own comfort, Rex slamming down onto the *face* of the flying craft, hands scrambling across the surface as he slid along its rigid armor, the blackened fist barely able to create enough of a handhold.

His right hand immediately pulled free one of the three blades strapped to his chest, and with it, Rex tried to pierce the surface of the creature, failing miserably, snarling and trying again ferociously. The tip of the knife bounced from the carapace and suddenly jutted into the edge of the large, globular, and multifaceted eye nearby, and the creature responded instantaneously. Deep bellows began from within its being, the large cannon now firing sporadically in multiple directions. The beast threw its own flight into a hard barrel roll that seemed to go on forever, like a crocodile trying to drown its prey, flopping into the wind brutally. Rex then used his right hand to pull free another of the blades, and with every bit of possible force, burrowed it deeply into the second eye, the thrashing becoming more erratic now and threatening to tear his precious grip free.

Levering his body up with one hand on a blade shoved in all the way to the hilt, and the blackened fist reaffirming its grasp, Rex used the second blade as a foothold and whipped around atop the creature as it moved, now sprawled belly-down atop its face as it swung and buzzed madly. Bracing himself with one foot still against the grip of the knife, Rex freed his right hand and pulled the third blade from its sheath, and slammed it down into a new position on the second eye. The noises emanating from the craft grew into a massive roar, echoing off of the huge snowed-in mountain side base, blasting waves of thick snow down the mountain, exposing ridges, caverns, lattices, and doors leading to the inside of the structure.

The entire creature wavered now, and Rex was uncertain of what he'd done until the beast reared back abruptly, then swung forward, face first. The lower portion of the face just in front of him smashed into the side of the mountain, ripping a walkway free, mashing rock and snow together, crushing part of an outer observation point, and burrowing into the mass of earth momentarily.

The beast was now squelching and screaming instead of roaring, and Rex could feel the thing attempt to gather momentum below him, and as it began to pull free, he could see the damage that had been done to the Dragon. The tip was now crippled and torn, the front completely crushed, exposing leaking machinery and bleeding flesh as it worked in unison. Rex abandoned his position and leapt into the cavernous opening left behind, and as he did so, the fore of the craft tore free, a weight of uncontrollable mass.

And as the beast attempted to swing around to limp away, the crippled Dragon finally gave up and simply stopped trying, and plummeting to its death. Rolling to a halt, Rex was exhausted and angry, the cold biting at his extremities, the implant bouncing to the beat of his pulse. Heart running ragged after the harrowing encounter, thoughts tinged with fear and regret, Rex numbly realized he'd lost every weapon left. He pulled himself together mentally and made his way back to a proper walkway. It was a rough go at first, still shaken from the impromptu fight, and Rex almost teetered his way off of the side and a second time it occurred he chastised himself. But a short pause was all Rex needed, affirming the fact that he did not want to see the bottom of this mountain the fast way.

Leaping to the solid concrete path bored into the side of the cliffs ahead, Rex took a good look around, and located the only entry he could feasibly reach. Rex began to approach it, following the exposed corridor, open to the snowy Russian winter, the weather creating an eerie muted calm after his intense arrival. It was a nice change of pace, and deep down, Rex hoped it didn't turn bad. He needed a short break from the ruthless tempo of combat, and even though he yearned to see Molly and Maurine, the breakneck speed of his travels was slowly eroding his will to fight.

Part of it was his fault, rushing in to complete the task at hand and ignoring the severed connections with people around him, fading the victories into harsh memories, losing pieces of himself along the way, imperceptibly. Rex quickly finished the approach to the large hazard door, the metal surface marked with a Lambda symbol as well as words in Cyrillic. Rex opened it with a wry grin, and felt a little stunned at the absolute silence from the interior.

There was an empty corridor ahead, but there was no hum of electricity, no echo of footsteps or voices, not even the skittering of bugs or critters from a mothballed facility. Instead, there was simply darkness and silence, and as anxiety gripped him tightly, Rex found himself moving in almost by autopilot. Rex had already faced some of the worst situations by simply launching into them, and it was now beginning to be an instinctive reaction.

The darkness was deep and impermeable, except by a small trail of strips burrowed into the concrete, the orange lights either a backup system or merely passive energy-absorbing gels, glowing in the dark, like some type of toy. Arranged in a straightforward path, Rex continued moving along them steadily, ignoring the repeating feeling of eyes upon him. A few times Rex halted his progress to stare into the blackness, unable to do anything else to respond to the sensation as it broke through his barriers of concentration.

Finally as the light strips made yet another turn, Rex could see flashing red emergency lights in the distance, and as he closed the length of corridor between him and the source of illumination, he found himself frowning in puzzlement. Everything was intact on the power generator mounted on the wall here, except for the single fuse jutting from its placement, twisted loose but left in the socket. Something was not right at all with this situation, and it unsettled him deeply even as Rex began to reach for the fuse, twisting it back in the proper direction, and pressing it home with a loud click. The machine paused, hummed deeply for a second, and finally rumbled to life, all of the lights snapping on at once incredibly fast, causing Rex to squint at the brightness, and adjust his vision.

Turning his back to the equipment, Rex found himself looking into a lab room littered with remnants of work undone, but no thick layers of dust untouched, pristine items and tools lying about, and a lack of cobwebs familiar to a mothballed facility. Had he been lied to, yet again? Approaching one desk, Rex found a computer up and active, and as he tried to access it, age finally showed with the technology here, the monitor snapping loudly as the display died inside. With a curse on his lips, Rex moved on to the next computer, found it more willing to be operational, and delved into the user interface, attempting to locate some kind of layout or building plan.

Instead, as he stumbled into a directory that was labeled *architecture*, Rex found notes on the installation that provided much more than simple schematics. Research labs, work bays, cargo manifest stations, specimen stores, and a *tech dump* all were situated on several floors, with the arrival terminal at the top, once connected to a *port* system and doubling as a helipad. The port system was now obvious to him, the connecting transporters routing together two sides of the world, but only the tech dump escaped his grasp of understanding. Focusing on a floor-by-floor scan of the area, Rex located the second floor area, and frowned in puzzlement. Labeled as the tech dump area, he began to wonder why it was so close to the receiving zones.

The next floor down below that was also confusing, with the specimen stores location in relation to the dump, and main access to the lab a bit too close for comfort. And as soon as Rex scanned the third floor, he came to the conclusion that the entry to the research labs was the reason for the awkward placement of rooms. Below the labs sat paired-off work bays of several sizes according to the building layout, and on a second-to-bottom level were the cargo areas. The last level refused to show up on the schematics and as he tried to access it further, the computer requested a restricted information code.

Rex began to estimate his chances of properly coming to the password's correct guess when something, several rooms back, landed against a solid surface with a metallic reverberation, closely followed by the shattering of glass. Rex's blood ran cold at the thought of enemies here, now, with no weapons on his person, and he scanned the upper entry to the facility for an exit or escape route, finding the alcove to the next level marked back at where he made his grand entrance. Turning slowly to face where he'd come into the facility, Rex began a slow, cautious walk to the source of the noise, spotting something odd at the corner ahead, his grimace becoming a snarl as he recognized the sight of blood spatter.

Finishing the approach to the edge of the wall revealed the spatter, and it became bloody drag marks into the next room. And as he moved into the connecting area, Rex bracing himself for what lay ahead, the stale smell of crimson still caught him off guard. The blood here wasn't fresh at all, but the sight of the mangled bodies, various unrecognizable hunks of flesh, and internal organs were still more than disturbing. Desks and consoles had been obliterated by, what appeared to be, scientists and guards being used as human sledgehammers.

One body had been slammed against a wall, the upper half collapsed in on itself, streaks on the wall leading down from a massive impact point that looked like a bloody sunburst, the metal wall unharmed yet marred by the remnants of the violence that occurred here. Another large workstation that once looked to be the sturdiest piece of lab equipment he'd spotted so far had been almost cut in half by another scientist used as a large destructive tool. The thick metal was sheared by brute force, layers of peeled away skin matting edges and pulverized sections of bone dotting the rest.

Locating one of the security guards' corpses, Rex found that they'd tried to defend themselves to no avail. A fiberglass and metal baton lay shattered on the ground next to an outstretched hand grasping what was formerly a handgun. The weapon and the limb were now meshed together, appearing as if whatever caused the damage here merely stepped on the offender to cease the fighting. Scavenging the tactical belt was useless, everything useful stripped off, and Rex found it pointless to try. Locating the only other guard here was just as disappointing, bearing a complete lack of weaponry, but a keycard remained jammed into a pouch, which he eagerly grabbed, slipping it into the same pocket with the transporter data.

With no weapon and more strange sounds of shifting feet coming from the areas ahead, Rex grabbed at one severed leg where the flesh and muscle had been, and breathed a sigh of relief at the fact that most of the wretched work had been done. Freeing the large femur from the remaining trappings of rotted meat, Rex found the lack of insects made the job no less revolting, especially as he broke the somewhat still-resilient knee in his hands and yanked the bone free. Grabbing the bloody end where the kneecap once connected the lower leg, Rex tested the bone club on one worktable's ruined surface, and found it to be somewhat reliable. The noise was loud and no doubt attracted the attention of the mystery guests, but as Rex began to advance to the next room with his left hand prepared and right hand grasping the femur, he knew it was inevitable.

More disaster greeted him in this area—corpses and more—but one item differed: A large marked cylinder had been placed at the far end, but was now tilted over with the front panel smashed, once made of a high-density glass, the remaining portions stenciled with Combine lettering and the Wrench. Memories flashed before his eyes, and he took a step back—Rex knew this container, what was inside, and as his memory leaped back to the first escape, part of it slipped his grasp. Indeed, whatever was once inside was a threat, true and clear, something small and afraid inside of him quivering.

Agonizing anticipation rocked him as Rex approached the once-intact container, examining it as close as possible, finding it more than intact for its already mangled condition. And as Rex reached to check the hinges, the container slid slightly, causing him to jerk backwards. The once-jutting hinges slammed shut with no glass panes on them to form a door, and dawning realization came to him. The container had opened inside this room, here in this facility, at some point. With how it had opened almost impossible to determine, this container had come from the facility in New Mexico, all the way to here, just like he had. Only its arrival was clearly sooner than his own, and the mere fact that there were casualties in this so-called *mothballed facility* was now a dark side note to what had come out of this pod.

Standing up, Rex realized the location of the inhabitant of the pod was now primary no matter what, even if the invader at the door was merely more Combine reinforcements. Angling around the container in his path, Rex moved into the main entry room where his journey in the pitch-black had begun, and what he saw there made his mind stop and his breath pause. At the very doorway where he once stood, a towering figure made an imposing stance, his back to Rex, the door open, arms in the air, appearing to enjoy the cold wind and snow blowing in from the Russian exterior.

Whatever it was wore black combat armor from head to toe in the shape of combine Judicators, but the armor was no longer completely flat black in several places. Coats of red covered hands up to the elbows, toes to knees, and as the bastard turned to face him, Rex could see blood had been smattered across the chest piece as well. The headgear was also different: A large green lens and two smaller satellite lenses to the two and four o'clock positions on the face, bearing a swept-and-slicker look than normal, gleaming like plate armor in the light.

It carried no weapons, only it's large musculature and blood-smattered visage were clear examples of the violence it could cause. Rex was forced to shift his footing to avoid the first thing thrown at him, and all he could do is snarl as the damned thing moved with blurring speed. His opponent had flung a large chunk of desk, which clipped Rex on his right shoulder as he moved, spinning him about, but narrowly avoiding the full force of the hit. Heels slamming down to dig in and give him purchase on the slick floor, Rex choked back a verbal barrage of verbose curses, forming vapidly on his wrangled lips as they strained to erupt between clenched teeth. Kicking out at the piece of desk as it now impeded his path and centering himself for the next attack, Rex had little time to prepare as it came even sooner than the last in comparison to his level of expectations.

The damned creature was almost on Rex as it moved forward with alarming grace, hefting another slab of unrecognizable metal to use as a large broad-faced hammer with one hand and trudging the rest of the way in a simple three-step stride. Rex rolled to the side and felt the air compact against his body as the metal and floor became one where he once lay, levering himself up with one leg and lashing out with the other as he moved. The bastard took the thundering kick to the side in ease, like it was a simple glancing blow, and as Rex raised the bone war mace to strike, the creature reached up for the head of the femur weapon as it swung down.

Although there was a visible sign of will in doing so, the creature halted the path of the makeshift club in its grasp, the sound of tearing muscle or tendon in its arm and shoulder drowned out by the sight and echoes of the mace shattering like it was glass. The impact sprayed the area with bone dust and fragments, sending Rex recoiling backwards, coughing and rubbing his exposed eyes to get the filth out of them, to see clearly before a fist of armor and mass force smashed into his features as Rex tried to wipe the dust away, and only the fact that his hands were close to his face saved him from a mashed nose and one eye socket caving in. His left hand was fine, but now his right began to throb, the hum of the implant dull to the roaring of blood in his veins now, trying to recover his stance, get up before another strike, this time an armored boot driven by tensed muscles slamming into his side, driving air from lungs and making the worst cracking sounds as the blow literally bounced him from one wall to the next. Rex managed to get to his feet quickly, despite having been kicked around like a soccer ball, stumbling away from the tight corner here to get at the room behind and beyond.

His enemy did not make a single sound, not uttering a word as the humanoid form approached steadily from the rear. Rex found himself spinning to face the large container in his way. Just as he began to attempt to pass it up, the booted foot struck him dead center in his back. Rex was still gasping for air as he collided with the container, folding over it and driving it forward with the force delivered, and as it pinned him to the floor with a resounding slam, he felt grateful for the chest armor: Without it, his internals would no doubt be gelatin by now, and before thoughts were still racing through his head as one hand grabbed his foot under the container and yanked Rex back, slamming the back of his head into the container, rolling over him as he was dragged under it with one massive pull. Consciousness now severely threatened to slip from him, and as the opponent hauled the container up with both hands, lifting it up over his head, Rex lashed out wildly with his right foot and caught the knee of the offender on the inside. The hit finally caused the leg to bend and the creature lost its grasp as it slipped forward to its knees, the heavy container slamming down and pinning the bastard to the floor.

Scrambling to his feet in the time he was suddenly allotted, Rex could feel the floor vibrate as the creature growled, something slamming into the doorway just as he cleared it. Rex tore along the bend into the final, clean room, eyes searching frantically for something to use, anything at all. But before long a section of the container slammed into the bend and the creature soon followed, hot on Rex's heels, and as he grabbed one large monitor and flung it over his shoulder, he heard it strike something, but was unsure of the object's destination. Clearing the edge of the final desk in his path to reach the power supply for the facility, Rex winced as a jagged edge rushed by his head, unknown furniture remains barely buzzing his skull but alarming him nonetheless.

A shoulder struck Rex in the center of the back this time, and he smacked the floor hard, skidding on its seamless surface, and slamming into the base of the power controller. Grimacing as the sight of the creature rushing him filled his vision, Rex forced himself to at least get to his feet before the first strike was thrown at him. It was a glancing punch that he deflected with the left arm, but the following right uppercut he couldn't stop, and Rex felt himself lifted off his feet as it connected. He was thrown bodily into the corner next to the power supply equipment, arm bouncing roughly from the metal exterior, and the creature still advancing steadily.

Another fist connected, and Rex found himself trying to blink away blurred vision, hands out, grasping for the headgear and edge of the chest plate, fingers finding purchase. They were working as his eyes couldn't right this moment, locating exactly what he was looking for, and gripping tightly. The beast knew what Rex was doing and batted his arms up and away, and as he brought his arms up in front of him again, Rex did his best to avoid the sledgehammer strike headed for his facial features. He could feel himself starting to ebb and fade from pain that wasn't there, the roar of the sea that was the implant's sounds drowning out everything else, making his fingertips feel numb, his toes almost like they weren't there…

Metal shrieked as the offender's fist collided solidly to Rex's left side, paint chips spattering him, the moment exposing a weakness in the creature's stance, which he immediately exploited by stepping closer. Rex wrapped his right arm about the neck and shoulder of his enemy in an awkward grasp, feet moving to leverage him around, and twisted hard, lifting the massive being from its stance, and slamming it into the power supply panel resoundingly. Rex reached his left arm up, and tore the metal casing off of the wire pipeline, leading up into the ceiling, slamming the scrap of metal down on the ground before reaching in, and pulling free one of the thicker cables. Rex easily snapped one end loose resoundingly and dragged it across the slick surface of the enemy body armor, slamming it home into the throat of the creature.

A ragged roar began emitting from its mouth as it jiggled on the live line, the lights now jittering erratically, casting odd shadows, yet not triggering the emergency lighting either, throwing other areas in total darkness. A shove from the beast came weakly and barely severed the electrical torture, stumbling feet attempting to back away from Rex now, whom simply did not allow it. Striking back at the creature with his left arm, the blackened fist bounced from the strong headgear twice, the beast recoiling physically from the hits. But the alien armor did not mar whatsoever, and Rex found himself bellowing a war cry as he continued pummeling his opponent, kicking out dead-on with a straight shot to the mid-torso.

The creature was lifted off its feet from the force of the blow, and Rex felt a smug sense of satisfaction as it collided with the exposed corner of the nearest desk, the surface buckling under the impact and sending the creature rolling to the ground. Rex approached his now-weakened opponent slowly, pinning the beast down with a knee to the chest, his right hand grasping purchase on the collarbone section of the plated chest armor. His left hand snaked toughened fingers up under the edge of the headgear near the bastard's chin, and after a slight pause, Rex pulled the two grasps apart, hearing an instantaneous wailing and screaming from the monster as he ripped the headgear free.

This time was much more dramatic than the last time he'd unmasked a Combine soldier, Rex himself gasping as he saw a larger portion of the face had been replaced with tech and cabling, but the eyes stuck out resolutely in socketed ports. Noticing Rex was bemused from the discovery, the beast had a chance to wriggle free from his grasp, and began to attempt to flee. Rex attempted the same maneuver his opponent had failed to pull off earlier, wrestling the chunk of broken desk off of the floor next to him, and flinging the mass of metal and wood at an angle along the beast's path, laughing aloud as it struck home, pinning the creature to the floor.

Rex was fully aware that he was roaring obscenities at the creature now as he moved. "You want to start attacking me then run the hell away?! Where do you think you're *going*!?"

The rest of the words blurred together to form a solid string of curses as Rex tore the desk free from the wounded beast, one furniture leg exiting wetly from a gaping shoulder wound. Rex knelt down now, still spitting vapid verbal venom at his crawling opponent as he tore more of the armor from the screeching, screaming creature.

"How do you *like* this eh?! Do you enjoy it as much as you did killing all these people, you piece of trash?!"

As he began to tear the torso armor free, the bastard tried to sit up, and Rex grabbed a fistful of the loose facial wiring and features, pulling the head up slightly, and then slamming it back down onto the slick metal floor. He could hear bones crack and metals whine, continuing his destructive, bloody work once the fighting ceased. Just the mere thought of what the thing had done to all the people working here in the facility was enough to keep his blood rage going, as Rex used his hands to continue removing the armor plated bodysuit, pulling free the last few pieces from the legs.

The creature began squirming madly now, attempting to scrabble away across the floor, its muscles and sinew blackened like Rex's arm, and slick with thick, vile blood. It now looked strange and alien, instead of neatly conforming, and Rex grimaced as he held the legs under his right arm, and tore the end plate from the shins and feet, ignoring the screams of pain. "Stop fighting, damnit!"

Hauling the now-weak-but-still-squirming beast up over one shoulder, Rex began to drag it, kicking and screaming to the entry where it once stood, gazing out at the snow with arms outstretched. Pausing once with the creature grasped in his left hand by the base of the neck and his right hand pinning the hands together at the base of the exposed spine, Rex felt the cold wind blast him as he opened the entry again, smiling as the bastard shivered in his grasp. And he spoke to it one last time, "One cold grave coming right up; make sure to say 'hello' to your friend at the bottom for me."

Bracing himself against the doorway, Rex leaned back, then hauled the creature up and forward, watching it pinwheel as it flew through the cold air awkwardly, smashing against the rocky outcropping that was the edge once before slipping over the side and out of sight. Chest heaving, breaths coming in long, harsh draws, Rex drew himself together raggedly, and shuffled back to the pile of armor, sitting down.

The fight had taken everything from him, and now he began to actually feel sore in certain places, the implant winding like an old toy in his chest, grinding in his ears, and drowning out his pulse. It was getting harder to breathe now, and as Rex put one palm to his forehead, he pulled it back slick with blood and a cold sweat. His heart was still pounding, like an endless drumbeat, a pain in his neck as Rex fell backwards from his sitting position, rolling back and forth on the floor, feeling like he was back in the cage again, pinned in by invisible walls, his innards roiling...

Rex was groaning as he began to convulse rapidly and uncontrollably, panic rising in his mind to drown out all rational thoughts and normal reactions, until that, too, was taken from him. A spike of pain raced from his chest up through his throat and into his head, where an explosion of extreme agony hit him, and he blacked out.

FADE TO BLACK

—∞—

*R*ex rushed up out of a sea of blackness to the surface of what was actual water—an ocean of it—and as he began a slow swim to shore, he noticed this was the shore he'd been to before. A flash, and Rex was killing bug creatures on the shore now, and he stopped, confused; another flash and he was on a grassy knoll, covered in yellow splotches of…blood? At the center of the island stood the spire that rose into the heavens, and laying about the bottom were humanoid forms, leaking the yellow blood and cooling internals, and as Rex approached the towering object, reaching out to touch the entryway, the sea of blackness rose up around him, strangling out the gasping noises he made as he struggled…

—∞—

Jerking awake gasping, Rex looked around nervously. He was still in the odd facility, but as Rex looked to his hands, he could only feel a shiver crawl up his spine. His right hand now was just as blackened as his left; only the skin wasn't mottled, still thick and impenetrable, but smooth and formless, making his left arm look crude and poorly formed in comparison. And as his hands came up to feel his features, Rex noticed the skin on his face, head and neck felt rougher than normal, and a wave of sadness began to flood him.

He was losing everything that made him human, morphing into something akin to what he'd pulled out of the armor suit and flung into the snowy crag below. His mind wandered for a moment, and Rex couldn't help but wonder, how was he supposed to look at Maurine like this, let them see him so far from what they remember as Rex, as humans were supposed to look. A wry grin touched his face, as he realized he'd never appeared wholly human to them before, and here he was now, considering how agape they'd be that he'd changed so much. It was still sad, yes, but it was becoming less of a problem and more of an obstacle to be overcame...somehow. Gathering himself together, Rex checked his pulse, found it strong and steady, but a bit rapid, and collected the pieces of armor from the floor, moving to half of a remaining desk and setting them down loudly.

They were heavy pieces, and after Rex stooped to tear fabric free from one corpse, he used the former scientist's lab coat remains to wipe the disgusting black substance out from the interior of the armor pieces, reflecting that if this was the ultimate transformation of humans, it was very bug-like, with an exoskeleton-type bodysuit wrapping about a weaker body inside. Recalling the brutal struggle, Rex wondered just how much of the fight was the creature, and how much was the suit. But as far as he could tell, there were no connections to underlying receptors in the armor pieces, only the familiar sight of the cables in the headgear meant for the ports that were apparently commonplace among his enemy now.

Examining each section cautiously, Rex finally decided it was clean enough, and began to place the armor on himself. It was an awkward task of wrapping the parts around his battered camouflage pants and combat boots, but they sealed tightly after a short struggle. As he examined the chest piece, Rex removed his father's armor, strapped the newer plate into position, and slung the heavy MCV over it. Placing his right arm into the proper suit piece, Rex decided to leave his left arm exposed, dropping the left-arm section of the armor suit to the floor. Grabbing up the headgear from the desk, Rex took one last look at the armor suit on himself with his own eyes, determined features setting a grim line on his face as he studied the black surface, attempting to ignore the spatters and smears of blood still on the exterior.

Looking up and ahead, out at the snowy expanse through the doorway, Rex fit the headgear on, mated the port and plug, and felt his vision change. Everything stayed in normal scale now, except he could see the headgear's HUD constantly adapting, sensing cold and heat, giving him blurs of output that made him glad to know it was all wetware. The information was almost overloading his senses, and any attempt to absorb it by normal means was far past being possible. Rex almost stumbled over as a wave of dizziness hit him, and for a second, his reaction was to pull the headgear up—it was still plugged into his skull however, and gave him the weird black-and-gray-scale view, seriously disorienting him.

There was a short pain in his forehead that ceased almost immediately, and Rex looked down to the floor to see the spatter of his own nosebleed. Taking a few steps back with his head tilted up to the lights, which continued to strobe every few moments, Rex refitted the headgear over his eyes, and began to concentrate. He certainly did not want to wander into a combat situation and suddenly feel nauseous or collapse from sensory shutdown while lives were on the line—especially his own, which had become a tool he did not want to lose until the last absolute moment. It took several moments to halt his racing heartbeat and calm his thoughts, control the flow of information before him, and absorb it; the interface was blazing fast and rough on the mind, doing its task harshly and with no remorse for sensitive human neurons.

Rex began to refocus on the task at hand, found the keycard from the corpse he'd looted earlier, and made his way to the entry, locating the secondary passage, and running the card once through the scanner. It blinked at him and waited expectantly for something so Rex examined the card itself, spotted a five-digit code, and punched it in. The whole complex seemed to black out for a moment, and Rex could barely contain his worry, until the lights came back up, the console beeped, and the door slid open, revealing a small shaft of stairs to the next floor, which he began to go down.

The first thing to be noticed here was the awful smell of burnt plastics and carbonized metal, and as he descended the poorly lit stairs to emerge into the large room beyond, Rex could see the discarded remains of computers new and old. Shattered Combine items such as scanners, mines, and the annoying flying mecha-razorblades, piles of ruined Combine pulse-rifles, one sniper rifle with its stock removed and barrel bent, large hunks of Combine tech ripped from gateway fields and other sorts of machinery, a mashed communications console standing out amongst the rest. Continuing along, Rex noted that there was a small security station here, too, yet it was devoid of items, looking like it had been stripped bare by someone else already, and it made him wonder if all of the security guards upstairs had done the looting or if someone else was still inside.

The area ended abruptly at another access door complete with console, and as he ran the card and punched the numbers in, the damned thing took an extraordinarily long pause without a blackout to go with it. As it finally blinked and cycled the door open, Rex found his concern rising, the smell getting substantially worse, streaks on the darkened walls here that could have been blood if there was better illumination to see the colors. As he crept down this set of stairs, anticipating any enemy to strike as he came to the bottom, Rex tried to ignore the eye-watering stench of decaying remains, looking ahead at the cages along the walls. It was an area almost identical to the cage zone back in New Mexico, a large, long room with a path leading down the center of the specimen tubes and restricted zones.

Rex moved forward slowly, headgear scanning along and showing him outlines of husks that remained in each cage, trying to identify them with a trillion other images blurring through his mind, and failing miserably. Rex reached the midway point and he had flashbacks of the doors, slamming shut on him and the cages opening to reveal the waves of mawmouths, and as he passed that point, it took every bit of effort not to run to the other side as fast as possible. Rex paused only once as he was within steps of the doorway to the next level, at one cage near the end, to peer in and see what the remains inside really were—the glass portion of the specimen cage shattered as the thing reached up out of the darkness, grabbed his wrist on the right arm, and jammed it's head through the safety glass, wedging it solidly between two bars.

Blood spattered everywhere and Rex could barely drown out the sound of it screeching with a roar of his own, his body recoiling as his left hand grabbed onto the neck of the creature within, found it sickeningly thin and emaciated, and ripped the head from shoulders, ceasing the cacophony of noise abruptly. Standing almost unbelievingly still with the disembodied head in his hands, Rex began to examine it closely, and found what little of it was human had left long ago—identical to the wiry, starvation-thinned creatures he'd encountered in China, this too had the odd band of equipment bolted to its face where the eyes once rested, now only a surface of scanners and what might have been an IR array remained where human features would have stared back at him.

Dropping the remains of the creature to the floor, he heard it land in something with a disgusting squelch, and Rex had no desire to go hunting for the source of the noise, bringing up the keycard again and running it once across the scanner. Nothing happened this time, and Rex had to quell the surge of unease that began to emerge, running the card again, and waiting for the flashing light. The console confirmed his actions this time and as he began to punch in the code on the card, the whole level went dark again. Power surged and failed repetitively for almost a solid minute as Rex stood stock still, cursing amid the total blackness. As power came back on solidly this time, there was clearly something wrong. Yellow warning lights above the two entryways began to strobe, and a male voice droned out over a loudspeaker, digitized and distorted, vaguely reminding him of the passive, soothing voice the Combine enjoyed to employ.

"Deploying purging process, beginning now."

The hiss of fumes or gas escaping nozzles and vents began to fill the room with noise, and a bitter tang in the air had him coughing, as he recognized the taste of fuel, but not sure what kind. The hissing was suddenly cut short by a massive *whoosh* of igniting fumes and superheating air, and Rex was violently thrown backwards as the heat rushed him, mashing into the card reader and turning it into a plastic mess of shattered components, and bending the door inward just enough to ensure that it wouldn't slide properly into the wall recess.

Cursing while trying to ignore the heat warnings flashing in the headgear, Rex peered around in the now-illuminated room, noting that the bottom of each of the intact cages had become flaming encased torches, blazing away with insane intensity and fire-blasting what little remained of the creatures inside. The ruined cage closest to him had ceased functioning properly, but fuel still poured from a bent nozzle on the floor, pooling in the bottom of the glass liner and seeping out through the cracks to the black filth surrounding it, whatever the liquid at the bottom was.

Further down towards the entry he'd used to get into this area, the specimen cage was not so content to be broken to the point of being inactive—no, instead the fire had caught properly from the starter near the fuel nozzle, and a literal wall of flame was erupting from between the hairline cracks in the glass. Rex had no doubts that the fuel would continue to flood the room from the broken nozzle on his end, filling the area with flammable liquid just soon enough for the wall of flame to ignite it and not only ruin the area for good, but potentially blow out a few holes in the sides of the mountain.

As Rex turned back to the bent door and the crushed card reader, he realized the facility was a ticking bomb, and his only path had been crippled by a chain of events he couldn't reverse or even prevent from the beginning. Hoping that his much-abused biology was in for another load of overworking itself, Rex began by examining the thickness of the door, the size of the dent he'd managed to make just by being blasted into it, and took a spare moment to wish the reader wasn't turned into little plastic bits that now decorated the poorly lit, and for all he knew, filthy flooring. Kicking the solid panel once with a straight punt, Rex grimaced his teeth for what was about to come, and began to bash at it with his left shoulder like a battering ram, hearing the sounds of the metal complaining in echoes throughout the darkened room.

Repetition became second nature as Rex ignored the potential death by fiery explosion continuing to fill the flooring below him, with his feet now moving somewhat slickly across the mesh floor. Finally the damned thing began to give in some headway, and Rex changed maneuvers, now using the sole of his foot to kick the center of the dent further in, the edge of the door beginning to pry free from the insets sealing it shut, sparks emitting from the shattered console and making Rex freeze. He did not want to ignite the fuel right underneath him, and the increasing smell of fumes was wearing on his physiology. There was only so much he could take without being able to breathe real live air, and while dying from fire and pressure forces was bad enough, suffocating in the process of trying to extricate himself would be even worse.

With both time and exhaustion bearing down on him, Rex forced his left hand into the crack where the door and inset came apart, and pulled as hard as he could. The crack barely widened, the edge of the thick door slightly curling, just enough for him to fit his right hand in now, too. Bracing his feet on the mesh flooring as best as possible, blocking out the *slush-slush* sounds it was making as he moved, Rex roared as he pulled on the edge of the ruined panel, with all of the force he could muster left. And as the damned door finally folded in on itself, he lost his grip, stumbled on his own legs as he tried to compensate, and struck the ruined cage with his back, shattering more glass.

The bars underneath bounced him away like a toy striking a concrete wall, and Rex ended up taking a face first fall into the wall next to him, hit it at an odd angle, and fell down sideways into the murk, splashing down solidly as his head cracked against the wall again. The headgear saved his face and skull, and didn't seem fazed by it, but the feeling of the dank cold seeping into his clothes had him jerking up from his position, thrashing about to find purchase, and beginning a blurring panic. Rex wanted up off the floor *now* and nothing was going to stop that except maybe himself, if he couldn't control his motions, gagging as the fuel-mixed filth splashed up against his chin, threatening to flood his headgear with the nasty fluid.

As Rex's mind came actively up to surge with rational thought, he lashed out and grabbed onto the rough glass edge of the cage, hauled himself up shakily, and stumbled towards the doorway physically drained, forcing his body through the hole, and tumbling down the flight of concrete stairs beyond. Rex couldn't hear the implant making any noises now, but still couldn't feel any real pain, only a detached sense of awareness that his body was paining for relief, calling out in agony for a rest.

Rex couldn't even take time to think about that at this moment, hearing the trickling sounds of the hellish mixture of fuel and other bile fluids coming down the stairs he'd just fallen down. And the sickening *slush-slush* of the liquid permeating his clothing, making him smell like a walking specimen lab mixed with aviation petrol that accompanied every movement now made it all the worse. The area beyond was very well-lit for the power problems the rest of the facility was encountering, and it would have been comforting if it wasn't for the fact that these research labs seemed to contain genetic diagrams on boards.

Jarred bodies, ranging from fetus to almost full-grown adolescence, lined a large central cylindrical machine, and something made his innards churn with dread realization: A facsimile of the implant he'd seen forced into him, the same shape he'd witnessed on the x-ray scans, a body of liquid metal with tendrils of nightmarish flowing steel that seemed to be alive, ending in sharp, ugly, and painful-looking connectors. Looking over his shoulder, Rex watched as the horrid fuel mixture now pooled into the labs here, and he wasted no time in moving to the next door, tearing his sight from the tables and displays. The sight of an upload console caught his gaze as he moved, and finding the output devices, he loaded one in, hit the only button on the exterior, and watched as the display lit up. At the same time, Rex located the keycard, to his relief not lost in the room above and undamaged, ran it through the reader by the door, and punched in the access code again.

Success occurred on both machines, and Rex couldn't divide his attention fast enough for himself as he used the upload device display as fast as possible, and held the door open with one foot across the infrared eye in the recess. The device took longer than he expected, and at 75 percent completion, he forced it to eject, and hauled ass through the now-closing door, hoping that the research lab would take plenty of time to fill before the purging process backfired and blew up. Rex took this set of stairs to a small lift at the bottom, which he had to call up, stood around worriedly as the grinding noises took forever resulting in little action, the rusty door cranking open to reveal a much-abused cargo lift which he climbed onto somewhat reluctantly.

Death was chasing fast behind him and his only bolt-hole turned out to be a lift that appeared to want to fall apart at any moment now, the whole thing rattling loudly under his feet, and raining red rust rain down from between the two bare bulbs mounted above. It moved far too slowly for the racket it was creating, and as the next level finally grinded down into view, the sight of shattered windows in braced-apart doors didn't exactly set a comforting tone to the area; Rex eagerly moved off of the lift, however, no matter the condition of the hall ahead—it was far better than staying in the deathtrap of a cargo elevator. Beginning at a slow jog, Rex noticed the metallic walls here were clean and unmarred, the lights were bright and active, and the area hummed with a strong source of power.

Coming around one bend of the huge hall, obviously meant for shifting cargo through, despite the cleanliness around him, Rex realized he knew the layout intimately. It was almost identical to the torture rooms in what was left of Black Mesa, the work bays sitting behind safety glass and their own personal self-sealing doors, instead of security windows and bolted wooden entryways. And while several rooms were empty, completely devoid of what was once inside and potentially being worked on, the last two were full. On his left stood a room with banks of computers and metal working machines, and on the right sat a component manufacturing device, one he could almost recognize as a processor assembly and finishing system.

Interesting banks of items, they were, but nonetheless, they were all useless to him now. Rex had no time to sit around and examine them further either, not with the research labs above him now surely beginning to fill up inch by inch with runoff fuel and a source of fire eagerly waiting to set it all off, and Rex made no more pauses in his motions as he completed the trip to the far end. Identifying the sloping floors and raised ceilings as a path once used by cargo lifters to make it to the bottom level, the glimmer of hope began to brighten within him.

Hustling along a bit faster, the fuel squelching in the bottom of his boots as they dried, Rex made note of the spaced ventilation system here, and the walls shifted from metallic, bright to dull, and concrete, lined with hazard markings, safe distance highlights, hard-hat warnings, and at least one biohazard symbol. Eyes peeled for anything of use or interest, Rex moved down the sloped ramp of poured concrete to the main cargo level, a snarl forming on his lips as he emerged into a massive room easily comparable to a small parking garage, already knowing that it was going to be hard getting past the door to the next level, let alone locating it.

The fact that it was in this area and led to an unmapped area of the facility was enough to lower his chances of finding the damned access to numbers and percentages, far too low for him to dwell on with any regularity. And as Rex made his way to the first long row of cargo containers along one wall, he began by opening up the first of them, and starting a thorough search. He found one full of filled gasoline and diesel canisters, another full of '46 Willys Jeeps sealed in old drums, a few packed with crates marked sterile tubes and test beakers, another piled with red and gray crowbars; one of which he happily helped himself to: sealed EVO suits, stacked furniture, stored software and hardware for computers, dozens filled with uniforms, and even one with a damned forklift inside of it.

After having opened every single cargo container he could locate a latch for, Rex started in on the larger units located in the rear section, bypassing dozens of unlabeled and unsorted crates and boxes in favor of the hatches dominating the rear wall. These cargo rooms were built into the back wall, with their doors flush with the surface, and marked with powder-blue stampings. The first was a true pain to open, and Rex finally found the crowbar somewhat useful. The hatch finally cracked open loudly to reveal a walk-in gun nut paradise, dozens of odd weapons, half-assembled and uncompleted rows continuing into the real weaponry sealed in containers smelling faintly of Cosmoline.

The most disappointing fact, however, was that there was absolutely no ammunition stored here; rifling through several containers of mags, Rex found them to all be empty, greased, and waiting for a batch of various rounds to be placed in them. But there was not a single bullet amongst all of the weapons, and as Rex backed out of the collection to close the hatch behind him, he felt wistfully saddened by the load of items, and to be passing them up.

Barely motivated to keep going on, now that he'd bypassed what he considered the most useful tools he'd stumbled upon so far, Rex began to eagerly hope that he'd find a box of ammunition somewhere to use, and as he opened the next hatch resolutely determined, he found what he felt was vindication inside. Only a single gun rack lined this container, and against the far wall sat a diagram he'd seen at least once before. Slick metal-gray body combined with a fore and rear pistol grip, long and mean, two barrels encased without shell ejectors, forward magazine stocky and lengthy, rear magazine obscured but bulging.

Making a quick search of the room, Rex found the racks full of them, sealed in navy-blued metal stamped with Combine seals of manufacture, and he spent little time in tearing one container off to get to the weapon on the interior, hands grasping on solidly. The headgear identified feeding port and magazine receiver for him automatically, and the surplus of crates in the room contained what he hoped, rows and rows of varied ammo, specially fitted for the newer Combine weapon. Pulling free magazines loaded with the caseless 4.3mm rounds he could easily identify from the special Combine modified MP7 weapons, and odd half-moon shaped stripper clips of the energy pods used for the Combine pulse-rifles, Rex began to load the weapon in his hands awkwardly at first.

Ensuring the weapon was ready to go and the round was chambered before shouldering it once to peer down nonexistent sights, Rex began realizing the weapon was not meant to be used without an integrated heads-up display, much alike he'd co-opted the mounted pulse weapon from one Combine APC. It took him only a moment to locate the proper cable in the remains of the case he'd torn free, ported it into the headgear, and plugged the weapon in.

Immediately, the weapon became part of his sight all the time, and even as he hung it at his side, a smaller display-within-display showed him what was live. And just by mere thought, Rex could raise the view up to dominate half of his vision, the other half showing him a typical face-on view of the container, disorienting him somewhat, and marveling him at the same time. Rex stood in awe of what the Combine had wrought, despite everything they had done, the technological wonders they could create and implement still impressed him.

Passing the thoughts aside as he gathered more ammunition, almost more than he could adequately carry, without sounding like a walking drum set, Rex moved onto the next hatch, slinging the rifle across his back, and considering a good name for it. Except all of those friendly, nice thoughts about the Combine vanished as he opened this container, finding himself staring into the creation of madness. Grown bodies locked in some sort of stasis contained in metal and glass containers, reminding him of the casing covering the first of the Judicators, displays and monitoring equipment silently pulsing. Horror turned into realization as he peered in through the glass, and saw a reflection of himself, before the madness began, before he'd felt as if he'd aged and grown beyond human proportions in the matter of days and weeks, a shadow of what he was now, the pure human part separated from the monster.

Each of the other six containers here had the same contents, and revulsion crawled through him as Rex noticed that this was not Combine tech, but instead, it was much more homemade, Earthen touches, human controls, and the mark he'd witnessed in the bowels of what was left of Black Mesa, the loud orange Lambda symbol scrawled in military-styled paint on each container. Backing away slowly as dawning light came to his mind, he realized all of this; the containers, the weapons, the research lab, the specimen rooms, all of it started out as programs by scientists at Black Mesa.

Rex did not want that to be the truth, and certainly didn't want his entire existence to have started at the bottom of some goddamned petri dish in a lab somewhere, splitting genes and cloning his ass...was he even the original? Was there another person out there that used to be Max and was running around now as a psychopath in Combine armor? And what, out of all of this, did that make his father? If the men in Latvia pointing out the combat vest as an MCV, belonging to some type of warrant officer, wasn't enough for Rex to be suspicious, just the existence of these containers and the contents was enough to rock the entire origins of his life, and cast doubt on every word his father had said to him.

With his mind trying to follow the unraveling strings of his mere creation, he forcefully remind himself of what he was supposed to be doing, and Rex tore his eyes away from the containers as the rage built up within. If he stayed in this container anymore he was likely to start smashing things, and he exited quickly, the hatch clomping shut behind him. Pushing the life-altering problem to the backburner, as he moved to the next hatch, Rex realized this was the last in the entire cargo area, and it was frankly the last place he could look for an alternate exit. Something shuddered above him inside the building, and he knew he'd spent too much time already.

As the hatch opened, Rex found only a single container inside, this one larger, and on the far side, to his relief, was another door inset into a concrete wall, complete with card reader and keypad. Closing this hatch shut with himself still inside, Rex hoped the damned door worked, and as he passed by the cylinder in the middle, he couldn't help but notice the size of the humanoid inside was comparable to him now. Except whoever it was wore an orange and black bodysuit that looked solid like armor, comparable to the EVO suits he'd seen before, vaguely recalling that the Vortigaunts called them the HEVs, whatever that meant.

Continuing to the door, Rex slid the card, punched in the numbers provided dramatically, and as he moved through the still-opening door, he knew what was coming next. As he saw the stairs to the next level, Rex hauled his ass down them at blurring speed, entering a pitch-blackened room lit only by the enhanced vision of the headgear, showing him the location of a light switch, which he smacked on absentmindedly as he continued to attempt and identify the machines inside. The switch controlled more than just the lights apparently, and machines lit up across his room, reinforcing a solid sense of hope he felt concerned would be torn free at any moment.

Rex moved to the cage-bound transporter he recognized right away from Kleiner's lab, located equipment that was similar, but in far better condition, and pulled free the note the doctor had written down for him, locating the proper input, and denoting the destination in the right columns. The cage for the transporter opened up to greet him, and as he turned to step in, the entire facility rocked back and forth, flinging him to the floor. Another jolt could be felt this time, closer and louder, and as Rex stumbled into the transporter, hauling the gate shut behind him, he hoped the power didn't cut out. Before he could even wonder if the machine would fail and he'd be trapped here to die, everything flashed brighter than his eyes could resolve them.

ALIEN REVISITATION

Vision cleared to blackness again, and Rex could only wonder if he was dead, injured to the point of blindness, or in the darkness that the man in the blue suit enjoyed to employ so often in their meetings. As his eyes adjusted and the headgear compensated, Rex realized he was in an identical form of the cage-bound transporter now, except this one looked ancient and decrepit, outdated and worn down. Moving this cage door to the side, instead of up like the other transporters, Rex heard the rustling of feet and the sounds of altered voices emitting through vocoders.

"Did you hear that? Sounds like someone is in the oldware room."

More shuffling of feet, and the cocking of a weapon followed the interrogative.

"No, but better check it out anyway, those bastards might be trying to sneak in again."

Remembering to jam the slip of paper back into the designated pocket, Rex slipped out of the cage system softly, keeping the new rifle slung behind him. His hands were much more in the mood to strangle the life from his next opponent, rather than spraying off rounds he potentially couldn't replace. Attempting to remain as still as possible in the darkness, the headgear amped up his vision, preventing him from running into more items and potentially causing much more noise to give away his location.

As the two Combine came around the corner ahead, weapons to their shoulders, Rex leapt into action. Jumping up over a short stand in front of him, he flat-palmed the first enemy in the center of the chest, hearing the Combine spit out his breath with a *whoosh* of air and ribs crackling like leaves in a compactor. The second enemy soldier was unable to respond as Rex backhanded the traitor with his left fist, the enemy stumbling over to crash into a pile of stored equipment. Rex moved over to him swiftly, placed one foot on the supine soldier's back, and grasped a fistful of forehead with his right hand.

Pulling up and back until blue eyes looked back up into his, Rex snarled as the neck snapped loudly, the light behind the neon eyes fading to black. Policing bodies, he found only two Combine pulse rifles, no sidearms, and no grenades, and Rex reflected that perhaps the soldiers he'd face here weren't so well-equipped, wondering just where the hell the coordinates had taken him. Rex did not remember entering this room before.

Picking up both of the rifles, one in his left and one in his right, Rex hefted them up to the crooks of his arms, and moved ahead to the entryway the Combine had used. It was a sparsely lit hall lined with poured concrete walls, and he felt slightly disoriented as it became a wide-open area ahead. The ground here was made of the odd marbled rock he'd seen before, the area Tank called *Xen*. The open area was cut off by endless space beyond, and as he turned to examine to his left, Rex found himself looking through a man-made archway of rock over at a group of blue-eyed Combine standing around the equipment that clearly didn't belong to them.

One of them turned and threw some kind of salute, and the others seemed to be waiting for orders from Rex. He refused to allow them to recover from their deadly mistake, whipping both weapons up and triggers ready, bearing down on all of the solders that remained as they expected a much different response, blue-eyed enemies toppling over to the ground. The Combine armor was an advantage this time, but he didn't expect it to be much more than a hindrance from here on in when encountering human fighters.

He dropped both of the now-spent pulse rifles, and gathered up one more from the corpses, removed a few energy pods for the weapon, and checked the machines here. None were powered on, and as Rex examined each, he found they'd been simply disconnected from one another, and began another arduous process, this one locating the proper ends, and matching prong to port properly. Once each were routed to the next correctly, Rex expected them to start up, but the anticlimax came when he realized that he was going to have to go hunting for the damned power source. His hindbrain at least made a stand, and pointed out that he needed to scout the area anyway, being pretty much lost in what was supposed to be familiar territory to him.

Moving up through the machines to the far areas of this floating ball of rock, Rex found the room connected into a tunnel burrowed down into the surface, then back up once it reached the bottom, lined with chem-light strips. And as he moved down to check the other side of the short tunnel, Rex could see the pathway leading back up to the surface ahead lined with three bodies, all in large white hazmat suits, dotted with plasma wounds that the hazard suit self-sealed around.

Unfortunately, the smart fabric couldn't repair the hollows in human tissue as well, and the three people died as the deadly ammunition tore through their vitals, long before the hazard suit could repair itself, leaving behind only blackened dots where the suit had filled in portions with instant-drying epoxies. Rex didn't bother examining them further. He had other things on his mind now, and as he reached the apex on the other side of the tunnel, Rex located a smaller opening here that lead to a short pathway around the edge of the entire floating island of odd faceted marble.

As he gazed out onto the somewhat colorless emptiness around him, Rex realized the colors were shifting and phasing, and it wasn't pleasing to his innards, which threatened to rebel. It took a moment to realize he hadn't eaten in a while, and what he'd consumed couldn't exactly be considered a real meal. Ignoring the sick pit in his gut from hunger that he'd no doubt have to solve at some point, Rex tried to focus on staying on the path, halting as he heard the sound of boots scrabbling on the pitted surface ahead. Kneeling to a firing position, Rex kept his vision ahead, pulse-rifle leveled. Two of the blue-eyed bastards came around the bend, hugging the path tightly as well, and as they spotted Rex pointing a rifle at them, they couldn't react fast enough.

It was almost amusing to see them struggle to move back as the soldier ahead called for retreat, and the man behind took a few stumbling motions before falling over the edge, to what was probably an endless trip to the bottom of the abyss. Rex didn't let the other complete his tactical reversal, using the pulse rifle to pick him off and sent him tumbling down as well, then continued moving around the side of the floating island at a kneeling-step pace, careful to keep an eye out for more incoming soldiers, and maintain footing on the ugly surface of rock. As Rex finished taking the path around, sighing as it lead to a small cavern in the side of the rock wall, he took note of the power lines snaking out of the side of the cavern, the box that obviously looked like a power-routing conduit, and the doorway inset into the rear wall of the cavern, frowning in concentration as he attempted to recall any of this from his previous trip to Xen.

Hooking up the lines to the routing box and starting it up, humming began to rise from all around, loud and deep rumbling, and a light sprang to life over the top of the doorway. Approaching it cautiously as it opened automatically for him, Rex found walked into a room of man-made proportions, walls of poured concrete, floors of yellow lamellar plate, and four pillars of machinery, larger and more complex versions of the power generator he'd seen the extraterrestrials utilizing in his previous visit.

Only these boasted larger feeders with automated crystal conveyors, obviously working after all this time, and clearly pre-Combine constructs. Taking the pathway through the room that was growing increasingly warm and loud, the humming and rumbling turned into a grinding racket that dominated his senses. Rex opened the next door to exit the power room with relief, even though it led into another clearing, this one with two stations of monitoring equipment, another transport pad, and more Combine shuffling about.

These four blue eyes seemed to be oblivious to the gunfire he'd used on the soldiers on the other side of the power station, and again confusion seemed to reign as they looked at his armor with curiosity and ignorance combined. Rex took full advantage of the situation, walking forward a few steps before aiming the alien rifle again, pounding out the rounds from the waist this time. Three of the Combine died without a word, and the fourth took a screaming fall over the edge as a pulse round caught the offender on the shoulder, spun him about, and sent him tumbling head first over the side of the transporter platform.

Reloading the pulse rifle with the last of the loose energy pods, Rex ensured the monitoring equipment and the pad itself were unharmed. He easily plugged these into the trailing power conduits as well, and began to cycle each of the stations on, smiling as the transport sparked to life. The glowing orb of familiar green, orange, and white phased into existence with a loud snap that sent a static charge through the thin air. Hopefully, the other side looked far more familiar to him, he mused, and Rex held the rifle at the ready as he stepped in.

After a sensation of weightlessness, nausea, and shock combined together, Rex stepped down from this platform as he arrived. The platform didn't seem to be fully operational on this end, dotted with debris, burns, stains, and bullet holes. It was combined with the sight of a humanoid in white smock coat lying against one wall, holding his bleeding abdomen, which didn't seem to be helping. Rex moved over to the man and knelt down, reaching to slip the hand aside, and almost fell back as the man brought up a weapon in the other hand, a revolver that Rex identified almost immediately as the .357 custom he'd liberated from Doctor Hernandez's old office. Recognition was not in the old man's eyes as he leveled the weapon at Rex, preparing to squeeze the trigger.

"…you'll…not…take me with…without…a fight…you Combine bastard…"

Rex grabbed the revolver and moved it over his head with the left hand, wrenching it free as gently as possible before the good doctor plugged him in the forehead. Pulling off the old man's coat, Rex tore it into some impromptu first aid, searched the small devoid space for more assistance, and failed to locate anything.

"Jesus, Doc, you look like a mess."

Rex muttered it low, but the old man heard it anyway, and as his head craned up from looking at the floor, Rex saw recognition strike the old man's features. Suddenly, Hernandez was grasping him as tightly as a wounded man could, one hand on each shoulder.

"Oh, my God! It's you! It's really you!" There were tears in his eyes, but the blood on his cheek turned them red as they streamed down his face.

"Are you hurt anywhere else? Or is that it?"

The doctor winced and shrugged off part of his shirt, exposing a nasty electrical wound to his shoulder, which he quickly recovered. "They…they nearly killed me outright. Then they gutshot me and I did the only thing I could think of—I portaled out." Hernandez coughed raggedly and threatened to pass out, but Rex managed to keep him comatose, checking to see if it was alright to move him. After a moment he decided it was better than leaving him behind, and Rex hefted the older male up, carrying him over to the doorway leading out, following it down to a small

T-intersection. The punctuating sounds of Combine radios being keyed and silent conversation through vocoder voices had him halting his forward progression.

As Rex lowered the old doctor to the floor, he checked the load in the revolver, and found it loaded full, eight rounds of .357 goodness flush home in the cylinders. Closing the weapon, Rex examined what the doctor was wearing, saw a bulge in one pocket, and checked it quickly, finding a speed loader clipped to a full moon of extra rounds. There were no more lucky stashes of ammo on the doctor, so he made sure Hernandez had his attention before he moved away.

"Stay quiet and still. Going to clear the main room."

Taking the path of the intersection that led to the left first, Rex crept around silently, spotted a door ajar at the end of the hall, and slipped in with the revolver gripped tightly. The room was dark and small, and as he moved in, closing the door behind him, the headgear attuned to the blackness, and he found himself in a tomb. A large man lay on the floor spread eagle, facedown, a wound in the back of his head that resulted in the mess that was his features being smattered all over the floor beyond. The kill was still somewhat fresh, and as Rex examined the body, he noted the similar security armor and uniform his so-called father once wore, and skipped over that fact in order to focus on the intact pistol belt.

Reaching over, Rex pulled up on one side of the body to roll it over, shrugged off the sight of the cavernous hole where the face once was, and unbuckled the belt. He casually tore the ID badge from the pinned-down spot on the torso armor, and tugged the belt with loaded pistol and clip pouches free. Slipping it on through the old gear belt he now wore, Rex hung it down to his right side and buckled it into place, the holster well within his reach. Looking at the tag with half-interest, he tucked the revolver and speed loader into the older gear belt pouches, reading off the name softly aloud.

"Otis Berenger."

Pocketing the badge, Rex pulled the pistol free of its holster and examined it in the dark, gazing at the Desert Eagle .357 with some amusement, the five-inch barrel and slide assembly slightly different than the typical model, more military-styled and utilizing a laser sight. It was all flat black, loaded with a seven-round magazine, and had one in the chamber, which he confirmed by tugging back the slide to ensure it was still operational, reloading the weapon and replacing it into the holster. Examining the magazines, he found them all intact and loaded, six of them. As Rex took one last look around the room, devoid of much else other than spare electrical components, he grabbed up the pulse-rifle loaded with its last pod of energy rounds, and left the small area behind him.

Moving back out into the T-intersection and taking the right path this time, Rex made sure Doc Hernandez was still alive and breathing as he moved onward, rolling his footsteps in order to make minimum noise approaching the next bend. The chatter of the Combine could be heard ahead louder now, and as he crept to the edge of the wall, he peered out along the corner as he listened, crouching and waiting.

"…took this place back in no time. No idea why we didn't earlier, like these pests were even a problem."

"Yeah, the resistance was pitiful. We must have caught them off guard to have taken it though—we had very strict orders to be cautious. This little group of rebels has cost us dearly recently. Never mind the facts of what they did surface side; what they caused up here alone was reason enough to be careful."

"What do you mean? It's just some oldware crap these monkeys developed before everything changed."

A contemptful snort followed the last comment.

"If you don't understand it yet you won't get it by me explaining it to you now."

The conversation took an abrupt end as Rex raised his rifle, looked through the doorway ahead, and opened fire on the occupants beyond in his sight. Two of them died right away as far as he could tell, the pulse rounds making short work of Combine headgear, and it wasn't unacceptable for Rex to keep firing just now, emptying the weapon into the air over the machinery he could see, trying to keep heads down, but maintain the level of preservation of equipment he'd seen so far.

Rex needed every bit he could access to get home, and as he let the empty weapon fall, the larger .357 automatic was in his hands first, emerging into an area he knew well now, blue-steeled walls and phased-glass fields used as décor even now, blood still spattered on the floor and walls from previous engagements. Two other soldiers with the neon-blue eyes stood behind one of the barriers, weapons leveled, and as Rex moved into partial light, they froze, trying to piece together what was happening. Both of them acted a hair too late, dying as they tried to take cover.

Rex moved to their bodies, ensured they were down for good, and tromped across the large room to the next doorway, footsteps on the odd ground making echoing noises from ahead, having no doubt that someone was coming to respond to the sounds of gunfire. Leaning around the corner to greet them with a hail of fire, Rex let the remaining rounds in the pistol serve as a minor distraction, jammed it solidly into the holster, and pulled up the newer Combine rifle.

The sight auto-resized in his view on the headgear, allowing Rex to use it as a scalpel on the incoming enemies, incising them open with energy rounds first, then excising them like tumors with the second trigger, 4.3mm caseless ammunition taking them down permanently. Moving ahead down the large dark tunnel here, Rex recalled the last time he was present that he'd used a rocket launcher to destroy a titan of an alien, and now nothing but scorch marks and bloodstains remained.

Stepping over bodies to reach the opposite side, Rex found this area empty of enemies now, and jogged in with the weapon half-aimed at the ground, looking over old computers, and the original platform he'd used to arrive here so long ago. He could feel a sense of ending, but was it real? Was this his finishing line, where he would go home and write the final pages? As he checked equipment still humming with power and ticking away on its endless task, Rex heard the distant sound of electricity discharging, saw power dim amongst the machinery, then rise back to full, questions racking his mind, including the interrogative of whether or not the transporter was safe to use, even after all this time, was it worth risking everything.

Turning around slowly, Rex listened intently for whatever was making the noise, and as something walked into view on the far side of the tunnel, emerging at the doorway of the barrier room, Rex re-gripped the weapon in his hands tightly. The co-opted Combine headgear tried everything possible to enhance his sight and identify the humanoid at the other side, only there was an odd hump on his left shoulder that obscured easy recognition. Rex had the unfortunate decision to take his opportunity now, charging in and potentially dying before finding out who it was, or stand and wait for their approach. Choosing the latter, he took position behind one piece of oldware, tactically reloaded his weapons, and prepared for the worst. The humanoid shape finally moved out into the light of the odd sky, stepping from the tunnel solidly to reveal what it was.

The suit was still reminiscent of the HEVs he'd seen before, and the size was indeed matched to his own. Doc Hernandez was slung over one shoulder, and as soon as Rex recognized the shape of the old man being carried about like a sack of wheat, the newer Combine rifle was up and aimed in a heartbeat as he stood up.

"Interesting."

It spoke with a deep basso tone that reflected a vocoder perhaps, or a completely mechanical voice, and the fact that it was more than just another Judicator or neon-eyed foe shook him to the core. Rex refused to budge however. "I suppose you're the one to thank for releasing me from the chamber."

Revulsion hit Rex as the conversation continued. "Don't. I left you behind to die. And if you don't let him go, I'm going to finish the job right now."

The response seemed to set the newcomer aback a bit, and as Doc Hernandez was lowered to the ground, Rex could see the walking HEV suit was armed with at least two of the alien pulse-rifles.

"Odd. A Combine soldier killing other Combine. This was not calculated in my preparations."

The HEV suit took a few steps away from the doctor, and turned to face Rex head-on. "And such a strange reaction, acting to defend a human scientist: This must be noted when I report it."

Gunfire was suddenly heading in Rex's direction faster than *he* could respond, feeling very much as if the shoe was now on the other foot as he felt the pulse rounds knock him down, and heat up the armor around him. The air tasted like ozone, and for the first time, he knew what it was like to take one of those shots in the face. Roaring as he rolled and stood up, he could see and hear the HEV suit firing away endlessly with one of the weapons, pinning Rex down behind the machinery. But with the weapon raised in both arms and the heads-up display sight working overtime, he picked the HEV's joints along the elbows and knees, and used the Combine-made rifle to his advantage, knocking down his enemy, and crippling him severely.

Movement continued, and Rex could see his opponent attempting to lever free the second rifle, and he solved this by blasting the HEV's shoulder until the weapon was dry of 4.3mm rounds, continuing to approach. The struggling had ceased, but still the mobile suit attempted to at least roll over and face his enemy, and Rex obliged him once, using the toe of his foot to roll the squirming suit over. Blood that was not entirely red poured from wounds, and breath came in ragged draws to the prone offender through the vocoded voice.

"That…gunfight…did not…last as long…as I thought it would. Outcome…unexpected…"

Rex supposed he was dutifully resigned to feeling some measure of regret at the interaction, but it faded fast. "It never turns out the way you think it will."

Gripping the rifle tight, Rex finished the job with a whole stripper-clip of energy pods for the rifle, ejecting the old strip and tucking it into the ammo belt as he reloaded the weapon resolutely, leaving the body behind like so much discarded Combine trash. Instead, he was more intent on the condition of the old man, and as he moved to Doc Hernandez, he found nothing but an elderly corpse remaining, and cursed under his breath. Rex had gone through a lot so far, but the death of the good doctor in front of him was wrenching at his innards, welling up emotions that he swore he wouldn't show in outbursts.

Rex moved away from the body before things grew uncontrollable, restraining the rage he felt as tightly as possible as he moved to the machinery, verifying things were in place and working properly. Attempting to shut out the sight from his memories, Rex started up the transporter, waited for the familiar glowing hum, and stepped into the pulsating orb of greens, oranges, and white.

COMBINE CONTROL

Dropping down into a sparking, shot up mess of a room was not pleasant, and as Rex stepped away from the transport, he could see a horrible gunfight had taken place here. There were a few of the human rebels scattered about, bodies decorated with wounds and scorches signaling that things were not alright here. And as he heard the sounds of Combine radios, Rex scrambled out of the transport room and down the catwalk to the old armory rooms he'd raided before, grimaced as he found one door ajar, and slipped inside, flicking off the interior light. Darkness surrounded him now as he stepped further inside, and the headgear altered his vision ever so slightly.

He could see that the corpse of the assassin that once lie along the far wall was now missing entirely, leaving behind only puddles of dried, caked blood and the skeletal remains of the baby headcrab. Footsteps continued in the area outside, and as the sounds of the armory door being pushed open echoed into the small room he'd moved into Rex slid around to the side of the room's entry, and slung the alien rifle in favor of a more personal approach. The door to the room slowly pushed open, and Rex grabbed the exposed muzzle of a pulse rifle as it moved ahead of the bearer, reversing it upwards and grasping the pistol grip of the weapon with the Combine still holding it, the bore coming to bear under the half-breed's chin as Rex squeezed the trigger.

The blue-eyed bastard dropped like a rock, and Rex relieved the still-falling body of the pulse-rifle, advancing back out into the hall and finding a second Combine soldier there, waiting for the first to emerge, and Rex killed the bastard with several well-aimed rounds. Crouching down, Rex moved to the next body, found a severe lack of ammunition available, and crept up to the transport room door, peering around for the sight of more enemies. Right on time, several came running through the doorway at the far side of the transport platforms, and he let the muzzle of the rifle speak for him, using the doorway as cover to pick off the offenders as they moved down the catwalk from the door to the floor below.

Two died right away as he opened fire, the other three seeming confused at first, before falling back behind a row of machines and returning covering fire, and Rex slammed the armory door closed long enough to take the impact of the rounds first. Taking a few steps back to the storage rooms, he opened them both up, leaving the light off in the first, and flicking the light in the second on. Moving into the darkened room, he waited for the enemy to approach, and wondered if his ploy would actually work, dragging the corpse of the dead Combine into the room with him.

Two more blue-eyed soldiers made their way to the armory door and kicked it open loudly, and as Rex stayed crouched in the darkness, weapon raised and ready, he began to time the approach of feet, listening to the rustling of equipment intently, focusing on the location of the others. Slowly they moved past the darkened room, ignoring it in favor of the lit storage area, and as they passed his door, Rex took the opportunity into his grasp, firing into the half-breeds from behind and snarling as they fell forward, one striking the wall and barely avoiding his well-aimed fire.

Continuing to squeeze the trigger till the weapon was spent, Rex reloaded it with its last energy pod, and began securing corpses, as fast as he could without being sloppy, flicking off the storage light as a last thought before returning to the transporter area. The Combine radios behind him could be heard as someone keyed up for a report, and Rex ensured that he was double-timing his motions as he policed the transporter platform itself, looking for any signs of Lena or the others, and found nothing but rebel corpses, people he didn't know. Either they were new recruits or people he'd never had the chance to meet, and in both cases, it disturbed him that they felt unfamiliar to him. Checking consoles, he found everything shot to hell and mostly unable to be fixed, large sections of circuit board melted away, and controls burned, smashed beyond recognition.

Moving hands across the panel, something caught his eye on the edge, and Rex forced away a section of cover to reveal that it was actually on a hinge, a large red panic-looking button inside. With nothing else to lose, he pressed the button and held it down until he could see the effect, and an almost-imperceptible click came from the wall inset on his right. Rex moved over to where an analysis screen hung off of the wall on broken mounts, pulling it down the rest of the way to reveal the hidden panel he'd just unlocked. Inside sat a huge metal crate he'd sworn he'd seen before, and as he reached in to pull it free, the sounds of more feet approaching had him rushing to yank it to the floor.

Hustling across the transport platform with his newly acquired prize, Rex found the test rooms for the transporter unlocked, and he moved into the first swiftly, setting the case on the floor and shutting the sliding door. Flicking each of the lid locks open, Rex opened the metal crate, and felt his mood darken. Inset on foam portions sat something he could recognize as Combine in origin, but it was now heavily modified and as he reached for the newer Combine weapon he'd stolen from the previous facility, he found they were close matches.

The weapon inside the crate had polymer alterations to the exterior where the weapon in his arms did not, and no forward grip, things that appeared to have far more human touch than the

Combine-prototype he now carried. Unplugging the Combine rifle from the headgear and pulling free the human version from the crate, careful to avoid making more noise than necessary, he made his motions quick and efficient. Checking to ensure they used the same caliber rounds and the same stripper-type clips for the energy pods, Rex held back a wry grin as he noted a third barrel mounted on the right side of the new weapon, the large bore of a 20mm grenade launcher, the caliber stenciled across the stubby, exposed barrel.

The top of the weapon had a large black unit attached to it, and as he examined it closer, Rex found it had the same cable used to plug into the headgear. He did so this time, and he could see the black unit was a heavily modified scope, peering through it and seeing strange readouts. The headgear melded his HUD with the newer weapon, and as he began to load it, he swore he heard a whisper of a voice, and began to stand in the small testing booth, peering through the window on the door.

Two blue-eyed Combine followed a third, this leader wearing the black jumpsuit and sporting a mask with green eyes, tactically approaching the armory door he'd used as cover. Ensuring the weapon in his arms was operational, Rex opened the door and started firing with the new rifle, realizing as it spat pulse rounds at the three half-breeds that he'd forgot to use the fire selector.

The two blue-eyed soldiers dropped fast, but the Judicator refused to do so as well, running through the path of fire and slamming into the armory door, rolling through the opening to barely avoid more of Rex's shots. Waiting a heartbeat for the Judicator to peer around into the open, Rex patiently aimed the weapon, and then swore as he noticed a red glowing streak of light from the bouncing Combine grenade, sliding the test room door closed and wincing as the device exploded, his ears ringing as the walls shook violently, gritting his teeth.

The headgear muted the explosion, but it was still strong enough to stun and affect him, and even Rex could realize it left an opening for the enemy. Despite his rattled senses, Rex slid the door open with the rifle at the ready, and emptied the rest of the energy pod at the armory door. Taking a moment for a tactical reload, Rex leaned over to the metal crate and peeled out the top foam insert, seeking replacement ammunition, and finding it. At least two boxes of 20mm explosives sat inside, and as he popped one box open, Rex could hear rounds bouncing from the test room wall and shattering glass observation windows.

Opening the short breech on the side of the weapon, Rex slipped one of the grenades in and clipped the slide shut, taking aim again at the armory door. Letting loose the single shot at his target, the armory door came off its hinges and the doorway itself warped impossibly, with concrete shattering, metal frame twisting, and the muted scream of the Judicator permeating the dust cloud that filled the air. Rex could see debris toppling away from the piles, and he quickly emerged from the test chamber while flicking the select-fire switch to the 4.3mm barrel, aiming dead ahead and waiting for the first of his opponent's body to emerge, squeezing the conforming trigger solidly and watching as the weapon shredded the top of the Judicator's head open.

Snarling grimly, Rex kept the weapon at the ready, returning to the test chamber. Quickly emptying the metal crate of its supplies, he left it behind him as he came back out to the transporter room, hustling along the metal-braced flooring, stepping over both Combine and Rebel bodies alike as he made his way to the bottom of the catwalk, running up with anger driving him. This was supposed to be safe grounds, home for the people Rex considered his own, and one was dead already, the others not even here. Biting off the growl that threatened to follow, he rushed up to the exit, and moved past double doors he recognized, a bloodstain on the floor he'd created, and a second set of doors that he swiftly moved through.

Here stood the research room, except it wasn't much of a room anymore, everything scorched to a pile of ashes, craters of weapons fire reforming the walls into what looked like natural cavern interior. The only thing remaining was a Combine control console, powered off but intact, and as he moved over to it, Rex kept his senses alert and ready for signs or sounds of more enemy troops. Connecting the power supply here, the console came to life, and he navigated the controls with ease as the HUD translated it for him, trying to access the data logs and finding them absent.

Switching over to the monitoring screens, he opened them all and set them to order, recognizing each of the rooms, and finding many of them destroyed. There were no visible corpses in camera range, and Rex soon left the console alone in favor of moving on, his rifle at the ready, finding the door to the mawmouth corridor now wedged open with a navy-metal brace of Combine origin. As he stepped in, he could see the room had been cleaned out for the most part, leaving behind only stains and rumpled hints of what once happened here.

Stepping through easily, Rex moved along the metal flooring with his weapon ready, trying to ignore the soft, streaming whisper at the back of his mind, torturing him with its inability to be distinctly heard, hoping beyond hope that it wasn't a hallucination and confirmation of his craziness. If there really *was* a voice in his head, he certainly didn't want it to be there. Something else going wrong in his mind at this point that was way too much for him to handle. Once he was on the other side of the headcrab room, Rex moved into the familiar sight of the control room, lights darkened here, something thick and sticky on the concrete flooring.

Rex didn't want to know, but soon he found the source, Colonel McClaine laying on the floor with his chest torn open, telltale marks of a larger energy weapon, with what was left of Lt. Wallace not far away, his face and upper chest gone, but still wearing Scottish fatigues. The screens that were once mounted in here were gone, even though they'd been hastily constructed last time Rex was present, and the two-way windows were shattered. There were a few other bodies here, no one he recognized, plenty of spent casings, burns, ruined equipment. It was an utter nightmare, a total wreck, and weapons fire ahead had him moving again, reloading both magazines while he thought of ways to torture Combine soldiers with anything he could get his hands on. Moving out of this small control room, he pushed open the bullet-ridden door placed here, memories of the surgery that occurred in this dank, dark room still vivid and fresh, the smell of blood, the blade opening flesh, something that felt *alive* crawling through him.

Snarling, Rex had to visibly restrain himself from his outburst, before continuing on to the source of fire, weapon begging to kill, everything about him willing to comply, loading the launcher a second time. He moved out into the control room here, noted it was torn to shreds as well, and moved past, through into the half-and-half hall, the metal still present, as well as the older human construction, except there was no progress of Combine tech here. The construct meant to replace older human buildings had been destroyed here, and it was the one room that remained the same for the most part.

The major difference was the far doors being open and braced aside by a pair of blue-suited soldiers, opening fire on one of the many rooms in the extended corridor ahead. Rex halted as he raised the rifle, waited for his brain to decide what to do for him, and let the weapon hang on its sling, deciding on a personal touch. Kicking the soldier on his right forward, Rex switched targets, side-kicked the second Combine in the throat as the soldier spun to face the disruption, and moved to the first, watching as enemy hands slid across the grimy concrete floor here, drawing the .357 auto easily, and taking aim from the hip.

Two rounds to the back, and one to the neck was all it took to stop the movement, and Rex kept the weapon up and prepared as he stepped over two more corpses, ignoring twitching feet and gurgling, as well as the fallen rifles. Scanning the area ahead, looking into each room with the headgear assisting him, he couldn't find what the soldiers were fighting with, or firing at. Plasma rounds had left scorches everywhere along these rooms, rooms he remembered as torture and observation bays.

The last room at the far end was the worst in terms of damage, and even there the scanners detected nothing whatsoever, perturbing him even further, curses under his breath as he finished the trek through the hall, and through doors here to the man-made catwalk. The ruined energy field projectors still stood like long-dead monoliths, covered in dust and far past being operational. His footsteps made muted sounds here as metal and concrete merged again to form a floor, the familiar sights of glassy surfaces below him and the wrecked Combine replacement equipment slumped against the far rock wall still.

The halls felt like they stretched across forever, and as he reached the opposite doors that finally led into the staircase leading upward, he felt like he'd substantially achieved something. But the continued sounds of moving feet above him inspired him to speed up his own pace, a door being kicked open then slammed shut echoing down to greet him as he ran. Pounding out the steps with rage building at the unknown, Rex began to feel a need to kill something, anything to ebb the flow of anger about what had happened here, what was *still* happening. And as he kicked at the door here at the stairs, his result was much different than just opening it up, the door tearing open, ripping hinges in the frame, shrapnel from a portion wrenching free and flying loose.

Nothing special could be seen here, except for the fact that all the rooms had been emptied into the center, forming what was probably a large pile, but now was only a lump of burned plastic surrounded by a scattering of ashes. It was simple enough to take a quick scan of the rooms, all empty, darkened, and not containing the stranger making noises. If this stranger was anything like the last two, it would show up at the most awkward moment, declare itself an enemy, and try to frag his ass.

Continuing motion to keep pace with the opposition, Rex could hear muted thumping sounds drifting in from the distance, and after securing his rifle again, he charged through the remnants of the door beyond that had been shredded long before by the Combine. He easily dusted his way through the tight concrete corridor to the vehicle bay, and felt relieved that his memory was still functioning. Of course, that thought evaporated as he spotted the chief engineer for the rebels, MacMullen lying amongst four blue eyes, a bloodied wrench still gripped in one hand.

The bodies of his engineering team were close by, as were several more of the red-eyed soldiers, all killed by electro-torch or torque-hammer. Blood was dried and the bodies seemed old however, the smell restrained in the room, and Rex could see more of the blue-eyed soldiers scattered about the far door of the bay to the security room beyond, all dead, fresher blood still pooling. Rex could tell that the killing shots were precise, and as he scanned the area, he could see a casing or two, the others obviously policed up by the marksman. Rex retrieved one, noted that it was a .30–06 caliber round, and grimaced, remembering the last person to use that type of rifle around him. "…if they've done anything to you…" Rex said it so quietly that it carried a very short distance, and instead he let his feet carry him forward, a new motivation rising in his currents, to find the would-be sniper still in front of him, and figure out just who they really were. He plucked at his weapon absentmindedly, still believing something could be left intact here, but it was something in the back of his brain, and he couldn't grasp it easily, already caught up in the building tension of the moment, his body on autopilot willing him forward.

Pacing steadily through the doorway scattered with bodies, pulse racing where it was once steady and calm, eyes searching for any trace of the person he was trying to pursue, Rex felt elated that no rounds were fired to greet him, especially as he charged through the security room and beyond, out to another half-and-half hallway. Opening the door on the left, he found himself in the exit room, more bodies of the blue-eyed bastards lining the floor. There was a surprising lack of Elites and Judicators present here, not to mention his unseen opponent, but from the looks of the opened doors ahead, perhaps even that stranger was gone now, too. Leaving with a single glance behind him, Rex knew this was no longer his home, if it ever was, and he stepped out the exit into the desert.

Vehicles were lined up here, again, and all were emptied of personnel and items; the only thing remaining were footsteps leaving the area, and instead of leading to where he could clearly identify, they tracked off into the distance to places unknown, and he refused to take them as his own. Focusing on his own trail, Rex stowed his gear, and began to run to the compound.

DARK HOMECOMING

Sweating profusely and cursing just as much, Rex felt exhausted, overheated, and sore. The Combine equipment pinched his skin, rubbed roughly with the clothes he wore, and flopped against the combat boots now, the strip of cloth he'd used to tie them down with broke free. And as he came into view of the compound, he realized it was beyond ruined now. The entire group of structures have been reduced to craters, leaving a few walls standing and little else, with a smattering of scarred and burnt bodies bearing the orange armbands. The corpses were in positions that suggested they were trying to reinforce the area or perhaps search for something, scattered but behind what was once cover, until the whole area was pounded into submission.

It wasn't a marvelous conclusion to arrive at, but he wasn't going to get a break here, assistance, or even a moment of rest, if he stayed at all. It would take an eternity to repair something enough to use as facilities, secure a safe spot to sleep, or make something to create heat to cook. But before Rex could even change his track of mind, realization struck him—he'd refused to stop, to think to rest for a long time now, and it was hanging in the back of his consciousness where he'd shoved it, preventing himself from feeling it like the implant dulled his pain. His adopted daughter was primary on his mind with Maurine right there with her, the only two he'd spent a long time with after the world had scrambled for him, his only family. And he could restrain it no more, he needed a moment.

Moving into the cluster of ruined homes slowly, Rex located what remained of his own house, and walked inside, realizing the roof was gone now, and the front exterior stood only due to sheer force of will, the entry carpet scorched and windows reduced to a once-liquid glaze. The condition of the home felt like he did—battered, overheated, worn down, falling apart. Rex began to snarl, trying to keep himself from sobbing, and failing as he turned the familiar, still-standing corner, looking at what was left of his father, still on the floor where he'd left him.

With what he learned traveling so far, Rex still couldn't stop himself, even if he was unsure who the man really was. The moment was cut short as he tripped into the room, collided with the doorframe, and found himself lying across the top of the desiccated corpse, rolling off and recoiling at the smell and thought of touching it. Anger flared at the lies he was told and Rex found himself kicking at the body ruthlessly, without measure or understanding, and stopped himself before he went too far. The head lolled on torn skin and broken bones, and insects crawled away from the violent motions. Backing away slowly, Rex left the body behind and retired to the charred interior of his own room, looking out at the sky with a mix of despair and a good measure of menace, the stars coming through as just more scans and a list of identifiable planetoids.

Standing up on the ruined bed to get a better look at the stars, he was in the process of reaching to remove the headgear, when rounds began to shatter the burned walls, dusting the area with shrapnel and causing Rex to roll headfirst across the filthy floor. His hands reached for his rifle and found it missing, the sling cut to ribbons by the hail of fire, the weapon itself bouncing across the carpet. The .357 Automatic was next in his grasp as the bullets continued to rain around him, and as Rex ensured a fresh magazine was in the receiver, a ready round in the breech, Rex turned to face the source through his own shattered bedroom window.

Three shots followed his movement and the projectiles struck his chest armor before he could see the flashes popping off from the shattered rubble of the tram station, forcing him to double back, taking cover within his own mauled house. He could feel the fire behind him trace through the home for his location, kicking over a larger piece of the roof that had fallen down through the home, Rex twisting it behind him and standing it up as a decent cover. The brace of lumber and thatching was hopefully thick enough to stop a few of the deadly projectiles from reaching him. Sitting in the dark, breathless, weapon ready, Rex could do nothing but wait for his opponent to reach his position, prepared for any sight or sound that was within range of his attention...

There was a shifting of dirt across carpeted floor that was far too close for comfort, behind him, quicker than he could have imagined. It was joined by the sounds of a blade dragging its way up his back to his lower ribs, then the pressure of an edge on the armor sheathing his throat, all of it blazingly fast and occurring before he could respond, and again, Rex could do nothing but wait. Letting the weapon drop from his hand, the heavy thuds of the pistol striking the carpet were quickly followed with it being scooped up out of sight, and the pressing of the edge became tighter. "Filthy half-breed."

The words came in as a whisper, the voice familiar, begging to reach through to him; it didn't matter that he was being held violently at this point, if the voice was the hint he needed, but he still didn't know, didn't have enough information, and felt lost, and found at the same time. A hand forcibly ran down his back in the same location the blade drew its path, and Rex could catch the barely audible curses that followed as the hand discovered there was no wound on his back, and a punch followed by a stunted grunt. Rex could barely feel the strike through the armor on his chest and back, and he recognized the motions, the patterns of attack on himself.

He'd taught those motions, passed on those brutal tactics, including the throat to the knife that held him back now; the word that followed escaped from his mouth before he could restrain it. "Molly." The violence increased dramatically now, with something whipping across the back of the headgear, a knee slamming up under his right arm, and a foot kicking him forward onto the floor, Rex rolling to see the muzzle of the rifle aimed at his throat, mirror actions of what he'd just done to the Combine upon his re-arrival to Old Black Mesa. The one addition was a booted foot slamming down onto his chest where he'd shot the Combine soldier instead, and the headgear could clearly identify what was hitting him in the faint light.

It was the black-clothed assassin he saw dead inside Old Black Mesa, complete with night vision goggle assembly over the eyes, and the familiar sight of the M1 carbine, except now it had black cloth wrapped around its exterior, with a larger scope mounted and wrapped as well, perfect night camouflage. One gloved hand ran the short slide on the rifle, hiked the sling, and hung it across a feminine shape, the same hand tugging free a pistol and returning the aim to Rex's forehead, the silenced bore coming to bear on his face as he lay there, wondering how the hell this ghost had come alive, and if it was the one that killed Molly...

"How the hell do you know that name?"

The pistol affirmed her question by jamming up against Rex's armored chin, and he responded as best as possible, still wondering who was doing the interrogating, "She was my daughter...a long time ago."

The pistol lowered, the stance changed, and the assailant removed her foot, taking a step back away from Rex now. "That's...impossible."

Rex slowly got to his feet, towering over her now, looking down at what he'd missed for so long, and as he removed the headgear to look at her with his real eyes, she pulled up the night vision goggles, and opened her own mask.

"Molly." He smiled broadly, and put hands on strong shoulders, a proud sight before him: A strong young woman that got the drop on him.

"Daddy?" She was crying now, and dropped the weapon to the floor, grabbing him close in a tight hug.

Rex responded and they stood still for several moments, reunited after so long...she was older than he remembered, and he couldn't recall the amount of time that passed, or where the strange blue-suited man would show up next. None of that mattered now, as long as this was real, and she was here, the blue-suited man could go take a flying leap off a cliff somewhere.

Backing away one step to get a better sight, he took a look at her again, and Rex could see the changes in her, the same coiled look behind the eyes he'd seen in the mirror, and the assassin's bodysuit fit her perfectly; ridged across the back, torso, and upper legs, Rex could see the suit had been enhanced by the thin body plating the Judicators typically wore. And as he bent down to retrieve her pistol, he could see the same mind at work on the handgun, the 9mm altered to make the suppressor integral with the slide and barrel, extended twenty-four-round magazine sitting in the double-stack receiver.

She exchanged it with his .357 Automatic bearing a wry grin on her face, returning a large, wicked-looking combat knife to a sheath on her upper left shoulder, while holstering her customized piece. Rex did the same with the Desert Eagle, slowly walking back to his old room with Molly in tow, no doubt just as surprised to be seeing him again, let alone still alive. Finding his rifle where it lay, Rex hefted it back up and began to repair the sling, sitting on the bed, Molly sitting next to him.

"God, how long has it been..." He said it gently, finishing the repair on the weapon and strapping it across his back akin to how Molly had her rifle shouldered now, glancing over at her and realizing how obscenely unnatural this was: A bond borne of war and death, one he almost ruined by stepping onto that teleporter pad, and relieved to have again, just by seeing her.

"Almost a year." The answer was not one he expected, and Rex could see the sadness her eyes carried as Molly said it aloud. It was clear things had not gone as well as they could have. Doctor Hernandez was dead, Old Black Mesa was littered with bodies of revolutionaries, the transport device was far beyond reclamation, and his former home was in even worse state than he'd left it before, one of a few structures remaining in a giant crater full of more humans whom died under the Combine scythe.

"Where's Maurine?"

Molly's features darkened now, and she looked away.

"They have her. And the others. The Combine took them only a few hours ago, in the middle of attacking the transport station. I haven't been back to the silo yet. I heard them taking it over through the Combine frequencies."

As Rex responded with a questioning, concerned look, reloading his weapons and standing, she continued.

"We figured out how to decrypt their radio transmissions. We've been using them for more than a month now. They helped out a lot when the Combine first began attacking the transport station, but somehow they got inside using the teleporter pad, when we had it all locked down for repairs."

Rex looked at the floor as he spoke, "Doc Hernandez was at one of the relay stations for the teleporter. I think they'd found something out when the Combine reverse-engineered the unit to get in; a lot of the bodies I found were wearing the Lambda-style HEV suits, and carrying scientific gear. Doc...didn't make it."

The reaction on Molly's features was unreadable, but as she stood, securing her gear and stowing spare ammo, Rex could come close to reading her thoughts, his observation confirmed as she put her mask back into place, and pulled the goggles down, ready to go. Doing likewise, he remated his rifle with the port, slid the headgear into place, and reestablished the heads-up display, looking around cautiously.

"I guess we both know what has to happen next."

Again there was a slight whisper in the back of his head, something he couldn't quite hold on to or understand, but he dismissed it as soon as possible, with other things dominating his concerns. Moving outside of the ruined home and hearing Molly do the same, Rex ensured his gear was in place and began to jog in the direction of the main highway, finding it half-covered in sand and unkempt from years of abuse. He was surprised when she took the lead and began to move along the road towards what he hoped was the city that remained, with the silo base nearby, and as he ran behind her, he questioned why. "Some reason you're taking the lead here?"

She didn't even look back as she spoke. "Things have changed, and you're still wearing Combine gear, now even more of it than when you left us. I didn't recognize you until you said something. We're heading into one of our zones that have been attacked, and neither one of us knows what we're going to find. If Tank sees you like this, trying to lead the way, he's likely just to blow you away from a distance."

Rex slowed his pace a bit, made sure there was a slight measure of distance between them to match what he felt in his mind there was, and continued along, understanding clearly what she was saying, and the reason behind saying it. He didn't like it, but he'd probably have to live with the fact that the blue-suited man had ruined everything that remained connected to him here, and felt weakened somehow by it, a feeling he couldn't grasp onto matching the whisper in the rear of his skull that refused to resolve.

The two of them moved on in silence, with only the sounds of booted feet on the sandy paved road to accompany them, and the rustling of air past the pickups on the headgear. Just as they began to approach the battered road sign, signaling the mile marker into the city proper, and the details of City 4 came into view, the massive frame of a modified Combine armored personnel carrier came streaking out into the open, dotted with blackened scorches and rows of bullet holes, but still flying a white flag with the orange symbol scrawled onto it, a large mounted pulse-cannon assembly swiveling to face them. Molly stopped where she was, and held one hand to his chest to still his motions, waving one arm to the vehicle as it roared to a halt before them. The cannon focused onto Rex and refused to move an inch, even as the canopy of the driver's section opened, and Rex found himself looking at the same Tank he knew before, except the battle scars on the armor bodysuit were somewhat more increased.

"Who the hell is that, Molly, and what're you doing with it?"

Molly seemed tongue-tied momentarily, as if she knew what she was about to say was highly unbelievable, even to the man Rex had known long enough to consider friend.

"It's Rex, Tank. I…found him."

The vehicle backed up even as Tank stayed motionless in the seat, the cannon remaining focused on its large target.

"Impossible. He's gone, and you damn well know it. Now seriously, tell me who that is."

Molly stopped as she began to respond again, looking back to Rex resignedly. He reached up and unsecured the headgear, pulling it off to reveal his features, the skin mutated to a dark tone, but the face remaining the same.

"Hello, Tank. It has…been a while."

Tank stood up in the driver's seat, leapt down with the cannon still auto-targeting Rex, and stepped forward. "You dumb son of a…you got a lot of guts coming back around here. We went through a ton of crap trying to find you, and now you just freaking show up out of the blue. How the hell you're here I have no idea, but you better damn sure realize this is not a happy reunion."

Rex held still for a moment, replaced the headgear, and nodded to the towering Tank just a few steps away. "Fine. I get it. Just tell me what happened here, and what's next."

Tank turned away half a step, looked off into the distance, and spoke coldly. "And now you want to help, or you think you do, and we're supposed to go along with it, just like before. You left us in a big lurch, Rex, you freaking *bailed* out on us almost a year ago, and now everything is ruined because of it."

Tank spun about violently, swinging one fist at Rex's head and snarling when he missed, Rex rolling back and to the side to avoid the next incoming kick. Grabbing the large foot as it came at him, Rex lifted as hard as he could, and watched in amazement as he hauled the massive Tank up off his stance, the large biomech body tumbling once in the air, before slamming down to the sandy pavement. Rex was immediately in motion, moving over the top of Tank, bracing him down to the ground, and snaking his left hand into the tight gap on the suit's neck, pulling free one of the cables, and hearing Tank snarl in response.

"Both of you, stop it now!" Molly said it with much anger, her pistol drawn and aimed at the two of them. Rex backed up and away, hardly believing what was happening, that he was manhandling someone that was once his trusted combat team member, but as the situation stilled, and Tank still lay there, unmoving, Molly took charge again.

"Why the hell aren't you getting up, Tank?"

The angry voice rippled with unseen rage. "*He* did something to me, I can't freakin' move!"

The silenced muzzle came to bear on him again and Rex calmly moved over to the prone form of Tank, reconnecting the cable, and backing away swiftly. The large biomech body made no more motions at him, but the look that crossed the distance between the two of them spoke volumes, including that this fight was only over for now.

"Now let's go, damnit, Maurine's in trouble, no one's responding over the radios, and the Combine are sending patrols along the route from here to Old Black Mesa. That means I want us arriving to the silo base as soon as freaking possible, and you two monkeying around in the dirt doesn't help me solve any of that."

Molly began approaching the rear door of the APC, and stood there for a moment before emphasizing her position. "Well?!"

Rex didn't know what to expect next, but Tank dutifully approached the APC, hopped back into the driver's seat, slammed the canopy closed, and opened the rear bay for Molly, allowing her up onto the ramp and inside. As Rex approached the rear, the tires spun in the dirt, and kicked up a cloud as it tore away, the rear doors closing shut even as the vehicle sped off, Molly loudly cursing. Furrows forming on his features under the headgear, Rex began to run hard, ignoring the slight sense of tiredness plaguing him, concerned only with Molly's destination, and followed the tracks and dirt cloud.

All along the run, Rex snarled in reflection, knowing this was way too wrong, everything was off, happening faster than he could change it, and it wasn't slowing or stopping for him to adapt to it. Far from it, the whole situation had accelerated beyond understanding, and the personal changes he'd gone through had not an inch of help to add to the length of difficulties ahead. Now his journey had taken a turn he could not correct the course of, and recalling his bestial dreams, he could only wonder if that really was how all of it is supposed to end, on some nameless shore, killing things that weren't remotely humanoid whilst losing his own state of mind and being in the process…

The tracks took a slight deviation through the sands, and Rex altered his path to match, but he rapidly lost sight of the APC even in the broad daylight, and tried to orient himself to prevent from losing his way to the silo base proper. He moved on in silence, while still trying to consider what to say or do next once he finally reached them. Nothing was coming to him easily, thoughts roiled and tumbled, and he barely noticed that he'd crossed a tripwire, until the first round came searing over his head and he rolled back, shoulders landing across the wire itself.

The rounds fired were loud and distinct, the second round bounced from the dirt to his immediate left, and he spun away from it, tearing up the tripwire with his left hand and winding it around toughened fingers as he ran straight ahead. Zigzagging once midway, Rex leapt up over the mound of sand, a round being fired underneath him midair, with the wind being struck from him as he landed upon the surprisingly hardened dune. Instead of soft sand rising to greet him, he met with a rigid ridge of cresting soil, packed together like the underground bunker he'd visited when he first met Molly. Forcing himself up, Rex leapt over the top, drew the Desert Eagle .357 in his right hand, and slid down the short set of hardened stairs, matching the basic layout of the other bunker, finding a single sniper inside.

The muzzle of his pistol was the first thing the sniper focused on, and the attention on it allowed Rex to identify the man, and decide what to do all in the same moment. "Hello, Harry." Rex felt that the sucker punch he delivered with his wire-wrapped fist was more than a bit unfair, especially as the sniper dropped like a rock, but as he located and smashed the only radio on him, Rex knew it was necessary. Leaving the scoped Winchester behind and intact, he decided not to leave the poor bastard completely defenseless. "Good-bye, Harry."

Running back up out of the small bunker, hindsight reminded him that he should have just taken the radio with him—Rex had no idea how often Harry reported back to the silo, and he could have used it to perhaps locate Molly, but it was far too late for that now. Running along the tracks again, realizing that Tank had led him around to the path of the sniper position, he let his memory follow its own course, moving away from the tracks, and quickly stumbling upon the small campfire and ammo stash. Holstering the pistol, Rex cranked open the lid, and found the old Samsonite leather briefcase sitting in the bottom, next to the only other weapon left, an ugly UMP45 with four magazines of ammunition.

Focusing on the case, he reached over, and opened it up, sighing to find it empty. If it had Tommy's weapons, it would have been a dead giveaway that the older male had bit the dust. True, his whereabouts and condition were still unknown, but this was better than nothing at all as a sign of his absence. Tightening the sling on his rifle along his back, Rex grabbed the machine pistol, and stuck the magazines in his almost-overloaded ammo belt before continuing on, unfolding the stock and holding it in a double-grip. Even as he ran the short distance to the base, he could see the tracks and dust left behind by Tank's APC, leading away from the base, and Rex had to make a decision on the fly, picking the route through the vehicle bay rather than going down the main shaft, or following Tank's tracks to the city right away.

Sliding across the dirt and sand onto the large metal platform, Rex kicked at the vehicle control once, snarling as it tilted, then lowered awkwardly, the far end digging into the wall as it moved, creating a horrible sound that echoed down into the silo and more than likely reverberated out into the desert above for a great distance. Rex doubted that Tank had booby trapped the lift like this, but he wasn't so sure now. However, he did not see entry tracks for Tank's APC, and that meant he was coming into the bay before them.

Rex was seeing the interior of the silo attack before either of them, and that insinuated that the situation down here was still potentially hostile, unsettling every nerve that was remaining calm in his person. Leaping over to the railing as the entire lift groaned loudly and tilted at a horizontal, and missing his grasp, he slid down off the edge, slammed into the far wall, and took a huge drop below. Striking metal at the bottom, Rex rolled into the vehicle bay, pieces of the vehicle lift falling down behind him as he stumbled away from the growing cacophony of sound, limping without pain, but feeling stress on his muscles that prevented his movements from completing. Falling over roughly, bruising again his body without the pain to accompany it—he was missing the sensation of pain now, especially as telltales or a demands for rest, a need to relax and repair that was quickly vanishing from his life, creating a nonstop nightmare with no breaks.

His weapons surpassingly intact and his body recouping with the sensation of motion from the device in his chest, Rex forced himself up, realizing the vehicle bay was darker than it should have been and glanced back at the fallen vehicle lift. He knew now the only way out of the silo was through the front entry lift, continuing his way across the concrete floor to an ajar door, surprised as he located the hidden kitchen area. The last meal was still in the middle of a preparation here, and one of the chefs laid dead on the floor, a spent shotgun in her arms and her body riddled with blackened holes, no sight of Nana with her young apprentices.

The doorway to the next area bore handiwork of the victim's empty weapon, along with the bodies of two Combine soldiers, and Rex felt a little disappointed that there were only two bodies here—they'd overwhelmed her by charging the entry, and the bulk of the shotgun's spread had peppered the doorway and wall, no doubt missing much of the incoming enemies. Of course, someone as skilled as Nana or her students were in cooking shouldn't necessarily carry over to a penchant for firearms, and even as he reflected upon this, he did it coldly, and it weighed on him more than he knew. Stepping away from her corpse and over the two enemy bodies, Rex moved out into the cafeteria area, and winced as he saw the trail of dead leading away, scattered rebels here, not a single enemy soldier in sight, signs of battle everywhere, craters from bullets in the concrete walls and light fixtures shot to hell to darken the area.

Making his way around to the entry lift, Rex found it jammed halfway up the shaft to the surface and made an about-face to see if there was an override anywhere close by, when the sounds of gunfire beyond the armored checkpoint door began to blast out. Rex doubled back to the checkpoint, ensured the UMP45 was operational, and took in the things around the desk: The mounted weapon sagged downwards, non-operational, the metal fencing was gone completely, scorched edges all that remained, the desk itself riddled with holes and dents, including scorches from pulse-rifles and plasma grenades.

Blood was everywhere here, under his feet as he moved, and along the side of the desk as he crept around it, matted with hunks of unidentifiable materials at the sharp edges of the top. But it was soon pushed out of his mind as the door on the opposite side of the desk tore open, and a rebel vaulted over the top, carrying around a lightweight backpack and a full-frame M16A2. The man slid across the cafeteria floor to one of the vending machines, tapping on the wall next to it apparently randomly. Instead of the typical nothing happening, the wall slid open, and Rex couldn't help but wonder what the hell was going on down here, the rebel slipping into the opening.

Several blue-eyed Combine ran out from the room behind the checkpoint, fanning out into the cafeteria area. Lifting the machine pistol to his shoulder, Rex began to fire rounds at the trio, the .45cal bullets knocking one Combine down, and scattering the other two. The secret panel opened back up, and the muzzle of the M16A2 emerged alone, firing upon the enemy soldiers. Once the blue eyes were dead, the muzzle turned on Rex. He found himself leaping through the torn security fencing and across the checkpoint desk, shoulder crunching against the one-way door to the storage room beyond and tearing it down with his momentum as rounds seared by.

Rex froze as the firing ceased, out of view, yelling aloud to the person targeting him, knowing that the Combine suit he wore wasn't assisting in the situation, yet again. "Goddamn it, stop shooting! How many freaking times do I have to say that?!"

As the pause in gunfire continued, a question shot back at him through the emptiness. "Rex?!"

Peering out through the doorway, Rex found himself looking down the muzzle of the M16 again, but this time the firing didn't continue. "Yeah, it's me!"

Stepping out, weapon lowered, Rex began to walk out from the checkpoint, when the rifle bearer yelled again. "Hold it right there. How do I know it's really you and not some Judicator using a vocoder?"

The voice was tantalizingly familiar, as was the weapon.

"A Judicator would have shot you as you leapt over the checkpoint station instead of firing on other Combine," he said it calmly as he tried to identify the person holding the weapon, walking out further into the cafeteria area. The shooter finally stepped forward, and Rex could see a slightly more-haggard Sarge O'Hare than when he'd left, three or four days' worth of stubble, a disturbed grimace, and several wounds on his face.

"Christ, it is you."

Rex noticed the rifle wasn't moving away. "So you gonna shoot me now?"

The response was not what he expected. "Maybe I should, just to be sure. It's not like your return is going to be heralded. You left the night before the attack that killed Thompson, and you show up here the day after the base is attacked. I don't know if it's coincidence or not, part of me doesn't even care. You're actually here, in front of me now, and I could make that decision."

Rex spun to the sound of the blue-eyed soldier on his right, scrambling to pull free a handgun, and emptied the magazine into the supine form, reloading the UMP45 with O'Hare standing and watching. "Yeah, well it wasn't by choice that I left. I could come up with some excuse for it, but I know who to blame—"

O'Hare interrupted him in mid-thought. "Yourself maybe? Lena told us what happened, and from what I understand, you could have told them 'no.' They had their own savior show up out there, we needed you here, and you were absent. Any *blame* you want to place, you can shove it up your ass. We trusted you and you abandoned us."

Rex snarled as he turned away from O'Hare, walking to the lift shaft. "I don't have time for your failure to understand. I'm sorry for what happened here while I was gone, but I had no choice. You can either face that fact or go on pretending to know what the hell you're talking about, but I've got people to save, a tower to destroy. Since you seem so intent on telling me how I'm not welcome here anymore, you can clear the damn base alone. Good luck." Rex strapped the machine pistol to his torso, turned to the lift, and stepped inside, grabbing the rungs of the emergency repair ladder, and began climbing back up to the surface. Under the calm exterior however, he was shaking. With fear at the fact that the Combine had totally violated the base, making it no longer safe, with revulsion at the thought that all of his friends and what he felt was extended family would hate to see him again, and with rage at the fact that Thompson was dead. He couldn't even remember the man's real name, it had been so long since they'd talked for the first time, and the sorrow piled onto him.

Rex arrived at the jammed lift and reached up for the latch controlling the floor hatch, and found it with one hand, trying to hold back the flood of emotions that were worse than the last time he remembered feeling pain, and almost failing, losing his grip on the rung in distraction and slipping almost a foot down the ladder. Resolving his actions separate from his thoughts, he put his train of thought on how to save Maurine and find Molly again, if only to say "good-bye." He could tell now, by the difference from his dreams, this wasn't the end. He had a task to complete, and he'd do it and move on. Recovering himself, Rex climbed up the ladder rungs to the lift, pulled himself through the hatch, and examined the machinery.

It was all still in order, and looking up through the hatch, Rex saw a Combine-stamped rope ladder hanging over the edge, confusing him. Did they use the lift to plug up the shaft and power it down to prevent escape? What did that mean about the garage lift being jammed as well? The only thing that it could mean was the Combine surrounded the surface, blocked the exits, and tunneled in somehow, although hearing that the Combine had accessed the transporter to get into Old Black Mesa, he couldn't help but wonder if they used the same trick to get inside the silo base.

Using the rope ladder for the sake of convenience, Rex reached the surface easily, and spotted the tracks of Tank's APC first thing as he emerged, realizing there were no footprints or signs of heavy braking. Whatever kind of stop-and-go run they'd done didn't include Molly leaping from the vehicle or Tank leaving the cockpit either. As he began to run alongside the tracks, he spared a glance at a site that disturbed him, fully taking notice of City 4 and what it had become. The tower was completed, and the first Rex had real witness to, even experiencing so many other zones. None sprawled into the sky like this one, and none had a massive ring rotating around it, clearly identifiable as the huge ship he'd first seen in the sky over the area.

The whole scene was completed by a domineering wall of navy-blue steel, almost twenty feet tall, towers stationed along at even points—none of the smaller towers had men in them; instead the turrets were automated, clear even from this distance, swiveling automatically with large, gleaming domes at the rear, filled with dozens of types of devices he guessed, from the size of the large objects. Turning his attention back to the tire treads, Rex focused on the job ahead, what it potentially entailed, and shuddered once before steeling his gut, pulling the UMP45 free just in case any Combine stumbled across him.

Rather, the complete opposite occurred, Rex finding a short trail of Combine corpses leading to another dug bunker, guessing it was a new addition that he wasn't aware of. The two corpses farthest away were barely intact along their torsos, having been hit by, what Rex approximated was, a steady burst from Tank's mounted pulse cannon. The power had increased further than he'd witnessed before, the damage burning through the typical Combine body armor, flesh, and most of the bone; leaving not much between the exit wound and the edges of the bodies, other than a few strands of cooked flesh and stubs of charred bone.

He hated to think if he was ever shot by the damned thing, and hoped Tank wasn't going to try something similar. Rex continued along the trail, finding three others spread around the entrance to the underground bunker, these riddled with smaller rounds, evidence of Molly's carbine, and the stamp of non-treaded rubber soles could barely be read in the sand, leading down, then up again from the interior of the bunker. The smell of hot sand and burning soil wafted out strongly, and one peek inside confirmed his suspicions—a Rebel was dead in one corner, his throat slit; two more blue-eyed Combine sprawled on the floor with carbine wounds; and a huge well-shaped tunnel ahead, collapsed only a few feet in by explosives.

Rex found it odd that the tunnel caved in upwards, as if Molly had taken the time to dig the device down into the floor of the tunnel, to prevent a telltale trench from showing on the surface. However, they hadn't taken the time to police the bodies that remained, and it puzzled him, until he shoved at the wall of dirt and sand blocking the tunnel. It moved almost too easily, and he could see the beginnings of a nasty trench under his foot, bringing him to only one conclusion: The device used to close in the tunnel was planted, as Molly left the tunnel, done to cover up the fact that they'd stopped here for something inside the base, and designed to create a trap for anyone else following, which meant *they planned on Rex being there.*

He gathered himself together, strapped the UMP45 to his torso again, and emerged to the surface, determined to find out how to do what was plainly next: Save Maurine and destroy City 4. Recollecting his bearings and examining the time of day, Rex located Tank's stop-and-go pattern with the treads in the dirt. Tracing the arcing circle, he found the proper set and jogged along the tread marks, one hand resting on the pistol grip of the automatic weapon. The sun had graced the sky past noon while being below ground, and he could feel the stiff air forming a solid breeze now, pausing just a moment to remove the headgear, getting instant blasts of cool along the sweat over his skull.

The suit was tough and useful, but it was insanely warm inside, and had stayed that hot for a long time now, obviously not meant for desert use. Nonetheless, Rex kept his pause short, the need to advance into the city greater than whatever relief he was gaining. As soon as he saw the tracks showing signs that the vehicle had slowed down at this point, he increased his own pace, until he arrived at what resembled a full stop, along with a small divot in the earth. Rex didn't examine the ground much at first, his attention riveted on what lie ahead. Three of the towers around the city were toppled and ruined along the wall, and the middle tower was nothing more than a smoldering pile of slag metal at the base of a huge hole burrowed through the wall itself, a column of smoke rising up into the air.

No alarms blared from the city, and the stark silence was surprising, only the wind whipping across the pickups of the headgear's receivers telling him he hadn't lost his hearing. Gazing at the divot under his feet, he could tell that someone laid down here, and it didn't take long to guess that it was Molly, not Tank, that used the trench. The ground was barely disturbed, rather than ravaged by Tank's huge mechanical feet, and the only thing left behind was a single Combine rocket magazine. Rex recognized it as used in the odd boxy launchers he'd utilized before, only this one had different markings that he didn't recognize, the headgear quickly translating them into the words *breeching charge* along with a string of letters and numbers, military-styled and foreign to him.

Tossing the casing aside, Rex bolted along the distance to the wall, noting that the treads of the APC crossed this way too as he made haste to the melted-down tower. Hurdling over it, he found himself following the treads of Tank's vehicle again. They veered to a halt onto an honest-to-God paved asphalt road beyond the gaping hole in the wall. The headgear or something he couldn't understand inside of it had begun to mark the path along the ground, pointing out Combine footprints, separating Molly's from the rest, tracing the treads of the vehicle, and estimating a path that Tank would have chosen. It also began flagging weapon casings, marks along the walls, craters, and a single trail of blood ending at a corpse crumpled against a building, the blue-eyed soldier shot to death at close range, lying on his rifle.

Rex moved past the crumbling remnants of the wall along the gaping hole, and as his boots hit the pavement, he smiled, recalling the last time he'd been in New Mexico City—the day at school before all of this started, thinking of homework he never finished, and the last real meal he'd had, even if it was during the portal storms—Chicken Pot Pie. His stomach reacted to the thoughts and his mouth salivated, but there was nothing here to eat, and he would just have to do with what he could find.

Refocusing his body to the task at hand, he wondered what was making his HUD so active, and why, after all this time, he didn't feel as if anyone was around him, but he certainly wasn't alone. Rounding the first corner Tank had taken, Rex could see two Combine bodies slammed up against opposite walls, this time bearing the unmistakable evidence of the mounted pulse cannon. Continuing past the two corpses, Rex pulled free his weapon again, flicking the select-fire to full auto, and preparing himself for the worst as he made another turn, bolting down the street, chasing the proverbial trail of breadcrumbs consisting of tire skid marks, and a lot of bodies.

The path finally ended at the entry to his old school, and he could only wonder why as he passed by Tank's APC. Raising the UMP45 and kicking open the right side door, it swung aside easily, a pile of rusted chains on the floor just beyond the entry, a padlock holding the chains together smashed into an odd lump. Disregarding the furniture that lay everywhere upturned, Rex moved through the first floor awkwardly, finding several more Combine bodies strewn along the way, smashed by one large fist, or crunched against closed doors and mashed fixtures. The trail of corpses ended at the boiler room door, and Rex pushed it aside to the sight of a smoking hole tunneled through the basement wall, sounds of gunfire not too far off in the distance.

Two of the navy-blue metal girders flanked the large hole, and he could guess that the opening was meant to tunnel under one of the security walls the Combine had installed everywhere, but Rex wasn't sure where it was leading to. Although, he began to get a pretty good idea as he moved in through the gaping hole, finding a single dead Combine soldier here already. The soldier wore a thicker suit akin to a riot uniform for policing, or maybe a guard in a prison, and had glowing yellow eyes on the headgear. The enemy appeared to be armed much simpler than what an Elite or one of the blue-eyed bastards would wear, and was barely comparable to the more complex types of gear the Judicators commonly employed.

Apparently killed in the explosion, this Combine only wore three things—a shock prod, a pistol, and a standard-issue pulse rifle, in addition to the riot suit. The left arm was stamped with a different band, this one with an all-black background with an orange sunrise of a sort, two words scrawled across it in the Combine symbols, headgear translating it easily for him: Nova Construxi. The walls here were of old poured concrete, similar to the school's basement, and all of the smaller windows to the surface had bars on them. This was a pretty deep basement, with the windows higher than himself, and the entire right wall was dominated by plumbing and various other utilities, ending at a sheathing that conformed with the wall, curving into the wall itself. Moving along the tight area here, surprised by the density of the facilities, Rex turned into a broader basement area now, barely recognizing the heavy doors as solitary cell hatches, tan metal exterior stamped with black painted-on numbers.

What disturbed Rex the most was the fact that all the power was still running to the cells. There was brand-new construction around the top of each, wiring and piping rerouted to each individual room, with obvious Combine-made pieces added to the side of each doorway. Approaching one and taking a closer look, he could recognize heart monitors, medication levels, even the state of consciousness, and what it told him was disturbing. The scans were similar to the readings he'd witnessed inside Doc Hernandez's hospital level so long ago and the rest were comparable to the diagrams, settings, and chemical combinations he'd seen inside Griswold's converted laboratory, indicating that everything here was an evolutionary leap of the technology they'd used on him.

It also bore signs of being far more progressed in growth, readouts he passed by dated at least a year old, all of that time no doubt spent in Combine captivity, every slight change or increase in activity monitored, unlike him. Any problems they encountered they could fix along the way, curbing undue tendencies or altering physiology to adapt properly, using up-to-date procedures and installing technology he could barely grasp the use for. Rex was broken from his deep thoughts by an explosion that shook the ceiling enough to drop concrete dust down onto his head.

And as it rained onto the metal surface of the headgear, he put himself into motion, running along the solitary cells and ignoring the sounds that were starting to emanate from each. Bolting up a set of stairs as they came into view, Rex paused at the top just long enough to identify another pair of Combine guards, shot to death in defensive positions along the walls, and the cage door at the far end locking off this section was ripped free from the hinges completely. It became clear where the door was as he approached, the object used as a projectile against the two guards on the other side, crushed to death under warped steel and bent bars, the bodies pinned against concrete and glass.

Rex charged through the scene, spun past another of the checkpoints that had been torn to ribbons, and began running past empty cells down a block labeled *V*. All of the inmates here were far past dead and rotten, most just skeletal-thin corpses that matched the untouched cells, paint peeling, metal rusting, light fixtures shattered from the last time the place had been used as a human prison, no doubt lasting signs from a riot that occurred the day the Combine landed. Kicking over the charred remains of a security desk, he hurdled over the broken bodies just beyond, following the cellblock as it turned left, spotted movement at the far end of the cellblock again, and cursed as he recognized Tank's massive frame, moving through another gaping tunnel, no doubt made by the same launcher.

"Tank!" He shouted abruptly, without thinking, and as the huge soldier turned to face him, Rex found himself avoiding a stream of the .50cal rounds from the huge altered general-purpose machine gun, the distinctive bark of the M60-modified lasting long enough to cover Tank's motions. As the firing stopped, Rex made to come around the corner again, only to see the gaping hole in the far wall collapse downwards from a smaller detonation. He couldn't stop the swearing rolling from his lips, snarling at the fact that Tank had actually fired on him now, machine pistol still at the ready, running up to the collapsed hole and shoving ruthlessly at the rubble.

Something fell out between crumbling rock and concrete, landing between his feet, an alert going off in the headgear and highlighting the item. The warning lasted less than a second before the next explosion followed, a massive, invisible hand of energy and force flinging him backwards with incredible speed, bouncing off of steel bars and racks to crunch up against a concrete wall. Coughing concrete dust from his lungs and shaking his head,

ears ringing and hands quivering, he made a quick check of the
suit and himself, grateful to find it intact, but he knew something
was distinctively wrong. He was feeling dizzy, nauseous, and
fatigued to the point of being almost unable to move, and his eyes
simply could not focus. He had to close them to stop the waves
of unease, but it didn't stop, overwhelming him for minutes that
felt like hours, body jerking in pain until it finally forced him to
black out.

NONTRIVIAL PURSUIT

Rex awoke with a start, gasping through the headgear, realizing that he had not dreamt, but as he gazed around, noting the sun had set through caged windows, he realized he had lost precious time, and began to stumble to his feet. His perspective was broken again however—he felt taller than before, awkward with his motions, unfamiliar with himself again, like waking up in the damned experiment cage all over again. The armor suit pinched against him in places where there were once gaps in size, something was distinctively wrong with his feet, two large clawed toes from each jutting through his combat boots, and his left arm now ended in razor-sharp fingers, the tripwire he'd wrapped around it broken and cut to pieces, hanging loosely.

"Cripes, not again."

Standing upright, Rex ensured the rifle was still strapped to his back and intact, still connected to the multiport, and relaxed as his eyes could focus, checking the heads-up display, and finding the UMP45 lying on the floor. The folding stock and the forward pistol grip were ruined beyond repair, but Rex easily tore free the composite parts, leaving the weapon itself in firing condition, still loaded and ready to go otherwise. Looking up to the collapsed wall, he groaned when he saw the secondary explosive had done more damage than the first to collapse the hole, now just a pile of rubble that would take an hour to move. The only good news was the explosion had torn open the outer wall leading into the inner yard, and he ran up to the ruined wall, leaped through the giant crack, and began running across a now-dead lawn that used to be an exercise yard.

Ignoring the large building marked *VI* and charging up to the opposite wall of the area labeled *II*, Rex began to use his left hand to batter at the caged, broad window in front of him, the clawed fingers allowing him to rip it loose from its moorings. Punching out the bulletproof and shock-resistant glass with his right arm, the left hand pulling him up, rolling inside onto a cafeteria floor, he began to examine the area, the weapon returning to his hands as he stood. There was dirt and filth everywhere, mashed tables, collapsed concrete beams, even a huge hole in the ceiling.

There were only two bodies here, both Combine guards, both long dead. Double-barricaded doors had been burst down along the far wall to his right, and down to his left, he could hear sounds of combat behind a door that had been braced shut with iron support struts. Disregarding the sealed entry in favor of the opened double doors, Rex found the HUD identifying the gaping hole in the opened doors as the same explosive that collapsed other entries he'd seen, and blown up in his face.

Grimacing as he moved through the new entry, Rex wasn't sure who he would encounter here, Tank or Molly, and at this point he much preferred to be seeing Molly. She would be the less likely of the two to fire at him on first sight. UMP45 raised and ready, Rex crept down a long, dark hallway to the very end, where it turned left, and stopped a short way down to a security station, complete with large steel door, pried from the hinges and slumped down as it hung from the latches, bent to the side with more explosives. The door read *Main Level*, but was also plastered and stamped with papers declaring it to be condemned.

Ignoring the pit that his gut had become reading the warnings glued to the painted surface, Rex edged around the door, weapon leading the way, surprised to see brightly its ceilings and mostly immaculate floors and walls, the only dirt present what was tracked in through the opened door. The area curved into a large open floor that had been reconverted to what looked like surgical wards, intensely illuminated and sterile, sectioned off with equipment and beds for at least twenty subjects, the machinery humming with no attendees. Entries branched off ahead and to his left, and as he moved to the left hatch, he found two Combine Elites dead here, inactive red lenses staring off into space, the wounds across their necks and faces obviously the silenced pistol rounds.

This hatch, however, remained closed, sealed with a Combine locking mechanism, a console embedded into the wall, readouts in Combine script translated only to say that the hatch was secured. Moving across the surgical ward to the other opening, he examined it as he found it forced aside, the locking mechanism bearing signs of being opened by a blade and the console smashed and shot to smoking ruins.

Pushing aside the large hatch and moving beyond, a short trail of blood led inside across a metal catwalk, but what had his attention was what the catwalk was suspended over. The cavernous area here had to be the work of the Combine, the length and breadth of the room comparable to football fields, a massive oval lined across the walls with individual pods, all identical to the reclamation pods he'd witnessed being transported across the country in the Ukraine, all stamped with the Combine wrench.

A single machine moved around, a large arm ending in triad of hooks, obviously used to pick up individual pods. Gazing over across the platform where the trail ended, Rex saw Molly standing behind the controls, one hand operating the machinery, the other holding the silenced 9mm firmly to an Elite's forehead, the soldier holding red hands to a bleeding belly. It became clear that she was interrogating him as he listened.

"Give me the access code for the restricted cells."

The soldier refused to move, and she shot him in both legs.

"Now I'm out of extremities to shoot. You might as well tell me before I start going for body shots."

The Combine grumbled the passcodes through gurgling mumbles, and as she entered them, ensuring they were the right codes, accessing the restricted pods, Molly then shot the Elite in the forehead, holstering the piece as the body slumped down. The mechanical arm grabbed a pod in the rear, hiked it up from its position, and began to pull it back to the platform, and Rex stepped forward at the thought that Maurine would be in that pod. Molly swung around at the sound, pulling a pulse rifle from the console and aiming it. It took a moment, a long pause, but Molly recognized him finally, in the darkness.

"Dad?"

Rex took another step forward, let the weapon hang on the sling, and nodded. "Yeah. It happened again."

She didn't look comforted by the fact that the change had occurred, but didn't keep the rifle aimed at him. Instead, she finished working with the machinery, and turned back to him, pulling off the night vision goggles and opening up her mask.

"We have a moment to talk; the pod put her in hibernation. How did it happen?"

Rex wasn't sure how to say it, but spoke anyway, "I saw the two of you going through the hole in the prison block wall. I yelled out at Tank and he started shooting at me. Then he collapsed the hole, and booby trapped it so it would blow up in my face when I tried to shove through," he said the last while removing the headgear, letting it hang from the multiport, looking up as Molly approached.

"I'm so sorry, Tank said there was a Judicator behind us, I collapsed the wall and booby trapped it."

A grimace touched Rex's features, and he shook his head softly. "How did things got so screwed up? Tank would never have done that before, would he?"

Molly's pained expression didn't change as she spoke now, and he could tell that even his return was creating shockwaves that his departure couldn't cover up. "When you disappeared in the teleporter, Rex, Tank took it hard. He searched for you the entire first month. Multiple trips to Xen, back and forth, trying to fix the devices, and when you didn't come back, he assumed you didn't want to. I tried to tell him, you weren't like that, but he wouldn't listen. I remember the dream with the blue-suited man, I remember being there while you talked, I know it wasn't your choice, none of this was, but Tank just wouldn't believe me, and eventually bad things happened over the year. We lost people. Prisoners were taken. Huge advantages were lost because we couldn't complete the task at hand. We've struggled against that tower being completed for a long time now, and we didn't stop it, the Combine finished it and they threw a mass of soldiers at us and we failed, and now I'm here."

There was more to be said, but the console buzzed loudly, and Rex followed Molly over to it, stopping short of the pod. She made a couple of motions on the console, and the pod hovered over the platform, opening up as it lowered. Maurine stumbled out from it, wearing combat boots, and a modified Judicator bodysuit, scratched and torn in a couple places, but clearly battle-ready. Her hair was still clipped short, and as Rex saw her, he couldn't help himself from dropping to one knee, the armor making a loud sound as it contacted the catwalk, moving his clawed hand behind his back, craning his neck to look up at her, tears in his eyes now.

God, it felt like an eternity the last time he'd seen her, but she only looked slightly worse for the wear, even after being captured. As Maurine turned to look at the command console and the two standing there, Molly ran up and held Maurine in a hug for a moment, then handed her the pulse rifle she'd pulled from the Elite, and helping Maurine forward. Maurine did not seem particularly happy to see him however, not at first.

"Who is this Molly?"

Molly seemed startled that recognition did not come so easily. "It's Rex, mom, Rex is here."

Maurine seemed to wake slightly as she looked at him now, as if she was clearing a druggy haze.

"Oh, my God." Maurine ran over and almost tackled him in a hug, and Molly spoke, "She must be still somewhat foggy from whatever they pumped her full of, and you'll need to get her out of here."

Rex stopped looking down enough to see if she was serious. "What? Are you sure? You're coming with us, and we can deal with the rest later."

Molly didn't budge. "Go, Rex. I need to make sure no one else we knew was captured, and I need to deal with Tank. Haul ass."

Rex couldn't believe it, but he stood and followed her orders, replacing the headgear while looking into Maurine's eyes, grabbing the UMP45 with his left hand, and pulling Maurine to his side with his right, guiding her to the hatch. With a confirming nod to Molly, Rex slipped through the hatch with Maurine close behind, and he began to guide her along the lab in silence, exchanging glances as they moved into the cafeteria to the sight of Combine soldiers starting to poke around, three in the thicker riot suits with yellow eyes, two in white Overwatch gear. Taking up positions along two of the remaining columns here, Rex opened fire first with the smaller weapon at the Elites, while Maurine began to use the pulse-rifle to chew through the thicker body armor on the others.

The surprise attack worked well for the moment, but the underpowered UMP45 wasn't dropping the Elites fast enough, and Rex found himself getting frustrated, flinging the empty weapon at one and rushing the other, ignoring the pulse rifle rounds that missed him by hairs in favor of the sensation of ripping Combine armor, breaking bones, rending flesh. Pulling the left leg from its socket, as he stood over the struggling soldier,

Rex swung it like a large golf club, snapping the Elite's neck and caving in much of the facial features even through the headgear. Tossing aside the disembodied limb dispassionately, Rex moved past the corpses, waving Maurine forward, and raised the customized combination rifle. Checking both magazines and the fire selector before stepping into the clear, he turned and grasped her hand as she offered it, helping her through the emptied window frame, and hauling himself through afterwards.

Maurine was already firing as she landed to the inner yard, dropping three Combine as they stood around the gaping hole in the outer wall, covering Rex as he finished coming out of the building properly. "Where in the hell are we, Rex, I don't recognize any of this."

Weapon raised and feet in motion, Rex ensured no more of the Combine were in the cellblock beyond before climbing through. Pausing to kneel so that Maurine could use his knee as a stepping-stone, he responded while tactical-stepping along the filthy concrete. "It's an old prison facility. I remember seeing it before all of this happened. It was closed during the portal storms, and afterwards they built a school down the street, and sealed all of this off permanently. I'm surprised to see that they've restored power to areas and changed the interiors. They've even repaired the solitary cells in the basement, and it was my first time seeing that area. It stretches all the way down the street from the school underground, and Tank and Molly knocked down a foundation wall to get in, tunneling beneath one of the huge barriers."

They made the turn past the second checkpoint, and began to move down the stairs here, when the sound of a door being unbolted had even Rex halting in his tracks. Rifle raised and one hand holding Maurine back, he advanced first with a snarl under the headgear, turning down the stairs and reaching the bottom to the horrid sight of one of the creatures crawling from behind the cell hatch. It was a smaller, nastier version of himself, yellow, feral eyes, jutting jaws with sharpened teeth, blackened, mottled armor hide skin, and angular, pointed ears forming a slick, edged profile. Four-fingered hands ended in razor-sharp tips, and the eyes bore a clearly intelligent mind. In seconds, it registered Rex's presence, spotted the rifle, and had decided how to use the hatch as a shield. Tearing it free from the moorings and holding it up, the creature began charging forward with the hatch held high and in front.

Rex held his ground, switched to the 4.3mm ammo, and blasted a burst off of the concrete floor to ricochet up under the hatch, and heard the little demon squeal in pain, motion stopping abruptly. Kicking out at the hatch, Rex followed up as the creature stumbled back, firing more of the rounds into its chest, until it stopped breathing and fighting altogether, allowing him to shove the hatch to the side to clear the path. Dumping it into the opened solitary cell, Rex ignored the sight of all of the machinery inside in favor of moving back to gather Maurine, seeing the surprised look on her face as they ran down to the basement together.

"Run ahead of me in case any more of these damn hatches open up, and cover me, I'll try to drag this dead one so you have something to look at later with Lena."

He didn't add the part that he wondered if Lena was still alive or not. Instead, he let Maurine pass him easily, grabbed the ankle of the strange creature, and began to haul it as fast as possible, waiting until he reached the cramped section with the utility lines to haul the body up onto one shoulder to make the travel easier. Barely able to keep a proper grasp on the rifle, he reluctantly let it drop and hoped that Maurine was out of the haze from the hibernation well enough to cover them both.

And as they moved from the basement of the prison into the boiler room of the school, Maurine's mettle was tested as the first scout came in through the open doorway at the top, neon-blue eyes searching the dark concrete basement until they died out, the pulse rifle in Maurine's arms punching holes through the thin armor. She kept up the steady fire as two others tried to make an entry as well, giving Rex enough time to advance halfway up the stairs, set the body down, and pull his rifle up, covering her as she grabbed onto the lower rail of the staircase, and pulled herself up past Rex, rolling through the doorway. He heard more gunfire, and could barely pick up the body fast enough for his own relief, heartbeat racing along with his feet, and each breath like fire now.

Something was still wrong with his body, but he had no time to stop and examine himself or start some ridiculous self-realization trip, not now with the stress of new creatures, old friends becoming new foes, and wanting to keep Maurine safe all weighing in on his mind and body. Shoving aside the ajar door, to the sight of Maurine shrugging off weapons fire in the Judicator suit, he could see a group of Combine scouts slowly dying under her withering gunfire. Rex was relieved to see they were using small MP7s, the live round much safer to absorb under armor than the more-than-deadly pulse rounds, but it still disturbed him to see her taking any damage at all. As the fearsnake ran through his gut, his mind leapt his body into action, shoving through the doorway and throwing the strange creature's corpse directly at the group of enemies.

Grasping and lifting his rifle, he switched to the pulse rounds and emptied thirty shots into the group, wincing as he hit the corpse a couple of times, but not letting it wear on him. Sure, Rex wanted them to have a body to examine, figure out what the hell it was, but he wasn't going to be pressured by the fact that it was going to be riddled with all sorts of bullet holes. Quickly reloading as the situation settled, Rex swiftly made his way to the enemy soldiers, shoved the creature's body aside, and shot each of the Combine as they lay on the floor ruthlessly. Turning back to Maurine, he stepped over to her and helped her up, examining her suit and relaxing a hair as he noticed she was alright.

"C'mon, let's get you out of here. This is quickly becoming my least favorite situation."

They both charged down the school halls, Rex carrying the creature, trying to pretend things were somewhat resolved, and failing miserably as he let his gaze stray to his own left arm. Switching the creature to haul over his left shoulder, streamers of yellow blood running down his armor surface, Rex snarled and focused on the heads-up display as it registered heat signals up ahead. The pickups on the headgear were apparently catching a radio conversation he couldn't hear, or at least that's what it sounded like, searching shortly for a volume control before concentrating his energy on bearing his own weapon, selecting the caseless rounds with one thumb while holding the rifle.

Opening fire at the slight silhouette of heat registering on his HUD, Rex stopped as the target moved out of sight again, and Maurine began to creep to the edge of the school hall, avoiding lockers as she moved, Rex now following suit. Maurine began to open fire as she emerged from the corner, and as Rex rushed up to the corner to assist, he turned to the sight of two more scouts down, done easily and well, a solid burst to the upper torso and face for each. Smiling as he advanced first, the weight of the body suddenly being an accustomed object, the rifle slipping solidly into his grip, his center of gravity changing oddly, Rex found himself standing on the balls of his feet now, advancing quickly down the hall, the sounds of Maurine reloading just behind him, as well as her increased heartbeat and rate of respiration.

Was she afraid of something? Pausing momentarily, he scanned the area, and swore he could smell plastics and the heat of another energy weapon up ahead around the bend from himself.

Ensured that the area was secured, Rex began to move again, asking the question and surprising himself with his own voice, raspy and forced. "Are you okay?"

Her response also sounded forced, but had an attempt at being reassuring. "Y-yeah, I'm fine. Keep moving, soldier."

He liked the way she'd taken control again, just as if he hadn't been stranded in portal storm hell for almost a year now, but knew it was false bravado: The HUD was telling him that her pulse was ragged, she was sweating profusely, and she was dehydrated. Her body temperature had spiked, but she was still operating under fire with a fever, and she wasn't showing signs of overbearing weakness, but something was still wrong. He could feel it in himself now, a disquieted void instead of pain that would typically throb, and it grew stronger, despite the fact that he was attempting to keep Maurine closer each moment. Halting and pausing on one knee, Rex watched as Maurine took the lead readily, leveled her weapon ahead, and made the next right down the school hallway, pointing out the exit that had been broken open.

"Is the field still up?" Rex asked without pausing, moving up alongside her with his own rifle still at the ready, watching her movements, and waiting for her response.

"Yeah, how could you tell?"

Rex focused the aim of his weapon on the open doorways, and slowed his pace, Maurine matching the speed. "It took finding you for me to start to figure it out again."

She turned and smiled, but immediately returned to her concentration, and Rex knew why now as he caught another heavy whiff of synthetic materials and weapon oil from up ahead.

"Judicators, has to be two or more, up through the doorway, carrying conventional weapons instead of pulse rifles."

Maurine gave him another quizzical look as he moved ahead of her this time, dropping the heavy body to the filthy floor, and ignoring the smears of yellow blood all over the armor as Rex double-gripped the rifle now. Shouldering it and letting out a burst of caseless ammunition at the right door, which stood slightly ajar, the door now slammed closed as whatever was on the other side slumped down against it, Rex moving again. Blood had barely start to pool on the ground under the doorjamb when Rex kicked the door with his left foot, watching as it snapped back out of view with a blur, a black-suited body tumbling away to wedge under the rear end of Tank's APC, and a second Judicator sidestepping into cover behind an additional armored personnel carrier.

Maurine hustled to respond to the sudden movements, opening fire with her pulse rifle to keep the Judicator from popping out from cover, while Rex located a way to swing around and flank the soldier. Instead of patiently taking his time, Rex chose the easiest route by leaping up onto the Combine APC, noting subtle differences even as he aimed the rifle, scooting along the roof, and firing down into the black-clad enemy from above, clearly not expecting the attack, a few clean bursts to the skull all it took. Rex swiftly reloaded the conventional magazine, switched to pulse rounds with one thumb, and leapt back down onto the still-falling body, claws and booted foot smashing bone as he landed, rage in his head guiding his actions now, hearing the beating of metal wings, and discovering what was truly concerning him.

There was no alarm here, no broadcast alerts, no sirens, no heavy sounds of additional reinforcements, just the echoes of the approaching helicopter rebounding from between buildings to reach his ears. Rex didn't like the implications that the Combine had done so much now that even breaking into one of their high-security complexes was now a barely noticeable event, like a mosquito trying to kill an elephant by extracting a bit of blood.

The approaching helicopter did so lazily, as if it wasn't expecting an armed reception, and sluggishly hovered over the area at first, sliding open one bay door, and deploying a set of descending cables over the street. Rex lifted the hybrid rifle, switched to the 20mm launcher, and squeezed the trigger as the bore came to bear on the open bay, the first resulting explosion muffled by the interior of the craft, but still sending it pinwheeling out of control. Leaping away from the Combine APC as the flying vehicle made a belly landing on the intersection, Rex rolled under Tank's APC and found himself lying next to Maurine, already way ahead of him in gaining a useful cover, and the two of them held extremely still as the helicopter exploded again.

The tail rotor slammed into the front of the school building, blades snapping off from the top of the craft as it sputtered in place, a flaming ball of burning metals and plastics. Weapon returning to his grasp as he crept back out from under the APC, Rex paused on one knee and reached out to Maurine to help her up, finding her hesitating to grasp his left hand, before reluctantly emerging on her own. He could tell that things had taken another step back between them, her witnessing his crazy actions and insane reactions to things, coupled with the body that refused to stop changing on him, it was no doubt wearing on Maurine's thoughts, affecting her views of what Rex was now.

Still she said nothing as she stood, holding her weapon at the ready, moving over to the crumpled remains of one of the Judicators, and exchanging her spent pulse rifle for what looked like a larger-than-usual M4 carbine, the item intriguing Rex and inspiring him to move over and examine it as she gathered ammunition. The weapon *appeared* to be a man-made Colt M4, but it was easy to pick apart the differences right away. It used the same caseless 4.3mm ammunition the Combine used for the modified weapons he'd run across, composites that were similar, but replaced metal portions on the original item, a single peep scope with red compound lenses, cables that were meant for use with a Combine port, and the Combine wrench stamped under the fire selector instead of any human manufacturing marks.

"Damn, Combine-made M4 rifles? What the hell, isn't bad enough they're turning us into weapons, now they're converting our own goods."

Maurine didn't respond as he spoke, and instead, she continued to gather the rifle rounds together, stealing one of the magazine sling assemblies from the corpse to replace the one on her own torso, now just tatters.

"When did you start wearing the Judicator suit?"

She looked over at him now, loading the carbine and chambering a round, a neutral glare on her features. "The week you left. Molly found hers a few days later. You leaving *changed* us, Rex. Hell, you just being there in the first place, around us, is what changed us, and we're altered, just like you are now. We didn't have to be tortured by some mad scientist experimenting with alien technology, combined with archaic human procedures to be different: All we had to do was meet you, Rex."

Maurine followed the statement up with a slight caress to Rex's armored face, before pulling away abruptly, pain in her eyes. He wasn't sure if it was a compliment or an insult, but he wasn't going to be offended, not after what he'd done, leaving them all.

"Go ahead and get aboard Tank's APC. I need to get back in there, find out where the other section of that building leads, and you need to get Molly home. I'll send her back here as soon as I see her."

Maurine nodded once in affirmation. "You stay safe or I'll kick your ass myself, mister."

Raising his rifle and looking away, trying to blink his blurring eyes free of tears under the headgear, Rex rumbled his response, squeezing her hand in his for a moment. "Always, love, always."

Standing and running before his mind could convince him to do otherwise, Rex kept the weapon close, passed through the opened school doors, and grabbed the creature's body still here, dragging it out to the APC and tossing it into the rear as Maurine opened it from the cockpit. Spinning on his heel once more, Rex made his way into the school, and started the long trek back through the winding corridors and halls. He was so confused. Things were better now that he was here and worse at the same time.

With no idea how that was even remotely possible, he collected his thoughts and rifled through them as he ran, shoving them aside as he saw Molly up ahead, leaning against the wall of lockers, nursing her leg, sobbing. Running up as fast as possible, he let the rifle hang on the sling as he slid to a halt on the filthy floors, grasping her shoulders and checking her body. She looked like she was also carrying bruised ribs, and a snarl built on his face to match what he was feeling now, holding her close.

"Are you alright?"

She cried harder for a moment, then stiffened up, and shoved Rex back. "I'm fine. It was Tank, he…he shot me. The Combine were flooding the area we were in, same spot he got pinned down into, and he told me to haul ass; I came back not twenty minutes later and he's lost his mind—there were bodies everywhere, even more Combine than I thought possible, except some of them were twisted, emaciated, and others weren't anything I've ever seen before"—Molly took one look at Rex from head to toe.— "you look a lot like them now," she said the last with apprehension in her voice, and it broke something inside Rex, ruined a part of him he couldn't grasp, turned it sour and ugly and devoid of life. The Combine had won their battle against him, turned him into something that wasn't considered human by any stretch of the imagination anymore, and in doing so, had injured connections, ties to other people, and hurt him more than the implant could drug or numb away. Molly spoke again now, the timbre of her voice distant and wavering. "I tried to help him, I killed one of these…things that were attacking him and got close, and he swung his weapon on me and knocked me down, and fired at me as I ran."

Rex's voice was cold, carrying traces of nothing as he looked away, squeezing her right shoulder once, and gesturing her behind him. "I'll deal with it. Go on, your mother is waiting. You need to guide her out." He walked away without looking back this time, only speaking once more. "Be good, girl. I might see you again."

Kicking open the basement door and running down the stairs here, Rex ignored the spots of blood on the wall, just about thigh height of Molly, and passed through the boiler room, and past the gaping hole in the wall swiftly, stopping at the wall of lines for the facilities. Using his now-sharp fingers on his left hand to gouge the casing on the cables open, Rex tore into them until none remained connected, smiling as the lights began to dim. Rounding the corner to the solitary cells, Rex growled as he found most of the cell hatches wide open, only a half-dozen sealed and locked with the indicator screens going red from lack of power, and as he shoved two of the hatches out of his way, he realized that the many that did escape were no doubt what Molly had encountered, finally making the connection between himself and the description she'd made.

He was such a fool, thinking she'd compared him to another one of the black-armored Combine test-tube freaks he'd killed before and stripped the armor from—she meant the beasts here, bred the same way, but taking a very different path than his own. Navigating through the cells and reaching the ground floor, Rex could hear the sounds of combat amplified now, a loud rumbling akin to a small earthquake echoing through the cellblock, reverberating between ruined bars, rusted fixtures, shattered concrete, and long-rotted corpses, followed by heavy gunshots. He moved as fast as possible now, trying not to trip on the bodies that littered the path, and finding the hole in the outer wall without conflict.

Rex could hear the scratching of feet across dirt and filth up ahead, reverberating through the window he'd broken out, the HUD highlighting strange talon tracks through the inner yard, separating his and Maurine's path out from Molly's footprints, and the tracks of the other creatures. Careful to ensure that nothing lay behind as a trap this time, Rex sprinted across the main yard, slid along the dirt ground, and leapt up through the window in one motion, landing in a rolling crouch with the rifle ready. Only after he'd steadied himself did Rex realize there was no enemy present here, only the growing cacophony of destruction emanating from the formerly barricaded doors on his immediate left, spinning to the sight of one of the little demons charging away into what he could only guess was Tank's location.

Standing up and checking his ammo stores as he crept to the now-broken down doorway, the sounds of combat suddenly amplified greatly, then stopped completely for several heartbeats. Rex halted to avoid making noise, the startling silence carrying on for long, eerie moments, until there was only a grinding sound that he couldn't identify, long and sharp, making his ears wince as he listened to a jagged surface being worked over with some kind of rock. There were also sounds of labored breathing, heavy, cavernous gasps for air, interspersed with a grumbling or growling, maybe even sobbing.

Rex moved firmly now, rifle held at waist level as he bypassed the opened doors here, gazing around at a hellish battlefield inside this zone, *IV* spray-painted at intervals on the walls stencil-style, next to smatters of blood, craters of bullet ricochets and grenades, and hunks of remains. The floor and ceiling were just as bad, bodies and pieces of bodies everywhere, flesh and internals matted and hanging down from sparking light fixtures, corpses wrapped around stone pillars and crumpled in corners, muscle pulled from under skin and armor suit then tossed aside in a single pile, biceps and ligaments, the air heavy with misted crimson and powdered bone, cordite and hot metal.

Sitting on the stump of a shattered concrete pillar, surrounded by disembodied corpses, Tank slowly ran a large hunk of the pillar's concrete across the edge of a torn iron strut, now forming a long, wicked-looking blade of roughly hewn proportions gripped in his biomechanical hands. It looked like it had been used already, spattered with blood, dotted with pulverized hunks of unidentifiable flesh. The big man was indeed sobbing and laughing at the same time now, louder than before, almost as if he was deliberately focusing attention on himself. Rex raised the rifle, and was about to step out of cover, when two of the smaller beasts came out of the shadows behind Tank, both growling at the same volume, opening hands and stepping in close to use them like knives.

Tank moved like a blur of raging steel, cutting both of the creatures in twain before they could react to his speed, torsos going one way, and legs toppling down the other side, yellow blood forming pools that mingled with the red of human and not-so-human Combine. Tank looked up to the sight of Rex stepping out from the pillar, weapon shouldered, feet braced and prepared, and he calmly spoke between sobbing and laughing, past the point of hysteria, into a whole new scary realm that made him look manic and twitchy.

"I shot at her, you know, almost killed her when she tried to help. I suppose you already know that. You wouldn't be here otherwise; you would have just left me behind. She's the only real reason why you came back at all. Both of them, none of the rest of us; we were never important enough for you, Rex. We weren't them. It took me a while to realize it, almost two months of thinking why you left early, left before we were *both* supposed to be at that transporter pad, and it dawned on me, you didn't want me there, and you didn't care enough for anyone else to say 'good-bye.' Except for maybe Lena, of course, she knew you loved Maurine, and still you said 'good-bye' to her, she never forgot that. I never forgot that."

Tank held the huge weapon at the ready now that he'd stopped speaking, and even through the transparent armored faceplate he wore with the suit, Rex couldn't mistake the look of anguish and hate the other man carried, and didn't budge from his position.

"Then I guess you know what's next, Tank."

Rex pulled the trigger on the rifle as he moved closer to the pillar, and as the pulse rounds began to bounce from Tank's exterior, the large biomechanical body leapt into motion, swinging the crude blade at him and being intercepted by the concrete pillar. Rex ducked down as the preformed pillar took the weight of the strike, a plume of choking dust and hunks of rock roaring away from the impact. Rex did not roll away this time, or try to gain distance. Rather, he let his weapon drop from his grasp to hang on the sling, and stiff-armed Tank once away from the pillar, forcing the grip to free from the crude sword. It gave Rex the opening to uppercut Tank with full force, his left hand making the strike. Tank reeled from the impact, rocking on his heels, before finally taking a backwards header, striking the paved floor and staying still for a moment before beginning to get to his feet.

"What the hell did you hit me with?"

As Tank turned, he looked utterly dazed and shaken, pale behind the now-cracked faceplate, blood streaming from nostrils, one arm hanging limply, dragging the foot on the same side. He truly looked at Rex now, saw his left hand, the size of his frame now, the talons that erupting from under steel-toe boots, and the blood splayed all over the surface of the armor suit, and he began back away slowly, horrified.

"Who-who are you? What do you want from me? Stay away!"

Rex hadn't moved an inch after striking Tank twice, but still the big man acted terrified, and launched himself at Rex again in desperation. One limp limb swung helplessly, but the other hit Rex solidly, knocking him back as the reaction surprised him. And as Tank reached to pull the huge blade from the concrete pillar, Rex lashed back out with one foot, talons gripping the arm reflexively and Rex arm-standing himself up, the weight and force pushing Tank from his feet and slamming him down onto the floor again. Rex landed with both feet on the one free arm, crushing it as he crouched down, putting all the force he could manage into his position. Tank was crying now, bawling loudly from the loss of motion no doubt, back to the strange feeling of paralysis he'd been feeling ever since he lost both real arms and legs, and as Rex stood over him, he ensured the crushed arm was moderately mobile, and shoved Tank over.

"I'm not going to kill you. You can crawl your way out of here. You've already killed off most of the creatures, and I doubt the Combine will be swarming the place like this again. Alarms aren't going off, and there's no army outside waiting, so you're probably safe. Until Molly finds you, and then, you really are on your own."

Rex walked away from Tank now, and following the route he took in, ignoring the sounds of sadness behind him as he reloaded the pulse rounds for the rifle. Shaking his head solemnly, Rex went over the complicated conversation again and again, finding no other way to have ended things differently—it had taken a turn for the worse the second the transporter malfunction had occurred for the blue-suited man's benefit and now Rex didn't know if it was his decision to comply or the blue-suited man that was to blame.

They were invariably tied, inseparable and one simply could not occur without the other—could it? If he refused, would the unseen conjuror still have sent him spiraling off into madness? Or would he have killed Rex outright, ported him into space and watched him suffocate to death? And how would any of it change the outcome of the fight he just had with Tank, he didn't know, except for the fact that the other man was barely communicable, things could have ended in a much-friendlier fashion, but Rex couldn't imagine the sequence leading to that.

Things had been ruined and corrupted between the two of them over time, and Tank lashing out at Molly only made things harder on him. Tank knew Rex was coming, knew what was going to happen ahead of time. Maybe he guessed that Rex would kill him outright rather than leave him to his own devices, three-fourths crippled, but still alive, but that still didn't change much. Tank was still in the land of the living, and he would find a way to get back to the silo base, Rex knew that much, and as far as he was concerned, he hoped it would be the last time he ever saw the other man.

ARTIFICIALLY INTELLIGENT

Moving past more stilled Combine bodies, Rex put aside his thoughts in favor of focusing on the HUD, which was now more active than ever. It was trying to provide some kind of amplified reading of sounds that he couldn't hear, and as he searched the heads-up display, Rex focused in on the audio receivers, and with a thought, managed to turn them up.

I was wondering when you'd figure it out, Rex.

The voice caught him completely off guard, and he began spinning about to locate the origin of the sounds, weapon moving wildly, searching for a target that wasn't in sight, heartbeat suddenly through the roof. Whoever it was, they were close, and Rex couldn't see them. The voice had no determined echo point, no source to track, and his mind began racing alongside his pulse, trying to understand what was happening. The HUD wasn't pointing out the possible trail of the sound, and the familiarity of the voice was haunting, something he couldn't pinpoint, but definitely tugging at his memories.

I'm right here with you Rex, I've been here since the transport lab.

He felt something *alive* crawling through his thoughts almost physically now, the sensation like talons raking up flesh and sorting through it with invisible eyes. He dropped to one knee, snarling at the contact with his thoughts, knowing now that he wasn't alone in his own head.

"Who the hell is that?!"

Rex roared the question aloud, hearing it echo from the room like the other voice did not, and felt his own confusion rising. Something was distinctly wrong with this, and he didn't understand what was going on.

You know who this is Rex, how could you forget?

Recognition hit him with the force of a gunshot, and everything snapped into place. "Lena." He thought she was still alive, but how was she here? Inside his skull, roving through his neurons as they fired, tracing his brain cells and tracking his thoughts.

I'm here, with you, inside the weapon.

Rex knew exactly what the voice was talking about: the rifle, he'd plugged it in himself, watched the HUD come alive, and misunderstood the reasons behind it all. That meant it wasn't really Lena, but somehow, it was. Confusing and understandable at the same time, he lowered his voice an octave as he spoke, continuing to walk along the now-darkened halls, holding his rifle reverently now, trying to examine it as he moved.

"How? Computer simulation? Artificial Intelligence?"

A little of both and neither of the two. Brain-scanned copy with a self-realization program, best that could be achieved considering what now resembles modern technology.

Hunkering down at the doorway to the laboratory, feeling the HUD activate itself, his vision amped up the light, and a tracer began to move in the direction of the sounds he was receiving into the headset, the Lena-AI continuing to respond to his thoughts as he moved.

Power source, still active, has to be on a separate circuit.

Rex frowned under the headgear as he moved, following the wall on his right and trying to get used to the feeling of something else walking around with him in his head, responding to everything that came up, and felt almost overwhelmed. How was he supposed to get used to this? He'd been alone so long, separated from everyone, and now he had something that was nigh-inseparable from himself, and it wasn't Maurine. Even worse, he couldn't derail his mind, it refused to be pushed aside and hung there even as he continued to aim the weapon and check his surroundings.

The hatch along the far wall of the laboratory here was still sealed shut, and the console next to it mounted on the wall was dead just like the rest of the circuitry, yet the humming of whatever power source was beyond, grew in measure as he crept closer, finally placing one side of the headgear to the side of the hatch itself to listen through the surface. There was a faint thumping interspersed with the sounds of humming from within, and before the AI could try to respond with an analysis, Rex opened fire on the dead console, blowing the surface open with a burst of pulse rounds.

Then proceeding to use his left hand, he tore up the circuitry, located the latch deep inside, and ripped it free of the wall and door, rending steel and plastics effortlessly, tossing aside the length of navy-blue metal and watching the hatch slip aside, opening with minimal effort. Giving it a sturdy shove, Rex peeked beyond the edge of the doorframe, looked around quickly, and identified a few pieces of equipment that could have been generators, pumps, storage containers, and stasis canisters. There was no sign of living Combine or any of the creatures, but he wasn't going to hold his breath.

Motion sensors active, no life signs indicated.

Stepping into the all-white room, he was surprised how Spartan it was, clean and organized. It seemed like a bio-development facility, but what purpose it had other than to create the creatures he'd already encountered, it spoke nothing of the kind, left no evidence of even being monitored. It made little to no sense, a fully operational facility, only manned by guards, with no maintenance abilities or drones or even self-diagnostic programs, connected underground to a school beyond a barrier around the complex itself...

It seemed sloppy, or overlooked by arrogance, and it insinuated that the Combine had a firm grasp here, added to the fact that alarms still had not gone off, and the extent of the reaction to his presence was a single chopper and a few scrubby scouts accompanied by a couple of Judicators. It made him wonder if this area was of any priority now at all—perhaps they'd gotten their use of the place, and now simply used it as a biomass storage facility, prisoners, materials, labs, all sealed and secured for future utilization, all sterilized and set to hibernate for what could potentially be a return trip to the labs to continue further study or experimentation. Walking through the only doorway here inside the room led to a command-style console system, powered down but all sitting at a startup prompt, and immediately the Lena-AI was excited.

Plug the rifle into the ports here, I can copy myself into their system like I copied into you.

The information that she could copy herself, and had done so once already, surprised Rex—everything he'd read about AIs had them as singular entities, but perhaps it was the nature of this creation that was the Lena-AI made it different. Just a self-aware program using a scan of Lena's brainwaves and activity, it was still strange to have a part of it in his skull. Unplugging the rifle from the port on his head, Rex snaked the small fiber-wire connector over to the console and plugged it in, watching as the console came to life, and began to blur at amazing speed. There was a gentle tone to notify him that the transfer was complete.

Rex unplugged the weapon, reconnecting it with his own headgear, and felt satisfied that the HUD had united with the rifle before he continued wordlessly, examining the room. He found another hatch here, sealed shut tight with no access console, no visible hinges, and no manipulative handholds or ridges for moving, seamless with the wall, but obviously used, a very small path formed into the floor where the panel had opened before. Shoving it once on instinct, the door popped open slightly, allowing him to get his left hand into the crevice, gripping the door tightly, and then yanking it back as hard as possible, hearing the hydraulics inside pop and hiss as he tore it free. That was obviously not how it was supposed to be opened, but Rex stared at yet another dark corridor of poured concrete and navy-metal braces leading down a few meters to another basement area.

Ensuring the headgear was still correcting the light amplification, Rex checked his weapon and amount of ammunition, and continued moving deeper in, taking each of the steps cautiously. He was crouched low even as he moved down the flight in order to get a better view of the room below, finding it oddly familiar, a long, dark corridor with bare walls and ceiling. Thoughts becoming somewhat downcast, Rex realized that the area was far too simplistic in form to be much more than cookie-cutter design, perhaps replicated in an untold amount of places, and it didn't comfort him much.

Taking the path across the distance slowly, he approached another set of stairs, and ascended to the top, finding an unmarked door with a waist-level opener. Pushing it in and opening the door slightly, Rex cursed under his breath as he found a large warehouse-sized room beyond, fenced off with steel cross sections, and topped with barbwire. The area itself was patrolled by at least a dozen of the Civil Patrol with their white masks and reflective eyepieces, accompanied by four or five of the yellow-eyed riot guards in heavy gear, using suppression sticks on a line of people in blue jumpsuits…

Rex had to shake his head as he tried to recall where he'd seen that before. His moment of reflection was interrupted as someone pulled the door open from the other side abruptly, and he fell into the room firing the rifle awkwardly, shooting up at a CP as he tried to bear down on Rex with one of the glowing shock prods. All hell broke loose as the guard struck the ground, sliding across the floor as Rex kicked the soldier away, and the prisoners saw the streak of vivid, red blood on the once-immaculate floor here, spinning in their heels and running right into the group of riot soldiers.

The Combine immediately began to beat on the prisoners to make them submit, and as they crouched down under the guard's beatings, Rex opened fire across the top of their shoulders, killing three enemies easily, and pulse rounds ripping through riot gear. Two more Civil Patrollers fell as they attempted to intercede on the situation, the rifle bearing on them and dropping both with the end of the magazine. The rest of the Civil Patrol began to scatter, and as the prisoners stood and bolted towards a pair of double doors behind a steel partition, alarms finally began to blare. The neutral feminine voice started up a new warning to repeat endlessly, just like before, mirrors of his first experience with the Combine.

"Noncitizen Alert, Nova Construxi. Requesting Judicator Assistance, Zeta Unit Inbound."

This broadcasted alert was rather short and abrupt, in comparison to others that he'd heard before, Rex pausing just a moment, the echo resounding. There was no following speech by Dr. Breen, and he could only wonder what happened to Freeman and City 17. Not one to wait around for the answer to come to him, Rex pushed aside a length of the steel interlinked fencing, and began to make his way to the double doors, leading out into the street, when a yell to his left caught his attention.

"Stop right there!"

Two of the Civil Patrol that had fled the fight now returned with two more, and they all leveled pistols at him, waiting for his next motion, prepared to fire, but obviously more interested in arresting and processing him alive, rather than scanning in a cold corpse. There could have been no other reason for their holding still and refraining from opening fire immediately, having witnessed him kill several other Combine already.

"Do not move and do not attempt to resist, you will be arrested!"

Rex watched them approach at first bearing only casual disinterest, hoping to catch them off guard as he tore into motion only a few seconds later. Stepping up over one body and grabbing the top of the fence with his left hand, his feet pushed down onto the top rail as he balanced, then leapt off of it, landing in a tuck-and-roll with the sounds of warning shots in his ears. At least he thought they were warning shots, until the first one grazed his shoulder, and he refused to look back as he bashed open the double doors here, finding a once-neat courtyard now trashed by burnt vehicles, corpses, rubble, and craters, even the solitary tree left half-scorched down to bare branches.

Two other CPs stood out here, patrolling warily—they'd no doubt heard the warning, and as Rex emerged, they had their own pistols up, and started firing at his legs as he ran. Running to the left out of instinct, Rex found a smaller steel wall segregating the area from the streets beyond, and immediately doubled back across his own path, bolting down to the right and hurdling over a bombed-out wreck, sliding down the side of a crater beyond and leaping up onto the ridge on the other end.

He began swearing as more rounds struck the armor suit, this time along his back and right, entering the alley ahead with only thoughts of escape on his mind. And even here, as he stopped on a dime, he found another of the navy-metal walls, boxing off the alley, and turned to a closed door, gripping the knob and finding it locked. Beginning to run back out of the alley, he was forced to stop again. CPs and a single Judicator filled the entry here, fanning out and rising weapons, Civil Patrol pistols and a Combine-made M4 clone. The Judicator said only one word with the weapon leveled at Rex's chest.

"Halt."

The moment froze for far too long, Rex staring through the three lenses at the Combine lining his path, and as they made a group effort to begin to back him down the alleyway, he reached out to his right, grabbing a length of a steel pole from a street sign, the sign long torn free, but the base still coated in a few inches of concrete from where it was once dug in and planted into the pavement. Bringing the makeshift mace up and to the left, he easily knocked the M4 clone from the Judicator's hands, ignoring the pistol rounds that struck and ricocheted off the chestplate. Reversing the mace in his grip in order to bring it down and to the left this time, it crushed in a skull of one CP, the mace moving faster now as Rex collected momentum, destroying two torsos with one strike as he whipped the head of concrete and steel to the right.

The two CPs on that side smashed into the wall of the building and created a crater as they died together, squelching through their vocoders, even as Rex continued to move, the mace whipping up and to the left again, missing the Judicator by centimeters as the soldier reached for his weapon. But the mace made solid contact with the neck and face of the last CP, whirling the head about on shoulders and letting out a horrid cracking as the neck snapped effortlessly. The Judicator was yelling inarticulately through his own headgear as he knelt down to grab the fallen rifle, the yelling turning to blood-curdling screams as Rex swung the mace down onto the upper thigh of the enemy soldier, shattering the femur in one stroke, and the pain driving the thought of the weapon deeper from the Judicator's actions. The yelling tapered off just before Rex hefted the war-mace up again, and ended the enemy mind by obliterating it, the head popping loudly as he brought it back down for the last time.

Backing away from the collection of corpses as the whine of assisted landing jets sounded off, Rex ran to the closed door on the side of the building. He mashed the doorknob off with a solid swing of the makeshift club, and damn near tore the door off its hinges with the left hand, carving fingers into the gaping hole where the knob had been removed, clipping free the locking bolt and entering the doorway quickly, slamming it shut behind him. Using one end of the pole as a brace against the door, Rex kicked the opposite end against the floor twice, wedging it into place to prevent the passage from being useable again, then about-faced, and hauled ass up the staircase here.

Reaching the third floor as the sounds of pounding finally started in on the door below, Rex arrived quickly at the crumbling remains of the fifth-story staircase, and began to climb up it awkwardly. He found the roof and several other stories completely missing from the building, the fifth floor literally the new roof, stripped of everything and burned down to the concrete flooring. Thankfully it hugged the navy-metal blockade wall well, and as he paused a moment to gather his bearings in relation to the tower, he judged an awkward guesstimate of about 2.7 miles, and leapt off of the building over the security wall, barely avoiding the top-lined energy barrier in the process.

Landing on both feet in a crouch on the opposite side, Rex smiled smugly as he ran, feeling a sense of satisfaction at having lost his pursuers for now, but felt somewhat confused as to how he would bring down the tower here. Locating a particularly sturdy structure several blocks down from the secured areas, Rex ensured the ground entries were all sealed and used the remnants of a fire escape to get in through the third floor window, balancing off of a dumpster to reach the locked ladder.

Picking the darkest of the four rooms on the interior here, Rex sat in one corner tiredly, relaxing for a spare moment, one he hadn't taken for a long time now, and slowly ensured his rifle and pistol were still loaded and on his person. Resounding trains of thought ran through his mind now, and it wasn't long before he felt the wave of coldness sliding along his thoughts, examining them, and leaving them to their course, creating a complex pattern he couldn't quite concentrate on.

"Lena, you there?"

There was a slight pause before he heard the voice in his thoughts.

Yes. I've been sorting through your concerns...

It felt strange to respond aloud, but he restrained his voice to a whisper to keep the sound down. "Have you come up with any ideas? I need to take down that tower and I don't have any conventional means of doing so with me..."

A map of the area leapt to life on his heads-up display in the headgear, an overhead view of the zone he'd looked at while estimating distance to the tower. Rex realized that the AI was watching everything through his eyes as well, and it felt eerie. Markers and coordinates popped up over several areas, and a path lit up leading from the building he was in, over to a smaller building across the street, down into a restroom on the first floor, and through a ventilation shaft into the next part of the same building, bypassing a guard tower.

Taking the path I've highlighted is the quickest route while still under cover. It gets tricky here however...

The path through the building ended at a large ruined structure, at least a hundred yards of no cover at all, across bombed-out remnants of what had to be a recreational area or something similar to be so huge and have nothing left inside to provide any cover at all. The AI estimated the former building shape as the same height as a two- or three-story residential complex, but with a much wider area, perhaps a series of apartments. Whatever the case was, the destruction had created a *killzone* area, where people running along the surface could be cut apart while trying to cross. The estimated path was the quickest route across the zone, but Rex could still see likely areas for ambush teams, and looked back along the building entry, hoping he was seeing the right solution.

"Highlight manhole covers for me along the street just before that second building across the way."

The AI responded immediately, and he smiled as he found the location correctly.

"Do you have maps of the tunnels there?"

Sewage tunnels led a partial way down, a claustrophobic passage he really didn't want to take, but it was the only other route he could see past the killzone. The small tunnels led along the streets in a mostly straightforward fashion, following a couple of turns until it led straight to the base of the tower itself, estimations of the former street ghostly echoes under the massive footprint of the Combine structure.

"What about maps of the tower itself, anything?"

One moment.

As the schematic began to load, Rex continued scanning the tunnels, and moved to the next room in order to look out the window, finding his entry down: A manhole in the center of the two-way street below, luckily not covered with debris or bodies. It was getting darker outside now, and he was losing time—surprise was fading from his entry into the city, and it had turned into a full-blown alert before he'd escaped. No doubt the soldiers were scouring the area near where he'd been last seen, but thankfully it had not escalated beyond that.

Rex began to wonder what was now leading the Combine still here, what their goals were. As he'd slogged through Europe, hearing Breen spew trash and the remaining rebellion praise Freeman, he had always wondered if Freeman would succeed, and if he did, what was the top of the Combine power structure now? And not only that, what was motivating them to remain here, if by choice? If he could somehow find a way to strike at that, he considered to himself, perhaps he could find a way to drive them off the world.

He felt tired of burning through so many pawns like there was no end to them, tiring of the waves of soldiers, guards, converts, traitors, and half-breeds the Combine employed and created, and each terrifying new discovery of gene manipulation, weapons duplication, and mass destruction he stumbled upon, it only wore on him worse. Slumping down now to one knee and breathing a bit slower, he felt the weight of what was happening here compound it, the fact that so many friends were gone, or different after he'd left. It tore at him relentlessly, and as he tried to shuffle the thoughts aside, he heard the sounds of movement along the base of the building, someone kicking at the solidly barricaded first floor entry.

Tracing more sounds as they reached him, Rex moved through the rooms of the third floor, until he reached the window with the fire escape, and peered outside. A trio of the Combine scouts, neon-blue eyes easy to spot amongst the growing evening, moved along the dumpster and the half-dropped ladder, one beginning to climb up. Rex backed away to the doorway leading into the room, thumbed the 20mm launcher open, and reloaded it with another grenade round, holding the rifle carefully, and waiting patiently for his target to reach the top, concealed in the darkness. More feet joined the climb up onto the dumpster and the fire escape, creating a muffled, controlled series of sounds outside the window, and soon the heavy breathing of the soldiers reached his ears, too.

One scout cautiously peered through the open window at waist level, and Rex began to wonder if they had night vision or light amplifiers to see him, but relaxed as the scout began to attempt to open the window wider for entry, obviously not aware that a grenade launcher was aimed at him. As the window reached the top of the frame, and the scout began to put one leg in through the window to step inside, Rex fired the launcher. The explosion tore the frame and window free, detonating the charges in the scout's pulse rifle with a series of smaller popping sounds, and shook the entire side of the building, the fire escape wrenching loudly from the force, groaning from the weight still on it.

Rex had no idea if the other two Combine with the scout were still conscious, but without waiting to find out, he swiftly reloaded the launcher, and set the rifle to conventional rounds. Approaching the gaping hole in the wall, where the window once sat, he began firing into the two other scouts lying supine below a couple of times, kicking once solidly at the fire escape. Rex couldn't stop his grimace as the entire wrought iron and steel construction tore free from the building as well, crashing to the ground below in a massive cacophony of sound.

Running back through the third floor, Rex let the rifle hang loosely as he approached the window he'd been observing the street through, tore one of the 2 x 4 timbers free, and ran to the door to the entry to the floor, jamming it under the staircase door before returning to the window. The sounds of banging and violence on the ground entry below increased now, and as he tore the second piece of wood blocking the window off of the frame, he waited half a heartbeat for the door below to crash open, ran his left hand through the glass of the window, and pulled it off of the wall as well, shattering glass and wood as he threw it to the floor, and leapt through the opening.

Landing roughly in the street below, Rex dropped his rifle and the length of wood, but rolled to his feet, urgency overriding the need to stop a moment, and grabbed both the fallen weapon and the board, running to the ground floor entry that had been pried open. Lifting the rifle in numb fingers and hands, Rex forced his fingers to use the select-fire switch, and fired the second 20mm grenade into the staircase, barely able to close the door before the blast caught up to the doorway. Jamming the length of timber under this door now and ensuring it was shut for good, Rex stumbled to the manhole, reloading the rifle, and taking aim on one of the second-story floors where he guessed the kitchen might be, he pulled the trigger.

The grenade round set off a series of explosions that rocked the exterior of the building on that end, and smoke bellowed from the ruined window, a sure sign of fire. Using his left hand to pull up the manhole cover, Rex snarled at the sight of darkness below, and climbed down, sliding the manhole cover back over as best as possible before dropping to the bottom, headgear amplifying his vision to help with the dank, dark tunnel here, barely big enough for him to move through. Alarms began to blare now, inspiring him to begin to move faster along the tunnel, as quick as possible in his case, his shoulder brushing harshly against one side or another every few steps, Rex wishing the tunnel was wider. The building he'd just fired into would no doubt burn to the ground, hopefully with the Combine trapped inside, but he began to wonder if it was a good thing that he'd started it ablaze.

There was little doubt that it would add strength to the previous alerts out for his presence, and would create a huge signal to the Combine that he was there, but it also served as a distraction. If the Combine were stupid enough to send more troops to that location, then perhaps he could get into the base of the tower with little or no difficulty whatsoever. It stood to reason that the tunnels had a potential of being guarded or booby trapped as well, but he wasn't going to let that stop him now—he'd gone too far for that already, taken too much time in planning a route.

He wondered when they would find the slightly ajar manhole, and send troops down after him. Rex supposed he could try to collapse the tunnel behind him, but it would only bring the street level down to the tunnel itself, and instead of properly blocking off the tunnel, he would be giving them an entry at street level with no manhole cover or entry to limit them. He could try blowing the base of the tunnel upwards, or caving in one side, but he had none of Molly's shaped charges handy, and no time to improvise a grenade round into something useful. Shoving most of the thoughts aside as he followed each turn and curve the tunnel took, Rex noted that the headgear had to keep amplifying the lenses more and more, and as he looked up, passing one manhole cover, he found it completely blocked off, no light escaping through. Attempting to use the HUD to guide him, he called up the tunnels map, and ensured he was going in the right direction, when the AI spoke again.

Sorry for the alarm. My copy was detected while gaining the tower interior information. I caught the main power circuitry and the first seven levels from ground, but the copy was terminated before it could broadcast more.

Rex found himself responding to the AI aloud again, breathing harder after speaking to keep his pace up. "Sorry to hear that. Tuck them away for me until we get there."

The AI didn't respond as he kept running, focusing on the direction he was supposed to be taking, swearing as he heard something up ahead precisely where he needed to get by. The headgear leapt up sensitivity of the pickups to try to identify the sounds, but it was Rex that remembered them first, the buzzing of the mecha-razorblades, the flying *Manhacks*. Rifle up and pulse rounds selected, Rex advanced into the wave of sounds, returning the gain on the headgear to normal as he reached a *Y* in the tunnel. It was a larger maintenance section with an electrical panel long past being useful, still sealed behind plastic but all the lights and telltales dead.

It didn't take long for the section to become more than just a larger area in the tunnels as the red eyes of Manhacks came screaming around both corners ahead, bouncing from the metal walls and sending sparks everywhere. Opening fire as soon as the first reached his view, Rex did his best to hold them back. But he began to realize how many of the little bastards were flooding in when he expended the first pulse round magazine for his rifle, blowing off ninety rounds like nothing into the waves of flying razors, being forced to switch to conventional rounds rather than reload the spent mag, and backing up a bit to force them to a pinch point in the tunnel.

Of course, as they kept coming and he began to reach the end of his second magazine, he made a split-second decision. Calling up the schematics for the tunnel ahead, Rex chose the path in the *Y* he didn't need to take, and fired off a grenade at it just before the waves of mecha-razorblades forced him to fall back, the maintenance area out of his line of sight. Running back away as he reloaded both magazines and slapped a fresh grenade round into the launcher, Rex dug his heels in, crouching as he waited for the waves to continue to come for him, rifle up and eyes ready. They continued to follow his path, and as they struck the ceiling ahead, he let the conventional rounds speak for him, the 4.3mm bullets doing the job well in short order, a few bursts till the magazine was empty again.

He tactically reloaded rather than switching rounds, beginning a crouching advance as he kept up the pressure, the tunnel now littered with at least thirty or forty remains of the buzzing blades, and he crunched them underfoot as he moved, switching to pulse rounds this time as he began to make progress. Edging into the maintenance zone again, Rex could see that he'd collapsed the side to his left, and much to his relief, the debris had caved in to an angle favorable for him, with the street remnants above blocking off the tunnel without allowing access in on his side.

Breaking into a full run past the thinning mob of Manhacks, Rex strapped the rifle to his chest to free his arms to gain better pace, pumping his legs harder to gain distance between him and the little flying razorblades, when three ahead dropped down from a grating or narrow in the ceiling. Rex gritted his teeth as he attempted to leap through them, arms up crisscrossed to protect his chest and face instinctively. Something got close to a pickup on the headgear, and he tried moving in midair, when an invisible hand of heat and energy propelled him forward, slamming him to the ground of the filthy, yet thankfully dry, sewage tunnel. Hands sticky with blood and eyes swimming under the headgear, Rex tried to identify the source of the explosion, and found one of the magazines for the pulse energy ammunition torn open.

However, there was no continued reverie to pause in before the cracking sounds above began, sudden weight and force overwhelming him and causing him to yelp as his legs were pinned down. Glancing back, he could see the tunnel had caved in here, blocking off entry from the other side, and slamming a meter-long slab of concrete that ramped up to the surface down onto the back of his body. The implant was heaving in his chest now, harder than he could recall it ever doing so before, and he began to feel actual pain, but nowhere near the injury. Instead, his fingertips and toes began to tingle and throb endlessly, and as he redoubled his efforts to get himself free of the hunk of poured concrete, the intensity increased, and so did the sounds from the implant under the armor.

It finally broke out into a roar as he shoved at the ground with pinned legs, tore at the surface with scrabbling fingers and pulled himself through. The slab made rough noises as it made contact with the ground, legs escaping quickly from the weight, and causing Rex to limp around to stand up and walk, until he ensured his limbs were still intact and functioning, no jutting bones, no joints pulverized to dust. Pausing once to examine the map still up in the headgear, Rex decided to get a ground-level look, and walked up the ramping slab of stone, just enough until his head peered out through the cavernous opening, ducking back down quickly as an APC roared over his head. Looking out again quickly, he could see it was a normal Combine-controlled vehicle, pulse weapon swiveling about independently as the APC disappeared around the bend of the massive building.

Examining the wall here, Rex found it to be impressively dominating, creating a large space between the tower and itself that could easily be used as a killzone against any large force attempting to breach either the wall or the tower, and it was littered with a good portion of windblown debris and trash. Again, hearing the roar of an engine before it reached his sight, Rex pulled himself back down into the tunnel, listening for the sounds of the next patrolling armored personnel carrier as it tore along the broad zone, and marking the area off in his mind, he began to bolt through the tunnel again.

The tunnel stopped twisting for the most part, taking only slight angles now, and as he moved past one angle, he hoped his vision was wrong of what lay ahead. The tunnel here had been mostly replaced or covered with layers of the navy-blue metal, and was immaculately clean and well lit in comparison to the dried-out sewage tunnels behind him. None of this concerned him like the thick sealed hatch that the tunnel ended in, obviously not on the map, the tunnel not taking a sharp turn to the right like the schematics indicated.

"Lena, please pull up some of those tower blueprints you got."

Doing so now. Levels one to seven are the only available information.

Rex cursed to himself as he realized the basement zones were not on that map, and continued towards the hatch unabated by the lack of diagrams, charging the hatch shoulder first. The AI might have been saying something before he moved, but he ignored it and slammed into the two sections of Combine-marked metals with his left shoulder, hearing it complain loudly, and smiling. Sharp fingers on his left hand and armored fingers on his right pried into the alien steel where it met in the center, bending the two edges away from each other, the fingers on the left hand tearing through and giving him a handhold strong enough to rip the upper panel away completely, the hatch's former recessions sparking and squealing loudly as he put both hands on the second panel, and tore it loose as well.

THE TOWER

Throwing the metal sections ahead of him as he looked up, Rex found himself staring into a massive circular fissure, going both skyward and downward at once, the blue-hued metal providing a catwalk to navigate the exterior of the hole. Light was but a pinpoint speck above him, barely visible, and below the hole glowed and seethed with heat from what had to be under the crust of the damn planet itself. As he took the catwalk around to his left, noting it descended further for quite a bit until it reached a solid cage-bound lift, Rex found himself reading the panels bolted to the machine, sorting Combine symbols into normal words with the assist of the headgear. Using the lever on the lift as he climbed in, he half-closed the cage and unslung the rifle, cleaning off refuse and other materials that had scraped it as he ran through the tunnels, Rex ensuring the weapon was loaded and ready to fire.

"This is supposed to be one of the three power levels, according to the equipment. See if you can map some of this out, in case there's another tower like this somewhere out there."

The AI didn't respond this time, and Rex assumed it was hard at work, crouching down in the lift and waiting for it to arrive— the length of travel it was taking was ridiculously long so far, the lift moving along at quite a clip. Peering over the edge, he realized the bottom was the only place left to go, and as it began to slow several hundred meters above a searing red glow, he could finally identify the source. A large hunk of insanely thick rock along the left had at least three or four massive conduits running down into it, and along the right, a gaping pit of molten metal and mineral could be witnessed churning away at the underside of the huge rock.

It took a second for realization to hit him—he was staring at a tectonic plate that had been shorn along the edge with some type of weapon perhaps, and if it wasn't for the long distance that was still between him and the real bottom, he would be roasting alive in the armor. Already the heat had taken a marked increase, and his ears had popped at least twice during the trip down—the pressures were slowly and steadily increasing, and as the lift finally ground to a halt, his thoughts ended with it. Here were at least a dozen of the skinny parodies of life, meandering about endlessly from one machine to another. Stepping off the lift was enough to catch the attention of the closest to him, several feet away, and soon Rex could only hear the screeching of a strangled, machinelike voice box as the entire room turned to face him.

He emptied the entire magazine of energy rounds first in response, several stumbling around still and colliding with the walls from stray fire, or shots that had glanced from the bones that stood out horridly under pale flesh of all colors. The fact that some of the pulse rounds had glanced from the parodies' skeletons concerned him at first, but his hands were too busy switching the weapon to conventional fire and aiming to do more than compartmentalize the information away in memory for examination later, killing the last three former humans with a trace of disgust crawling across masked features. Tactically reloading the weapon as he glanced at the equipment here, he used the heads-up display to the best advantage he could manage, identifying equipment and containers, before turning his attention to one row of equipment, finding them to be temperature rates of the geothermal tap.

It began to make a little more sense to him now, supercooling a portion of the plate to run conduits through safely, yet keeping one portion heated by exposing it to air and caustic chemicals to keep the *fire stoked* so to speak. Locating the pipelines that flushed the chemicals into the hot zone, Rex began to check the regulated amounts, and then looked at the cooling system. He could try to cause an overload, shutting down the coolant taps and opening the seals on the chemicals, but he neither had any idea the time it would take, nor the aftereffects of pumping hell-knows-what inside the chemicals down onto a portion of exposed outer core. Guessing it would work was all the effort he could spare to take right now, and as he ran the plan over to the AI in his mind silently, it responded crisply.

Overload of core would take approximately 1 hour 22 minutes.

Setting his features into a determined grimace to avoid roaring aloud at the sound of a solution to his problem, Rex pulled up his weapon, set it on the panel, and began to shut down the coolant lines, telltales lighting up all over the place across the room's machinery. Automated response protocols began to engage, shutting down the chemical lines and rerouting available power to trying to restore the coolant—except Rex had sealed the main lines for the coolant, there was no excess for the protocol to flush into the lines. Tearing the lever for the main lines free from the panel, Rex picked up his rifle, and let the equipment for the coolant have a steady burst of 4.3mm, which punched through the modified human control panels without effort.

As he approached the caustic control zone, he found it was all made of newer Combine equipment and panels, most of the major computing power tucked away in a tiny box flush with the wall beyond, the visible controls all on the face of the monitors. Fingers dancing along controls he could barely identify, Rex began to touch systems that he could reach through this one, deactivating telltales, and rerouting the self-repair systems to the lowest level priorities first, starting with a loose grate some twenty floors up. He increased its tasks up from minor repair all the way into full diagnostic and replacement of material, hopefully buying himself plenty of time before the software found out what he was doing.

Deactivating and locking as many of the alarms as he could locate through the network here, Rex suddenly found one screen barred off after reaching a higher-priority security zone, and tore it off the wall with his left hand angrily, flinging it over the edge into the open pit. The remaining screen focused on the coolant levels being breached, and it took him almost a solid minute of fumbling with the awkward controls to get it to resume monitoring of the chemicals in the lines. He cursed loudly when he found that the self-repair system had royally screwed his plan, back-sealing the caustic lines in the same way he'd locked off the coolant streams. Tapping into the seal controls for the chemical lines was essentially not an option from here, and as he pulled this screen sparking from the Combine-made sectional socket, he flung this one too over the edge, watching it bounce from several containers before making the final fall.

Rex moved to these containers and smiled, finding them brimming full of, if the labels were correct, toxins too caustic to be used in the lines, by-products of the energy reactor above. Shoving at these, he easily unbolted them from the floor, and tipped the sealed containers down into the glowing heat, seven in all, not bothering to stay and watch the fireworks. Rifle up and feet moving, he hustled up into the cage-bound lift, and slammed the controls angrily, the lift taking off with a start, sounds of searing metal and popping seals precursors to what happened next, raw, angry explosions sending shockwaves up the tunnel.

Rex was rocked from his feet and spent the next few moments, hoping the lift wouldn't fall away, until it reached the next level and he dove out. The metal screamed loudly as stresses tore at it, the lift and most of the catwalk surrounding it breaking free from its moorings on the stone and tipping over, slamming into the opposite side of the huge circular hole, before collapsing completely and tumbling out of sight. Running up the remaining catwalk and leaping over a section that had come free, Rex bolted past the tunnel opening without stopping and kept going, the catwalk still shaking, but clearly firmer here, where it bolted into the sides of the huge cylinder that was the tower's central interior.

With any luck, as he ran into the first level of the tower, the building wouldn't alarm or call for emergency repairs any time soon. Emerging from the catwalk into the only doorway out of the central cylinder, Rex kept his rifle up and at the ready as he scanned the surroundings with his eyes and the HUD's displays, realizing there was a rather large absence of troopers here. Navigating the maze of navy-blue metals and peering over bottomless edges, Rex began to study the awkward and impromptu placing of walls, panels, shafts of metal that moved upwards for hundreds of meters, and deep, vast pits of blackness which no amount of light managed to penetrate.

Comparing his location to the Level 1 plans for the tower the AI had retrieved, Rex zeroed in on his coordinates and then rotated the map to match the overlays around him, a small green highlighted path marking its way through the semi-maze to the next floor entry for him. Following the path around several dominating pillars that seemed to be main supports for the tower, Rex found himself backpedaling as he reached the location of the second level entry, rolling behind cover just as two machines turned to approach, narrowly avoiding their sight, the boxy machines with red eyes floating by, automated sentries scanning and patrolling the zone around the door here. Bolting past before they could finish their circuit and complete a turnaround motion, Rex slipped through the door easily, the panels opening to greet him as he approached, sliding resolutely shut as he walked away.

Taking the ramps up as he met them with his feet, Rex moved to the second-level entry here, and couldn't help but grin to himself. This tower, this place of unholy alien hell and breeding and other unmentionables would finally be dying tonight, would at last be a smoldering ruins in the face of what the Combine wrought upon the planet, and he could only hope that this crater would serve as a symbol big enough for the half-breeds and traitorous slavers to see, and fear.

Tactically reloading again in order to keep his hands from clenching up on the rifle, Rex flexed his fingers once before approaching the doorway, the panels slipping aside into their respective recessions to expose a much-different-looking configuration. Tight hallways formed of towering metal walls hugged what appeared to be a stone floor, but even as his talons and boots touched it, he knew it was painted metal, spotting spaces along the walls where it peered right back down into the darkness below, other depressions in the walls containing strange pillars of contained light, orbs bouncing around inside endlessly, with no purpose he could readily identify. Everything here was immaculate, but buzzed with the sounds of roaring energy, and instead of a complicated maze, he found himself slowly following the hall, sniffing the air once and finding it to smell heavy of ozone, thick and swampy with each breath, the heat of the area incredible and dominating.

His feet made loud noises on the faux stone, even amongst the sounds of power coursing through the equipment around him, and it didn't take long to realize his feet were not the only ones moving on the floor, quickly looking around for a place to hide or dart out of sight, and failing miserably as the source of the footsteps came around the corner ahead. A very surprised red-eyed Elite in white armor spotted him and they both froze, the moment hanging on incredulously, the Combine soldier actually going so far as to question if Rex was friend or foe, weapon pointed at the floor, but slowly making its way upwards. Rex, on the other hand, had his rifle at the ready, and answered the interrogative by firing once, catching the Combine in the padded throat, firing again to ensure the bullets were penetrating the suit, the second shot throwing the Combine from his feet.

Disregarding the corpse and focusing on the turn ahead, Rex peered around the bend and found another long hall, devoid of soldiers now, but who knew how long that would last, having just killed one patrolling Elite. Rex knew they all remained in radio contact constantly, and if there were any signs of alarms going off, he couldn't see them. What was going on here? The flood of enemies he'd been met with time and time again was not here, and it was a growing concern chewing at his underbelly. The Combine were appearing to be weakened drastically by something here, and despite all the havoc he'd brought to their other installations, he doubted it was the source of the problem that the Combine were facing now.

Attempting his best to move the thought aside where it belonged, Rex left the body where it lay, and continued down along the halls here, the layout diagram of the level showing him that the second level zigged and zagged all along the zone, a strange circular pattern that actually connected it to the third level at the end, like a coiled spring. Hustling up his motions in order to keep a brisk pace, switching to pulse rounds absentmindedly while watching the schematics for the second level, Rex flat-out ran into the next Elite, bowling the enemy soldier over easily, and didn't bother firing his weapon.

Instead, he grabbed the soldier by one foot, the left hand slicing through armored leg as he gripped tightly, and slammed the soldier into one of the corners on the wall, the entire body going slack like a ragdoll, Rex flinging the body aside without paying attention to what he was doing. The former Elite bounced off of a jagged edge of a recession and flew right into one of the pillars of energy, Rex recoiling and expecting an explosion, but instead only felt his jaw drop as the energy arced out and vaporized the body.

Shaking his head at what he just saw, Rex ignored the possibilities of that kind of energy being fired from a weapon at him, and broke out into a full run along the twisting faux stone floors, breezing through the rest of the way and arriving at a hatch inset into the wall ending the long hall. Using the Combine-designed activator for the door, Rex watched as the indicator turned from orange to green, the door panels cycling open to reveal another of the faux stone floors and arcing hall.

Except this did no turns or twists other than a long sloping curve going up, the hall broad and tall for an unknown complement of creatures, guessing that it was probably the end of a particular security zone, the layouts provided by the AI giving little more in information other than this was the largest level he'd been on so far, the curving hall approximately a mile in length moving to the next level of the tower, the fourth zone marked better on the map.

Taking time to pause and examine the schematics, Rex poured over the ID signatures of each marked lab on the fourth level, finding many to be just relay stations for something he didn't know, and the AI had not guessed when marking zones. Other areas looked to be repair stations, with the ceiling topped just as high as it was here. His moment to pause was interrupted by a horrid screeching that caught him off guard and made him grasp the sides of the headgear, and soon heavy stomping could be heard, along with the sounds of buzzing, echoes easily identified as Manhacks, but the stomping still puzzled him.

Weapon at his shoulder, Rex cleared his heads-up display, and crouched, waiting for the source to come to him. The mecha-razorblades came around the corner into view first, and with careful aim, he was able to pick a good half dozen out of the air using pulse rounds at maximum range. As more joined the first wave, he began to increase his rate of fire, backing up a few steps while what appeared to be a swarm of them came into his sight, and loading another of the pulse pods as the first went empty. Continuing to fire, Rex could see that the source of the approaching stomping was not the worst of his worries, and began to back up to the hatchway in order to use it as cover against the flying razors coming at him in larger numbers than he'd experienced before.

With the entire magazine of pulse pods empty, Rex took the time to turn to the hatch to open it and bit off a roar as he found it locked tight. Switching to conventional fire on the rifle and charging away from the hatch, Rex did his best to carve a path in the cloud of swarming enemies, and shoved through them. The feeling of the carbon fiber blades as they scored the armor was enough to make him shudder as he ran through the small fliers, thankful that only a few around his extremities were still alive to attack him as he ran. The path he cleared was not all too perfect, but just enough so for him to make it past the dense cloud of Manhacks that were trying to sweep around to his original position at the hatchway. Continuing in a full breakout speed, Rex passed a good portion of the mecha-razorblades while running along the curving floor, but even that minor accomplishment was buried by the sight of the true source of the stomping noises:

Another of the towering, three-legged monstrosities were here, this one covered in bluish armor plate, swiveling an uncountable amount of weaponry on a multi-turret, deep orange eyes hooded under navy-metal plates regarding him with a look reserved only for the lowest common denominator, before bringing about the bristling weapons ports at him. Rex kept hauling ass, pretending that he wasn't hearing the sounds of gunfire hit the deck right behind him, but acknowledging the fact that he certainly did not want to be the receiver of such lethal ammunition.

The ground was starting to shake under his feet as he ran now, waves of heat shoving against his armored back and legs, and he let the weapon loose from his grasp, the rifle bouncing wildly on the sling, as he pumped his arms for speed. One giant leg speared down next to him and missed by a mere hairsbreadth from knocking him on his ass, almost allowing the weapons to do their deadly job. The buzzing of the Manhacks was long gone, but now the whine of the implant was in his ears. And as something grazed his right side, superheating the armor for a second and causing it to sear against him underneath, Rex screamed at the pain not from his side, but from his hands and feet, which were now ablaze with roaring nerves.

A strange, cracking feeling emanated each time he put one foot in front of the other, feeling it slowly crawl upwards through his body. The pain was soon dying to a dull throb that continued to ache, but it was dampened enough that he could focus on running again, increasing his pace yet again in order to attempt outrunning the beast over his shoulders, and as it stomped twice more, extremely close to him, still firing, Rex knew it was impossible. He had to wound it somehow, scare it, or stop it entirely. He couldn't keep running from it at this speed, his body was aching from all of the effort he'd poured into his actions without rest, and the fact that the implant was acting even stranger than usual was not helping matters.

Timing the stomps nearest him, Rex held his breath as he waited for the leg to get close, then leapt at it in an insane maneuver, left hand barely closing clawed grasp about the armor sheath along the limb, whipping about it wildly. Suddenly he was thrown to his feet and bounced to one knee as the limb shifted dramatically, and Rex forced himself to roll it out instead of face planting on the faux stone floor. His eyes got only a slight glance of a massive streak of black blood along the floor before he could stop.

The ground was heaving as he stopped himself and turned about to face the large beast, and found himself cheering inarticulately as he spied the damage he'd brought upon the three-legged titan in his crazy move. The weapons had clipped the beast's own leg in an effort to track-fire on Rex, and cut the footpad portion free easily. Before the giant could halt its motions and realize what it'd done to itself, it tried to step down on the wounded limb and toppled over. Rex jogged along the side of the titanic bastard lying on the floor, retrieving his weapon into his grasp, and smiling as he looked at what gravity had done to the *head* of the beast, half of it flattened and crushed inside of itself from the weight of the impact upon falling.

More of the ichor it used as internal fluids were running down the ramping level away from the massive corpse, and as he watched them trail momentarily, he heard the sounds of the Manhacks again, and decided to keep moving ahead. As annoying as the little bastards could be, he had no need to face them head-on again, knowing full well that if there were more ahead, he'd rather get them behind him as well, way behind him. Motion was slightly less stressful now without a titan bearing down upon him with a multitude of weaponry, but still he ached from so much time spent on the run, fighting, nearly dying, killing, using muscles that had no common use anywhere else in life.

Calling up the schematics of the tower was easy, but it took a long moment for the map to resolve itself on the third floor, and then track his motions to compare to his location, only the sight of the end of the hall on the map brightening his mood. The large end of the corridor was coming into his own view quickly enough for his tastes, and as he examined the enormous double-panel door here, one that towered nearly twenty feet tall, he realized he was correct in his earlier assumption. The giant would have continued to stride over him right to this door and beyond if need be.

Slowing himself as he closed the distance to the massive doors, Rex pushed the small access button at shoulder height once, and when it didn't budge, kicked at the door as hard as possible. It still didn't move, and he jammed his hand down onto the access panel again, shoving at it with a snarl. The sounds of the mecha-razors closing in behind him distantly inspired him to beat at the panel, when it finally began to move aside. Squeezing in between the two panels as soon as he could, Rex hauled into the next room and spun to the controls here, kicking at them once solidly, and grinning as the doors responded faster this time, halting and reversing direction to slam shut once again.

However sudden silence was permeated by the sounds of metallic tinkering and the odd box-lung breathing of Combine, and as he slowly turned away from the console controlling the door to take a look at what was waiting for him there, he cursed under his breath, taking a headcount as fast as possible. At least a dozen of the skinny human parodies of life were manning numbered alcoves along both walls here with three strange Combine constructions he'd never seen before present. Strange, heavily armored, and squat-statured, they moved about amazingly quiet and efficient for their frame, standing about the size of the typical Combine or CP, but wide and heavy, with no real visible head, only sloping metal covering the torso.

Hands ended in articulated tools of almost a million types like Swiss-army knives from space touching consoles, and the giant living Dragons were in some of the alcoves, the others containing the Whale-carrier creatures, and one holding another of the towering tri-legged mobile weapons platforms. The moment lasted far longer than Rex even considered was possible, the closest few of the strange parodies of human life pausing in their work on the alcoves to turn and face him, the others continuing to grind away, the flying constructions moving downward in the alcoves, only to be replaced by another. And as those closest to him faced his presence, Rex could hear them *sniff* at the air around him, focusing intently, and the first of them made the realization that he wasn't a Combine with a maddening screech though a ragged voice box.

The screaming worker flung himself at Rex physically, throwing lashes from deformed limbs, and as he cut the ragged creature down, the sounds of gunfire attracted the attention of everything else in the room, all the other workers abandoning the alcoves, and the strange metallic bots turning to face him as well. Continuing to fire with the conventional rounds still in the magazine, he knew he had no cover, and distinctly did not want to go back through the door behind him, already hearing the scrabbling sounds of the buzzing devices attempting to get through.

Several of the workers died in the insane charge they threw at him, but the resilience of the skinny beings was incredible for their condition, and Rex found himself hemmed in, weak hits battering the armor surface, until they pinned him back, and Rex could focus on the larger repair bots. All three of the bots had opened from the center, metal plates sliding away and back to reveal the glowing white power sources in their chests, and he felt his fear surge as one of the bots began to hum louder, the glowing becoming increasingly intense. Shaking the workers from him, as they held him against the door, Rex forced his arms up and used the butt of the now-empty rifle to remove them one at a time.

The weapon cracked loudly as it came into contact with the strange plates bolted to their faces, one head actually popping like a zombie, and making him recoil as the gore splashed all over the once-clean weapon. The nearest bot was unable to be seen behind the aura of power emanating from the core at its center, and Rex barely managed to shove off enough of the workers to attempt to avoid what came next: A massive pillar of light and energy erupted from the core of the robotic machine, and as he fell backwards, he could see the tops of the creatures around him disappear, torsoless legs toppling onto him. He almost panicked as he shoved them away and attempted to crawl back from the blast of energy still going on over his head, fingers searching ammo pouches and finding all of the pulse ammo completely gone.

Only three of the conventional magazines remained, and as he slapped one of the forty-round clips home, Rex attempted to blink his vision free, focusing on the other two bots, and firing on them with a few controlled bursts. The rounds did nothing to the metallic exterior, but as he refocused one burst, and struck the core at the center of one, the explosion blinded him. Curling into a ball and hoping the armor was tough enough to withstand shrapnel from these things at this range, Rex snarled as two more eruptions followed, blinking rapidly to restore his vision, and relaxing as it returned. The effect caused the HUD to blank the receptors as they were nearly overloaded, the lenses covering themselves until they could readjust.

There were now three shining craters where the bots once stood on the metal deck crossing the area here, and the consoles and railings around the craters had been turned to molten slag long enough to reduce them to piles of sparking materials bonded together by immense energy. No moment of relaxation followed this discovery however, Rex facing at least a dozen of the Manhacks as they poured into the large room, through a meter-wide hole in the massive door. As a reaction, he began to plink several with conventional fire, before halting abruptly at the expense of ammunition, eyes searching the room as he attempted to avoid the mecha-razorblades.

Running ahead to the catwalk and leaping over one smoldering crater, Rex grabbed onto the curved edge of one console at a nearby alcove, and managed to tear it free after much-concerted effort, pulling off a wide, slightly curved section of the navy-blue metal. Gripping it in the center where it was once fused to the other pieces, Rex used it as a giant flyswatter on the Manhacks. One slipped by and attempted to intervene on Rex's next motion, and with his left hand, he reached out, and crushed it like it wasn't there, but snarled as the rest of the mob forced him to fall back further, amassing through the gaping hole and forming a thick cloud of themselves to rush him with.

Bracing himself, Rex cleared a path in front of him with three wide, sweeping arcs of the large metal section, cleaving and crushing the flying razorblades easily, dully noting that there were dozens upon dozens more still coming through the hole, but with no other clear choices, he was going to finish them all off. By hand if necessary, and he emphasized this with each brutal swing, feeling exhaustion upon him like a parasite, slowing his speed, making him sweat, and while it carried on further, it began to enrage him. He was not going to die to some swarm of mechanical insects, and the feeling of pain creeping back into his awareness was like salt in his wounds, roaring aloud through the headgear as he charged back into the cloud, the section of navy-blue metal up like a battering ram now, bouncing and crashing the mecha-razorblades everywhere.

Digging in his heels in the center of the massing group, Rex swung the slab of metal around as viciously as possible, blurring the object back and forth now, sparks and sounds of screaming metal and smashing parts like a whirlwind of noise, drowning out everything else. As a group of the mecha-razors attempted to flee back from the aura of destruction around him, Rex snarled and leapt up to meet them in midair. Bringing the improvised weapon down upon the Manhacks, and landing on a scattered pile of bits and pieces, he almost lost his footing completely, spinning and backing to the wall abruptly.

Forcing a halt without falling, and pretending he didn't just bruise his back horribly, he dug in again, and flung the slab at the remaining swarm, charging in after the flying object as it mashed a handful of Manhacks out of the air, beginning to finish off the rest with his left hand, the right batting them aside as they got close. Finally the last of them died under his brute force, and no more swarmed through the hole to meet him, Rex standing there gasping, chest heaving, sweating profusely, mind swimming. He shifted back and forth from taloned foot to taloned foot, doing his best not to fall backwards from the level of energy being drained so thoroughly from him, and felt no singing songs of the implant in chest, instead only a soft whisper rolling through him.

Balancing carefully while walking, grasping at the still-intact portions of the railing to stay upright, vision attempting to focus and failing, he stumbled once, stopped himself, and kept moving carefully, trying to understand why he was feeling so tired all of the sudden. But he was unable to remain on the track of thought, drifting slowly every time he tried to remain on the line of thinking. He was seeing spots in his vision now, and he knew that wasn't good, and Rex finally took a header, collapsing on the catwalk for a moment, trying to relax, closing his eyes, pacing his ragged breathing, losing grasp on being awake just long enough...

The alcoves ground into motion around him, and he leapt to his feet amazingly fast, clearheaded, focused, ready to roll, and the awareness of it had him puzzled and confused, but looking around the huge manufacturing or repair room was enough to hint him to haul ass. The biomechanical creatures were being pumped through here like crazy now, as if someone knew where he was, and was trying to amass as many of these before he could destroy them. As if in response to his train of thought, the last of the alcoves ahead, the tallest of them all, opened to reveal another of the tri-legged weapons platforms ready to move and kill, refocusing onto him and warbling loudly through some strange means.

A blue pinpoint beam began to sweep towards him, and as it approached his feet, Rex turned and ran. He didn't know what followed the beam, only knew that he felt the force of an explosion, and his ears were ringing now, the deck shaking underneath him. He had no weapons with him that could deal enough damage to the titanic bastards, and once again, he was forced to flee instead of standing and fighting, and that was worse to him than the exhaustion, being forced to run away. Leaping through the meter-wide gap as he came to the oversized door, Rex rolled to his feet on the other side, ignoring the huge blue pulse of energy that narrowly avoided him and struck the wall a long way distant, scoring it and turning the navy-blue metal searing read hot for several moments.

An idea leaping up in his wracked thoughts, and Rex grasped onto it, tearing into motion for the prone corpse of the second three-legged walker, stopping quickly as he approached and ripping through the exterior with his left hand as best as possible. The HUD was immediately attempting to identify circuits for him, locating a power control box buried into the oversized skull, and picking leads that were still connected to the uncrushed power source within. Tracking them to the exterior of the huge skull, Rex heard the sounds of the other Walker now ramming at the door he'd leapt through, the heat-bored hole in the center no doubt fusing portions of metal together and making the panels struggle to slide open. Locating the weapon along the exposed portions of the turret on the corpse he had his arm buried into, Rex grabbed together the cable and feeder line, and grasped onto the base of the weapon with his right hand, trying to quickly pinpoint the triggering mechanism.

The sectioned doors ahead squealed loudly as it began to separate, metal tearing, stresses causing hydraulics or whatever they used to moan and grind behind the walls, the ramming noises continuing all the while. Hands slick with dark-blue ichors and other internals, Rex gripped the weapon underneath the mashed skull, trying to force the weapon loose from the body, and failing as the doors ahead literally began to bend back away from the Walker battering at it, hands almost losing grasp. Mind racing, he shifted his plan slightly, grasped where the manual trigger should have been, and waited for the second towering creature to burst into view, pieces of the sectioned door being flung aside brutally, several bits narrowly avoiding him.

The bestial warble that followed was similar to before, except this one held slight tinges of desperation in it, as if the creature was begging to kill him. And as it finished its vocal announcement to him that it was angry, the turret mounted in the center of the odd triangle-shaped head swiveled to face him, and he leaned just enough to rotate the barrel of his own makeshift weapon in return. Squeezing the manual trigger with both hands, he was almost afraid nothing was happening as the blue pinpoint beam came to bear on the underbelly of the other Walker, yet did not fire.

He felt the surge from the power supply through the energy and feeder lines, resisting the urge to jerk back as the massive pulse of blue energy erupted from the barrel. Heat splashed against the side of the skull opposite of Rex, and he realized the other Walker had gotten off a shot as well, but not nearly as devastating in location as Rex had chosen. The other Walker was stumbling around awkwardly now, the underside of the creature molten and dripping, components splaying out, searing hot sides burning cables and frying electronics as it came into contact.

And as it suddenly balanced itself, refocused onto him resolutely, and chose a different weapon from the turret, Rex didn't wait for the effect, only ran. Instead of running the rational direction, one most people would choose, away from the thing trying to kill him, Rex made another beeline for his adversary, sweeping in amongst the trio of spine-like legs, grabbing onto one. While it attempted to shake him off, he leapt bodily at the next leg, moving up the limb like it was a length of rope, until he was within arm's reach of the gaping hole at the center of the underbelly.

At this height, the view was impressive and hard to avoid—whatever weapon the Walker had chosen to fire next, the spot where he stood once and the corpse of the enemy he'd used to his advantage were both nothing more than charred smears on the blackened metal floor. Returning to the task at hand, Rex pushed away from the leg and tore into the loose cables and hardware dangling down here, climbing up into the cavernous opening, and finding a tight crawlspace-sized area where all of the now-hanging cables and lines once sat. There was several other objects bolted down to the interior, navy-metal sealed tight with power and transfer lines snaking out, all leading to another thick metal plate above his head, ports spread out along the bottom.

Using his left hand in an entirely vicious and brutal manner, Rex tore one of the larger lines free from the connecting plate, and once he was ensured there wasn't a solid source of power running through the exposed socket, Rex braced his feet and rammed his left hand up through the connector. The razor-sharp fingers and armor-like skin ripped through the materials like they were made of tissue paper, grasping onto something somewhat solid on the other side, and pulling it through as hard as possible. A thick streamer of the blue internal fluid spat from the ruined port, splaying the ichor everywhere, the warbling turning into a high-pitched scream of agony through still-unidentifiable means, and he had to clasp his hands over the pickups on the headgear to try to cut off the sounds.

Kicking out at one of the bolted-down, navy-metal objects, he heard the scream pause then start again, and began to batter the module as hard as possible, tearing it loose from its moorings and throwing it out of the gaping hole, leads and cables severing as it fell past their length to smash open on the metal floor below. The screaming had stopped, but now the creature was swaying again, and it wasn't stopping to rebalance itself on the three legs. Instead they began to stiffen and shake uncontrollably, causing the entire interior to shift, and before he could consider leaping back out, the entire body had shifted, turning it into a ceiling as it toppled over.

Rex might have been yelling as it fell over, but none of that mattered when it fell twenty feet to the metal ground, and crushed around him like a can. The rush of pain, surprise, and terror at being trapped struck him all at once, and there was no moment to black out or lose consciousness, not when his body was jerking and moving to get the hell out, or the way his limbs thrashed at bent walls of metal and piles of jumbled equipment or components around him, or when he began growling like a wounded, caged animal, desperate and raging. Something smacked against the side of the headgear and it served only to anger him more, lashing back out and feeling the satisfying squelch of something that was once alive being crushed under his hands, and tore into it with fervor, hands bursting through whatever it was out into the exterior of the mashed skull of metal and organics.

Using his arms and legs to pry the exit wider, the upper rim of the hole broke free, and he found himself flinging it out angrily, following up by leaping out with a nasty roar. Both feet landing on the solid floor was enough to steady him, even as his talons secured his stance further, and Rex shook the disgusting internals from around the armor, ignoring what might have been blood just to get back and away from the creature, to keep moving, keep the adrenaline flowing. Rex could think now, could feel actual thoughts flow again, and as he began to jog away from the bodies, he hated the idea of what just occurred. He'd lost every semblance of rational mind when he was trapped inside the body after it fell, and the sheer animalistic fury of it scared him, shook him to his core at the thought of losing all control of his actions, especially after the weapon the Combine had turned him into.

Breaking into a run, Rex ignored bodies and craters, leaping past a fallen console, hauling up a railing in his path and grabbing it like a club, and heading straight to the next towering pair of doors. Desperately he wanted this all to be over, to find an ending to this suddenly, the beast he'd just become worse to him than every alien or human life he'd taken, every motion of violence he'd used or lashed out with, none of it felt like the sheer emptiness of falling away as his body took over.

The massive doors parted ways here. He looked upon an area that was like an oversized manufacturing conveyor, hooks carrying pods and flyers; others hauling around the towering Walkers, Dragons, Whales…the pods were humanoid sized and clearly distinguishable as conversion or prisoner containers he'd seen before, and could contain either future traitors, prisoners of war, or both at the same time. Taking a quick sweep of the room, he found himself edging away, creeping along the shadows, trying to find an exit rather than dealing with the units being pumped out here, and the discovery created a well of self-disgust, rising to revulsion as it struck him. He was running from the enemy now, not just himself, and that was completely unacceptable. Halting in the dark and whispering to the AI, he hoped it had some useful information.

"Can you locate munitions reloaders or suppliers in here?"

The AI brought the map of the level up to the forefront, and began to mark alcoves in the room that formed an exact circle around the center of the tower. As Rex located one nearest him, he moved to the alcove silently, and examined the machinery, which seemed to be nothing more than a fancy box with loading arm. It took a moment for him to identify the types of ammo being deposited into each of the units as they rolled by, mounted sections of turrets passing along one set while sections from the forward-mounted ball turrets for Dragons and the Combine-altered helicopters passed along another, and it wasn't long until he'd found the more standard fare, sealed-off conveyors loading magazines and pods for various weapons under solid, translucent panels.

Unfortunately for Rex, none contained the 20mm grenades or 4.3mm conventional rounds. However, there was a conveyor running the pulse pods through, and he eagerly ripped it open, hundreds of the energy pods scattering across the floor. These were unloaded casings, and he cursed as he discovered it, battering at the conveyor to release the loaded pods. It finally took ripping the entire machine from the floor and flinging it down for him to finally get something out of it, four filled energy pods. It was about 120 rounds, and as he gathered them together, loading his nearing-empty weapon, he was determined to make each round count.

Hauling back to one of the turret-loaders, he spied one that was using liquid fuel for some type of gas-compressed weapon he couldn't identify, and tore into this machine as well, but going into the conveyor portion first this time, scavenging six of the large canisters of greenish-blue liquid. Smashing the metal lid of one and pouring it all over the turret loader still functioning, he ensured that a good portion of the liquid made it inside the machine and onto the outer surface as well, leaving a trail to the next machine from which he'd liberated the liquid, clearly caustic, making the metal warp as it pooled and roiled across the navy-blue steel.

Rex switched to the pulse rounds on his trusty rifle, took aim, and fired once at the green-blue ooze, smiling as it erupted into a green-hued flame, raced across the surface, into the machine, and detonated without warning. He found himself shaking his head and standing up from the floor several feet from where he once stood, glad he'd moved the other canisters of the fuel away first. Repeating the process with five of the other loaders with heavier ammunition, this time quite a bit more cautiously than before, he'd managed to destroy a lot of munitions, and started six very nasty fires. At the end of the task, he was more than happy to haul ass away; the air was getting thick with smoke he couldn't breathe for long, already seeing spots and sparkles across his vision, unsure if it was from his somewhat disoriented state or just the fumes of the fuel and fires.

Upon reaching the next door here, human-sized and with a typical Combine-created controller panel, Rex began to key it open, when another, louder explosion rocked the room, and flung debris into his line of sight from around the corner. Doubling back to check the damage, he found that one of the artillery loaders he'd sabotaged had trailed some of the fiery fuel or something down into the metal deck, and began blowing up stored munitions there, sending the whole unit tumbling down a smoldering hole and blowing up what was left on the level. He could see it wasn't the only thing that was beginning to do so. All five of the other machines were starting to do likewise, and as he began to back away, alarms blared.

His fusing of the alarms in the basement had come to an end—they'd found a way past the telltales with this last act of destruction, and he found himself mildly surprised—not that the alarms were blaring, but that they hadn't done so earlier. And to accompany the alarms, a bright red trail of metal began to head up *under* the plate flooring in his direction, moving for the next machine. It struck something vital in its path as it continued to crawl, the metal floor surface turning into a searing hot bubble of molten slag before popping explosively, sending bits of hot steel in his direction and a streamer of flame jetting straight upwards, gasping for more air and fuel before dying out slowly.

Running was now the only option, and as another *pop* of heated air and metal sounded off, Rex kicked at the door ahead, glad that it responded by opening up instead of refusing to budge, as so many other Combine-made doorways seemed prone to do during extreme situations. Emerging out into the center of the tower, standing on a translucent catwalk, he could see Combine coming to greet him. It was only three Scouts in thinner suits, each carrying the modified MP7M weapons with longer barrels and heavier ammo, but they were nothing as Rex fired into them with the pulse rounds, their thin armor not sufficient to withstand thirty rounds precisely flung at them. Tactically reloading, Rex retrieved one of the nicer MP7M sub-rifles, and as much of the 7.62mm ammunition he could.

It wasn't a very elegant solution, but it solved his lack of rounds soundly, and as he kept up the pace across the catwalk, it led into a tighter corridor that set a staircase up to what he didn't know, taking it anyway and emerging onto a second catwalk above the first. This had a massive machine in the center, dozens of screens, controls all along its surface, all lights and liquid crystal displays. Two Combine Scouts were milling around beyond it, and one white-suit Elite stood behind a panel, tapping away at what was probably a tactical order console.

The situation looked tenable until the door on the catwalk below burst from the doorway itself, shattering the lower catwalk and spraying hot metal out into the emptiness of the tower's center, alerting the Combine ahead and spurring the Elite to bark orders through the radio, tapping faster at the commands before him. Backing to the darkness of the stairwell, Rex waited for the two Scouts to approach. He doubted they would try to go to the bottom and cross the ruined catwalk, but as he listened to the radio traffic pass between the Elite and Scouts, he knew they'd be coming to check the damage.

Right on time they came around the corner and damn near ran into him, Rex grabbing the soldier on his left by the neck, and dumping pulse rounds into the chest of the Combine to his right as they gasped in surprise. His left hand easily pierced the seals around the half-breed's throat, and crushed the windpipe without any concerted effort, letting the slack body fall as he reloaded the rifle again, kicking the corpse to his right over and emerging out onto the command platform. The Elite was too busy to notice the re-entry until he was dying, Rex firing through the command screen the Combine soldier had up and his face buried in, pulse rounds cutting through the equipment and the Combine easily, sending the soldier toppling back to the armored glass floor.

Charging up and kicking the pistol out of the Elite's grasp as he drew it, Rex finished him off with a shot to the face, and slung the rifle to get his hands on the command controls. Entire screens were focused on the silo entry rather than the tower, and he realized they were going to attack the base yet again, even weakened as they were. Accessing hatches and bays for the vehicles and biomechanical creatures, Rex locked them down as tight as he could from here, the HUD showing him what to press and where to set things so the encryption on the locks were top-level, ensuring no regular flunky traitor or half-breed could access them.

He hoped it was enough to delay most of the heavier equipment from being used in the attack, and began to shut down as many of the smaller devices as it would allow him to. Decommissioning dozens upon dozens of the prepared Manhacks, and directing them to the trash compactor, deactivating the slower, more annoying floating cameras where they hovered and simply let gravity do the rest. He could see now that one screen was dedicated to the power levels and routing systems, and as he moved to it, he plugged the rifle into the console, the two technologies working alarmingly in unison.

"Try to get the info on the other two power levels. I've located a lift here we can use, so we don't need to haul through all this crap on foot."

It was a very slight feeling as the AI broke from his consciousness momentarily, and as it returned, Rex found himself looking at schematics for the two other main power stations in the tower, and grinned wildly. Grabbing up his weapon and leaving the command console in a state of uncontrolled chaos, Rex leapt up onto the lift as it ground down to meet him, running fingers across the simple console here, and activating it, selecting the 8th level, where the energy reactors were located. A deep, rhythmic hum began to signal as the lift was starting, and just in time apparently. He wasn't more than ten feet up from the command platform before more slag and hot metal erupted from the side of the tower two levels down, clipped a support he couldn't see, and sent part of the translucent catwalk from the second level bursting into shattered fragments down below.

The Command console he was just standing at also followed suit, and as it disappeared from his view, Rex focused his attention on what was up above him, pushing aside the fact that if he'd been a bit slower, he too would be falling down an endless pit right now. Ensuring the compound rifle was loaded with pulse rounds, Rex slung it across his back in favor of the MP7M, running the short slide once, and making positive the combat weapon sight was functioning, before extending the collapsing stock, hands tight on the double pistol grips. There was a long pause as the lift kept moving, and nothing flew down to greet him, moving ever upwards and gasping at the inside of the tower.

It was as technologically packed as possible, every wall laced with diodes, cables, conduits, others covered by the navy-metal plating, but bulging where a particularly large piece of operating equipment might have been stashed, and the stillness that emanated from all of the operating machines, it was disquieting and peaceful at the same time. There also seemed to be a strange haze to his vision gazing up and down along the center, as if the air had something fog-like in its consistency at a distance, but completely unnoticeable up close, no strange odors other than the faint taste of ozone, possibly from the equipment itself. Returning his gaze upwards, he found the lift coming up to another level, alarms still sounding, and crouched as he saw Elites running across the translucent platforms, no doubt being spotted himself.

Just as the lift crested the level to keep going, a hail of conventional fire was at him, and it took all he could manage to avoid it, lying flat on the lift and swearing that the rounds better not hit the lift controls, unable to even return fire as hot air surrounded him, the rounds cutting by, and one even glancing from the side of the headgear precariously. As the lift kept rising and rounds bounced from the underside of the lift's surface, Rex could only be thankful that one of them hadn't gotten the idea to leap aboard as the lift passed by. It took a moment for him to begin to piece it together as he considered why the last floor was so packed, but dawning came to him easily.

The AI was captured attempting to access schematics of the seventh level, and someone had the intelligence to lay a trap for him, but had not anticipated his gaining control of a lift and a command console with more schematic access than the AI could muster. Still the idea that he was fighting someone with brains was counter to the situation here as far as he could figure. The tower was weakened, the city was possibly being pacified by force or just in a state of complete disarray, and the amount of soldiers he'd seen lately were not as many as he'd had gunning for him before, a dramatic reduction in personnel. And the tower was throwing all its remaining resources at a silo full of human revolutionaries that were almost certainly already dead from the last attack where they'd taken so many people, and killed others without counting.

Was it a final attempt to win? Or to just defeat the adversaries in its path, win or lose? And even in a more extreme case, was this all a distraction to prevent him from getting to the top of the tower, a diversion to peel him away from the task at hand and go running to help his friends? His train of thought was interrupted as the lift halted at the 8th level, a straight navy-metal deck bolted along the center of the tower, several others stretching up above his line of sight, each at a placement that he guessed denoted another level. Ignoring the sights above him in favor of the solitary door here, Rex approached it carefully, pressed the button that opened the door, and stood puzzled by the way the door seemed to fold in on itself, tucking away to the sides, and unfolding as he passed by, sealing in the same strange fashion.

The lighting here was so intense the headgear actually had to polarize the lenses a bit, at least twelve to fifteen of the tall pillars of energy here, the strange orbs floating inside each, bouncing up and down rapidly, slowing, then repeating the process by speeding up again. It looked like molecules on a macro level, the orbs like giant atoms surrounded by pulses of light, trails of orbiting orbs...it was enchanting to look at, and as he snapped himself to the situation, he realized it was far too easy to be distracted by bright, shiny Combine lights. And perhaps that was precisely what the entire Combine technology basically came down to— get the subject to look away while you work them over, provide a focus that allows them to ignore what's happening.

It was the only thing his mind could circle to every time he tried to consider one of the half-breeds or traitor's positions, something had to be impairing rational thought in order to hand everything, lock, stock, and barrel, to the invaders after only seven hours of sustained combat. And soon, his thoughts rotated back around to what had started all of this—the orbs of energy. The pillars were no doubt powering something, and the volume of them meant they were important, no matter the fact that they had a single pulsing orb of energy in each, with fifteen of them in a massive circle around the tower. They could have been providing everything required beyond what mess he'd done to the geothermal tap below, and determined to figure out how to move or remove them, he opened fire on one of the orbs first, and felt disappointed that the rounds merely vanished.

Looking around for something to use as a club was almost entirely useless in effort, locating only a cable dangling from the ceiling, which he eagerly snapped free, and swung at the orb. The metal-encased cable made no noise as it too became nothing but a scattering of molecules, and the immense power behind the orbs disturbed him. He still didn't want to touch it, and he needed to figure out how to displace them without turning into nothingness, a cloud of ionized particles or whatever was happening to the objects he flung at them. Watching each orb as it sped then slowed, he heard the rush of gasses from equipment somewhere, and began to consider how each orb of energy was being slowed down after moving with so much power. The AI was in these thoughts, swirling about like a physical being in his mind, and he found scans of individual energy cells being displayed on the HUD, marking locations of pressure nozzles, energy siphons, and tanks of gasses embedded into the walls.

"What the hell...?"

It was hard to piece together what he was looking at from the start, but it soon snapped into place: inert gasses were continuously being pumped in and out of each 'field' around the orb. Each time the inert gasses were introduced, it stopped momentum inherent in the orb's production of energy, and then the gasses were removed before all momentum halted, allowing the orb to bounce rapidly against the energy collectors again. The AI could not identify the type of energy it was, but the use of power seemed incredibly efficient, and he realized each of the pillars he'd seen before, were no doubt powering something inside the facility. The concentration of the orbs here, not to mention the size of the energy collectors, were impressive for any display of alien technology, and he could only guess at what portions of the tower depended on such a source. A plan started to formulate again, and he consulted with the AI on how long it would take for the tower to destroy itself if he'd punctured one of the gas tanks or simply set all the gas levers to max.

Puncturing tanks would result in a six-minute countdown to overload on this level. Setting tanks to max dispersal would exhaust gas supply in twenty minutes, resulting in an overload seven minutes after that.

Rex moved away from the energy orb here, searched the room until he found a control console, and maxed out the gas output, watching as each of the orbs slowed then stopped entirely in the center of each cyclical field, all of the lights dimming to half power at once. He was completely and thoroughly stressing the tower's capabilities now, the reactions on the console slowing to a crawl, and the once-strong alarm reducing from a blare to a weak moan, a small timer appearing on the heads-up display signaling how much time he had left to get to the last power station and the hell out of the tower before it collapsed. Rex hoped his timing was perfect; otherwise, they'd potentially be picking pieces of him out from under the tower's remnants, and as that particularly unpleasant thought roiled past, he found himself snarling at the possibility, opening the door he'd taken to get in and emerging out onto the metal deck here.

Stepping onto the lift, which was still gratefully where he'd left it, Rex turned to the controls to move to the 17th level, the location of the last power station, when something swung down and landed on the surface of the lift. He was spinning with the

MP7M at the ready, muzzle sweeping the lift back and forth, as he squeezed the trigger on instinct. The first Judicator to land was surprised to arrive being fired upon, and the black-armored bodysuit tumbled out of sight as the 7.62mm rounds flattened against chest plate, but propelled the enemy backwards, over the edge of the lift. Rex never allowed the second to make it on his own, raising the sub-rifle and firing on the rappelling line instead of the soldier itself, and smiling as it snapped loudly, the enemy falling to the lift in a belly flop motion. Hauling his foot back like he was about to punt, Rex kicked the fallen soldier square in the face, the head whipping about wildly on shoulders and everything in between ripping loudly under the surface of the skin and the suit.

Weapon still aimed upwards, Rex crouched down next to the fallen adversary, eyes darting between the timer on his display and the emptiness above him, cautiously leveling the rifle at each platform he passed in case anymore unexpected company decided to arrive. He was realizing the lift's slowness as he began to get a bit antsy, foot tapping the glass, hands grasping and releasing the weapon in his hands over and over, a slight trickle of sweat running down the side of his head in the headgear, the temperature of the tower actually rising now. Trying to divert himself a bit by examining the dead Judicator at his feet, he found himself mildly shocked as he located one of the Combine-created M4 carbine clones, and quickly relieved the corpse of the weapon and all of the 4.3mm ammunition he carried, stealing one of the upper torso magazine slings to add to his own collection.

Soon he'd passed all of the platforms, and now there was an odd carrier system moving past and around the tower, into its walls and on an unseen course, the human-sized objects unfamiliar to him, but similar to the hooks that carried objects through the conveyor area below. All of them were empty now, but still mobile. The heat level was starting to bother him severely, and suddenly the lift kicked back into faster motion, the carriers speeding along normally, and the heat continuing to rise uncontrollably. Each breath was heavier than before, and sweat began to pour down his sides, the lift halting at the specified floor, not too far away from the peak of the small human-sized carrier track, Rex watching momentarily as they rose into the ceiling past a tight opening surrounded by dangling cables and other lines.

Finding only a door ahead, rather than a catwalk or platform to walk on, Rex moved to it and accessed the console controlling its opening, granting access with a few quick presses, and stepping inside as the panels separated, the immediate area beyond empty of a reception crew, and making his motions in easier. The heat was insane in this room as well, and he wished only that his sabotage had overloaded the air-conditioning system, instead of the thermostat going in this direction, the clothes he wore under the armor now sticky and matted to his skin.

It was hard to see anything in the zone, the lighting amped to max now, instead of dimmed, and he could only guess that the gasses from the energy fields below were starting to finally dissipate. The room led into a boxy chamber just beyond, a tall ceiling dominated by some type of grating that appeared to be sectioned, and operable, the walls decorated with catwalks and consoles. A smattering of the meandering parodies of life he was beginning to call *Workers* were manning several screens, positioning giant pillars of tech that ended in pulsing prods, four of them aimed at a massive globe of golden energy, translucent but swirling, hazy and distorting the view beyond of a large shaft from the room above.

MP7M still ready to roll and in his hands, Rex moved around the corner he was peering from, walked out into the huge chamber, and took careful aim on the furthest of the adversaries, firing once. The round was barely heard through the blasting of the enormous probes, and the Worker took the shot in the chest and toppled from the catwalk, the probe continuing uncontrolled. It took killing two of the others closest to him to finally grab the attention of the last Worker, pumping a few rounds into the scraggly form and watching it fall backwards, craters where its torso once was.

All of the probes now dominated the globe's surface, charging it wildly, and Rex observed it as he moved about the room, checking panels and controls for any sign of what this was, and failing until he came to the shaft at the back of the room. This was obviously a lift, and while he guessed it led only to the next floor, as he examined some of the oddities about the shaft, he realized that it was some type of emergency escape hatch. It had to be, with precautions in the odd Combine scrawl on certain sections indicating use only by a word he couldn't identify or pronounce, not translating into a language he could understand like the rest, remaining in Combine text.

Scanning a few other panels, he could see these were access controls for the lift, and had plenty of Do Not Touch labels on them in various forms, and a quick examination of the panel further allowed him to bolt the level closed from above, refusing access to anything. The locking bolts slid into place loudly and solidly, even from this distance visible as yellow-and-black striped bars of metal moving and slamming still, and he felt that he'd accomplished something just now, only he wasn't quite sure what it was. Turning back to the giant ball of orange light dominating the center of the room, he couldn't help, but gaze into it for a moment, and touched a not-quite-solid surface, withdrawing his hand before it entered the orb.

His examination of the energy ball ended as he began to walk away from the device, and swung to face the doorway beyond, only to find himself taking cover behind a panel, rounds searing by his head, thumping heavily against the torso armor, and one cutting by the Combine equipment and striking his left shoulder. There was no pain, and no wound, but a slow reverberation echoed through his body from the hit, and suddenly his hands and feet were on fire, pain lashing its way up his forearms, causing him to yelp in surprise, and almost dropped the MP7M as his fingers recoiled from the shockingly intense jolt.

Rolling back and away seemed to be the only option to gain any sort of view of the source of weapons fire. He did so cautiously, but quickly, picking out two soldiers—both Judicators with Combine-carbines—crouching at the entry, plucking one enemy up off the ground with a burst of the heavy ammunition, and barely making it back to cover before the next wave of rounds found its way to him, cutting up plastics and rending metal all around. Slapping flush to the floor and rolling back out, weapon raised and eyes down the CWS, Rex found his next target's forehead with a double tap, the body whipping wildly backwards to crumple to the deck.

Immediately, he was up and moving, one-handing up onto the console, leaping over the railing beyond, and landing onto the mesh deck around the orb itself, skirting its outer edge to police the Judicator bodies beyond, adding several more magazines of the wonderful ammunition to his now-restored stores of munitions. Where the hell had they come from was the only question in his mind as he moved to the door, accessing it easily and moving back onto the translucent lift, looking around for some sort of route to continue progressing by, knowing he was close to something, he could feel it in his bones. Spotting a pair of rappelling lines draped down the center of the transport shaft above, Rex hauled himself upwards until he was within reach of the moving conveyor of human-sized transport devices, grabbing one as it sped past and hearing it complain from the sudden addition of weight.

Holding on tightly, with his weapons swinging wildly on their slings as the device made each movement or adjustment in its path, he watched in silence as the device carried him up past the tighter entry, straight up for some twenty or thirty meters, before flattening out its path, each carrier taking a turn at stopping at a platform ahead, swinging open. Leaping from the carrier as it approached the platform, Rex landed solidly on both feet, hands still freed, weapons slung, and he softly closed the distance between the carrier line and the door ahead. This entry was intensely different, the first actual decorated door Rex had seen the Combine ever use. Panels of brown-patterned steels intermixed with the blue, a large white orb in the center of the two entrance panels glowing softly, perhaps a scanner or identifier of some sort, the only obvious piece of technology on the door's exterior, no knobs and no consoles within any distance of the door.

Without warning, the door scanned him, and for a second he froze, complying; would the device find the port, the implant, the armor, and decide to let him in? Or would it take one scan of the blood all over him and decide that anything draped in the internals of other Combine wasn't exactly something to permit entry to the room beyond? Standing totally still for several breathless moments, Rex was more than surprised when the doors only reaction was to slowly open, and softly strode into the chamber beyond. The room was intensely bright, brighter than it was supposed to be, Rex looking ahead and feeling very confused as his eyes tried to piece together what it was seeing. A creature of large proportions stood in front of a massive multicontrol panel. Covered in a strange metallic skin or armor, the creature had almost forty or more little limbs along its undercarriage, and even from the view from the rear, he could see the upper limbs were much more spiderlike, long and segmented, tapping at dozens of buttons.

"Just what the hell are you supposed to be?"

Rex had spoken partly to break the silence that drifted down, partly to ensure he was still capable of commanding his mind body into motion, the ghastly view before him disturbingly alien enough to cause waves of revulsion and disgust to crawl through him, realizing just how insectile this thing was. The size of its bug-like nature made it even worse for him, feeling as if he had a giant roach turning to look at him as it shuffled digits, forced huge muscles along the underside to shift, and spun incredibly fast for something so large.

The head and neck were both covered in a dome of transparent materials, and a pair of small, segmented eyes glared at him from a long forehead and short jaw, forming an odd set of what could be called facial features. And as the bug saw him, it took a step back, and began to screech in a horrible warbling voice, almost sending Rex pitching to the deck with his hands over the headgear's pickups. He couldn't remove his hands until the headgear resolved, and the screeching became a background noise, replaced by the sounds of a machine-like translation reaching his mind.

"...Noncitizen...in our presence...intolerable...intrusion of our space... demand...reason..."

It trailed on for several moments, making Rex's head swim trying to piece together the later parts being slurred and almost unintelligible. When the headgear finally resolved it, it developed into spoken words he could understand, chained together properly instead of sounding like it was coming through a translator having difficulty with the words being utilized.

"How dare a noncitizen enter our presence!? You have not been allowed an intolerable intrusion of our space! We demand a reason for your disruption before we recycle your components for nutrition!"

Clearly, the bug was not happy to see Rex, and it was getting rather forceful with him even from the beginning. How it knew he was a noncitizen, Rex had no clue, but the suit obviously did not fool the insectile creature behind a very human-looking desk like it fooled the scanner at the door. One spindly limb slammed down on a control on the panel behind the creature, and Rex could hear the door panels shut closed. Not bothering to turn around, or respond to the barbed interrogative, he began to walk forward slowly, hefting the composite rifle and switching the select-fire from the almost spent pulse rounds to the conventional magazine.

He began to take aim carefully, when the creature pressed another control on the panel behind in the same strange backwards-bending motion of segmented limb. As soon as the button was pressed, it began to travel away faster than he thought that size of mass could even think of moving, and Rex was mildly surprised that there was no trail of green slime as he tracked with the weapon. An intense hum from the door behind him had Rex spinning to face it, and just as he completed turning, a pillar of the white energy licked out from the orb, and struck him in the chest, flinging him backwards against the metal desk and control console, almost blacking out from the sudden intensity of the pain.

Spots danced before his eyes as he stood up slowly, the chestpiece of the armor ticking as it went from searing red-hot to a much cooler state, but thankfully it had stopped the energy blast instead of allowing it to carve straight through him. His hands were still gripped about the weapon, and as he stepped away from the massive crater where the desk once was and the panel once stood, his eyes tracked the giant bug to where it now reared, along the left side of the room, where two massive sealed panels placed over the entries in the walls began to slowly open.

As Rex raised the weapon again, he found both the energy emitter and the conventional barrel fused shut from the heat, and let the weapon hang on the sling instead, reaching for another. The giant insect-like creature was slamming angrily on consoles with all of the segmented limbs in a flurry of motion, the screech emanating loudly still.

"What have you done to our systems?!"

It was obviously trying to get the lift ready to lower into the rooms below. Rex could tell as he heard the lift jam against the emergency locks several times, and as he finally got the MP7M back around to bear on his target, pulling the trigger, he'd barely managed to clip off a few of the larger segmented limbs before the bug leapt into the lift, and slammed the panels shut.

"You will not stop us!!"

It didn't take a genius to see what the oversized insect was trying to do this time as the lift moved up and away, and the opposite panel unbolted just enough to show the glowing orb below, the massive floor beginning to grind open. Immediately, he was backing away and running towards the door that led him here, and as it refused to budge with him standing in front of it, he lashed out at it with his left hand clenched into a fist, and smiled as the orb's exterior shattered, and the ball of energy leapt away, bouncing off into the distant darkness of the tower's interior. Peeling the doors open to get them out of his way, his mind began to map the decent furiously, kicking the right panel as it refused to move, until it slammed flush with the wall.

The trip back down was going to be insanely difficult, he could tell, as he leapt out at the first of the carriers, and attempted leapfrogging to the next ahead, the movement of the carriers in the opposite direction which he needed to go, hampering his efforts. As he barely managed to not miss one carrier, he only hoped it got easier, continuing along. And then suddenly the conveyor stopped moving entirely, and he almost missed his target again, but did not curse this time. The fact that it was not moving was going to speed up his progress dramatically, and as he braced himself, he tore into rapid motion.

Going from one to the next without pause, finally he leapt all the way down through the tighter passage, and grasped onto one of the rappelling cables again, sliding down swiftly. Pace continuing without halt, Rex moved through this doorway, found the orb halfway up through the ceiling, and hiked up onto one of the nearby platforms, one-handing up…and suddenly, he was rolling onto the mesh flooring the orb sat on, standing up *inside* the swirling globe of orange energy. His breathing was an unending rattle, catching up with his exhausted mind, and as he kneeled now, his eyes drifted to the counter on the heads-up display.

He had less than three minutes to finish his time here before the tower overloaded, but he doubted he was going to get away. Why bother at this point trying to escape? There was little he could do to make it down to the ground floor without being dead first.

"What will the overload look like?"

Unknown, I only concluded that at the end of the timer, the tower's primary systems would be disrupted and begin a rate of rapid decay, either by explosive force or—

The rest of the response from the AI was cut off as the globe of energy passed by the tight chamber, the large powered probes falling silent and tumbling away as the platform entered a spire. The circular platform continued moving up around a hollow center, the top of the tower opening, and he could see the stars here, past the cloud cover, achingly close even from the bottom of the large shaft. The globe around him shifted colors, and became a blazing golden yellow, sounds of gunfire bouncing from its surface inspiring his reactions to aim on the source and pull his own trigger.

His rounds shot neatly through the energy barrier, while the Judicator beyond was not so lucky, dying from the three-round blast to the facial features, the headgear cutting apart. Even more rounds peppered the surface of the energy sphere, and he responded in kind, reloading as the weapon emptied, barely conscious of how many Combine were now flooding the section. They were expecting him to be *on* that twisting outer platform, running up through them, stopped by their makeshift barriers, repelled by their resolute stance in his path. But instead he'd found a different way up, one that involved less of a impedance, and more of a protected position, even if it was unintentional, it was now serving its purpose.

Scores of Judicators were dying now, and his MP7M fell silent as the last of the rounds were expended, letting the modified sub-rifle drop to the mesh deck, the Combine-made M4 clone ready and willing. Pounding out a string of the caseless rounds at his next target, Rex felt the air around him shudder as a pulse of white energy struck the surface of the sphere, turning a section darker orange. It temporarily allowed a clump of enemy fire through to ricochet around the interior, and forced Rex to hit the deck as the others around attempted to take advantage of the hole in the field. He kept firing up through a still-protective section at one of the repair bots on the edge of one platform, moved into position by Combine soldiers.

The bot detonated like the others he'd fired upon, killing several more Judicators, and starting another alarm that had Elites in white armor, red-eyes staring endlessly, flooding the upper platforms he hadn't reached yet. But as the field regenerated itself and sealed shut, it became a series of attacks like shooting drunken fish in a barrel, pouring out almost every last round Rex had in an effort to expend the ranks of enemies before him. And the facility began to help in his conquest, the lights yet again blaring to full power, consoles overloading, cables setting alight from the power being pumped through them, panels of interlaced equipment and monitors exploding outwards, until finally much of the platforms themselves began to weaken and topple, devices attached to them overpowering and detonating or ceasing to function altogether.

Sparks and flame shot everywhere, fires starting alight blazingly bright, melting navy steel, shattering lights, monitors, diodes, everything left intact, spraying groups of concealed soldiers, destroying mounted guns, and sending bodies tumbling down the shaft below with a storm of other debris. His weapons were now empty, but the tower itself had become his weapon. It was going to die today, and it was going to help him while it was doing it. It had no choice now, he'd demanded of it, and now it was going to give him what he'd asked of it: Destruction.

Fires and flames belched from conduits, more explosions, dancing lights, sparkles, bouncing from the orb and adding to its glow, creating a maelstrom of chaos, noise, objects, light, and death. Combine were dying all around him now in increasing measures, and the timer grew precipitously close to its end, signaling that his final confrontation was either now, or it was truly never. Right on time, the lift came to the top of the spire, three points of the tower around the circling platform, and a translucent catwalk leading from the orb, to a series of expanded controls, a bank like none other, a screen dominated by the night sky, mapping the stars, and only the Combine knew what else. The massive creature stood at this console now, and the chittering, warbling screech of alien language could be heard even over the din of the whirlwind of destruction below. The headgear again had problems separating out the sounds and making it into a proper string of language, but he could see now, the voice was coming through the console.

"Must…now…we cannot…no other option…delay too critical…time of…essence…"

A single probe of energy hovered over the face of the orb, and set one of the sides to the permeable state of darker orange-hued, and as the creature whirled about, Rex strode from the center, onto the catwalk. The being screeched horridly at him, a second one emanating from the console in similar form, and he ignored what the HUD tried to translate to him, only yelling aloud.

"There is no escape. Not from me, not anymore!"

And he charged into the creature's width, weapons empty but mind uncaring, body raring, hands willing, blood pumping. Adrenaline was his ammunition now, and it fired into his arteries like nitrous into an overpowered, overworked engine, and he exploded into frenzy, feeling his thinking-self drop away, but allowing it this time, reveling in it, in the sheer brutality he began to employ. The insect towered over him. Its tonnage was that equal to several of the armored personnel carriers stacked onto one another. And it attempted to use this to its advantage as he slammed into it, all of the remaining limbs latching onto him, and the sheer weight of the creature pressing down.

Shoving back intensely, raging aloud, he shoved his right fist into the abdomen as hard as possible, and felt the metal material of the fabric rip like paper under the force, the suit popping like it was pressurized, a blast of air and green blood spattering Rex as he continued assaulting. His left hand of blackened claws became a reaper's scythe, cutting the sectioned limbs from sockets almost too easily, grasping onto great handfuls of the suit and ripping it away. He kept doing this until finally, he had enough foot and handholds to physically climb up the front of the creature, and smash his armored boot through the faceplate, shattering glass, and crushing the creature's head in one motion.

The entire corpse fell, and he toppled back with it, pinned to the surface of the catwalk as it landed, cracking loudly along its surface, and the immense weight was now more threatening than before. He had no leverage to get the damned thing off of him, and the only saving grace was the green ooze pouring from the wounds, which smelled rancid, but made the motion easier to slip away, the blood making the catwalk slick enough to get free.

Stumbling back to the sphere, Rex stepped back inside resolutely, and as an afterthought, reached for the Desert Eagle pistol still on his hip, and fired once at the probe aimed at the orb, smiling as it shattered, the globe of energy returning to its golden state. The screeching was still coming from the console on the platform ahead of him, but as he holstered the pistol, and stood waiting for his destiny, he was glad this was finally over. He would die in the explosion, but it would take the tower with him. It was good enough for him. Molly and Maurine would be safe. And he wouldn't be here, another monster gone from this world. Crouching down and whispering to himself and the AI, he knew he was ready.

"And so it ends…"

The tower below him shook. Metal toppled. Light flared. And he gazed upwards, staring at the stars through the energy, hoping that this was enough. Rex could feel the explosion, felt it in his bones the instant it happened, and the force of it threw him around the inside of the orb like a toy, blacking out after the third or fourth bounce, he couldn't tell.

FALSE BOTTOM

Something was distinctly wrong with the outcome. Rex was waking up. Rolling over and feeling agony ripple through his muscles, dirt and debris scattered from him, and as he stood, he found himself in the center of a crater, where a two-story building once sat intact, now just a pile of rubble. Kicking rocks and concrete from his path, Rex moved around a wall that only half-stood, resting against another. Passing by another toppled section of wall, he limped out through the doorway, and into the street. The tower was gone, and the massive orbiting halo was no longer a perfect circle, now two larger halves and a dozen or more fragments raining down to burn in the atmosphere.

There might have been cheering somewhere, or it was just the dull roar of the wind, and Rex didn't take the time to differentiate the two—he was too busy leaning against the wall, trying to recover—he felt like he'd been bruised every possible place there could be a location, and even a few new ones. The Combine clone rifle was shattered to nothing, the MP7M was nowhere in sight, and the composite rifle the AI was housed in had been mauled badly. It was mostly intact but by no means functioning, and he was unsure if the AI was safe inside of it. The Desert Eagle was still amazingly buckled into the holster, and he thanked his lucky stars for the belt, counting the remaining .357 magazines softly to himself as his body sang songs of agony to him. He was beyond tired and wired, unable to close his eyes, but so close to passing out again, he teetered back and forth on the brink.

The tower was indeed nothing but a few spires of bent steel that jutted from the ground in various places, fires glowing in the coming dawn…and he had no idea how long he'd been unconscious. Forcing himself to his feet, grimacing under the surpassingly intact and functioning headgear, he took a long look around, snarled once for good measure and began to slowly walk away from his landing site. He wasn't exactly sure where he was going, but as his body led him away, his mind knew he wasn't supposed to have survived. This wasn't supposed to be happening this way. There was something distinctly disturbing about still being alive after having given up on the chance of it, and now he felt lost, rudderless in a sea he had not anticipated.

One thing was for certain, he didn't know when it was coming, but the man in the blue suit would be showing up again, he had no doubts of it. That was the one factor that could have done anything to help him survive the explosion he'd just caused—his line of thought was cut by a sound of a string of detonations going off, and immediately he was into motion. The streets were littered with more debris than usual, a line of fires alight along one wall, under the furniture, and quickly growing to encompass the whole building. Rushing by with the wave of heat pressing down on his side, a pillar of stone threatened to fall onto him, and he shoved at it subconsciously while hauling ass, watching it arc away from him and shatter into the street.

Coming up onto a large pile of remnants, resembling a thrashed Combine APC covered with trash and burning refuse, Rex slipped around it and came to one of the former *safety zones* the Civil Patrol had set up. He found it was a chaotic mess, civilian survivors rioting against anything that resembled Combine tech or emplacements, CPs dead and bleeding out, scattered around the former control zone in a pattern of when they were killed.

The blue jumpsuits were still prevalent amongst the people here, some openly weeping over corpses, others smashing consoles, burning Combine bodies, and collecting fallen weapons.

But all wore a grim mask of victory, no matter how pyrrhic, the destruction of the tower and its horrible halo a permanent sign of humanity's dissatisfaction with the alien invaders. Of course, none of that mattered when the first of them saw him, and all they could see was the armor, and there was no second waiver of thought or spoken word. Instead, he found himself running the opposite direction as a mob of rescued humans began to chase him, and in a split-second decision, he leapt to the top of the ruined APC, climbed the refuse that wasn't burning, and rolled onto the roof of a ruined building, amid a forest of antennae and piping, long useless but enough to slow him down as he ran.

Grabbing a particularly nasty-looking section of wrought iron pipe, he tore it free from its rusting base, and kept moving, reaching the edge of the building and leaping off, into the center of the courtyard the group once occupied. The others were far too busy trying to climb the APC he'd used as a stepping stone to see him hop back down, and as he bolted across the clearing, leaping over dead bodies and running past one mourning woman, he ignored her screams and stopped at the one intact panel remaining, the controls for the huge panels that formed a blockade here.

Wedging the broad end of the makeshift club into the console, he quickly tore the cover of the console off, reached in with his left hand, and grasped as many of the cables as he could. Clenching tightly, Rex could feel the strange limb do its destructive work to the electronics, and overload the device. The opposite side of the panel exploded outwards, and the giant barricade ground open. He had no time to celebrate the action, ripping his hand and the wrought iron free from the console and running through the opening, the mob now following him again, albeit a bit more puzzled at why he'd broken open the barricade placed by the Combine, causing several to pause in their chase, and shrug him off.

Rex kept up his pace down the center of the street beyond, weaving past one pair of wrecked cars, and leaping up across a third vehicle rolled over in the center, and found poorly aimed rounds coming his direction from ahead. CPs had formed their own secondary holdout area here in a four-way intersection with two lanes completely blocked off, and fired pistols at him from their makeshift cover, at least five of them huddled together to protect themselves from the rioting citizenry.

Bodies were splayed out on the pavement where others had stumbled upon the Civil Patrol, and the sight flared like a nova in his head, roaring without slowing down, leaping up over their barricade and killing the first with a side swing to the head, the wrought iron club ripping off the skullcap of his opponent, and drawing a gasp from the crowd of pursuers behind him. Many had halted completely behind the vehicles he'd moved past, and others stopped to watch as he tore into the five CPs ruthlessly. Not a single enemy had anything more than a pistol or a scream to lend to Rex, killing all before they could respond, a whirlwind of angst unleashed on the nearest target. Flinging one battered body away from him and leaping up onto the barricade around the dead CPs, Rex took a single, long look behind him at the crowd there, felt the chilly air brush along his gaze, and turned away from the stunned audience.

Charging along the surface of the thrashed vehicle he stood upon, he spotted a city transit bus, and leapt atop of its still roof, bolting across and landing roughly at a cul-de-sac as he jumped down, recognizing the gaping hole in the wall here, and running through. It was a stark contrast to the ruined city, being back out in the desert just on the opposite side of the wall, but one very familiar thing still remained, the blasting of weapons, the chattering of pulse rifles, and the sources of light they caused when being fired. Running towards the sounds of combat was all he could do presently, passing up the bunker that had been deliberately collapsed from the inside in favor of the wrecked APC just beyond.

This one had been spray-painted with the orange symbol the revolutionaries used, the forward end mashed by an unknown means, but the rear doors and ramp standing wide open. Heading in, he found it stank of corpses on the interior, and immediately doubled back, headgear scanning the sands as the sun began to dawn to the east. A trail of footprints and tracks led him back to the main entry of the silo, where he found a small ground war carrying on, defenders around the main vehicle bay of the base instead of around the tight path leading to the ground-level lift. They were holding off a mass of the swarming Combine scouts, one Judicator, and a handful of Elites organizing the remaining bunch together into an assault team.

Moving up silently as he surveyed the zone for surprises, right on time one lit up on the far side of the group of amassed Combine, a turret on one of the APCs using the combination launcher and pulse weapon to blanket the area with explosions and dirt, making return fire nearly impossible and kicking up a lot of sand, allowing the ground pounders to slowly approach. Eyes searching for something useful this time, he found the shape of the VW bus dragging his attention away, and ran across the dark desert to the shattered hulk, roof turret ruined, and wheels on the right side melted down to puddles. But in the rear, still safely secured in the shockproof container, sat the LAW tube, and he snatched it up eagerly, hoping the damned thing still functioned after all this time, feet scrambling across the dirt.

Someone noticed his presence and the turret lit the remains of the VW bus up, but the soldiers were far too focused on the assault at the main bay to stop Rex. He slid to a halt on one knee, unlocked the ends of the light armor weapon, extended the tubes, took a solid grip and sighted through the viewfinder, then mashed down the ignition trigger. The aging one-use weapon leapt to life in his hands, and as the rocket sped to its destination, he let the dead tube drop, grasping onto the Desert Eagle and watching the explosion tear the turret loose from the remaining APC, and set the surface ablaze.

Finally, some of the Combine deemed him enough of a threat to focus on, but by then he was already running forward and firing with the heavy pistol, killing three Scouts before leaping into the group physically. Letting go of his weapon in favor of grasping onto the Judicator in front of him by the shoulders, Rex whipped the Combine around into a pair of others, heads coming together with much force and driving them backwards to the dirt, and knocking the Judicator senseless.

As the flow of enemy commands halted to the soldiers, panic slowly crept in across the remaining ranks, even as Rex finished the Judicator off with bare hands, twisting the neck until it turned twice, and letting the body fall. Pulse rounds struck the chest and shoulder of the suit now, accurate fire that forced him to fall back, and sent his nerves jangling as he moved, hands shaking, chest heaving. But the damage had been done to the Combine's stability, and it didn't take long for the group still behind to break out into a fleeing run, all of whom were quickly cut down as the revolutionaries closed the gap between the main bay and the Combine's former position.

Leaning back and sitting down on the rough surface, Rex attempted to force his body to relax, and failed miserably, feeling himself shake and shiver in reaction. Eyes searching the ground, he found his pistol and slowly limped over to retrieve it, bending down and grasping it to the sound of a rifle cocking in his direction. Standing to his full height, reloading the weapon cautiously, and turning about with the piece holstered, Rex faced a young man with an MP7 leveled at him, and couldn't help but scare him.

"You pull that trigger and you're going to regret it."

The revolutionary froze, reached for a tactical radio, clearly stolen from a Judicator or Elite, and spoke into it softly, voice wavering.

"I've got a live one over here."

The weapon aimed at him didn't waver, and he figured he should try to identify himself.

"Might as well tell them Rex is here."

Where he expected a look of recognition he found only confusion, the young man repeating what he just said into the radio cautiously, hands still on the weapon. The radio responded loudly, and Rex could hear Molly even from this distance.

"Do. Not. Fire. Get your ass to—"

Of course, the transmission was cut, and a quieter, somewhat garbled command came through, the words unintelligible, but causing the young man to stiffen, and steadily aim the weapon. Other revolutionaries near the bay door began to mutter over the communication, shifting about uneasily with weapons half-raised, but not approaching where Rex and the young man stood, clearly disconcerted about the exchange over the channel, but unwilling to forcefully intervene. Rex spoke during the tedium to the young man.

"Listen to Molly, you don't want to make me hurt you."

Eyes locked onto him with hostile intent as he spoke her name, and Rex kept on speaking, preparing himself, tensing for when he would have to tear the weapon from the young man's hands and...

"Who are you, don't you recognize my name? How did you get to the silo base?"

Somehow he'd managed to flip the situation around, and the eyes glaring at him softened, Rex relaxing a hair. It almost seemed as if the young man was going to respond to the question when the main bay became a center of activity, the lift was actually working now, lowering empty and raising with the sight of Molly, in her black bodysuit, approaching the area quickly.

"You belay that last order, you understand?"

She said it with finality, and the weapon lowered. Standing here, no facemask, goggles, or headgear to obscure her face, she looked determinedly gorgeous, and Rex felt a small hope inside of him that maybe—just maybe—she would see a day of normality soon, where she wouldn't have to carry a weapon just because she was human. Relaxing completely, Rex waited where he was, glad that perhaps things were over, for now. He almost took a step forward, but she continued speaking.

"Rex, would you mind waiting out here?"

Turning to the young man, she gestured him inside, and motioned around to the old campsite he'd remembered from before.

"We'll meet you back out here soon, just need to...settle something first."

Rex nodded again as they headed off to the base, and took his time walking back around to the campfire, retrieving the carbine-clone from the dead Judicator out of this bunch, ensuring the weapon was loaded and taking the rest of the ammo with him before moving away from the bay and the bodies around it. The small fire pit was dead and cold, leaving darkness on the area that seemed serene and threatening at the same time, and as Rex checked the area, he found the stash was still in place instead of being a crater, and hauled it open. It was still rather empty, but at the bottom sat some tinder and a starter box for the fire, which he quickly gathered up and took to the cold pit, helping himself to a couple lengths of hacked wood from the stash's interior as well.

He'd no more than started the fire when he heard the sounds of the vehicle bay moving, and an APC came around the bend from the dunes piled around the silo, halting at the former scouting position, and the rear opening up. As Molly and Maurine stepped from the back, Rex stood up from the spot at the fire, and removed the headgear slowly, wanting to see them with his real eyes again. They sat across from him, and he returned to a crouch, keeping the dwindling fire going until it finally burned under its own volition.

The silence that carried on was not unwelcome, but rather, accepted with open arms. He'd never had the chance for silence like this before, only the wind or the fire crackling disturbing the quiet for some time. No one came to bother them, and the driver of the APC sat behind the cockpit door without saying a word. Rex did take the time to gaze around him, but eventually his eyes rest upon Maurine and Molly, grateful to be seeing them again, to be sharing space with them, like Old Home Week, except maybe a little more skewed chaotically than any aging house before it.

They both seemed rather preoccupied, but each time they looked at him, he could see two things. One was the gratefulness to see him again, he could tell, the same feelings he bore for them, glad to be back around him again, glad to know Rex was still in the land of the living. The other, it spoke of apprehension and regret and maybe even the fear of the unknown, for he had changed greatly while he was gone, and the few alterations they'd been witness to no doubt unsettled them. Finally, he broke the long silence with a question that simply had to be answered, "Do you know if the suppression field is still up?"

Instead of answering verbally, Maurine simply reached out her hand and grasped his tightly, and he could feel the disquieting discomfort growing. Reluctantly he let go of her warm hand.

"Damn it," he said the words with a tone of finality about the subject, and as his mouth cursed, his mind raced.

It still was not over until that field was gone. Every Combine on the face of the planet could keel over from exhaustion right now and the field would still kill them, keep the entire population from ever growing past the battered number that remained now, and would suffocate the *last breath* out of the species as a whole. The mere thought was enraging, and they could see his disgust about the topic welling up in his eyes. Pulling the damaged and barely intact composite rifle from the sling, he held it out for

Molly to see, handing it over the campfire; she took one look at the beat-up weapon and grimaced, handing it back.

"We'll head inside and deal with that soon. Just giving people some time to rest, and be asleep when we head back inside."

Rex caught himself almost asking why they were waiting to go into the silo, when he realized he damn well knew the reason—he *was* the reason. And even that disquieted him further, knowing that while Molly and Maurine were here, it was only because they'd shared something with each other—if he was just another stranger, he would be out at this fire, alone, and wouldn't be seeing the interior of the silo, no matter how many people were asleep or awake at the time. The distance his humanity had traveled away from him, this whole time, it now weighed on him in totality, asked him what he'd become, and why. His self-introspective reverie was broken by the sound of the driver speaking over a loudspeaker to Molly and Maurine.

"O'Hare says it's clear now."

Everyone slowly stood from the fire, Rex enjoying the clear night, and the momentary respite, and Molly waved them towards the rear of the APC, climbing aboard herself and closing the door once everyone was inside. The drive was short and uneventful, and soon they were clambering back out inside the underground vehicle bay, O'Hare there to greet them, complete with his old M16. Rex took a gaze around the bay, and spotted two other armored personnel carriers, both damaged heavily, and both being repaired by a single technician each. O'Hare was busy speaking with Molly, and Rex caught him say something about how they couldn't sleep, and nodded to himself, knowing just how hard it had become to sleep lately, unless he was being knocked out by force or blown up. Ensuring the headgear was properly secured to the ammo belt around his waist, Rex moved off a couple of feet and spoke to the AI.

"Go ahead and secure yourself, and download to the rifle module."

Are you sure?

He smiled to himself, but felt no pangs of regret as he spoke again.

"I'm sure. Things are not well here, and if they...find me unsuitable to remain here, you need to stay and help them."

There's something you aren't telling me...

This time he responded without pausing.

"Don't worry about it, sort for transfer."

And without another word being spoken between them, the AI removed itself from his mind, and returned to the module safely. Locking off the rifle and removing the jack from his port, Rex slowly returned to the group and handed the weapon over to Molly, talking softly and mentioning food and a cot for the night. O'Hare didn't quite look at him while talking, but spoke to Molly when she turned to face O'Hare.

"We can't find Nana, but most of the food stores are intact, if you want to put something together."

O'Hare strode off silently after that, walking to the door to the kitchen from the bay, and leaving it open before moving to another door, going through and shutting it behind him. Molly and Maurine gave Rex an off glance, not understanding why the former sergeant left so brusquely, but not willing to carry it into an awkward conversation. Instead, they simply broke into the food, and trying to be careful not to overdo it, made large enough sandwiches to satiate them for now, using what remained and finding everything sealed and labeled where it sat. Clearing space around the huge metal island in the center of the kitchen each pulled a stool up, and they sat, and ate, in peaceful silence for some time. It was obvious no one wanted to ruin the moment, but Molly broke the silence with a question.

"So, where did you go?"

Everyone exchanged glances casually, Rex mostly trying to verify the casual part of the question before responding.

"China first then Africa, Ukraine after that, not sure how far to the east I traveled in Europe; landed in the Urals, in Russia, for a bit, and then Xen for a while. And from Xen, I got here, don't ask me exactly how, I'm still confused by it myself."

He had to stop to remember the friends he'd seen fallen in the Xen labs and in the former Black Mesa zone. It was a sad thing, to be forced to halt to be able to vaguely recall them, but he'd tried shoving the thoughts as far away as possible when he found those bodies.

"It was an uncontrollable trip for the most part. Once I got to the Ukraine, I began to try to change course on my own, get back here faster. It didn't exactly work out the way I intended it to."

More silence now drifted over the whole kitchen as they ate, and Rex knew deep down this conversation wasn't over, could tell the way Molly stood when she was finished eating, rinsed her plate, and left the kitchen. Maurine finished soon after, and as Rex stood from his empty plate, she turned to him.

"So when do you leave again, Rex?"

The way she said it crushed him, smeared him like a bug on the windshield of life, and he knew he was just a step away from being wiped from her life forever.

"I don't—I don't know if I'm supposed to leave or stay. It's not up to me anymore. It never was."

She wasn't buying the simple explanation anymore, and Rex could tell that she'd seen something, knew something about his predicament.

"He's been here, Rex, while you were gone. He spoke to me, I don't know how, not like he walked up and started talking, but you *must* know how he does it…"

And now Rex felt partially paralyzed by the fact that the man in the blue suit was interfering in the lives of those he cared about, invading their dreams personally. But she continued on anyway.

"Damn it, I know something was supposed to happen when you left, I knew that you'd come back, but I didn't know when, and now I know you're going to leave for the second time, maybe even before you do. But don't you dare let that mean to you that you shouldn't come back, Rex. And while I might understand it, there will be others who won't. Like Tank and O'Hare."

He felt helpless in this situation, and it ground at his will like shattered glass under his feet.

"I would stop this if I could, Maurine, you know that. And I would never stop coming back. What troubles me? What's going to happen while I'm gone? What if Mr. Mysterious shows up again, and this time he's not carrying happy omens? I already understand that my job isn't finished, and the task won't be done until that field is down, and maybe every Combine left is dead and buried. But maybe even then, it won't stop this stranger from interfering, won't prevent him from being able to bend us to his will, and force us to do his dirty work."

Shifting about slowly, he was unsure if what he said next was even necessary.

"Listen, I love you, gal, and there's nothing that will stop that. And when I do leave, if I have to, I hope you understand. I'll be back, again. Nothing will stop me, not when it comes to the space between me and you."

And with that said, he slowly walked up to her, embraced her tightly, and kissed her once softly. Letting go and turning away, he headed for the door, leaving her there alone.

"I need to talk with Molly. See you soon."

Rex headed away from the kitchen with a leaden anchor in his heart—he *did* love her, more than he realized at first, but it ripped apart his insides at the thought of what he had to do, being forced to bear the brunt of combat for the strange man, and being separated from this home was worse than being torn from his normal life with his father. It was like the goddamn portal storm in Scottsdale again, alien invaders corrupting people around him to try and kill him, others dying, even more suffering from the acute shattered humanity syndrome, uncaring but willing, fighting but not feeling. He'd been doing the latter for far too long now, and it had only driven him further away from his goals, to be here, to start anew after it had all been wrest apart. And now he was paying for it, the price being the friendships of others and the security of their well-being. Turning through the main hall, Rex approached the guest room, guessing that was where Molly would be, and found it empty instead.

A frown forming on his features as he left the room and closed the door, he began to walk back through the galley, when he felt eyes on him, and the shuffling of feet. Turning in the direction where the noises came from, he found himself moving deeper into the first floor, past a small station and a line of computers he didn't recall seeing before, and into a hallway of doors, a young boy standing next to Molly at one of the several doorways. He was looking up at Molly with despair hidden behind coiled eyes, and as Rex paused long enough to let the moment sink in, he realized the young boy was armed as well, one of the USP pistols tucked into a waist holster, and a band of the black, flexible metal armor wrapped about the chest. The sight was familiar, and the smile on Molly's face as she comforted the young man was not to be forgotten. As she looked up, the young man backed behind her just a bit.

"He can't speak. We found him in one of those elimination patrols you were so fond of hunting down."

She bent to one knee and pointed at Rex, her other arm about the young boy's shoulders. "That's Rex, that's the one I told you about, the man that saved me."

The young boy's eyes went agape, and his mouth formed a gasp as his jaw dropped. Rex held the question in his eyes as he looked to Molly to explain.

"He thought you were just another Combine. The armor confused him." She gently pat him once, and ushered him inside the room, closing the door. Turning back to face Rex, she waved him down the hall to the far end.

"C'mon down here. We have plenty to discuss." Rex nodded and followed her motion, noting that she had grown up in the time he was gone. How long had it been, again? He wasn't sure. For the longest time, things were moving so quickly, and he had no real sense of what time it ever was, what day it could have been—none of it mattered up to a certain point, the days blurred simply because they were hours spent under the harmful wings of the vulture-like alien species preying upon them. And even as they entered, despite her claims of all they had to say, the silence carried onwards for some time, Molly finally breaking it.

"So where did you really go?"

The question set him back a bit, and he tried to recover as best as possible as he responded, "I really *did* go to all those places I told you about. And it happened…faster than I care to think, slower on the other hand, far too slow. I spent all that time pursuing some way to get to you, to get back home, and somehow, I lost everything I knew along the way. And when I finally *do* get back to somewhere I know I've been before, it turns out to be something horrible beyond imagination, or even worse, like finding Doc Hernandez dying, after finding his security friend, revolutionaries everywhere, littered across every floor in every room."

Rex broke off for a moment, realizing his tone was rising, the intensity of the rooms coming back to him quicker than expected, then continued calmly. "And then I realized that it's not a Combine prison or battle site I've arrived at, its home, with all the people ruined. Tommy gone, Nana missing or dead, Doc dead, and an endless number I don't know about. All of our former military food chain gone till it's down to you, leading them with Maurine and several others being kidnapped, imprisoned in cold storage; a miserable, hatred-consumed Tank; and a darker, meaner O'Hare under your command as the only two people left…not even counting that hermit, Harry, that lives in the outer bunkers. And despite all of that, you pull survivors together, but certainly not because I've come back. Rather, it seemed that you could have done it without me here—and in the end, the only thing I can truly *know* is that you're all still alive. Beyond that, I'm confused as to what to expect."

She mulled over the comment only a second.

"If this is about that young man drawing down on you out there, I'll remind you, you run around in Combine gear. And you haven't been here; our descriptions of you don't exactly fit anymore either. You look like you took a return trip to the lab rather than anything else." The abrasiveness of her tone was unexpected up to a certain point, but the fact was Rex knew this was coming.

"It happened each time I blacked out or took a serious amount of damage, as far as I could tell. It's not amusing to me, either, Molly, but it just happened. It's not something I can control—if it was, I would not look like this—" Pointing at his left arm, he flexed the razor claws that his fingers had become, and the talons on his feet clacked against the concrete bunker floor nervously. "Well, whatever the hell I look like, it doesn't change the fact that I have come many a mile to be with my love and child." As Rex said that, he moved close, held her in a hug, and kissed her forehead. Maybe he wasn't crazy to want to be home, but he was certainly feeling insane right now, with only part of him relaxed. The world was still capable of taking a potentially nasty turn, and there was still the issue of the unspoken Combine threat, if there was one anymore.

"So what should we expect, Rex? What's next?"

She pushed him away a bit to ask the question and look into his face as he responded, and as he spoke, it was instinct that drove the answer out.

"We'll face it, together, until it drives us apart again, the only thing we can do, so we can strive to be together once more. It seems to be the brutal habit of this world to force that upon us."

Molly's eyebrows furrowed in concentration, and turned away, moving to a table of maps and diagrams, clearly already planning something, but they wouldn't be speaking of that, just yet. She waved to a chair, and he grabbed it, sitting down slowly for the first in ages, not for food or sleep, just relaxation. She began to take notes, and spoke absentmindedly as he watched.

"Let's go over a few problems I had, then we can sleep. I want you to take some notes for me if you don't mind. Maurine's room is two doors down on the left, by the way."

Rex smiled and motioned for her to continue.

FOREBODING REQUEST

Rex jerked awake in a crouched position, and groaned as he stood, feeling exhausted and sore. He'd been sitting outside Maurine's room ever since he finished the conversation with Molly, and as he shuffled to consciousness, he realized he must have nodded off. The hall was dark, forebodingly so, and he stumbled his way through the lack of light resolutely, moving back through the console room, ignoring readouts and cameras hastily put into place in favor of leaving the newer command zone for the cafeteria. But stepping into here was surreal in nature, the light bending and softening somehow, his movements slowing. He began to breathe harder as his adrenaline started off like a race car, and as he looked around the cafeteria, Rex could see wing-tip shoes being illuminated by an arc of light, everything else beyond shrouded in darkness. And when he spoke, Rex showed his displeasure.

"You. I was wondering when I'd see *you* again. Why the hell am I still alive?!"

There was no instantaneous response, no break in the silence that carried on long after his voice echoed away, and his lips formed a snarl, one catching on a sharpened tooth in his mouth, angering him further. He didn't understand why he was there, why he'd been allowed to return to this place, and see everything falling apart. And now that the bastard in the blue suit was here, he wasn't speaking, wasn't explaining, wasn't extrapolating on anything, and Rex could barely contain his fury. He wanted to fling tables, screens, and chairs everywhere, mash bone and rend flesh. But the bastard behind the table sat still.

"Answer me, now."

He gestured hard at the ground with his left hand, trembling with disgust and enraged beyond mere conversation. He wanted answers, and he wanted them fast. The lack of them was intolerable, destructive, and ruinous. And even as he thought the words, he *knew* the man could hear them, could hear everything he perceived, however he was doing it no matter to Rex anymore, not the primary concern on his mind. Instead, his mind was roaring on a path of disappointment, regret, and building angst— he'd been lied to, deceived, tricked all along, fighting what he *knew* was the enemy, but for all of the wrong reasons. And as those last thoughts trailed off into the darkness, the feet began to move under the table. The light trembled, the air grew thick, and a rush of pressure surrounded him.

Everything moved slower, achingly extending the motions the shined shoes made across the floor, the scratching of leather across concrete grating on his very last nerve, the light swinging gently as imperceptible motion struck it from a distance, and finally the blue suit could be seen, dark eyes in unsettling, smiling features.

"And here I thought you'd be more satiated at being home again, Mr. Rex. No, don't bother trying to respond. I already know what you've done, all the things you've been through. And you're right, I know what you think of me and all this progress…you might not see it, not yet, but you will eventually…and right now, you're wanting some answers. What shall I tell you, Mr. Rex? That this was all necessary? You know that. Maybe you want to hear me congratulate you? Well, congratulations, Mr. Rex. You've still not yet outlived your usefulness to…me and others. Perhaps you don't understand, perhaps you never will, and even then, there is the chance that you don't care…"

Rex couldn't exactly move, but he could track the blue-suited man as feet shuffled around him, light shifting, darkness fading.

"Well maybe I should give you the chance to change that, Mr. Rex. We're here, now, for you to do that."

And the man was right, he stood in front of the cages, the horrible, bloody, rusted cages, the younger version of himself twitching and snarling inside, unconscious. His hands gripped onto the cage door tightly, and he realized, he could set himself free, end it all for himself now...but even at this moment, he stood, unmoving, unable to continue. Here he was, standing at the ultimate choice, poised at the final decision, and yet he could not make it, felt his will refusing to budge. And as he stood there, dawning realization hit him like the sight of the sunrise. It was the sound around him, the cacophony of screams, wails, crying voices calling out.

Turning about, blurring vision hindering clarity, Rex felt his hands release the cage, and looked into the others surrounding him, feeling aghast—the children and young adults were still here, still alive. They had not yet given into starvation and torture, still resisting experimentation and transformation, but he knew, even as those thoughts crawled through his hindbrain, that it would not last, it was not their future to survive. Rex found himself roaming corridors, bursting doors aside, scrambling for what he knew was there, and as the shifting vision acceded to his demand, he moved into the torture rooms. The screams were louder now, and he realized he didn't want this. He was losing grasp of what made him in the beginning, and all along, he'd not paid attention to it, ignored it.

"Why don't you do anything, Mr. Rex? It's all at your fingertips now."

Rex felt sick, his guts rebelling. Looking down at his hands, they were covered in blood. It was pooling on the floor, running down his chest and legs, dripping from his chin, vivid, bright crimson.

"You've done so much already, haven't you? What are a few more forgotten bodies now?"

Turning about, his world spun, and he was again, standing in front of his own darkened cage, bloodied hands grasping the bars, watching himself quivering and twitching.

"I don't want this." The silence continued, and he spoke louder, feeling his unease grow. *"Take me back."*

He could feel the watching presence over his shoulder, whispering into his ear like the devil promising him something for his nonexistent soul, and the ill feeling in Rex increased dramatically.

"Are you sure? Nothing can stop you now, not even me. It's all up to you now, Mr. Rex..."

All this time, and he'd almost forgotten why he fought, the ninety other souls that died here to bend to the Combine will, almost pushed them out of his memory completely. They weren't related to him by blood, no, they were related by death, kin by mortality, and he'd attempted to shed them like a second skin, leave it all behind: A mistake. It was leaving him hollow and devastated, instead of fueled and satiated by their sacrifice, an offering he was using against the invaders that begged and pleaded for it so desperately, that they were willing to kill for it.

"Please. Take me back. This is all wrong, and I can't change this here, not now, not ever."

The change was slow and subtle, but again he was back in the cafeteria of the silo, watching the swinging light dangle over an empty space. The man in the blue suit could not be seen, but his voice could be heard, rasping in the darkness, unrevealing of the source, only there in the vaguest sense of the word.

"I hope you understand the choice you made, Mr. Rex. I will be seeing you soon. Make the most of this time."

His response went unspoken, the world snapping back into view almost instantly, giving him no measure of recovery or recall before he arrived in the cafeteria, alone, lights on full, mind swimming through a roiling sea of thoughts and memories. He could barely remain standing, his legs suddenly weary, and as he shuffled over to one of the cafeteria tables, he slowly sat on its surface, hearing it complain at the weight, but remained steady. One thing rang out in the thoughts that roared by his consciousness, and that was the rediscovery of his motivation, the ninety others that died so long ago, perished for creatures he dared to defy, turning their own efforts against them. Rex looked around the cafeteria slowly, knowing that while the people here were his motivation to return, time and time again, the individuals that bought the proverbial farm for his mere existing were the true motivation for him to fight.

But hadn't he fought off the Combine? What was truly left?

Of course, the answer hit him like a truck, and he felt himself lying back onto the table's surface, the slow aches echoing through his limbs, the intense pain in his extremities gone, but the dull throbbing in his nerves and head would not relinquish to calm, all effects of his proximity to others he cared for. It had been weighing on him from the beginning of his return, the instant he stood in the room with Molly holding the weapon to his throat.

A snarl built on his lips, and he felt his desperation rising. It was the goddamned field, the energy that sapped actual will and emotions, turning them inward like a physical force, battering the human psyche. It began to make sense, the fact that he'd not seen an infant or child under a year of age in all this time, only those already born remaining; the emotions that burbled up quickly being covered and masked by Maurine when they'd spoken were now hazy and buried like the conversation, but he knew that was not of his own volition.

He'd missed it just like all the other small things he'd forgotten along the way, and Rex began to ponder if the implant was having the adverse effect of wiping his mind, the slow and painfully unobvious way. Or if it was another effect of the field, warping thoughts themselves, in addition to how it supposedly bent and altered time. It could have been a fallout from weapons, resounding echoes from experiments, or any of the numerous outcomes he could think of being side effects from endless atrocities committed.

Just standing there, he could feel another change inside of himself. It was no longer an uncontrollable roller-coaster ride of death and destruction, something he couldn't step off of—it was a path he'd *chosen*, even before the realization had arrived, unconsciously he'd walked down this route willingly and with no amount of hesitation. The decision had been his long ago, and instead of being one to lie down, die in that cage or willingly serve some alien master, it was to resist what was being done, to fight. One thing was for certain now: He wasn't going to run at the presence of the enemy, no matter how many remained.

And Rex had a lot to do before the stranger in the suit reappeared. He would leave this time, but not before his friends were prepared.

WAITING GAME

A week. It had the weight of a month, but a mere seven days had passed since his arrival, and the escapees from the city were still showing up. Molly now had the additional pressure of a growing population on her hands, and the lack of food stores were showing. It was difficult to locate the stores in the silo other than what was in the pantry, and as each new arrival walked in, they were immediately put to work. There was no time for niceties or introductions, no psychologist moving from person to person, analyzing their stress after having survived such an ordeal, and there was no time to create such things.

Starvation had become a factor now, and the overpopulated silo was in desperate need of repair to become a functioning habitat again, having been reduced to a nightmarish jigsaw puzzle of warped steel, shattered concrete, molten components, and bodies, numerous corpses littered about the invaded wreck of the former missile silo. Time was weighing on him in particular, Rex having become increasingly aware of the passing of minutes, the fact that the Combine could be growing stronger from their possible crippled position, and the unexpected nature of his departures, forced or not, was something he doubted he wanted to face at a critical moment repairing things or defending the structure. Anxiety rising, he still found the time to assist in their endeavors while readying what he could; he was still an irregular sight amongst the people here, and the physical alterations helped none with his diplomatic measures to try and fit in once again.

The second that the showers were reopened, he found himself eagerly wanting a turn—the clothes he wore and the armor were filthy, and it was enough to drive him mad. Waiting until everyone had gone to sleep was a necessity for his psyche, unwilling to ignore the reactions of others again, and adverse to provoking anger or fear amid those he had to stay. But once he got under those streams of hot water, he stayed for nearly an hour, feeling as if he were washing away some great sin perhaps. As the blood and grime changed the water underneath him, he sighed to himself, noting that even water washed off as a different color, warped by his presence. Finally, when it ran clear around his feet, he emerged from the water, and walked numbly to the rack of dampened and ragged towels—they'd barely survived the rubble intact.

Ensuring he was covered mostly by the largest of the towels, he felt glad it was so late at night, allowing him to take the lift to the manufacturing level half-naked, and ran into no one as he pulled open the lift door, walking to the few intact laundry machines. When he'd pulled the armor and clothes off of himself, he'd found the black t-shirt he'd pulled on so long ago to be nothing but tatters and a collar holding itself together by threads. At least, the pants he'd chosen had survived somewhat as a whole, as well as the socks and boots amazingly, other than the holes created by the sudden presence of talons. Dressing silently, stumbling once in the dark as he nearly lost his balance, but finishing quickly, Rex gathered his remaining composure before exiting. Walking back to the lift, he strode in and took it back to the main level, still thinking about the time passing around him with no way to halt it.

Moving into the former armory section from the lift in several swift steps, Rex vaulted back into the bombed-out and looted room, stepping to the locker he'd secured before undressing, cranking open the door. Inside sat the hated Combine armor, black surfaces now shiny and clean, a sight that disgusted him inside when he saw it for the first time, after giving it a decent once-over with soap and water. All he could see when he gazed at it was the horrid monstrosity he'd encountered in the Urals, reveling in the feeling of the snow after killing all those men... it was like looking in a damned mirror, and it drove white-hot needles into his soul. Still, he did not stop his hand as he reached in, and pulled the pieces out, fitting them on once again, slipping the old military vest on over the chest piece, and buckling the pistol belt on last.

With a handful of magazines remaining, the .357 model of the Desert Eagle handgun was quickly becoming a fancy club with moving parts, and only one look around the thrashed armory was enough to stop him from searching for more ammunition or a replacement weapon. There had been a fire in one corner, and all that remained of a series of shelves were lumps of molten plastic and scorched metal pieces. Casings littered the rest of the concrete floor, spilling from overturned boxes, riddled with holes from exploding rounds. The state of things here were horrid, but slowly, they would rebuild.

Stepping away from the locker, he let it hang open behind him as he made motion for the armory door, emerging into the main entry area once again, with the sounds of people beginning to wake up around the silo surrounding him now. Ready to work, Rex hauled back onto the lift and prepared himself for another day of waiting.

—◁◁◁◁▷—

Seven more damned days, and Rex was beginning to become weary from being on edge all the time. They'd taken in nearly a hundred more survivors in the passing week, and it was quickly becoming apparent that the silo was not sizeable enough to remain a suitable home for the growing demand. So it was natural that he found himself in the belly of one of the few remaining APCs stolen from the Combine, traveling back to the old 187 Compound at full speed, six others sitting with him. A second armored personnel carrier trailed behind them by only a few feet, containing more of the rebels, and a few buckets of recovered tools to utilize on the ruined homes.

The hope was to revamp the former compound as best as possible, and start first on a smaller scale, to get some kind of idea the type of repairs that were going to be necessary once they began to reconstruct residential zones inside greater New Mexico City. Truthfully, the entire zone was still mostly unsecured, with reports of soldiers holding out in bunkers, stationary platforms, guard towers, landing areas, and other Combine-placed secure areas that survived the tower's destruction, keeping themselves intact like a splinter group.

Still, he'd come with them to ensure none of those remaining under the Combine's will had an easy target: Providing security for the laborers here would be a small help, but a help nonetheless. They would be sleeping and eating here, until the job was finished and the compound was once again secured and hospitable, and the likelihood of any attacks were high. Maurine and Molly were both in the other APC, monitoring and commanding the situation, the vehicles thundering across the highway until they made a sharp turn onto the desert sands, hauling ass for Compound 187 around the opposite side.

The idea was to take anything still living there by surprise, he could hear as the pilot spoke to Maurine over the APC's radio, and the instructions came across clear, concise, and punctual. And it didn't take long for the APC convoy to encircle the old compound, the passengers all easily able to see things through the shaped gun ports. Rex kept turned away, gripping one of the Combine-cloned M4 weapons in both hands, staring at his boots. Unwilling to recall memories of the area, he simply waited for the moment the rear hatch would slide open, and the rebels could spill out onto the concrete, securing the zone. Two of the people in his detail were raw, fresh recoveries from the cold storage prison.

They'd thawed more than fifty people in addition to everyone else showing up, and they'd left the prison locked down until they could recover this area. Most of those thawed were local authorities and ex-military, and even under extreme circumstances, their training and lives never prepared them for waking up from being frozen solid over a year in time. It was harder for the two in his squad, in particular, former local policeman and army sergeant, struggling with limbs they'd not been able to employ physically, and a sense of competition with those that had been mobile ever since the invasion began. Rex had to watch them carefully at first, but knew it was a good thing to have them in his squad—they would try as hard as possible and they could only get better. It was the younger man that worried him, the very same that had leveled a weapon at Rex and nearly refused to cease-fire; he could hear the cracking voice yelp aloud as the vehicle ground to a halt.

"Are we really gonna see any Combine out here?"

Rex frowned under the headgear, and he was grateful his expression was hidden from the others around him as he turned to the young man, speaking brusquely with a firm conviction in his tone, attempting to ease the nervousness. The expression would have only served as a counter to his words, and he knew he needed to solve that within himself, even as he spoke.

"I don't know. Chances are the undead and critters will be more of a problem."

Standing up and facing the opening hatch, he held the M4 clone at the ready, and felt the rush of adrenaline mirroring his experiences.

"Stay sharp, shoot anything that moves that doesn't identify itself, and don't freak out. Cover each other and listen for the workers to call out for help. They're depending on us."

Without a rearward glance, he led the way down the ramping hatchway, weapon raised, eyes searching, and body moving fluidly. He had the more immediate concern of the well-being of the arrival to contend with and as Rex swept his hand across the zone, the wave of men and women flowed out like an upsurge of security to close around the gaps in the structures. They completed surrounding the workers as their crack squad of makeshift engineers and volunteers began by breaking down the mass of fallen Combine copter off to one side, shoved away by brute force of something else that was thankfully no longer present.

Rex began his own patrol of the area, noting that O'Hare stood with the command crew to protect them, and starting to jog around the compound, sight peeled for any signs of life, or parodies thereof, and only twice did he see heat sources causing a pausing of his actions. Both turned out to be slowly dying fires, cooling metal surrounded by glowing coals of wood and steel shavings sprayed about everywhere, intensifying the static readings on the headgear. And both times he had to prevent himself from showing his frustrations at the odd readings, pushing it away to his hindbrain before resuming course around the compound.

The smoldering burnt out remains were a testament to the resolve of the Combine's efforts to wipe out anything resembling a former state of humanity, and by the same token, it represented the determination of humanity as a whole. Built immediately after the advent of the portal storms, Rex knew they were a glaring target on the desert's surface, but it was here purposefully, as was the trams existence. Humans refused to cower inside massive fortresses or city walls, and were absolutely set on being able to expand farther beyond their imposed limits, creating the Compounds scattered throughout the southwest to replace what was lost in the portal storms and their destructive nature.

And now, after they'd been scoured from the face of usefulness, persevering survivors were putting the wreckage and remains to use once again—they would never look the same, but the homes here would be standing again, soon. The APC quickly about-faced as the last of the guards exited, and the second vehicle followed suit as the final worker offloaded the last of the crates of tools and supplies. They'd been left to their own devices for now, and the wait for reinforcements began.

Rex halted at the furthest of the homes as he heard a scream, and turned to see the young man holding a bleeding arm, kicking at spindly remains of a human, the upper half grasping with bone-bare hands, screeching like a demon. The issued carbine was nowhere in sight, and as he raised the clone M4, another of the guards grabbed onto the dragging hip bone, and tore the monstrosity away, letting the young man run free. With the creature now in the clear, it was easy to shoot once, and the round tore the headcrab melded to the skull free in a single shot. The body flopped to the dirt several meters away, and it wasn't long until the young man returned with a bloodied rifle, the torn sling swinging wildly.

The stained weapon barked twice more at the body on the ground, and the young man finally relented, walking away and heading towards one of the medics. Frowning, Rex was unsure if he should let the moment settle, but he had to secure the other half of the compound—wherever the hell the creature came from, he wasn't about to let more of them fester. They weren't showing up on any type of heat or infrared register, and even the corpse on the ground was far beyond being cold and dead. Sliding in a grimy patch of dirt where a garden once grew, Rex regained his balance easily, and across the distance, pointed to the recently thawed recruits, both the ex-army man and the former police officer jogging over at the sight of the signal.

Approaching the middle home as the other two came up behind him, Rex turned back only once to nod, and as he received affirmations in return, he charged into the charred remnants, kicked over a fallen panel of scorched metal, and felt his teeth clench as one of the skeletal monstrosities leapt out to greet him. His left hand whipping up to defend himself, Rex grasped the skull, felt his fingers tear through the headcrab perched atop, and shoved the creature backwards with enough force to shear off its lower half on the metal panel, jutting over the edge of the staircase leading down. The upper half was still determined to growl and attempt crawling towards Rex, and the man to his left fired without a word being given, killing the creature, and allowing Rex to continue down.

Moving swiftly, but cautiously, Rex ensured the stairs weren't crumbling, and gestured for the others to follow, the clone M4 leading the way with its muzzle jutting outwards. As the three of them reached the bottom, the creaking from the staircase echoing in the empty room, the wave of smells that struck them had even Rex recoiling, coughing and gasping for something that didn't smell like rotting meat and molding flesh. Bones were scattered around the area here, with no signs of actual bodies or blood, no physical remains besides picked-clean calcium, a few traces of mottled, dried cartilage splayed on the once-clean carpet. Everything was filthy beyond the sense of the word, dirt and other unidentifiable substances caked almost an inch thick, the disgusting sight leading right up to a massive hole burrowed through the wall.

It took a moment before the sounds of shuffling could be heard and the creature that emerged from the hole could be seen, but Rex distinctly picked out the former police officer losing his lunch at the horrible sight. This version of the headcrab breed was another of the hunched-over carriers, only the headcrabs were huge, covered with molds and fungi, and crawled like massive insects across the hulking surface of the once-human carrier. It had no distinctive head anymore, lost in large amounts of garbage and clumps of feces or remnants of food, forming a grotesque body shaped like a rotten potato, stumbling and weaving with much difficulty.

It had only one arm now, the other either covered up, or gone by grace of gangrene, or being used as food. Dozens upon dozens of smaller, translucent headcrabs walked around their slow-moving feet, and they seemed to be emerging from the tops of the long, awkward legs, crawling from smaller holes in the larger mass. The sight was so amazingly perturbing that Rex neglected to open fire on first contact, and the singular arm bulged with effort as it reached up, and grasped onto the largest of the massive headcrabs, cocking back like a star pitcher.

"Fire at the crabs first, and then take down the…center mass."

Even as Rex finished speaking, his rifle continued barking for him, ripping up the throwing arm with a few controlled bursts, his fellow fighters swiftly killing all four of the largest headcrabs, removing a good bit of outer layers from the carrier mass. The ex-army soldier yelled in pain and ripped a smaller headcrab from his arm, flinging it back, and Rex noticed that they were trying to crawl up his own feet and legs, sliding on the armor plate.

"Back up, we need some room for a grenade."

Both of the others crept backwards up the stairs once again, and Rex made sure he had a bit of room as well before thumbing the fire selector to single shot, slid an old rocket-propelled stick grenade onto the muzzle of the M4, and instead of instinctually firing into the center of the creature, knowing that it would more than likely just spread the babies around the room, aimed at the ground near the beast's feet and let fly. The resounding detonation shook the foundation of the house, and spread green blood everywhere, adding a fresh coat of nasty paint to the already-repulsive area, including spatters that Rex was forced to remove shortly after the flare of the explosion.

As the smoke and clouds of dirt cleared, the others joined him in the basement, and they all took in the view, a snarl replacing shocked features. Dozens of the smaller headcrabs were still alive, crawling along the edges of the tunnel, making high-pitched squealing sounds as they moved. The carrier was nowhere in sight, only burning, charred remnants lumped on the walls further down into the hand-carved basement extension, and as Rex stepped forward, he wondered if there was a less-costly solution to the problem. They were going to end up expending far too much ammunition, killing the little ones a bullet at a time. Of course, the situation didn't have far to get worse, and it decided to do so just as soon as it could.

Along the far side of the tunnel emerged something far worse than the carrier, seven to eight feet of disgusting muscle, a massive maw down the center of the torso in a vertical snarl of immense teeth, dripping with vivid, red blood. The maw was engorged with parts and mutilated bits, but that was far from the worst—the bulging arms, ending in long claws, were also covered with blood, and each gripped onto halves of a torso. The legs were like tree trunks, ending in splayed, insectile toes, segmented but rigid, clacking on the floor in time with the massive thuds of the rest of the foot following each step. The angular, chitinous headcrab grasping to the location where the head of a human would have been was vicious in comparison even with the previous versions encountered, the parasite's former feet transformed into talons, curved forward as if to assist with slicing opponents or defending the neck.

And the ease which accompanied the motion was startling, shocking Rex as the difference between the titanic headcrab mutant and the carrier creature in their actions were as vast as the shape and size of their forms. It roared, moving like one of the skeletal parodies, ignoring its own size easily somehow and charging forward with an unnatural quickness. Even as it moved, the three of them were still reacting to the roar and its presence alone, and it was nearly on top of them before all three weapons opened fire simultaneously. The barrage was barely enough to slow a fraction of the momentum, and as their weapons began to run dry, sheer, dumb luck prevailed on their side as the creature stepped upon one of the dozens of translucent parasites roaming the floor.

The tiny monster popped loudly under the gigantic tread, and became an instant slick spot, causing all of the central traction of the heel to slide forwards. The smaller, segmented tendrils might've been intended to be more useful at a later stage of development, but at this point, all they could do under the changing of the center of gravity, and the lack of contact with the ground, was snap off like brittle twigs whipping away from a main branch in a gust of strong wind.

The momentum that once carried it so gracefully, so smoothly without effort, now hampered its ability to right itself in time, and it spun about vertically, the left leg whipping forwards as it continued its tread over the creature, the right bending at a severe angle for a split second before ripping loudly at the groin and flopping free wildly. The rest of the body simply carried the twisting angle to an extreme as it pushed forwards still, and it slammed into the three of the men like pins, bowling them over backwards and pinning them down. Rex wrested himself free from the tangle of grasping, elongated fingers, swearing as two things happened at the same time:

He stepped forwards with his right foot, instinctively to pin the creature to the ruined floor, and found himself buried knee-deep into the cavernous maw, several distinct jaws on the interior grinding together with the outer jaw to attempt to flay his leg clean off; at the exact instant this was occurring, the huge, groping claws it called hands, grabbed onto the legs of both the others, and with one pull, tugged them off-balance, weapons falling free from recovering hands. The blur of motion, the way it was happening so fast, it drove memories and flashbacks into the forefront that Rex refused to go through, but knew each warned him of the disgusting power this creature held. Snarling under the headgear once again, he roared in response as he prepared the rest of his rebuttal to the affront before him.

Left hand striking down like a scythe reaping the wheat, it tore into the side of the creature, along the outer edges of the multilayered jaw instead of along the interior, razor-edged fingers delving deeply into the resilient flesh, until they touched the back of the vertical maw, and grasped tightly onto the central, connecting jawbone. The headcrab controlling the beast began to squeal at the severe invasion of its central mass, and it finally fell silent for a second, as he pulled upwards with all his might, perhaps unbelieving of what was occurring, and powerless to stop him. The left side of the jaw popped deep inside the creature, and again the parasitic controller mounted atop the once-humanoid head began to squeal, only this was worse in the fact that its volume increased dramatically, twitching back and forth erratically as the assault continued.

Rex smiled grimly as he reaffirmed his grip, and lifted with every muscle his arm could spare, ripping the jawbone and a huge amount of surrounding, fetid flesh away from the massive monster, the titan spraying blood and other fluids onto the floor. With the beast crippled and unable to control itself, one could have said that Rex was finished with dealing out punishment to the mutant, but his emotions pushed him onwards, ignoring the fact that the two others with him were now free of the grasping hands, recovering their rifles once again.

Instead of calmly assessing the situation or even realizing that the corpse could be useful for study, he tore into it with voracity while it was still alive, still in its final throes, both hands about the sides of the parasitic controlling creature atop the broad shoulders, the left easily puncturing the armored surface to dig sharpened talons into the flesh underneath, the right squeezing so hard that the chitin on the surface cracked like glass, green internals oozing from between broken sections. Again, he yanked up with as much force as possible, and the results were similar, a loud snapping sound following as the head and much of the spine came free easily in his hands, the stiffened, razor-edged talons struggling to move after all this time growing and solidifying into place.

The screaming was down to a squeal, intermixed with horrible gurgling sounds, and yet it refused to stop, even as the skeletal remnants of the skull broke apart, falling from the nasty, toothy mouth under its belly. With a growl steadily growing, he began to pull his hands apart while still grasping the sides of the headcrab, and after a slight amount of effort, ripped it in twain, spilling more of the internals across the ground, flinging the now-motionless husk and remnants aside, kicking the massive Titan under his foot once before turning about to face the others.

"Go on up, I'm gonna be down here a while…"

Rex said it firmly, but still trailed off at the end of the order, slowly circling to face the growing mob of parasitic invaders. Grabbing one limb free from the deceased Titan, and tearing it loose from the now-mangled torso, he hefted it like a baseball bat and began smashing a few of the creatures at a time, plowing into them ruthlessly. By the time he'd reached the midway point down the burrowed tunnel, still swinging and killing, he'd thinned out the crowd quite thoroughly, but soon began to encounter several larger ones, including those that were typically crawling along a carrier's body, and it became tougher to kill them with the blunt force of the severed arm.

Grasping it in one hand and using it like a bent flail, Rex caught the first headcrab to attempt to leap at him with his left hand, and easily squished it between his long, sharp fingers on the mutated limb. Flinging the severed arm ahead of him, Rex smiled as the decoy worked, and nearly a half-dozen of the larger, crustier headcrabs pounced at once, exposing them and allowing him to run up easily. Punting the first, he watched as it arced up to smash against the ceiling, stepping on two more with his right foot, pounding down onto them like a sledgehammer, and grasping the last two by their fleshy tops, threw each of them against an opposite wall like a practicing pitcher, getting a thorough workout.

Soon the cavernous roof of the tunnel sloped down ahead of him, and the walls squeezed tighter than he could fit, forcing him to bend to one knee and peer into an opening the size of his waist, far too narrow for his shoulders. The sounds of movement on the other side had him looking around for some type of source, but the lenses were receiving zero light to amplify from the opening beyond.

Reaching back to his belt for a newly acquisitioned flashlight, Rex felt it slip through his fingers once, and turned back to see why, when something smacked into the side of the headgear with the force of a 2 x 4. Stumbling back and crunching headfirst into the wall beyond, he couldn't believe it, but he was actually starting to see stars from the double blow, shaking his noggin and struggling to right himself, backing away from the large crevice.

Grateful that the headgear could still keep this area mostly illuminated through the lenses, Rex reached back for the clone M4, slid the last of his RPG units onto the muzzle, and took careful aim. The view before him was disgusting, limbs that looked like living, virulent, diseased flesh wrapped in globs and layers about a deformed hand squeezing out from the crevice, a second limb of similar proportions joining it, three-fingered, stubby, mottled hands bracing against the floor with sickly sounds, spreading a thin layer of green ichor on the cavern surface. A body attached to the limbs was slowly following as best as it could, clearly a larger mass that was able to separate itself and *pour* through the opening, but as it began to fill the far end of the area, and still kept oozing through the crevice, Rex knew he'd seen enough.

Squeezing the trigger on the carbine, he watched as the weapon streaked to the target across the distance...and stuck in it, the rocket fuel sputtering as it emptied itself without contacting the wall beyond the creature. Snarling, he flicked his fire selector to full auto, and sprayed the torso of the creature where the grenade was, and felt the explosion as the grenade detonated, rather than hearing it, shoved backwards by the force, mashing against the far wall of the cavern painfully, the device in his own body barely able to compete with the abuse now.

Shaking and stunned, Rex coughed a few times as he got to his feet, looking at the spot where the crevice used to sit, now just a pile of rubble and burning ichor, sending a thick column of smoke along the ceiling. Collecting himself and grasping the dinged, battered, but still intact clone M4, Rex made much haste up through the tunnel of deceased headcrabs, waving smoke from his face in order to help himself breathe, charging up the staircase and into the waiting light of the surface.

The other two soldiers were here, the ex-army and former policeman both stepping back at the sight and smell Rex carried with him, but kept their weapons trained down the staircase just in case anything nasty decided to follow. Molly was also not too far from the front of the bombed out house, and as he motioned to the men to stand down, he walked over to her swiftly, hanging the carbine to his side, and wiping the worst of the oozes from the headgear. He spoke strongly, trying to avoid the fact he was covered in some very offensive-smelling materials.

"The basement of that became some kind of hive, killed most of everything still living down there, you might want to use a few charges, blow it up a bit more, and try to seal it off. Most of what's on fire down there was the worst of the bunch, might be a cavern down there too if you want to clear it out."

She frowned at the report, but nodded anyway, and waved to O'Hare to approach, inspiring Rex to walk the other way. Refocusing on the descending night, he located the nearest cooking source, and approached, hoping someone had a towel and some warm water to spare. The smell was starting to agitate him, and so was his empty stomach.

LAST GOOD-BYE

He'd been counting the hours of each day as it passed now, and the fact that so much of it had gone by without a word or a dream from the man in the blue suit to confirm he was still there, that Rex was still needed, that time was no longer a factor for his stay. Still he'd kept deliberately distant from the others, knowing that all the while, any second could be his last here for God knew how long. In that short time, however, things were looking upwards. Defenses were now in place around the compound, three of the seven homes were repaired to the point of being livable, and construction had begun on the tunnel below the last.

Carefully secured digging was being done in order to make a larger bunker under the compound, and also ensure there wasn't more of the headcrabs nesting underneath. Training had begun with all of the newer survivors and recipients from the city, many of them the first new arrivals to the compound, and all were working on the area, recovering what could be and reconstructing everything else. And as he paused in his rounds, early morning chilling the area despite the work still being done, he could see another APC was incoming, headed in hard and fast.

Rex wondered if there was a problem he wasn't aware of, but as he recalled his distance from the source of most information, he could tell there was plenty he wasn't in on. Returning to his patrol, he let his curiosity hide while he kept up his pace, doing as best as he could to keep himself in shape, alert, and ready without tiring down. It didn't last very long, the small radio in the headgear crackling to life. He was still impressed that Molly figured out how to utilize the communication systems they'd been stripping from Combine corpses, but that fact went to the side as a request for his presence alerted him.

Turning on one heel and facing the newly arrived vehicle, he ran as fast as possible, eager to do something other than run around the compound's outer defenses, scanning the area for hostiles that had not shown up so far. Several others were also heading inwards, by orders or otherwise he didn't know, and it created an odd sight, leaving only a skeletal crew behind on the defenses. Several standing here were the heavier armed of the bunch, and as the APC opened up, the bay hatch sliding down to a ramp, Tank emerged from within, the steel plate of his prosthesis body now restored, and painted black in certain sections. He was carrying a large section of computer core, and followed Maurine as she led the way to the first completed home. The rest of the vehicle was quickly emptied, and the contents transferred to the same home, but not before Molly began to talk in his headset.

"Once the bay is empty, climb in. Your crew will be joining you shortly."

Still somewhat puzzled, but entirely understanding of the situation, Rex checked his weapons and ammunition, grimacing at the short supply, but it wasn't something to be helped. Supplies were getting increasingly thin and no store of weapons and ammunition had been located as of yet. Looting of the city was slow and ponderous, with plenty of dangers still out there, ready and willing to pounce on anyone attempting to scavenge from wreckage, and the more people they found alive, the more disparate the lack of supplies became in relation. Reflecting upon this while he waited, he climbed into the vehicle's bay, and felt the doors close behind him, the vehicle starting up again.

It spurred into motion as he took a seat in one of the few on the interior, unfolding it from the locking mechanism. The ride was terribly boring, but it gave him plenty of time to think, the last thing he wanted to do, but it was not easy to stop the flow of his mind. Thankfully it didn't get far in a maze of emotions and buried anger before the vehicle stopped again, but the sounds of gunfire had him alerted and standing up, yelling out loud to the driver's compartment.

"What the hell is going on out there?"

There was another slight pause in the gunfire before it started again, the pilot finally responding in between bursts. "Sorry, sir, just a few of those skeletal skittering bastards out here, picking them off with the turret is all."

Somehow, Rex was not surprised at the presence of the monstrosities around the vehicle, any type of movement could attract them out of a nest, and there were plenty of nests around to be worried about. Of course, the pilot's reaction puzzled him— perhaps the driver was a newcomer, or simply did not know who Rex was, but sealing the bay prevented him from helping out.

"Open the bay, I can assist you."

Still the bursts continued, and no response came over the intercom, even as he yelled again, and felt the balance of the vehicle alter awkwardly.

"What are you doing? Open the damn bay, soldier!"

Again nothing replied and he felt the vehicle jerk awkwardly this time, and sounds of something slamming into it repeatedly reverberated throughout the bay. Not bothering to yell out this time, Rex turned to the bay door and raised one foot to kick at it, and felt his world warp around him, a rush of pressure, the growl of a larger engine, and wet, gnashing sounds combined with the bone-jarring impact of a heavier collision. The armored personnel carrier did a pair of three-sixty spins before tumbling once more, crunching to a halt on its roof, stuck in a very similar position.

Struggling to regain a sense of balance, he found himself standing up numbly without knowing it, already limping over to the bent bay door. Trying once again to bash the door down with one foot, he was allowed to complete the motion this time, and as it tore free from the moorings holding it in place, Rex could feel himself beginning to pull together, the numbness still on the edge of his perceptions however. It was pervasive enough to dodge every effort his mind made to identify it, but the worry was placed on his mental backburner as he emerged to a sight of more wreckage strewn across a very familiar entry area—green blood from the parasites and skitterers ran thick on the sands, along with burning fuel from the second APC, shattered canopy glass glittering in the sun.

Pulling up the clone M4 still strapped to his back, he found part of the stock bent, but the rest functional, and flicked off the safety as he began to move again, shooting at one mutant trying to crawl towards him, advancing onto a fallen form nearby. Maurine groaned as he rolled her over on her side, and found her swimming to consciousness, reaching for her own weapon, only an arm's reach away, jerking away from Rex as she saw him so close. Ensured that she would be alright now that she was awake, he moved away from her and ran to the next still form, finding O'Hare, coughing and wheezing, looking for his own weapon.

The last were a couple of bodies he couldn't identify, burning in a pool of oils and fuels, and the mashed canopy of the second APC showed telltale signs of gunfire, not to mention it was a crater mashed inwards, only a single foot jutting outwards. The situation looked nightmarish, but was quickly relieved by the oncoming presence of a third APC, the white flag of the revolutionaries flying wildly in the wind. It slid across blackened ground to halt just outside of the range of the wreck, the canopy and bay door opening simultaneously, Tank emerging from the front, and Molly stepping down from the rear with another complement of people. They were all heavily armed, and rushed over to the disaster site to see what was going on, Rex realizing that two men of the strike team were already dead, and so were each of the drivers for both APCs.

Maurine was soon at his side, with O'Hare not far behind, and neither looked too pleased at the situation, but both followed him resolutely. Rex began to approach the second group with some apprehension, not having spoken with Tank since their last fight, and wondering if O'Hare would open fire from behind at any second. However, things seemed settled, everyone acting coolly, keeping a reserved calm not often displayed around Rex recently—it allowed him to take a moment within himself, reserving his apprehension as he took each step carefully.

Both groups arrived at the entrance to the former Black Mesa area, the doors blackened by weapons fire, but still the same he'd seen so many times before. He was about to take the obligatory first steps in when a hand gestured him away, and he was shocked to see Tank moving him aside without a word, Maurine nodding as he was pushed to the tail end, O'Hare taking up second position. The noncommittal way he was moved to the rear of the group disturbed him greatly, but it was nothing out of the ordinary as of late, and he kept his mouth shut even as Molly joined the party, bearing a grimace after having examined the corpses in the flames. Pushing him forward as Tank lead the way, Molly said nothing either, and Rex took it as a matter of course, following duly with his weapon at the ready.

The heat from the evening was nothing compared to the unbearable warmth from the interior—the air recyclers or whatever conditioning system that was in place had gone down without being restarted, and the whole place carried the heat of the sun in the metal and concrete walls, the acrid stench of rotting things carried along in the tepid air. Blood and bodies from numerous encounters were spread along the route, but all the while, there was nothing new to find, no Combine running up to greet them or bursting out from hiding to fire upon their backs. The filth was certainly filling up, and rodents that somehow managed to slip in were making things worse, spreading what was left around to the corners and building nests.

Thankfully, none of the headcrabs seemed to be running loose here, but the amount of them on the exterior still had Rex guessing that a nest was nearby somewhere. The whole incident had blurred by without an explanation, but there was little to do about it now, both pilots dead, two witnesses burnt to death, the rest of them perhaps still in shock, angry at the result being more fatalities in a seemingly endless war, casualties of remnants of bioweapons, not even actual Combine. And the lack of actual enemies here only burned them hotter, blazing their internal coals—there was no bloodletting to relieve the pressure of the offenses committed against them, no easy valve to twist and let free a blaze of outpouring angst.

The silence carried on for some time, only their steps breaking the oppressive mood, and the occasional grunt as Tank whirled to aim at something, and shrugged it off as chasing shadows. This was certainly out of the ordinary as of late, not even a trace of living enemies to cast a doubt about the state of the facility, or the last time it had been put into use. More than likely, his last romp through here, and the brutal gunfight that ensued, was the last action that had taken place. The power was fluctuating, but refused to start all the way up, sparking consoles, burned-out computers, molten plastics, and slagged metals adding to the other permeating smells, causing each of them in the group to make remarks about the stench, but no responses came to each, the simple statements carrying no humor, only pointing out the abhorrence to the nastiness around them.

Burnt bodies, ashes, charred remains…it was an endless, repeating mural of death and destruction, abandonment and decay, with no content worth reclaiming other than the complex itself. That was clear enough as they passed the cells and moved into the control station, every console mashed, burned, or smoldered to ruin, screens ripped from their mounts and gone completely, double-thickness glass riddled with holes, and the screen of metal between the layers stretched around or torn through the spaces. The doors to the lab beyond were a bent and torn-free pile of debris, slumped against the far wall of the laboratory, the lab space itself now a giant crater, firebombed to nothing, and barely reminiscent of what it once was. The next doors that lead into the portal zone below were melted down to a solid steel bar, wedged in the hollow and fused to the surrounding metals.

It was, however, nothing to Tank, who merely shoved it aside, but paused for a long time without saying a word. It disturbed O'Hare, and passed to each person in line waiting, and as the giant refused to budge, Molly spoke up, "What's stopping you? Move in, Tank."

The big man almost didn't respond, but finally continued to move into the portal chamber, and Rex could hardly wait to see what could stop Tank in his tracks like that. Not many things could stun the giant, but after the earlier incidents, the phobias that could have surfaced or been created were numerous. Waiting patiently, he finally took his turn to step through the doorway into the room beyond, feet making hollow noises on the catwalk, matched only by the breathless view of the interior, the room burned and scorched so badly as to form a blanket of darkness covering the surfaces of metal and concrete. To top it off, the torn wires, holes, and shattered lights formed amazing patterns like stars, the only remaining illumination, forming a starry void that they could walk into, and stand amongst. And at the core of the darkness, capturing the attention of all of them, sat the much-abused portal platform, burnt and broken at an awkward angle, but somehow, still activated, a globe of the pulsing green-to-orange energy he'd seen so many times before. It haunted his nightmares, plagued his dreams, and turned his reality upside down each time he'd witnessed them while awake, and now to have it here, waiting for him after three weeks in the making for some kind of sign, he regretted ever seeing it in the first place.

Its mere presence shook him down to his core and he could barely approach it, all of the others waiting in a line stretched across the front of the machine, pausing, prepared. Rex refused to look right at it, glancing from person to person, realizing they were relaxed, and smiling at him, a completely different reaction than he'd witnessed before today, reminding him of the first time he'd ever seen them all together. Things had certainly changed, and taken its toll on each of them, none for the better, and all for the worse, but even now those changes were hidden, imperceptible to him at any distance.

And as he turned back to the sphere, still fearing any outcome that was the definite result of stepping into that mass of energy, he realized none of it mattered at this point—they all understood what was happening, all stuck waiting just like him. Feeling as if he was shrinking under their gaze, he finally walked to the energy portal, and there he stood still, taking one more moment to behold the defiance of nature and physics; turning slightly to look over one shoulder at his comrades, he felt a smile grow as he spoke.

"I will be seeing you all again. Trust me."

And without a second thought, pushing off his hesitation, Rex leapt into the light.

—◦◦◦—

Rebellion. Disgust. Emptiness. Despair.

They flooded him in this hollow pit, fighting over his tortured, cloned soul, battering it around with ease, no measure of resistance from himself—for far too long he'd avoided these emotions while feeling them, these driving forces that were easy to ignore, but impossible to completely abandon, and at long last, he wanted to fully embrace them. All that truly remained of himself while he was gone from his new home; they would now be his anchors in the storm, the solid base from which he would be able to strike, the immunization from the emotional assault that was sure to come later.

Collecting in the waves, they began to rebound inside his own globe of energy, expanding until he was overwhelming the darkness itself...

—◦◦◦—

GUARANTEED RESULTS

Appearing some fifty feet over the surface of a seamless, blue ocean was perhaps the one sight he did not expect, especially the freefall sensation afterwards, or the landing against the cold, salty water with enough force to cause him to see stars. The dive was a short one, Rex flailing slightly as he realized he could swim to the air with ease, and breached the surface for a satisfying breath, feeling slightly disoriented, and spotting the length of beach ahead. Understanding hit him with a remarkable sense of clarity, and he could feel himself echoing motions he knew instinctively, but had not yet taken, each stroke of swimming through the water predetermined, but never taken before this moment, washing up onto the shore confidently.

It was there, under the glare of a sun shining through a cloudy overcast day that he found himself recovering from more than just confusion, looking at the continuing bodily changes, his left arm now ending in massive, foot-long clawed appendages in the pattern a human hand would hold, each blackened finger morphed into a blade at least an inch wide at the base, tapering down to a double-edged tip he could barely distinguish, the point so fine. His right arm now ended in thick, rock-hide fingers, splitting through portions of the black body armor, turning the hand portion into something akin to a metal fingerless glove, the tips of his own hand bursting through bluntly. Both the older MCV and the newer bodysuit armor pinched tighter to him than ever before, the web belt strained, the boots split and clutching onto his broad, talon-toed feet for dear existence.

The headgear also felt tighter and strained, and as he stretched his neck, he felt the ends of the metal plates split ever so slightly to try to accustom the alteration. Rex straightened his back and stood proudly for a moment, until the overcast clouds returned, and with them came the strange sounds of insectile movement. Spinning to his left, he found a group of small, knee-high creatures bursting up from the sand, angular, chitinous armor glistening in the sun, strange, almost too-alien squeaks and squeals emanating from unseen orifices. The biggest threats about them were the razor-sharpened ends of each leg, and the odd fin-like projections, spines without webbing spread out between them, far more insect-like in nature than reptilian.

They moved faster than most of the headcrab mutants could, skittering across the sand and making a beeline for his position, still standing ankle-deep in the shore, the sun breaking through heavy storm clouds to cast an odd light on the area, rain beginning to patter down. Grabbing the first of the creatures to reach him, Rex began to move in the opposite direction, tearing the beast in his hands apart, and flinging the corpse into the water behind him. Spotting a wrecked shack of the navy-blue metal pinned against a rocky outcropping, connected to the reef itself perhaps, he began to run his way over to it. Of course, that was cut short as one of the creatures leapt onto his back, and as he was forced to cease motion and deal with the offender, two more joined the action, a third bursting from the sand under his feet. Kicking and thrashing madly was the instantaneous reaction to being swarmed, and he found himself roaring, shrugging off most of the minimal damage, green-yellow blood everywhere, bits and pieces of bugs strewn about, jutting from the surface of the sand.

Continuing to run for the shack, tearing up wet soil and kicking splashing shore as he increased his speed dramatically, he began to reach for a weapon that wasn't there, shocked to be grasping a shattered stock connected to his weapon sling, instinct drove him to reach for the Desert Eagle on his hip, and discovered his fingers couldn't slip into the trigger guard. Snarling louder as he kept up his pace, Rex leapt the last few feet to the shack, and as he found it empty, the rage increased even further, driving him to spin about and face the next oncoming wave of the insects. The rearmost portion of his brain was nagging the hell out of him, telling him that this was different than the dream, the nightmare, none of it matching the image he'd been presented with, the details skewed all wrong, like stepping on a broken mirror, the glass shifting, changing the outcome.

The bugs began to back away as a strange, strained-horn sound rung out, and as the navy-blue metal shack began to shake, Rex tried to move, and found himself failing as one plate of the steel slammed down onto his back, the feeling of nearly a ton trampling across it barely tolerable. Pinned firmly into place, Rex began to shake with a mixture of fear and desperation, and while he was struggling with this, elongated talons tore into metal, coming down only inches from his neck, scratching across the surface of the suit around his shoulder, crunching through the soil.

Rex forced himself to shove back at the earth under him, the plate of metal barely budging, and the pressure from above increased. Metal peeled and tore as he resisted the weight from above, and finally some semblance of balance above him tilted in favor of one side, sloping to the left, the distinct clacking of claws on the navy-blue plate turning into screeching as they slid across the surface. There was another rumble of commotion beyond the plate to his extreme left, and a large measure of the weight atop him reduced, allowing him to stand up, grasping at the length of Combine steel resolutely, exerting himself to the point of gasping for air with each passing second, the metal rising into the air over his head as he wrenched it up.

A trio of the insectile invaders burst from the sand ahead of him, a fourth and fifth already on the surface, leaping at him—slamming the plate downwards as fast and hard as possible in a motion similar to a combination of a giant whack-a-mole and an oversized flyswatter, a wave of ichor and bug parts burst out from under the length of steel, coating his legs up to his knees in green, and sending gobs of sand-coated blood off in the opposite direction. An inhuman groan from the source of the attack was next on his list of threats, and spun to face it. It was still on his left, still recovering from having its center of gravity disturbed, curled into a rapidly expanding ball of massive legs and limbs, all insectile, ten times the size of the smaller versions, almost eight to ten feet tall, a bulbous head draped with feelers swinging about viciously.

Gripped about the navy-blue plate of steel, his fingers and palms complained of overuse, vices about the weight of the makeshift bludgeon, another sky-shattering roar emanating from his lips as he whipped the metal about, twisting his body hard, releasing the incredible mass of steel with a precise velocity aimed at the beast before him. The makeshift projectile arced just slightly under where he intended for it to go, clipping through the neck and upper tendrils easily, embedding into the rock spire just beyond, and killing the monster in one strike. More of the creatures began to burst upwards, irritating him further, but he was in no mood to fight an endless battle on the shores here, wherever the hell here was, and decided to vacate the sands.

Leaping over a portion of the massive corpse, Rex stepped from one stone to the next until he had the height to leap upon the metal plate, going from the embedded object to the top of the rocky outcropping. Running over the ragged surface, Rex guessed it was exposed reef perhaps, and as he took a moment to look about, he noticed the insects refused to move beyond the sands, halting at the zones where it met the grass. It allowed him to move up onto the hill above, and take in a better sight of the area, spying a beach that carried on a short while in both directions before curving out of range of his vision, but the giant bunker in the center of the hill ahead, with the towering pillar of black, glistening metal jutting upwards into the sky, was the sign that caught his attention. Flashes of this sight ran before his vision, dredged up from his mind, realizing that while things had altered around him, the end was still the same, the tower to the stars, the bridge into the great darkness above, and whatever Combine it entailed stationed beyond.

The sun died now as the clouds returned to an overcast state, and it began to get very cold, wind whipping, rain beginning to fall. The droplets were like ice on exposed portions of his skin, and as he began to approach the final hill, the grass thick and wet under his feet, he could see the shadows of two others standing at the base of the bunker. They were only blackened silhouettes at this distance, but still fearful profiles, angular, sharp-edged looking rifles grasped onto by hands he could not distinguish. Slowing his steps, talons gripping the dirt, Rex halted himself while crouching, trying to focus hard on the potential targets, and felt his vision slip somehow, a combination of the lens and maybe something else, and he was looking right at them, up close and personal, disoriented and dizzy from the sudden shift.

He was falling backwards from the confusion before he could stop himself, and as his vision stayed zoomed out impossibly, he struck the dirt hard, landing on his back, shaking his head and rapidly blinking away until he could see from his proper perspective again. Biting back anger from the minor mishap, Rex crawled his way back to the position he formerly held, and attempted again to adjust his sight, this time trying to expect the instantaneous sensation of movement while standing still.

Containing his excitement as his vision magnified, Rex began to study the short, but powerfully compact soldiers at the bunker's base, seeing ringlets full of odd grenades, weapons with pulsing, white energy cores, and unmasked faces of horrid visage, animal-like maws covered with odd devices, eyes socketed with glowing yellow lenses. Suddenly the head began to turn…and he was staring down the enemy's lenses, eyes almost unrecognizable through the complex equipment, and Rex felt himself recoil inside as the angular weapon turned to his position as well.

Feet began to move in his direction, edged toes digging into the grass and flinging up clods of dirt as one of the soldiers began to run straight towards him, and he shook his head to clear his focus, sliding back down the hill almost to its hilt, an outcropping circling the small island he was on, a break between the sandy shores and the topsoil. Using it as cover and a line-of-sight break, Rex hauled along it like mad, dashing crazily about the curve of crabgrasses, wishing he had a useful weapon with which to retaliate upon his would-be pursuers. Settling for the makeshift nature of defense at hand, he gripped great gobs of the grassy topsoil, felt the thick mud of the root-entangled mess, and kept sweeping around until he reached the rear of the bunker's base.

Charging up while hoping he was still out of the opponent's crosshairs, Rex leaned into the windy rain, leapt over a shallow ditch full of water, and as he landed near the large concrete wall on the rear of the bunker, he realized his feet were leaving tracks behind. Circling around the bunker to the batten-down and sealed hatch, he began to use it as a ladder, mud and grass oozing between clenched fingers, complicating the task but not stopping him from reaching the top, crouching down to his belly, and waiting.

It took them a while, but the enemy finally began to approach the bunker again, following his steps in the soggy soil easily, and coming around the edge of the bunker in a tactical crouch with weapons raised and ready, the lenses spotting his handprints on the cement structure. Although realization hit them a moment too late as he stood up, and flung the mud balls as hard as possible, striking one between the lenses and spattering brown mess everywhere, the second throw almost off target, striking the other soldier in the side of the head, and coating one lens, but leaving the other relatively useful.

Roaring and leaping from the roof, a cone of white light seared by his left side, suit suddenly white-hot in an instant and causing pain to rejoin the battle cry. His left foot lanced down and crushed the torso of the still-able soldier as he landed atop, mashing the creature into the grass, and reaching out with his right hand, grasped the neck of the amazingly still-struggling enemy underneath him, and twisted a semicircle as hard as possible. Returning attention to the living Combine, Rex whipped the claws on his left hand across the muddied lenses, permanently blinding the enemy first, and allowing him to knock it down with a second swing, tearing the larger rifle from twitching fingers, and attempting to examine the corpse.

The armor on the creature wasn't really body armor, and the lenses, now hacked to pieces, were not part of a mask. The strange blackened skin that was similar to his left own arm covered his opponent's entire body, fusing wiring under the surface, creating a completely alien exterior. The hands were like talons, feet seemingly bare, but coated on the underside with actual treads, a mutated mix between a normal sole, and a combat boot, puzzling him thoroughly.

Acknowledging the fact that they somehow maintained a method of communication, Rex hurried in his examination, learning as much as possible, which was barely useful now that they were dead. Collecting both of the lighter, metal-edged weapons, shaped a bit like a heavy-bore rifle with no obvious parts, other than a trigger and grip, he tried to ignore the pulsing, globe of near-translucent energy throbbing within a pair of containment vices, slinging one across his back, and trying to fit his hands around the first.

The trigger grip prevented his fingers from being able to utilize it properly, and instead he focused on the long, sharply edged barrel and area under the forward grip, all-black metal a complete counter to the core of light at the center. Hoping it was as sharp as it looked and as strong as the navy-blue steels the aliens typically used, Rex swung it as hard as possible against the outer seals on the hatch. A blast of air began to jet from the ragged scar in the seals, and he jerked away, the rifle still jammed in between the two layers, creating a screeching whistle that rung his senses like his head was inside a jar, and someone was tapping on the exterior. Hands clenched about his head, trying to cover the pickups on the headgear, Rex moved awkwardly around the side of the bunker, the pressure first blasting the rifle from the gouge in the steels, and then ripping the outer hatch from its moorings, propelled towards the shore.

Wondering just what the hell needed a double-sealed pressurized hatchway for a simple bunker, Rex took the second rifle, still strapped to the sling, and held it too at the ready like a sword before approaching the still-venting lock. The inner door still resolutely in place, he located the panel on the interior, and cursed as it buzzed harshly in response to his hands accessing the buttons and touch screen, far beyond usefulness, the connecting hydraulics burnt and sparked out, shattered and empty of the fluid meant to ensure its operation. After a moment's thought, he wondered why he couldn't just proceed through a hatch without destroying it, once in his life, and reluctantly began to rip into the next door, surprised how much more integrity the inner door had in comparison to the outer seals.

The metal screamed as he carved the blade into it, and as he tore it free to swing again, a beam of light across the lenses had his attention turning to the alien weapon, seeing the crack in the exterior, and flinging it down without hesitation. Rolling out of the hatchway and scrambling down the still-sopping wet hill of grass and dirt, Rex belly flopped painfully in order to avoid an explosion he expected was rapidly incoming, and after a short pause, he turned back to see what was going on, and was flattened by the delayed detonation. Waves of hot mud, shattered concrete, and spikes of molten metal emanated from the explosion, wishing that he was out of range, and not surprised when, as he stood, mud began to slick down the back of the armor suit, pelted with rock. Looking over his right shoulder, Rex suppressed a scream as he saw six large, nasty spikes of the navy-blue metal jutting from his arm and back.

Slumping to his knees for a moment, breathing heavily, and trying to ignore the grinding sensation in his chest, while ensuring he was not bleeding too badly, Rex noted that each of the spikes were deep enough to puncture through the Combine suit, but were not deeply embedded into his own body. However, without decent means of first aid or other medical attention, he was not about to begin yanking them free.

Taking caution with each motion, trying to flex his muscles and stretch his arm, he made a positive confirmation that it could be done without too much difficulty. As he turned back to the bunker, the massive crater on the exterior was hardly a surprise, only the fact that the room beyond the hatch was exposed to the atmosphere, expelling oxygen still through cracks in the remaining surfaces. Wiping the biggest hunks of mud off of the armor suit, and clearing around the somewhat shallow wounds, Rex began to make his way back to the shattered bunker.

Balance still teetering off every few steps, he shoved it aside internally, scrounging around the debris while walking. Rex found nothing useful or remotely intact, even the secondary chamber now little more than four blackened walls without a ceiling, a connecting doorway still sealed tight, access panels bolted behind safety glass. Taking a short look around at the mess he'd made, Rex figured he'd already taken violence to another level on this structure, and decided not to stop there, using his left hand to easily rend the surrounding, weakened steels to get at the controls, chucking aside the glass panel complete with frame.

After a few more moments, the access console allowed him to use the next room as a backup airlock, and he stepped in as the cycle sequence began to restart, feeling lost all over again, wondering what kind of surprises lie in store for him next, and just where the island was, or how it could have been useful to the Combine. Unimpressed so far, the second hatch signaled the level of the process taking place, and Rex took his time to examine the slate-gray steel walls and matching concrete, stress fractures from the explosion spider-webbing along areas, but still held together by sturdy construction.

The machinery here was all of the typical Combine fare, flat-panel control screens along the left wall, larger pulsing conduits running vertically down the right wall, from ceiling to floor, surrounded by strange halos of light. It took him a second to realize it, as the air finished equalizing pressure, the halos were not dissipating or even being disturbed by the rush of pressures, the lenses allowing him to slowly adjust his focus closer, a jolt to his system as it went all the way to microscopic measurement, and he could only see swarming machines, a buzz of mechanical activity down to a level he couldn't recognize.

The harsh whine of the backup airlock completing and allowing him access snapped him out of his reverie, and he whipped his head around to the sight of a dank, rusted series of corridor panels leading up to the next room, and wondered why the rust had deteriorated the metal here so badly, complete opposite to the condition of the entry. The next door was completely untouched by rust, but a thick layer of grime coated control grips and levers, dripped from the hinges, and pooled on the floor, making Rex reluctant to touch it at all.

Still he opened it despite all of the nastiness, and the wave of stale air that greeted him was more than enough to trigger his gag reflex, choking back tears at the stench, coughing raggedly under the headgear. He looked ahead at an expanse of fencing and iron struts, formed into rough corridors, chain mesh floors and ceilings revealing little other than the fact that several stories ran deep underneath his own, circling around a central pillar of light.

The large mechanical source of energy seemed stunningly familiar, close to the individual power cells inside of the tower, and the unnatural throbbing it produced to the lighting fixtures seemed surreal, making the area even stranger, the blackened metal, stench, poor illumination counter to all his other experiences with the Combine. Even the shape and form of the soldiers, their weapons, the construction of the building, did not present a front he could face with recognition, blurring lines between alien and human and just plain filth, creating a maze of unfamiliar origin.

Just taking the first step into it was daunting enough, trying to force his body into action after having taken such abuse and neglect, shaking off the fact that the implant now made inhuman growling sounds rather than the angelic tones he'd listened to before, when it was first jammed into his torso so long ago, all adding to his worries. The lack of any additional weaponry became his primary concern, noting that he was going to solve that problem as soon as possible. Continuing in his forced motions, Rex kept following the bend and turn of the fenced-off pathway, looking at valves, switches, knobs, and other hand controls with very human influences, only scrawled with the symbolic shapes of the Combine language.

Heavy plodding sounds could be heard below, reverberating through the metal frames, shaking the area like a web connected together using the odd collaboration of materials. Despite it all, Rex moved as quietly as possible, seeking a source of all this; recognizing some things, others too dissimilar to compare with other examples. There had to be a reason he was here, and even as he snuck through the area, examining whatever he could pick out, dreaming of having hands able to use the weapons he had access to, wishing of having something that was proportional to the changes he'd undergone…

It was abruptly replaced by the sight of the little yellow-lensed demon just in front of him, carrying another of the rifles, shocked by the intruding presence. The enemy's weapon nearly contacting his chest, Rex smacked it aside, and winced as the blast of energy emptied into the machinery around him, dripping hot gobs of searing metal. Gripping the rifle in the same motion with his left hand, and the right snaking out, Rex grasped the lenses and cables mounted on the face of the new mutant type.

Rifle easily taken from the surprised clutch of the opponent, Rex reversed it and jammed it into the soldier's gut, tearing the accessories from the facial features, embedded circuitry and sockets popping loudly as they left behind gaping holes. It began to gobble and warble through a throat microphone, shaking on the sharpened point of the rifle, and Rex kicked it off and away, slicing the bladed weapon across the alien neck swiftly before switching it to his right hand, dragging the point across the metal surface of the grated wall.

Rex was tired of this, craving real accomplishment here so he could finish this off, needing to do this, but wanting it by him, in his past, a burden no longer there—derailing his train of thought, deeming it unnecessary to dredge over, he instead concentrated on the tasks upcoming at hand, the fact that the metallic corridor of parts made an abrupt turn here, going down to the next level. At the bottom of the long ramp sat a curved shallow basin moving out of sight, and Rex stepped down further to investigate, clacking of insectile feet on the bottom of the basin vibrating the metal and making it shake under his feet.

The pooling liquid on the interior of the basin was sticky and thick, giving strange intonations to the motions of the giant-legged slug up ahead, the large bug-thing turning to face him even as Rex finished stepping down the ramp, staring with multifaceted eyes, larger segmented limbs pulling away from controls. The motion to kill the creature was the first on his mind, an almost-instantaneous reaction as he turned to face it, wielding the weapon like a sword. He hacked off several limbs with the first swing, and carving a swath through the chest carapace, Rex wondered why it wasn't wearing an environment suit like the others he'd killed. A splash of thick, dark ichor spattered the lenses of the headgear, impeding the speed of his next attack as he wavered just long enough to wipe it away. Finally, he slammed the edge of the rifle down at a deep diagonal, cleaving in with every inch of muscle he could spare, nearly splaying the torso in twain.

Rex finished the motion by kicking his right foot high enough to strike the head of the giant bug, and the creature folded backwards in half, the body spurting jets of the bluish-green blood that he avoided. Hauling the bladed rifle free with a solid jerk and shoving aside the massive remains, watching them splash to the ankle-deep basin before walking by, Rex began looking at the few consoles that were present here, trying to match the strange motions he'd attempted to memorize as he encountered the creature using the touch screens.

Surpassingly they came back alive and responded to the touches he made to the control panel, showing him an odd series of overhead planetary views. They were intermixed with sonic readings, the headgear translating things into calculations and dividends he couldn't recognize, obviously advanced mathematics designed by the insectile slavers, written in their numbers and letters. Altering the readouts in order to locate precisely what it was measuring, Rex gasped in reaction to the size of the objects on screen. Three massive discs of the navy-blue Combine steels formed hulls of multiple craft, locked in a triangular position around a huge pylon of the same metals. All were connected, creating a spin that stabilized the three ships somehow.

Delving deeper into the console, he tried to desperately find more information about the objects he witnessed through the monitor, but spun to see another of the newer mutations walking up to step into the basin from a lower level, and flung the rifle at the newcomer. The trajectory of the rifle was horrible, but caused the enemy to attempt to dodge it anyway, and Rex leapt immediately thereafter, tackling the opponent and mashing the armament from the creature's fingers. The fight was interrupted by the sound of a second mutate, also armed with a strange energy cannon, aiming the weapon directly at Rex and pulling the trigger without uttering a word.

The charge of sound and energy seared the air around him, cooked the creature he still grasped in his hands, and flung him back against the far wall like an explosive force, sending Rex crumpling through the panel of consoles and down a floor below. He struck the platform with much force, body superheated, hands twitching, armor suit and mobile combat vest still smoking from the exchange of energy. Struggling to his feet, Rex shook stars from his eyes, flexed hands and fingers until he could feel them again, and forced himself to stand, bones and muscles so sore from abuse they felt as if they were creaking, aged wood under his skin. Sounds of feet coming back down the ramp had him rolling for cover, avoiding a shower of sparks as a wall beyond his position seared alight with red-hot directed power, and he made no plans to give up, even now.

Waiting half a heartbeat for the enemy to decide to close in, Rex gripped a fistful of blackened fencing embedded into the wall ahead, and with one foot braced against the base of the mounted equipment, leapt up, and pulled himself over the top of the wall, arms swinging his body and propelling him around the corner out of range of the rifle's direction. The maneuver easily allowed him to land atop the mutate, the weapon blasting off again as hands gripped the trigger, resulting in the lance of energy to sear ahead past Rex to once again strike the wall. Left foot pinning the trigger hand down and right foot crushing the chest, Rex leaned down and pulled the enemy's head up until the neck snapped, leaving the paralyzed soldier there to die while he walked back up the ramp to the destroyed basin.

All of the computers and screens blacked out—dead—obviously lacking power routing to them, the sparking, gaping hole where he'd been shot through most likely the source of routing that had been eliminated. Shaking his head, Rex turned away, stepping back down the ramp to the previous area resolutely. A quick examination of the layout revealed a strange *W* shape, the side to his right the location where he'd been forced to fall to, the corpse of the creature marking that passage as being the dead end. Choosing to move to his left, Rex cautiously reminded himself that, while information was of the utmost priority, he had to keep it intact long enough to read it. Not encouraging his unstable mind was the lack of computers, access ports, and machinery down this way, a complete absence of what he was focused on locating, sending his mood spiraling downwards.

A storm cloud rising over his thoughts, Rex began to let slip curses and guttural tones, coming to the end of the corridor of mesh and panels, and pausing in confusion again. The interior curved into a central, pulsing chamber, and he brightened internally as he found the chamber was an extension of the oversized power source below. The thrumming of the energy could be felt through the soles of his boots, vibrated up his legs, shook his spine, and pulsed through his veins, invigorating him through an invisible means. It was indescribable and powerful beyond measure, the heads-up display reacting favorably, giving him access to the entire data store, wetwire interface blazingly quick.

With a smile, he realized that the Lena-AI would have loved a database of this extent, and tapped into the functions he required, bringing up data streams from live feeds, searching through scores of files, and racing along bits of information. He rapidly collected a mass of the gathered secrets, and snarled aloud as he stumbled upon realization, locating the true purpose of the triad ships in orbit. They *were* the suppression devices, the three of them broadcasting across the entire planet, covering up so much of the planet in orbit that he could not recognize the landmasses nearby, the scale coming in from another satellite, locked to the large station by unseen means.

But all of the information, all the control, was meaningless here on the planet. The power needed to be connected to the central spire in orbit above him, and even as he received those thoughts, his mind spurred to action, charging along the system's controls. Finding the lift assembly for the power source, Rex began the process to raise the platform to orbit level, and then suddenly halted. Something else was just outside his periphery, and he felt giant hands of his own mind grasp the data stream, ripping it free from out of sight and back into plain view, shaking it as the encryption surrounding the characters refused to clarify. One solid jolt to the jagged collection of data files with a digital swipe and it formed into a proper message, unfolding into a stream of information, sound and visual overwhelming him through the wireless connection maintained by the headgear, activating the stored information.

"Hello, Mr. Rex. Just a short relayed message here for you: The lower levels have a few items you will need, and some assistance."

Rereading the message several times, Rex knew it was from the stranger in the blue suit even though it was not signed as such, and as he tossed the data aside, his mind mulled over the reference to assistance, in addition to other items. Never before had there deliberately been a crew of fighters working for the strange benefactor in any of his travels, and only once had he encountered anyone like him, as confused as he was now, it carried no wonder or disguised amusement as it always had before. Who exactly was he to expect to show up before him amidst all this blackened metal and strange steel, odd layouts forming the interior and even eerier creatures than usual filling it up?

The question went unanswered in the back of his mind, Rex focusing on the fact that any assistance was better than none, and sending the lift sliding down the shaft to the bottom, the decent taking an entire thirty seconds of complete silence to reach the very deep level. The connection with the data stream seemed to halt as the lift increased in motion, but the thrumming of energy did not cease within himself, echoing along the corridors of his body. It created a resounding sensation that reverberated through the implant, eyes growing wide as the grinding sounds grew louder and louder...

Grasping his chest and gasping at the sudden pain jolting through him, Rex felt his ribcage heaving, coughing like mad, lifting the faceplate to spit a streamer of blood, torso blazing alight with flame, arms and legs shaking with effort as he tried to stand, to push back the pain, when the grinding became the orchestra, the symphony of sounds he was so fond of before. Gloriously he stood without pain, without tremors, wiping his lips with the back of one hand, and replacing the headgear to its proper position, a smile on his face despite everything, gazing about at the lift as it came to a stop. One entrance sat here for the entire level, the glow beyond a strange white-blue light, source unseen, and as Rex stepped towards the archway, the power source activated the rooms beyond, consoles and architecture coming to life, LCD monitors, flat screens, touch pads, and command consoles all unlocking.

The floor here was the alien-looking brown-textured metal, walls of blackened steels, overhead lights stars in a field of darkness, a strange, almost-human feel to the construction. It had wide spaces between walls to accommodate large shapes, but not quite eight-foot tall, leading straight ahead to a deviation on the right, no furnishings other than the dozens of consoles and access ports at shoulder level. Ignoring the typical means of data access in favor of walking down the length of the corridor, Rex kept close to the right side, wondering where all the opposition was, now eager to embrace others in combat, any others. Even the giant, bloated insectile slavers would be a decent target for an outpouring of anger, something to generate a feeling of accomplishment, taking a deep breath and pausing briefly to stretch out, working muscles and joints that were once pained like nothing ever happened.

Taking the turn to the right as it came up, Rex smiled as he found it ending at a navy-blue hatchway, two of the advanced mutated soldiers standing here holding their weapons smugly, non-communicative, but connected without being vocal, broadcasting his position to each other as he came around the bend. Both soldiers raised weapons, firing simultaneously, and Rex stepped into it. MCV and Combine armor blazingly hot, but well within structural integrity, the power of both cannons stopped his motion as they came into contact with him. Still, as the moment of struggling forces passed, Rex charged the two soldiers, leaping the last few steps at his enemies, and slashing with his left hand, the large claws lifting rifles free from surprised grasps.

He landed just in front of them, slamming each into the thickened armor hatch briefly, and rebalancing himself for the next strike before they could recover, he took the side of one mutant head in his left hand, and pinned the second enemy to the door with the right hand. The Combine creatures struggled against him with a measure of calculatedly immense strength, and Rex had to hand it to the slavers, they'd converted the technology well. Unfortunately for them, the prototype did not agree with the master's will, and he showed the end results just how strong he was now, crushing skulls by colliding both brainpans, lights going dead in all lenses, Rex tossing the bodies aside.

In response to the deaths of the guards, the console for the doorway angrily refused to respond to his manipulations, and a sense of happiness turned to rage, smashing and kicking at the door. He peeled the metal open with razor edged fingertips, tearing out the tech and flinging it aside to shatter against the far wall. Turning his attention back to the door itself, he began to use a loose section of the wall to pry at the entry, jamming it into the latch until it stuck resolutely, then resorting to using his hand as hammers on the layered armor, bending the huge panel inwards measurably.

Shoulder down and aimed at the lever of steel jutting from the latches, Rex rammed it repeatedly to lever open the gap wider, metal whining in complaint as it finally relented, steel on both ends snapping, increasing amounts of sparks blazing from the gaping hole in the wall, and hydraulics bubbling over the top of the heavily strained hinges. Working his hands into the opening in a mirror fashion of other heavy doors he'd tackled before, Rex began to pull on the edge roughly, curling metal and splitting edges as it twisted around, barely forming a gap. Roaring louder, he continued raging against the resisting navy-blue steels, thrashing and kicking the center until the moored braces along the surfaces cracked and fell loose.

Backing away from what he could judge as a proper distance, Rex leaned in full force on a charge, leaping again just before the door, tackling the target evenly with all four limbs, fingers grasping the steel-like paper, and momentum carrying him transferred to the multilayered panels with ease, metal crumpling and popping. The huge section of alien material came free from the complex pressure pumps and hinges, coasting through the air a short distance with him atop, until it landed on the metal floor, throwing up sparks and a shower of heated bits, shredding the brown texture surfaces, and gouging out huge portions of metal from the walls.

Sliding for several feet until crashing into the furthest wall beyond, he began to laugh as he found himself on the other side of the seal at last, the chuckling interrupted by gasping and other confusing sounds on his left, pausing just long enough to stand before turning to face the noises. Several cages lined the left wall, each containing a single humanoid form, all facing his dramatic entry, looks of apprehension on their faces. Rex forced a double take as he realized he was looking into real human features, instead of a mask or a monstrosity covered with lenses, actual human beings, covered head to toe in strange, chitinous battle gear, black and red layers overlapping to present an out-of-the-ordinary sight.

Recognition soon followed the realizations, and he could feel his mind piecing together the last time he'd looked into the eyes of the people jailed before him, each approaching cage doors with clear doubts as to whom Rex really was, not appearing to be Combine slaves, but not being vocal about anything either, presenting a confusing situation. All five of them carried a question in their eyes for him, a question that had gone unanswered for a long time now: Was he Combine or Human, and despite either of those, wherein did his loyalties lie? Forcing his feet to move himself away from the forced-and-fallen door, and making his way to the right side of the room, he spied a few items to focus his attention on, remaining just as silent as the others imprisoned behind him.

Looking at a wall of secured and locked weaponry with a slight smile, the store of data in his mind described each, and the DNA lock for each reader revealed a list of numbers and letters instead of a real name. However, what drew him closer was the single unlocked compartment, almost beckoning him right to it without explanation, and he reached out to it slowly, opening the latch with his right hand and raising the lid. Fingers reaching deep inside, Rex almost jerked away as something snapped around his wrist, surprising him, the enclosing feeling crawling up his arm, mind racing.

Finally, he began to pull back, and the sight before him was even more shocking than the other discoveries so far: A giant mechanical spider latching around the forearm, crawling up to his shoulder; a massive white globe of energy embedded into it forming around his shoulder, another limb wrapping about his upper back, grasping onto his neck, and working up into the headgear to mate with the Combine multi-port on the back of his skull. Frozen where he stood, a mechanical scream reverberated through his body, paralyzed by the creature on his arm and unable to react, until he realized the voice had come from somewhere else.

A click deep in his head had the immobilizing effects fading, a wave of freedom working down his spine and allowing him to gasp for air, becoming conscious of the fact that even his lungs had frozen for that split second. And as he looked to his right arm, expecting a living being to be crawling and oozing along his limb, he found only a mechanical device formfitting to his body. The data store of info he'd accessed gave him enough information to piece together what it was for the most part, matching a prototype cannon in the Combine database only up to a certain point. Stretching slowly and flexing muscles to help accommodate the extra mass, Rex felt the device in his mind as well, responding to inquiries about charge status, ammunition, power source location, and even total condition, thanking the stranger in the blue dress suit unconsciously.

Looking back over his right shoulder now, past the pulsating core of energy now resting there embedded into the armor, taking in the vision of panic-stricken prisoners—if before they had some trouble of discerning who and what he was, the event they had no doubt witnessed could have potentially changed everything about him. Turning to face them again, he stopped to look into their faces, the headgear collaborating with the data stream to identify their retinal scans, matching them with numbered identities, identical to the DNA locks for the weapons behind him. The information came to him passively, and as soon as it hit him, he tried to look them up on the Combine database, matching IDs to reference files. The task became one he had to set aside, and allow running in his mental background, the oldest of the three caged males spoke for the first time. "I recognize you. The psycho Combine from the train wreck."

Rex couldn't help but chuckle at the description, looking up at the vaunted ceiling and breathing in deeply, wishing it was fresher air, something from the outdoors, but settling for the stale, over-recycled fog of swampy air instead, inhalation reverberating in his lungs, a calm flooding him with a cold chill, fires of anger becoming a tranquil heat.

"And I recognize all of you. The humans I saved, who so graciously left me behind to be captured; the five that bailed out on me as I was surrounded by Combine. I seriously doubted I would ever see you all again. I suppose this is some sort of odd reunion, but I'm not holding my breath."

The tallest of the three, the one he'd coined as *giant* before, growled audibly, the skinniest male shifting about nervously. Both of the females seemed eternally calm, still not saying a word out loud, but glancing at each other, clearly exchanging thoughts and perhaps more somehow. It was a conversation he could only participate half of the time in, but undaunted, Rex continued.

"I suppose you already know who sent me; it was more than likely the same...person...that sent you all. Curiously, he made little mention of who exactly I would find. Needless to say this is as much a surprise to me as it is to all of you."

The calm he felt seemed to exude outwards from his position, and spread to the others in turn, the eldest of them all smiling and turning to face Rex, seemingly in agreement with each other.

"We...understand. We all agree that what you have stated is correct."

Even as the words were spoken, Rex still felt as if there was a chasm, yet to cross between them all, and began again, in hopes of understanding more, and perhaps gaining a better grasp at what he should be saying to them next.

"Good, then I propose we work together. It's clear from the prison records the Combine have on you all that you don't agree with the alien invaders, and while we didn't get off on the right foot the first time we've all met, I'm hoping we can change that now."

Letting the words sink in, hoping the pause was enough for a moment of reflection, Rex spoke again a second later, "Anyone disagree?"

Once more, the question settled in the air, and the only grunt of derision came from the giant. Rex turned to face him, and the same part of himself that calculated the group was communicating telepathically or by another link, now intuitively knew that all the doubts, all the conflicting views, all the disruptive elements still resting within the group, they had been projected to the largest of them. It was similar to what he could guess, dealing with a hive mind would be like, and far be it from himself to not oblige them, responding to the nonverbal affront.

"Fine. Do you have a better idea?"

Rex already knew the response, could sense it coming a mile away, the exact same response he would have given if there was a Combine soldier standing outside his cage, asking him to cooperate on a task. He'd given them very little to actually trust him, and the blue-suited benefactor could have been a completely different type of patron for them, rescuer apparent even after Rex had been forced to go to all the trouble, accreditation going to the strange controller of time and space rather than to the person that had actually been on the ground, in the thick of it. And even as the heavy tone came from the giant behind the cage, Rex could think of every outcome of any conflict, narrowing them down to only one: he couldn't kill, couldn't subdue the giant. He had to convince them, somehow.

"I say, I kill you, take your weapon, release the others, and then we figure out what to do."

Rex turned to the console, and touched the controls for the cages. The giant seemed surprised that the cage door slid open, stepping out and snarling.

"What? You expected me to not let you out, even after threatening me? Perhaps I'm not who you think I am."

A roar permeated the air as the giant charged him, almost tripping over the fallen door, but still trying to shoulder slam in vein—Rex easily sidestepped the attack, a gentle push all that was needed to throw the larger male off-balance, crashing into the far wall with the sound of crystalline on metallic surfaces. Eyebrows furrowing as his opponent easily recovered, Rex spoke again, continuing his efforts. "I'm here to stop the field. And destroy the ships in orbit."

The blazing surge of action that followed from the giant seemed to construe that the spoken words were not being heard, but Rex had to convince himself otherwise—injuring or crippling the opponent was not an option, he *needed* him for the fight ahead, leapfrogging over the giant as another charge missed him. Dodging a backhand, and dipping away from a roundhouse kick, a solid shove was all that was required to again topple his opponent in mid-strike, and he spoke again as was becoming pattern, "You don't want to try to stop me. Or try to kill me; we all know what we want is the same, whether or not I'm alive at the end of it all."

At that, the giant paused as he turned, and Rex held his ground. But still, it was not enough, another attack following with an as-of-yet-unseen ferocity, Rex forced to swat away, block, parry, and stop most of the attacks with his hands, the blurring motions almost overwhelming, the smile creeping onto the giant's features…with a sudden countermeasure of bursting speed and shifting center of gravity, Rex bounced knuckles from his smartly, grasping both armored forearms. Feet planted firmly and momentum in his favor, he twisted about while lifting upwards, kicking the legs out from under the giant, and with a force of energy only fractional in comparison to what was being directed at him, threw the larger male across the distance to the furthest wall. Breathing slightly harder now, a single trickle of sweat rolling down his side, Rex spoke now to his recovering opponent, the resolve behind his voice like a powerful force of its own to be reckoned with, "We need to stop them together, or not at all. It has to be this way, and we cannot do it alone."

The giant stood again, showing signs of bewilderment, but eyes locking onto him as the words drove home.

"Do not make me hurt you, or we're all screwed."

Finally, the attacks stopped, but only physically—the verbal lashing that came next was harsh, but expected, and carried equal measures of indignation and refusal with it.

"Just what makes you think that you're so damned important, that *we're* so damned important that we have to work with you as some kind of team? What makes you so special that the five of us alone could not handle the task without your supposed expertise? We've gone a long way without your assistance, and now you insist so much while giving so little. What reason have you espoused upon us for trusting you beyond that doorway?"

Rex felt himself halting in his rebuttal before he could think of it, head swimming with words and emotions he dared not speak of now, hating the fact that things had gone so far only to come down to this, fighting someone that should have been an ally a long time ago, turned to an enemy somehow through lies and falsehoods, or simply mere misunderstanding. The worst part of it all being that he needed these allies, could not turn away from them, could not finish his task without the assistance they would provide, and if he killed them, all was lost.

"Think back to when I first saw you all. Was I trying to kill you? Or was I saving you from the hail of gunfire the Combine began raining down upon your heads? Who left who on a field surrounded by the enemy, which of us abandoned the other on that battleground? Now, realize that we were all suddenly thrust into this without choice, without even being asked or told what was happening, by one person, if it's really just a person, the same mysterious stranger that stuck my ass out on that grassy expanse to *save* the five of you. And now you finally might see, you left me there alone to fight the Combine, despite every effort I made to save you all, you *abandoned* me out there.

"You talk of trust? Understanding? You've taken no steps of your own to establish any of this to me, and here it is, the second time I've been put here to *help* you, and still you doubt me. What do you expect? For me to just give up, let you cage me? What else were all of you thinking when you saw me for the second time, that I had come to *end* you?" Arms at his sides, snarling with each breath, Rex finished the statement by stomping on the metal floor once.

"Well knock it off, now. You need to get your crap together, as a *group*, and finally start understanding what I'm saying to you. I'm not asking, just like the bastard in the blue suit, I'm telling you this is what has to be done. If I leave you in your cages or kill you, I'm eternally screwed, I'll never get home again, and I don't have to even begin to describe to you what that means to me. And if you kill me or cage me, you'll never get past the power lift to get to the surface, let alone getting up to orbit to destroy those platforms. Despite everything you might think or do, we need each other in order to stop this thing. If you insist on going your own way when we're done with this task, then fine, I won't stop any of you. But right now, you're all standing in my path to return to the people I care about, and even if I have to tie you all up and *drag* you into that lift to take you to those satellites, nothing, I repeat, *nothing* will stop me. There are no choices here. Either you're with me, or you're *with* me on this, no my-way-or-the-highway choice, just *our* way; with my insistence."

Rex was done, verbally spent and shifting on his mental tracks aimlessly, the giant clearly not his enemy, but unsure of what was to come, pausing his own physical pacing in order to grind over his moment of indecision, turning to the controls for the other cages as he made his choice, unlocking all of the barred doors and releasing the other four captives. Rex turned away from them, walking to the forced-open doorway, looking back only once over his shoulder with a sidelong glance, his comment barely audible.

"When you're done making up your minds, I'll be on the lift, waiting for you."

Striding out of the lockdown room and passing the gaping hole where the vault-like door once stood, Rex tried to quiet the voice in the back of his skull insisting he'd made the wrong decision, the devilish, toothy, monstrous grin insisting that he go back and eliminate them all, stop the fight through utter finality of death…

It felt like a physical shove to get it away from himself, back it off and box it away into a compartment of his mind not to be drifting into, anything to step away from it, flee as fast and as hard as possible from it, and when it finally retreated, it did so willingly.

Walking down the metal floor with eyes focused ahead, Rex made the turn back to the lift, and as he moved to the middle of the platform, he sat, cross-legged and head in his malformed hands, talons on his toes, clacking loudly against the metal with each motion. The vocal confrontation along with the attempt to avoid the fight drained much from him, but even as he considered this, he could feel the reserve of energy within himself, hardly touched, smudged, but ready, pulsing in his veins, mind with each echoing reverberation.

He'd gone so far for this, to argue with the people that were supposed to be helping? To become wrapped up in a discussion about who had displayed enough measures of trust, then physically fight over who was right or wrong…it felt eternally out of place, broken interactions with shattered dialogue for a ruined future. And still, he could feel the well of resolve within himself—he would not stop until he'd completed the task at hand.

But did that make him right? Was he correct in being so firm, so stubborn, so on point? Had he missed something, after all this time, attempting to be so reckless, but so analytical, what was the detail he'd completely avoided? One look at himself, and he could not deny he looked a very different part from the one he was currently playing, and even then, he had been wearing Combine armor when he'd first rescued them. Could looks be so deceiving that even his own sight had fooled himself? Dressing in the armor that the Combine used, it afforded him a deep amount of protection from most any weapons, but it presented awkward problems everywhere he went, turning friend into foe, corrupting communications, making horrible conversations, and as he was finally honest about it, revealed a monstrous part of himself behind the heavy-drawn curtains.

Was that monster the primary thing that scared his friends, eliminated cooperators, and ruined things from the very start? First sight of the creature within and a spiritual sign saying 'All those that approach, Beware' mounted on his chest was the most commonly perceived view he was beginning to notice, and it also mirrored the Combine's approach towards him at the same time. Kill or capture, eliminate or collar, containment by any means including slavery and death. The only kindness he'd known was his mother and father, and in the end, neither of those were really his parents, adoptive guardians that took him from the Black Mesa labs so long ago. He'd never found more proof than the clone of himself sitting in a government-sanctioned base, locked in a containment pod, but what more evidence did he need than that? And even as he thought it, there were other sources of care he'd known: Maurine, Thompson, Tank, and O'Hare before things went crazy, and the one constant since he'd found her, Molly.

But what did any of that matter now? He was stuck here, waiting on them, or an attack that might come at any moment, his course of action derailed by unexpected visitors and huge gaps in provided information, helped only by more Combine tech and equipment, given an immense source of knowledge that had nothing to do with the task at hand, being forced to adapt it to his will, bend it to his needs. A single damn note in a computer on an island in the middle of a sea or ocean, miles from any shore, buried thousands of feet deep underground, and that was the fullest extent of assistance he'd received from the strange benefactor so far, if he didn't count the mechanical spider nesting on his right arm. Or if he ignored the room full of people that consistently showed how much they trusted him by bailing on him, if that could be done at this point.

Still things could have been far worse, he guessed, knowing he could have been locked in a cage, under the knives of a torturous traitor, or even more horrid, leading assault forces from a tower somewhere to try and hunt out the remaining humans. The sounds of approaching steps on the metal tiles leading to the lift forced Rex into motion, and standing while turning to face the newcomers, he couldn't help but wonder if they were approaching as friends or enemies. He stood still regardless, waiting for the next string of words or actions to follow, begging the universe that things would go in the right direction...

All five of them were there, standing at the entry and waiting for him to face them. Unmoving, passive-featured, but equipped with their weaponry from the wall of locks, being led by the only man he'd easily rescued and spoken with before, the moderate-sized fellow putting up his hands, palms-out as he spoke.

"Enough, stranger. We've had enough fighting with you. Even from the beginning, when you saved us, we did not understand why. And now, after all this, we finally understand—it was not your choice to be there, not your choice to become what you are, but you did choose to fight the Combine. You chose to save us."

They all entered the lift calmly, encircling along the walls, speaking as the leader gestured to them in turn, after introducing himself first, "I am Emrich, you saved me first."

The giant spoke next, "Beremod."

Both women followed up with introductions of their own, nearly speaking simultaneously, almost giving off literal waves of noninterest at Rex.

"Aae."

"Bre."

And finally, the skinniest, shortest of the three males spoke last, his voice like a whisper grating against torn metal. "Skel."

After the speaking was over, a dead silence began to drift down around them, Rex adjusting his position, and understanding what transpired before him. With a curt nod to each of them, Rex finally spoke, gesturing them inside all of the way.

"Good to finally meet you all on friendlier terms. My…name is Rex. Let's get on with this so we can all go our separate ways."

Focusing his thoughts on the lift and up the shaft, he could easily sense the movement as they rocketed to the surface, Rex planning out the amount of time it would take to reach the orbiter and focusing on the creature latched around his arm.

"It'll take us about ten minutes to reach orbit. Quite an impressive speed for a launch, for no chemical rockets or engines that I can discern, but should provide us enough time to prepare for what we might meet."

The entire weapon about his arm stayed motionless as he flexed his muscles, examining fiberwire, noting armored portions, and locating an ominous-looking bore of an energy emitter at the back of his hand. The metal spines interlaced through his arm and the armor, interlinking the Combine suit with the strange device, readings coming through the heads-up display attempting to point out individual sections, but unable to distinguish it into sections anymore. Further scans revealed it wasn't even a separate, unified device connected only to the suit. It was now *part* of him, intertwined into his body, one with his mind, connected and inseparable. Looking around, he could see all eyes were on him, feeling put out of place, but knowing what he was supposed to be doing. As he spoke softly, he continued the introspective thoughts of himself, while attempting to maintain a modicum of balance.

"Not sure how long it's been since I've fought alongside others I've barely met before. I was defending a compound almost a week ago, had a few new faces, but nothing like this."

Smiles were actually spread around, except for the two females, eyes locked onto each other, and he could feel a small sense of camaraderie beginning to build up between everyone. Not positive if it had him included, but too far beyond the ability to change things now, riding out the current of the wave he'd been forced upon. One thing that calmed his nerves was the fact that his fellow fighters were now fighting *with* him, instead of fighting against him about combating the enemy they both had looming over them.

It set a serene tone to the moving lift, no windows, or ports, but plenty of thrumming from the power source under their feet to accompany them during the journey, hands shifting uneasily, fingers grasping weapons, hackles on the back of his neck rising to match his angst. Peace left his body as the countdown to arrival closed to the end, the empty reservoir filling with the darkness he'd kept contained, restricted away, piecing out the uncontrollable portions to protect the others around him from it, but wanting enough of the monster unleashed to assist his battle. Centering himself as the bestial form flooded his senses, Rex took one more opportunity to speak, voice pouring out like gravel from his parched throat.

"Alright. Keep cool, expect the best, and prepare for the worst. If we all let chillier minds prevail, we'll finish our task here, and be sipping martini's on the beach, if that's what you want."

Flicking on the arming sequence for the odd weapon fused into his arm and shoulder, and leveling the muzzle at the wide breach of the lift as it halted, Rex let only one word loose. "Action."

Both panels slid open, and the six of them fanned out into a broad, bright central chamber, connecting hatches, supports, and braces for each of the three craft connected to the platform jutting out in domineering angles and well-lit, consoles and flat screens chirping, and calculating away endlessly at streams of data. Rex felt his vision rise to the ceiling of the gigantic area, locating a tall control spire, hanging from the domed top of the structure by three large pulsating cables, and even as he did so, gunfire interrupted the tranquil sea of thoughts, a cone of energy searing the ground beyond his feet as Emrich and the two women took the left side of the zone, attracting attention.

Moving to his right, following both Beremod and Skel in pace and direction, Rex targeted one of the enemy soldiers blocking the hatchway ahead with the strange unified weapon, and let fly with a single eye-searing shot, surprised when the bulkheads blackened around the impact point, threw pieces of the strange clad mutate about wildly, and melted down the hatch itself, reducing it to a pile of hot slag at the base. Skel leapt through the burned-down hatchway without saying a word, and as Rex paused to wonder what was happening, Beremod gestured him ahead while whispering.

"He's going to try to interrupt the engines on that one, get me into the next craft, and you can head for the control cluster."

A short nod was all he could spare for the brief interim of information flow before his attentions were forced to the middle hatch, Beremod making short work of the two soldiers standing guard with the strange pulse rifle in his hands, before barreling through the metal hatch like it wasn't there, or sealed shut either. There was quite a racket as the heavy metal door flew off the hinges and bounced down the connecting pathway beyond, Beremod disappearing from sight as he turned around a bend, leaving Rex all alone in the massive, dominating area under the control spire. A quick glance to his left confirmed that Emrich managed to get both Aae and Bre through the locking mechanism on the far side of the station, and as he advanced his own stride towards the abnormally shaped platforms dangling from the central spire, he felt his hands grasping the supports as he kept his eyes up to the dome, tracing the path of the support beam to the control nodule with his eyes.

Ascending hand over hand, Rex brushed aside a conduit as it drifted too close to him, and as it did it again, he tore it free from the clamps mounting it above with a steady jerk, letting the thick cabling fall before resuming the rise to the top of the support. Finally ascending to the peak of the column, Rex reached his hand out to try and grab onto something, anything for a handhold on the base of the control spire, fingers sliding on the slick metal surface, forcing him to tear into the outer exterior of the nodule with his left hand.

The clawed fingers easily peeled the outer layer of metal free, flinging aside a length of the ripped material to get at the interior, grasping bodily onto another layer, this one a combination of mesh and cabling, far easier to pull away than the first stratum of steel surrounding the control nodule. Crawling up into the inside, elbows bouncing from jutting edges and socketed devices along the last layer of steel on the interior, knees banging harshly as he crawled further inwards, Rex ignored the pinching of two plates of metal around his foot in favor of battering the last section of navy-blued Combine material.

A couple of brutish shoulder slams on the final sheet of steel in his path bulged it outwards dramatically, and as he moved about in the enclosed quarters, he felt his head and back jutting out over the zone, grasping the lengths of cable and metal to each side to brace himself, kicking out madly at the steel until shafts of light began to peek through. Jagged edges appearing as the stress on the materials increased, Rex could hear himself roaring over the sounds of abuse he was inflicting on the structure, the fortified substance screaming as it tore, echoing in the tight enclosure and causing him to clench his jaw, gritting teeth in an attempt to muzzle the noise. At last, the ragged egg-shaped section of steel came free and was propelled into the control room. Rex rolled inwards, halting just inside and standing upright, more sounds of movement straight ahead, but the glaring lights forced the lenses to auto adjust to the intensity. Just as vision normalized and Rex could focus, the sound of metal cutting through the air forced him to instinctively back up, shoulders striking the curved wall as a metallic fist buzzed his head.

"You will halt and comply, or be eliminated."

The voice was just as synthetic as the fist that narrowly killed him outright, and the angular, sharp frame of the form before him bore a crystalline structure to it, and as the translation reached his ears, it carried an insectile nature, matching its creators thoroughly, and presenting a challenging target. Running instinctually and slashing at the right side of the crystalline armor surface with his hand of claws, Rex was amazed when nothing happened; no scratches, cuts, or gashes, barely a sound to match the attack. And as another swing came at him, he ducked underneath the strike to make another of his own, kicking out at legs like pillars, the enemy unmoving from the force, turning to face him, perhaps to lock on a weapon or merely take another deadly punch.

Rex responded by raising his right hand at waist-level, and as the muzzle of the strange amalgamation of weapon and armor came around to bear on the automated defender's chest, it removed the threat by smacking him aside bodily. Rex crashed into the only console on the entire interior of the strange globe, turning the bright glare above and the navy-steel walls into a field of stars. The amazing view included all three of the orbiting craft locked to the station, barely catching glimpses as he landed on the floor, shreds of glass and metal from the rest of the console scattering around and ruining his footing. Sliding across the fragments desperately while his arms flailed about seeking purchase, the defender pinned him to the side of the control room wall with a single limb, the satellite feeds interrupting and creating static in the display.

Shoving at the ugly, sharp-angled fist and arm holding him back, Rex again tried to kick whatever he could reach, the thrashing landed home with plenty of force, but providing little if any result other than marring the once-shining surface of the mechanical creation. As he tried to re-aim the mounted weapon once more in desperation, he felt the next strike hit him from overhead, but did not see it. Driven to one knee, arm still holding him at length, Rex's vision began to swim as another hit from above connected, one oddly-formed crystalline knee whipping up to land directly into his armored features, blackness forming at the corners of his sight.

Barely avoiding the next overhead slam by forcing his body to twist under the pressure pushing him down, Rex laughed as the defender struck itself with its own attack, freeing him to roll out and away from the corner he'd been pinned into, diving and sliding across the metal flooring. Hands bouncing from surfaces as he stretched out to gain a hold of anything, attempting to stop his momentum, Rex failed as he slid right out through his own handmade entry. He was barely able to grasp onto a length of loose inner mesh in time to hang stubbornly over the great distance, the layer beginning to pull free a foot at a time, jerking after each pause.

Still without hesitation in his actions, Rex held his right arm up, leveled the complex weapon at the gaping hole in the command nodule, waited a single moment of freefall until the next pause came, and fired again, trigger by thought, the bolt of energy nearly blinding the lenses again as it scorched the air, glazing the metal edges of the makeshift entry as it passed through. The heat from the massive round cut off the layer of metal mesh, sending Rex falling to the floor meters below, finding himself surprisingly grateful as he struck the metal floor on his left side. He still screamed as his body impacted, but the sound was dwarfed by the echoes and screeches of the exploding control room above, shattering sounds followed by a jet of flame and debris funneling out through the same entry point, spraying metal ribbons and shards out like a blast of birdshot, coating the area.

Rex forced himself to begin to move while still roaring from unstoppable pain, entire side alive with firing nerves, but still somehow intact, no broken bones in his legs, allowing himself to get out of harm's way. The explosion above continued as it found the power source of the automated defender. Huge pieces of crystalline structure and hunks of the exterior began to escape from the detonations by force, burying themselves in the rounded walls, cutting off power conduits, toppling supports, and starting an alarm. White lighting became orange and pulsating to match blaring noise. More of the strange Combine language began to broadcast angrily in rapid repetition, the headgear translating it as a single word:

"Emergency!"

Stopping himself as a section of metal attached to one conduit whipped by, sparking lively and casting shadows, Rex watched as it slammed into a curved wall beyond and stuck there, finally resuming his movement back to the control spire. With a solid two-step propelling him along the debris-strewn floor, he took one mighty leap, catching one of the remaining cables and quickly climbing upwards to again reach the spire, a falling support missing him by inches as he forced his body to twist. Still steadily ascending the cable, he was forced to swing about the last few feet to gain hold of stubby remains, all that was left of a support strut, which easily provided enough of a hand and foothold for Rex to get over the glazed lip he'd turned his makeshift entry into.

The metal deck of the control nodule was a mess, coated in a thick gelatinous material and shards of the automated defender, Rex guessing that the material came from the interior of the machine or was a flame suppressant, and either way, it made footing complicated. The console that was the singular access point for the entire control station had a good layer of its own, and the surrounding displays for the walls of the nodule had only half of the ring working, snow on some, space on others. Grasping a section of the crystalline material and using it to scoop great gobs of the neutral, clear goo from the console surface, he ensured it was in working order, and accessed what he could easily reach, the headgear and the wealth of Combine information assisting him to bring up the cameras. Very few were actually functioning, and he was glad to be able to see the views on the three hatches leading to the craft, and sectioned them off under live feeds from outer shots from space side on the hull, trying to find out as much as he possibly could.

Two of the craft were smoking visibly into space, creating an odd view of expelled materials, quenching vacuum, dying fires, and glowing hulls, detonations flaring from the topmost decks of the upper craft in the triad, metal humming and screaming. The view on the hatchway for that craft showed Beremod rolling out, spinning around with the same hatch he'd torn off to gain access to the ship. Just as the larger vessel split from the central spire, Beremod slammed the hatch onto the hole, and Rex watched as pressures stayed even for the spire while the ship outside pulled free. Almost fifty meters out and another explosion, this on the left end underneath the disk-shaped vessel, sent it spinning as it fell out of its orbit, and plunged down into the atmosphere. Turning from the console long enough to lean out of the nodule, head poking through the entry he'd created, Rex looked down to the hatchway, and yelled to the ally he'd just watched destroy a Combine spacecraft.

"Where the heck are you going?! What's the backup plan?!"

The giant slowed a moment, and gazed upwards at the destruction with a wry smile.

"Going to assist Skel, I promised him! Be ready to evacuate here to the tertiary craft!"

And once he'd yelled that, the big man pointed one arm to the rightmost hatchway, still intact but buzzing green for entry, and then disappeared through the left hatch without further utterance. Rex felt confused, but still determined to make his own position useful, he began to use the console input to access the enormous source of power within the lift system, the Combine architecture of design being resistant to what he was attempting, but finally relenting as he overpowered safeties and overrode control authorizations. Forcing every bit of available power to reroute into the third craft, he could physically feel ill at the Combine machinery insisting to refuse acceptance of his efforts, and as his connection clamped down like vices on the data streams, progress slowed to a crawl.

Another kind of enemy would have presented no problems whatsoever, but the cerebral opponent was proving tougher than the set of keys his patron had provided for him in the lift, and even with all the blunt force of throwing the block of data at the problem, he still found it strange to be forced to dissect the information, and he began to go through the code keys line by line. Staring at them for what felt like far too long, he finally grabbed a section of the first key, and snaking a line from the console into the port at the base of his skull, felt his mind warp the end of the key code, and jammed it into the digital lock on the connection. With a mental *snap*, the connections broke free and the power levels transferred recklessly, some spillover building up in a reservoir located on the spire's outer hull, just above the control nodule, the rest filling long-dormant pathways and engines of the enormous Combine creation still docked, still pristine on the monitors, no detonations as lights and systems came to life, strange drives warming up with blazing white illumination.

Abruptly the craft on the right side of the spire began to explode, starting at the very far end, and working its way across both the underside and upper surface of the craft, in the spire's direction. Beremod and Skel could both be seen as they dove out of the hatchway, the outer seal still present and holding. Rex used the station access to seal the spire and activated the minimal power on the detonating ship, firing whatever attitude thrusters he could find in the closest end of the craft, trying to spin it away from the control spire itself. The resulting detonation blew the now-rotating craft into a mass of debris and shockwaves, no sound, a strange, artistic display of fireworks far deadlier than any rocket he'd ever launched by hand, and it entranced him long enough to miss Beremod yelling up at him from below.

An alarm began to go off in his head as he watched the view on the screens, and his attention spun to the console too late to stop the reservoir of power from flooding his connection, roaring through the console and into the wetwire feed. A digital scream of his own roaring was all Rex could hear in his mind before everything around him exploded, the energy transfer thrumming into him like a freight train and shoving him out the upper portion of the control nodule, bursting clean through all of the layers to smack into the dome of the spire. Gravity pulled him right back down into the detonating control nodule, and barely on the edge of realization, he graced through it to slam onto the floor below, falling amongst a mess of debris, still picking himself up as the largest remnants fell atop him.

Rex shoving relentlessly at the metal and scrap pinning him down, he was more than grateful to see the faces of Beremod and Skel assisting him, heaving great hunks of debris away, and pulling sections of sparking wires and flaming mess to a safe distance, finally giving him hands with which to grab, pulling him up. Stepping onto the deck with wobbling legs and weak knees, he held onto the support from his allies for a second, and coughing into a laugh, he looked up at them, and asked a joking question.

"So, fellas, we got a ship with plenty of power, where do ya' want to go?"

No laughing followed as they helped him get moving on his own volition, and he easily followed them to the last hatchway, waiting for a response. When none came, Rex paused, and cleared his throat. Finally, Beremod turned, and without breaking a sweat or pausing, spoke evenly, "We're going to the next Combine controlled planet. Even their home world if we can find it."

Rex was about to protest, to say he wasn't going with them, but the alarm he once heard in his still-fuzzed-over head now blared over the emergency sounds. Orange lights turned red, and sections along the dome opened, exposing nasty gun emplacements, warming up to fire, and turning his next words into a warning. "Run!"

Beremod and Skel turned and bolted without a second word being required, and Rex forced his own feet into motion, shaking his still-buzzing head and leaping over a piece of the control nodule in his path. Both of his allies passed easily through the locking mechanism into the last ship, and they kept moving without looking back behind them, allowing Rex to pause. Making his decision, he whispered into the open hatch. "Good luck, my friends."

Slamming the hatch closed and locked, he used the nearby access panel to seal it off and detonated the explosive bolts on the upper half of the hatch first, hoping that it was enough to grant the mass of Combine metals beyond with some form of motion. He waited a half-second before firing the lower bolts, the central spire groaning loudly as it was tugged by the departing ship enough to begin to tear moorings and rip metal. The actions forced the docking tube to disconnect, sending the last craft gracefully on her way, and putting the spire itself on a slow rotation to meet the atmosphere itself. Rex spun to face the opening weapons ports, and with his right arm raised up to activate the weapon intertwined into his body, he snapped it into motion aiming and locking onto his first target.

The strange shoulder-mounted energy launcher proved to be dependable, eliminating three of the dome-mounted turrets, before they finished warming up and he was forced to move, return shots in the form of more white-energy cannon fire heating up the deck around him, scorching air to ozone, and melting pieces of scrapped metals to pools of reflective liquid. A single misstep had him sliding into one of the larger pools, and as the hot metal splashed the armor and some of his left side, he was forced to bite off a yelp as it sent his nerves racing with pain, tumbling over a section of the fallen control nodule, and into a pile of the equipment still soaked with the neutral jelly.

The goo sang aloud as it came into contact with the cooling metal on his body, and he rolled about in it for extra measures, thanking the source of heat-resistant material as he took another bolt of accelerated particles to his chest on the move. The force still tossed him back and away to land in a crumpled heap against another portion of the wall, but as he picked himself up and prepared for another shot, he smiled at the lack of heat transfer, grabbing a diamond-shaped panel of curved navy-blue steel.

Running along a path that was mostly cleared, Rex hopped onto the diamond-panel as he tossed it in front of him, and thanked the stars as the momentum he carried with him worked to force the panel into motion, skidding along the surface faster for several seconds before landing in the largest heap of remnants, energy blasts missing him by a wide margin, but still slagging components. He tore into the largest heap with both hands, digging inwards until he was satisfied to see the still-sparking console, only the personal display and a tiny portion of the keypad still working, all coated in the protective gel, inspiring him to laugh. The Combine equipment was proving to be some of the most indestructible tech he'd ever encountered, surviving even the worst abuse and damage he could manage to inflict.

The screen was hard to see even close-up, and the air began to heat up warmer and warmer around him, the remaining cannons no doubt still pounding out as much as they could at the metal scraps covering him and the console alike, and the sight of the spire dipping into orbit had his gut turning to lead. Of course, this all occurred just before power decided to die completely, the console going first, alarms next, lights after that, and last, the strobes of the turrets. Shaking the metal debris off of his back and standing, the center of gravity began to change, and it wasn't long until that disappeared as well.

Floating up into the empty air, Rex couldn't help but wonder which would become a concern first, running out of air or dying when he burned up in the atmosphere. It didn't seem like much of a problem to fret heavily about however, he'd done his part, and whatever came next, he would not be leading it. His only task was to go home. And as Rex took a good look around, debris and wrecks floating in the zero-gee environment with him, none of the systems active, metal wrenching loudly as invisible forces battered the exterior, he wasn't surprised when the whole section of the spire began to tumble.

It provided a modicum of force akin to gravity, which he began to use to his advantage, crawling across the pitching surface and attempting to make his way to the central lift, sliding into what he hoped was one of the safer places to be just now. Unfortunately, the lift was no longer there, and as he slid out to greet it, he was barely able to grasp onto one end of the wall, finding his lungs gasping as the oxygen continued evacuating into space, eyes staring out at the curve of the planet one moment, tracing the arc of the stars the next, and swinging back to the surface.

The tumbling created a bizarre view, metal surfaces shaking, connections vibrating madly, the outer layers of the spire around the area he was in beginning to fracture and break from the stress, and Rex could see something odd building on the horizon in Europe, but could not place the familiarity of the area, the continuing revolutions of the spire complicating his sight. Finally, he was able to piece enough together to make out thick gray swirls comprising something akin to a hurricane or typhoon, a blazing blue core at its center, touching space with a tentative tendril. Rex had no idea what the significance of it was, but it held ominous portent, something he couldn't quite touch in his mind, an almost tangible echo of what it was in the data he'd taken from the Combine database, yet he couldn't find it.

A disturbing shudder from the substructure had Rex abandoning his spot at the lift, especially as it began to tip back down into the atmosphere bottom first, metals and polymers superheating as it punched through Earth's thermosphere easily. The giant metal form became warm to the touch, and stars began to form along Rex's vision, the air now thinned out to nothing, except whipping pressure. He was now pinned to the far wall just outside of the dome area, gravity playing an increasingly important role that he could not avoid, trying his best to gouge out handholds and drag himself back into the main room. Finally reaching it was an exercise in punishing oneself, only the blood from wounds he could not see or feel gliding his path, leaving filthy streaks on the wall as he slid along it, drying quickly from the combination of heated steel and rushing pressure. His left hand ripped a long line of claw marks in the navy-blued material as he let his body drag with the gravity. He could no longer keep his thoughts lucid, and found himself losing hold of his mind...

Ripping free from the surface and flinging back with the rush around him, Rex finally awoke again as he slammed into the roof of the dome with incredible speed, only the intensity of the sudden pain unbearable being the jolt required to bring him back around somewhat. Rex came to just as real air began to break into the interior, whipping the contents of the ruined spire into a frenzy, entire sections of curvature squealing as bonded plates tore free, an odd checkerboard-like effect continuing to form as more tore away. The sight was intense, and brought a gleeful sight to his eyes as he realized enough had broken loose to provide him a view of Earth's surface rushing up to greet him.

It was coming at him far too fast, but with all of the other insane stunts he lived through, why not this one? Forcing his body to roll along the interior, Rex reached the uppermost central panel in the dome, and what he hoped was the sturdiest. It was still lined with ports and couplings for conduits and cables long snapped away, but remained connected to another, weaker panel to its left. Staring at it for a moment, mind working out his survival, Rex located what he was looking for, and paused. It took him a second to identify the correct seam in the layered plates, and bashing the almost-flawless surface while being buffeted with wind was not the easiest of tasks to accomplish.

His limbs were sore beyond relief now, aching with each continuing motion, Rex crumpling and bending the steel, until it not only presented a gaping hole, but also a solid handhold, mashed to the strut to provide a stronger composition. Gripping on for dear life as he began to move his legs through the newly created opening, forces threatened to fling him free from the shuddering structure, remaining sources of energy popping off, shards of metal screaming by, burning plastic and wiring forming clouds of nastiness darkening the sky around him, and interfering with his observation of the quickly approaching planetary surface.

The moment of muddled clarity presented a strange paradox of sorts in his mind, creating a translucent series of thoughts centered around his current situation, especially focusing on where the unknown benefactor that had trapped him so long ago in this horrid maze of events was going to show up next. In his most desperate times of need, some kind of revelation or plan would come to life, or even one of the alien portals could rip him away to another point of the world, but somehow he knew there would be no miracles this time, no spoken words or incoming thoughts. Just a permanent ending, more than likely one in which he would die, and the peace of soul he felt now surprised him.

His source of inner tranquility derived from the satisfaction that he'd completed his own mission to bring the field down. Humanity could once again get close to each other, and make love instead of only war. The species would continue on, the Combine be damned, completely now that five of humanity's best were making their way to the enemies' home world, and his own family would be safe, he hoped. The sight of the storm on the horizon disturbed him, but perhaps the blue-suited backer had his hands full there, and Freeman was their *hero*.

As the spire shook harder, a larger portion of superheated steel warped from the base of the falling spire, and pulled free from the force, smashing on the interior of the perforated dome, tearing Rex away from his reverie and forcing him back to reality. Gripping harder in order not to lose position on the falling object, he could feel heat moving up the claws of his left hand, and as it reached his wrist, he looked down to see the molten metal crawling up his arm as the wind shoved at the now-liquid material, rapidly cooling even as more pushed upwards. Rex also began to feel the suit heat up around him, and his body was sweating madly, attempting to compensate for the increasing temperature.

Sweat continued dripping down his eyebrows under the headgear and stinging his eyes to the point where it was impossible to distinguish what was going on around him, shaking his head and raising his chin in order to force air up onto his face. The cooling sensation was instant, and as his sight came back to him, he could see the beach meeting the shore below, groups of islands off the coast, the very tip of a peninsula approaching way too fast for comfort. Groups of buildings began to appear, and far too late, fear began to truly sink in at the pain he was about to experience, and as it finally came down to it, he was unsure what happened after life ended, not ready to meet it—but barring his panic aside, Rex prepared for the worst.

Vibrations made the steel sing, metal turning bright orange all around him, and the sensation of the air whipping by burned his skin, even the leathery hide beginning to feel pins and needles, lasting all the way until the first impact. Upon striking the surface, a gout of water and sand thrust up through the center of the spire, the entire object spearing in and shaking violently as it met the surface, shuddering and snapping even as a jet of water and dirt formed a mud geyser, blasting throughout the interior. Exiting from every hole in the dome where panels had torn free during the fall, the water and dirt rushed up with incredible force, popping his right hand free easily and leaving him hanging on with only his left, smashing into the panel again as gravity came about full force.

The spire's remains crumpled along the bottom, creating another freefall for a mere moment, bucking him upwards and back down as another layer smashed into the shore and waterline. Dazed and unable to keep focused whatsoever, Rex felt his mind swimming in a sea of confusion, losing control of his grip, only the cooled molten metal wrapped about his hand and forearm holding him in place. Again, the dome snapped along the center, still carried by momentum, water still pouring out in huge streamers, dirt matting the metal of the dome and the surface of his suit, this freefall enough to last several seconds, ended again by an abrupt stop. The metal holding him in place snapped free from the jolt, and he began bouncing across the surface of the dome, leg catching in one tear just long enough to send him pinwheeling, blacking out after the next series of rolls.

His body carried on for some time, propelled by momentum, and the dome completed its fall by cracking along the top fourth of the circumference. The end facing the sea compacted inwards and twisted metal as it broke loose, acting like a seesaw and flinging Rex, along with half a ton of sand and freed steel panels, through the torrid air. Shockwaves carried some and buried the rest into a swampy shoreline. Trees, mud, and other debris clumped together into a massive pile, before everything came to a steady halt. Cooling metal and steam created a fixed pattern of ticking metal and hissing, until it too broke down to a hum, and finally, nothing.

WAKING THE DEAD

Rex awoke with darkness surrounding him, gasping for air that was not there, thrashing about wildly as he felt his limbs return to his awareness. The thick, gummy nothing that surrounded him suffocated his efforts, pinned him down, trapping him and holding him despite every effort he made to move, to gain freedom from the all-encompassing mass squeezing him close and embracing him like the grasp of a warm, dark grave. Shoving at the moist matter with every effort in the world still remaining within him, he forced himself to a kneeling position, braced his feet under his body, and put his shoulder into bulldozing motion, sounds coming to him, plants tearing and something metallic screeching against wood or bark. Left foot sliding in mud and dipping down into a shallow mess of liquid, an animalistic growl soon followed, forcing Rex to pause completely, and listen for the movement of whatever else was still alive here with him, still knee-deep in muck.

But the next motion could be felt as that something rustled by his foot and Rex tore into the darkness faster, panic rising to match his stature, grasping great handfuls and pulling it aside, the air in the headgear now stale and smelling heavily of wet mud, driving him harder to reach fresh atmosphere. Kicking up out of the wetness and flinging himself bodily at the wall of darkness ahead, a trickle of light struck the mud around him, the lenses blurred and caked with wet material, but adjusting just enough to show him daylight, hands reaching out to meet it. Pulling down the walls around the small crack, Rex climbed upwards relentlessly until, finally, he burst through into the open, hands around the base of the headgear, and lifting it up to let his real eyes do the seeing, tears streaming down his cheeks as sunlight struck his skin and pupils.

Jaws akin to a vice had his smile disappearing as they clamped about his left ankle, and with power of a torque wrench, wrestled him about in a circle until he was on his back, pulling him deeper back into the darkness from which he'd struggled so mightily to exit. But with both hands firmly entrenched, Rex hauled back up, still fighting the pull of the creature, until he was able to use both forearms to lever up further, clawed left hand and armored right hand sinking into the layers of debris and mud around him to provide suitable handholds.

Continuing to pull at the uppermost layer of wreckage, he almost slid back again, but readjusted his hand and yanked harder, until finally he was waist-deep in the mess, giving himself another opportunity to reach out with his left arm first, gaining new purchase on the rubble of some type of structure strewn about with the trees, mud, and water, not a plate of the spire, but large enough to be useful for his right hand as well. One last steady jerk had him fully clear of the hole, dragging the offensive creature into the light, and securing a place for his right foot to brace itself, rejoining the struggle just as the beast attempted to flip him again.

It was scaled and massive; comprising three sets of clawed legs instead of two, and rows upon rows of teeth in the maw, it resembled a gator gone completely wrong. Compound eyes with reptilian pupils blinked back at him as it growled again, head whipping back and forth to allow hooked choppers it had for teeth to dig into the surface of the armor around his foot.

Rex knew the only solution, and rolled right up to a standing position until his left foot could press the lower jaw into the rubbish remaining from the spire's landing, reaching down with both hands to grasp at the upper jaw of the creature, snapping off teeth with armored and clawed fingers alike, until the tips could sink firmly into the gums, squeezing with intensity.

Hands solidly plunged into the mass, Rex lifted upwards with muscles beyond sore, roaring like the beast below him as he first popped the jaw out of place, then ripped it free from the now-garbling beast waggling and flopping with no eyes, no nostrils, brain cavity and mouth torn open to the surroundings, the motions driving mud and trashed structure into internal organs. Chest heaving and lungs gasping, Rex looked up to the sky as he slowly walked away from the dead entity, taking in the surroundings, and smiling that yet again he'd pulled through, on a doomed crash-landing even. But the sight of one of the three combine ships falling into the atmosphere had his smile fading, tracing the arc with his eyes for as long as it took, until it disappeared beyond a distant tree line, a resounding shockwave following soon after.

Wiping the mud from his left arm, now glistening up to the forearm with the surface of melted Combine metal, conformed to the rough hide-like skin over every clawed finger, he did the same with the right arm. Clearing out every bit of exposed circuitry still on the mechanical symbiotic device melded with his body, Rex picked off the worst from the container of blazing white energy pulsing over his right shoulder. Looking down at the tattered, scorched, and bullet hole-ridden MCV vest over his chest plate with a wry smile, he brushed the wet soil from it, finally turning his attention to the headgear still hanging awkwardly from the port. One massive hunk of topsoil, grass included, was still stuck across two of the three lenses, and as he pulled it off, wiping the mud from each crevice as best as possible, he took a long look at it before slipping it onto his bare head.

Eyes readjusting to the view, he oriented himself northwest, and began to walk slowly, testing himself out to see how exhausted he was; but after a few good steps along the field of wreckage, he began to run. His next quest was to get home.

After all, he still needed his family.

EPILOGUE

W ind whipped by hard and fast, buffeting the pickups on the headgear, matching the roar of the engine in front of him. The vehicle was old, battered, and rusted, decrepit beyond total recognition. He'd found it in the swamp near his crash-landing, and the humid, hot air of the southern peninsula had not treated it well over the years. Still, Rex couldn't complain too badly, as it started up after several attempts and a blast of black exhaust. Riding the car to its limits of speed, he could hear it groan and complain around him, shaking and trembling with each bump, squealing and tearing with each turn. But he was satisfied that it would get him where he needed to go. The stack of gas tanks in the rear compartment shook haphazardly as the vehicle roared onwards, secured down only by the rotting seatbelts.

It took him what felt like a week to traverse the country, leaving what looked to be Florida, through the rotting south, traveling on the crumbling ruin that was the interstate highway. Several times the vehicle had run out of fuel, and he had little choice but to scavenge for more, able to find the occasional stash for backup generators, abandoned fuel depots, and at least one rusting rig full of fuel. The almost-nonstop travel was wearing him. Rex could catch himself nodding, could feel sleep creeping in. But there was nowhere safe for him yet, no place that would allow him to relax and close his eyes. Several days later, he had no choice but to force himself to stop, his demand for rest on the verge of overwhelming when the car nearly tipped over on him. Stopping in the middle of the freeway, he took his chances to sleep.

His dreams were battered, torn, and scattered like the countryside, and refused to stay with him as he tossed and turned in the driver's seat, neck complaining of position and body sore from bruises, yet unhealed. Rex was surprised that he was able to stay out for more than a few hours, finally waking to the roar of an engine overhead, scrambling to his senses. At first, he'd confused the deep, heavy thrumming as the implant in his chest, but the blast of sound overhead nearly deafened him through the headgear. Blinking his eyes as he looked to the source, he almost wondered if he was hallucinating or if the headgear was broken, removing it long enough to confirm the sight. The jet that roared by had USAF markings, blazingly fast and leaving a streak of exhaust in the sky.

Hope soared and sang inside him, starting the car up again and stepping on the accelerator hard, chasing the trail of exhaust. Several times, he had to double back on empty exits and curving roadway in order to follow the trail, and as it pointed north, he finally gave up. Forcing himself to abandon the trail, he focused on making it as close to directly westward as he could manage. Shattered highway, broken freeway, ruined off-ramps, these things all impeded his path, but he could only feel relief as the exit for Albuquerque came up. He was rapidly approaching the place he'd left behind. It was cold ice water on a burning heat of nerves coiled deep inside.

Rex let his mind wander as he continued driving, trying to blur the time; he needed to let it wander and retain focus simultaneously. He was far too close to let the edge of discovery of home wear on him—he was frayed, tattered, almost broken. Things had changed so much, and he'd gone so far—

Another jet zipped by, but not so fast that he couldn't tell it was deliberately buzzing his car. It roared close enough that the sound made his ears ring, made his eyes water, and nose recoil from the stink of burning jet fuel. It shook the entire frame of the car. Twice he had to ensure the headgear was unplugged, that again, this was *real*, that humans were flying, that it wasn't some Combine traitor flying a copycat...

He nearly forgot to watch the road, and felt the car ramp up over a section of crumpled macadam at high speed, the wheels squealing and frame crumpling as he landed down, gripping the wheel with iron hands trying to avoid the crash that felt nearly inevitable. Left, right, left, right...

He could feel the control slipping, feel the pull of the forces beyond his ability to contort and handle...but as the wheels hit dirt, he slammed the e-brake, spun, gassed, all he could, and drifted the car into control, thanking the gods of gravity and motion as the wide-bodied car shifted and did as he asked. As control returned, so did his awareness of his surroundings. Rex knew this stretch of dirt. He knew his land.

The compound was ahead. It had to be his compound, had to be his home. Except...

It had towers around it, a wall around it, fortifications ringed the familiar sight of homes and the cul-de-sac...and as the jet passed right over it, the turrets turned and aimed at him...

"Oh crap!"

Rex could barely contain himself as red lines of fire tore up lanes of dirt around him, guiding him, warning him, and spraying dust and rocks against the car; the dings and cracks appearing on the windshield rattling him nearly as much as the sounds of the weapons echoing. It wasn't till he regained control of his senses as well as the vehicle that he realized he was holding his breath, and began gasping as the tunnel vision opened up, and he slowed down before the lanes of fire ripped up cracked asphalt in front of him as well.

By the time he had reached a few hundred meters from the main gates, the car was crawling, the guns still actively trained on him. One hand on the wheel, Rex used the other to plug in the headgear, and slipped it over his face. Whatever he was, they would have to accept that he'd come without the intent of violence carried upon his shoulders. It should have been a homecoming worth remembering. But he couldn't tell what would occur. The last time he'd been gone the changes had become so horrible that they'd forever altered relationships, and somehow he knew this would be no different,

The engine on the aging car began knocking loudly as he slowed it, coughing and sputtering loudly, until it finally died of exhaustion. At that, the gates finally cranked open, and Rex saw something he could not understand. Two of Tank stood there at the gates carrying identical weapons. And as they strode forward, he could finally make out minute differences in the armor, and the ballistic headgear they wore. Neither looked like Tank behind the headgear—neither looked old enough or haggard enough, even though they bore similar faces of distrust and curiosity mingled together.

The voices that boomed out were unidentifiable, but they said the same thing in unison, "Exit the vehicle slowly, with both arms raised in the air. Make no sudden movements and we will not fire upon you."

Still gripping the steering wheel tightly, Rex really didn't see much choice in the matter. It would be interesting if they tried to remove the symbiote from his arm, or claim his other hand was wearing a big black glove, but he'd know momentarily what would take place. Cranking open the stubborn driver's side door and shoving at the seat, he'd had to alter just to get in comfortably, Rex emerged to the sunlight and squinted in the glare as the lenses had to adjust. Arms up as he sidestepped from the vehicle, he stood stock-still as the two behemoths approached, and Rex could finally see, they weren't Tank, but they were damn close to what he was—duplicates or mass-produced copies.

Neither looked like Tank under closer inspection—each had different, unique markings, self-drawn scribbles on their gear, and features that were nothing like the man he'd known so many days passed ago. One spoke to him with the muzzle of his weapon pointed at the ground now.

"So. Who the hell are you supposed to be? Don't quite look like anything I've ever seen…or heard of for that matter."

"The name is Rex. I trust that will ring some bells."

Eyebrows on both sets of features hit the tops of their faceplates at the mention of the name, and cheeks turned bright red. Rex could hear them talking to each other in hushed tones.

"No way, man. No way."

The second man spoke with the same sense of awe and grasping of understanding as the first.

"It's gotta be him. No one is dumb enough to admit that and *not* be him, you know who would flip out if they found out."

The conversation continued after a short pause, wherein Rex could hear his own heartbeats.

"So what are we supposed to do, wave our arms in joy and let him in?"

"I'm not waving, but I'm sure as hell not making *Rex* stand here at the goddamn gate of his own home."

They continued arguing in lower tones for a long moment while he stood there, watching, listening, and standing in the hot sun. Finally, both of them turned to face him, and they had stoic expressions on their face.

"Welcome home…sir. We'll have to impound your vehicle, and when you come in, we suggest you make your way directly to command at the rearmost central house of the district."

With a perfunctory nod he gestured to the car.

"That rust heap is all yours to deal with gents. Now if you'd be so kind."

Rex walked by them, recognizing that he nearly matched their height and width, and wondered just how the hell he'd managed to squeeze into the hotbox of the car for such a long trip. Walking tiredly amongst the homes was a totally bizarre experience—lawns were flourishing. The houses on each side of the compound were rebuilt and interconnected, making massively long neighborhoods, kids, families, rebuilt lives here. Only the existence of the walls, the Tank-like guards, and the towers ringing the property made it look like the Combine were still a presence somewhere here on the planet.

While the kids and families did not stop and wave and celebrate his presence, they did not run away either. They stood still, watched him walk, gazed at him, and whispered to themselves. Rex was both embarrassed and proud at the same time. He was *back*, and these people were safe, whether indirectly or directly owed to his actions. He beamed in the sunlight knowing that humans were safe; able to breed, able to continue. The dirt road kicked up dust that was quickly blown away, but the cobbled sidewalks met the lawns neatly, and if he peeked just right, he could see the possible beginnings of community gardens at the corners, picking out corn, and squash growing in the soil. It was marvelous.

Heading straight to the rear of the Compound towards the biggest, most expansive looking of the homes, Rex gazed at its arches, clean corners, fresh paint, pillars, and distinct style. The numbers *187* curved in giant bronze pieces over the top arch nearing the peak of the angled roof, and he almost began to tear up. Walking up to the opened gates, in past well-manicured bushes and trimmed lawns, the large black-lacquered door opened up to the sight of a younger blond gentleman, well-dressed and groomed, ushering him inside.

Rex walked right in and was not remotely surprised to find that the inside was well-built and ornate as well; no staircases, only ramps everywhere. And almost on instinct, he knew what was next. Standing in the main entryway, gazing upwards, he heard the sounds of rubberized treads on the hardwood floors, and turned to what he knew was coming.

"You dumb SOB."

Rex turned and saw his troubled friend sitting in the mind-controlled wheelchair, hair grayer and face wrinkled and scarred.

"Tank. Jesus…Tank, I missed you, brother."

Tank had his jaw set, and tears were in his eyes. "Take that headgear off, you animal."

Rex did so and turned to face him, buckling it to what was left of his patchwork gear. Taking two steps forward and stopping in front of the chair, Rex didn't hesitate to pick up his friend out of the chair and hug him tight. Tank complained loudly at first, but finally relented.

"Awright, you giant pain in my ass, I missed you! Now set me down!"

Smiling broadly, and kissing the old man on the cheek, Rex did so, and followed his partner as the wizened soldier rolled back into the next room.

"Maurie's gonna freaking flip when she sees you. But have a cup o' what these savages call *tea* with me, Rex."

"I can't wait to see her and Molly, but yeah, we have to catch up a bit first."

Rex and Tank sat there for some time, jostling each other with vibes and sharing stories, and apologies, and information. He found out that Lena had re-created the process of the armor construction the Combine had begun, and anyone crippled or wounded with lost limbs became eligible for what they now called the *knights* program, which explained why he'd seen so many Tanks walking around. It was a huge step in protecting, defending, and eventually, eliminating what was left of the Combine on world. But Rex realized that it had been done with an expressed vehemence—the Combine could be back. They were not a destroyed threat, and even though their presence had been crippled, no one would risk another invasion with their hands behind their back and eyes closed.

And as Rex conversed with his old friend, he realized just how much he'd hated being alone all this time. He spent a good hour of time with him until finally his impatience won out and he had to speak out.

"Tank, I love that we've had a little time, but I really, really need to see Maurine and Molly. I'm not leaving again, we'll have more time."

"Understood, brother. Get yer ass on board the transport at the northern gate. It'll take you right to the silo. I guarantee you'll be pleasantly surprised. Now git!"

Rex smiled at Tank's way of saying he loved him back, and patted the old man on the shoulder before running out of the house as fast as he could.

———✎✎✎———

The transport was a re-reconverted bus made out of a tramcar that had been modified with brute force and creative engineering, and it powered through the desert sands of New Mexico without an issue on the way to the silo, the high speed and open windows blasting him with cool air and brushing the sweat off his body. As it finally pulled to a halt, Rex beheld something that he couldn't believe. The entire upper entry to the silo had been rebuilt and repaved, including bunkers where the once dug-out outposts had stood, towers made of the navy-blue scavenged metal, and an honest-to-God visitors entry booth. Knights and other soldiers patrolled the surface, and he was greeted by a pair of well-outfitted men carrying remade Combine M4s, whom gestured him out slowly.

Rex had to guess that the word of his return had to be spreading somehow, for the two looked at him with awe and bright eyes. Wordlessly, they both guided him to the booth, where he met another person he really didn't expect to see.

"Harry? Holy..."

Harry, now well-trimmed and prim-dressed in a uniform matching the rest, looked up with wide eyes and spaced eyebrows, one hand shaking as he held out a pen for Rex to sign his name on a check-in list. Wordlessly, he pointed out a space to sign, nodded numbly, and gestured gently into the main entryway, head craning as Rex smiled and walked past, the guards staying with Harry at the booth.

"You knew him, Captain?"

"You don't want to know, kids, you really don't."

Rex heard the last as he walked up to the glass-paneled doors of the entryway, onto patched and makeshift linoleum floors of a spartan military administration complex, now built on top of the silo. Signs directed him back to a rebuilt lift system, and he clambered onto the solidly repaired plate of steel before pressing the button labeled *Command*. The walls of the shaft were still open to view. As it descended, he watched as it revealed floor after floor of the rebuilt facility, including the laboratory, the kitchen, the power center, the rec rooms, dormitories, and finally down to the command center level, wherein he stepped out to brightly lit revamped walls of the Combine navy-blue steels. He had to give them credit; they'd scavenged and used whatever was available, and done an amazing job.

He followed the provided arrows painted on the floor, passing new offices, computer labs, and other rooms full of paperwork, until he reached a pair of secured double doors. He walked up to the recognition device, and wondered just how badly he'd screw this part up. Thankfully, it seemed his eyes were the one part of him that did not change all that much, and as he bent down to the reader, it scanned him in green, and the doors clicked. Pushing his way in, he found a well-organized hive that utilized both Combine tech and recovered devices from Black Mesa itself, a kaleidoscope of colors and a cacophony of sounds.

Everything however, came to a screeching halt as he entered, and silence filled the huge room. Only one woman continued talking in the center, gesturing to a console and talking to what was probably her aides with a rising temper as she realized they weren't paying attention. Finally, her focus was broken.

"What the hell are you people gawking at?"

Maurine looked up, and her jaw dropped. She looked incredibly sharp dressed in her feminine business suit, cut to her shape, even if there were a few patches in the gray fabric. Her hair had grown out to ear length, and she was still incredibly striking, yet bore a sharp, dangerous look in her eyes. As she began moving, Rex could hear that she still wore combat boots, stomping around the people in her way and making her way forward to where Rex stood. Stopping abruptly right in front of him, she reached out and smacked him across the face once squarely.

"You big lug, you kept me waiting."

She stood up on her tiptoes, arms around his neck, and kissed him squarely. They held each other for some time, kissing and holding with no side effects, no pain, nothing but pleasure, and a huge ragged cheer went up from the people in the hive. They continued for the longest moment Rex had ever felt in his life, until Maurine broke away, and turned to the people.

"Alright, Goddamnit, enough screwing around! Get back to it!"

Everyone was still smiling as they got back to work, including Maurine as she turned back to face him, and spoke under her breath, "You should only be so lucky that I'm holding you right now, mister. Take me down to the showers, now."

With a laugh, he swept her up off her feet, carried her back to the lift, and pressed the button with one hand, arms full of his love for the first real time, and obeyed without question.

After nearly using up all of the hot water in the entire facility, and then using one of the biggest rooms in the dormitories he'd ever seen, Rex felt clean, happy, and comforted. He lay with her on a massive bed, which they'd managed to break twice during the next few hours, naked and spun and twirled with her. They spoke in soft undertones, chuckled, giggled, and made love over and over. It was as near-heaven as he could ever guess he would get, with what left of his clothes in an incinerator somewhere, and the armor cleaned, she held him prisoner of sorts, until a wry grin crossed her features, and she turned to him.

"I think we're gonna make lots of babies."

"Are you sure you want them, babe? I'm not exactly the top shelf of the human gene pool anymore."

She propped up on one elbow. "Are you kidding me, *of course* I want them. And if you think for a moment your genes aren't important you've been lying to yourself, mister. I just waited until we could make them in person."

Rex smiled broadly, and stroked her cheek with his right hand carefully; but the realization of what she'd intimated hit his forebrain.

"Huh? Someone didn't wait?"

Maurine bit her lower lip, still slightly smiling.

"Lena didn't wait. She kept your…samples, and when you left, she made her first. She really did love you; but she knew who you wanted. If you desire, we can go see her and the new baby boy."

Rex lay there shocked, numb, and unbelieving.

"Maybe…uh, maybe later; for now, I want to see our daughter. Where's Molly?"

Maurine got up from the bed and dragged the sheet away with her, while Rex watched.

"Let's see if we have some clothes to go on under your armor…"

—⚬⚬⚬—

It resulted in an hour more of fumbling around and enjoying each other, but finally Maurine sat next to Rex as the transport rumbled towards New Mexico City, holding hands carefully as it moved. He felt nearly complete, almost whole. And in this moment, if the blue-suited man showed up, he'd shove the bastard's head into a certain black hole and flush. Rex felt nervous and excited as the transport rumbled into the new barriers around NMC proper, bypassing a checkpoint with a wave, and entering the first honest-to-God city he'd seen since the entire mess started so long ago. New Mexico City was back. People walked the streets. Homes and businesses glowed with power and activity. Small farms and food growing plots shone in the sun and gave off earthy and animalistic smells. The cobbled streets made distant, thumping sounds as the tires rolled over it. In the center, where they drove, a new defensive tower stood, ringed with weapons and preparations, keeping watch over the city.

The transport drove up to the entry, and the two of them stepped out onto the repaved concrete, bright, bronzed letters set into the stones catching Rex's eyes.

"For those that fell, fought, and rebelled. For those that stood, leapt, and charged into the breach. For Humanity. We falter, but never fail."

Tears were at the corners of his eyes. He was a wellspring of untapped emotions finally coming home. And Rex could barely contain it. He led the way into the building with Maurine running to catch up, his armor shining in the sun and cool wind blowing at his back, as they walked into the checkpoints. Check after check, they cleared through, deeper into the expansive, impressively built facility. Closer and closer, he felt it. His heart was hammering, the implant still beating its tune.

At last, the penultimate pair of doors stood before him, and he paused. Could he do it? What the hell was he waiting for?! And just as he began the step forward, they opened up to him and she stepped out. Papers held dropped to the floor. Jaws dropped. And she screamed for joy.

"Daddy!"

She leapt at him, and they embraced and he twirled with her, crying and laughing and joyous outpouring that shook him. He was Home.

And Rex would do whatever it took to protect it.